BLOOD HARVEST

Also available:

THE NEW

Doctor WHO

ADVENTURES

BLOOD HARVEST

Terrance Dicks

First published in Great Britain in 1994 by
Doctor Who Books
an imprint of Virgin Publishing Ltd
332 Ladbroke Grove
London W10 5AH

Copyright © Terrance Dicks 1994

'Doctor Who' series copyright © British Broadcasting
Corporation 1994

ISBN 0 426 20417 4

Cover illustration by Bill Donohoe

Typeset by Intype, London
Printed and bound in Great Britain by
Cox & Wyman Ltd, Reading, Berks

This book is sold subject to the condition that it shall not by
way of trade or otherwise, be lent, resold, hired out or
otherwise circulated without the publisher's prior written
consent in any form of binding or cover other than that in
which it is published and without a similar condition including
this condition being imposed on the subsequent purchaser

Never play cards with a man called Doc
Never eat out at a place called Mom's
Never lie down with a woman
Whose troubles are worse than your own

Prologue

The Doctor came hurrying into the TARDIS, curly hair standing on end with excitement, long scarf trailing behind him. K-9 was plugged into the console and lights were flashing furiously.

As the Doctor entered, K-9 unplugged himself and turned round. 'Computations completed, Master! Using information from the *Hydrax* data banks I have computed an infallible method of entering and leaving E-space at will.'

'Never mind that now!'

K-9 was hurt. 'Leaving E-space matter of highest priority, Master!'

'So is this! Romana insists on leaving us, K-9. She wants to help Biroc free the Tharils. I can't go with her. Will you?'

There was a moment's pause.

'She needs you, K-9,' said the Doctor. 'She's taken on a huge job and she needs your help. Will you go?'

K-9 said, 'Affirmative, Master!'

The Doctor picked up K-9, hugged him and carried him out of the TARDIS.

A few moments later he came back in, alone. He went back to the console and re-ran the data K-9 had just loaded, storing it in his Time Lord memory. It was an elegant solution – and very logical. 'Of course!' he said. 'So simple I couldn't see it! Clever old K-9. We can go back now.'

Somehow the idea didn't seem to give him very much pleasure.

Things would be very different without Romana and K-9. There was still Adric, of course.

Then came the explosion.

The hidden control room, deep in the heart of the Capitol, had long been cleansed, deactivated and sealed. Tarnished by a history of ancient evil, it was a place of unspeakable horror, no longer discussed, or even thought of by the civilization that had created it. Yet now it was in use once again.

Two black-robed and hooded figures watched a third as he struggled with a complex array of ancient equipment. There was a console, a variety of controls, a monitor screen bordered with elaborate metal scroll-work.

One of the hooded watchers spoke. 'Can it be reactivated?'

The one at the console said, 'It won't be easy. Flavia's lackeys were thorough.'

'But without the Time Scoop – '

'Visual function at least can be restored. We can observe. When the time comes, we shall find ways to intervene.'

The watcher raised his voice in a ritual incantation.

'Death to the Doctor!'

The second watcher joined him:

'Borusa lives!'

All three chanted the final, blasphemous line:

'Rassilon must die!'

The figure at the console returned to his work.

On the monitor the swirling mists of space and time cleared to reveal a city.

A city of towers beside a lake.

But down these mean streets a man must go who is not himself mean, who is neither tarnished nor afraid ... He is the hero, he is everything ... He must be the best man in his world and a good enough man for any world.

The story is this man's adventure in search of a hidden truth.

Raymond Chandler
'The Simple Art of Murder'

1

The Big Fellow

It was a bright winter morning, the sun shining with a sharp jab of cold in the wind off the lake. Chicago looked swell – like a beautiful woman with an ice-pick in her stocking top.

I was driving along Lake Shore Drive in my old Buick. I was wearing the new dark-blue pin-stripe with trench-coat and snap-brim fedora. I was everything the well-dressed private eye ought to be. I was calling on a hundred million dollars.

The invitation had arrived in my office a few hours earlier. It was my first day in business and I was sitting behind my new desk wondering what the hell to do next. The desk itself wasn't new, it came with the office. The previous occupant was in the insurance business, until someone cancelled his policy with three slugs from a Saturday night special in a South Side speakeasy.

Suddenly shy a tenant and a month's rent, the landlord had rented me the office at a bargain rate and thrown in the fixtures and fittings for free. I was now the proud owner of a hat-rack, a worn-out carpet, a cigarette-scarred wooden desk, one swivel and two rickety kitchen-type chairs and a beat-up green filing cabinet filled largely with Chicago air.

The desk was pretty empty too, except for the bottle of bourbon – well, the label said bourbon – in the deep file drawer.

I was just deciding that it was too early for a drink but I'd go ahead and have one anyway when my first business opportunity arrived.

It arrived in the shape of two hard-eyed characters in black topcoats and identical pearl-grey felt hats with broad black hatbands. The topcoats hung open to reveal dark suits, white shirts and striped ties. In certain criminal circles, gaudy vests, loud ties and diamond tie-pins were a thing of the past. The Big Fellow liked the hired help to look respectable.

The get-up had changed but the manners were the same as ever. They shoved the door open without knocking and stepped forward, shoulder to shoulder, sneering down at me. Both were beefy and blue-jawed, one tall, the other short and stocky.

'Morning gents,' I said cheerfully. 'What can I do for you? Lost dogs, missing mothers? You do have mothers?'

The tall hood said, 'They told us you was a wiseguy, Dekker.'

The thickset one said, 'We gotta come all the way downtown to this dump to listen to cheap wisecracks from a cheap peeper.'

He spat on the carpet, which needled me more than somewhat.

'Hang on till I send for a spittoon,' I said. 'Try to remember you're not at home.'

'On your feet, shamus,' said the tall one. 'We're going for a ride.'

'One way?'

'Someone wants to see you.'

I stood up, hands on the side of the desk.

'Clients are welcome in office hours,' I said. 'House calls can be arranged by appointment.'

'Cut the wisecracks, Dekker,' said the stocky one. 'Move your ass or we'll move it for you.'

I picked up the desk and threw it at them.

The desk smashed them apart like ninepins, knocking them to the floor. By the time they made it to their feet I had the .45 out and was covering them both.

I felt under their arms and took away their guns. I knew they'd both have guns, just as I knew they'd both have

6

permits. I grabbed the thickset one and shoved him down on his knees.

'Clean up the carpet,' I said. 'Clean it up, or I'll scrub it with your face.'

He took the display handkerchief from his pocket and scrubbed away at the spittle. I let him up.

'Get your hats, you're leaving.'

They grabbed their hats, getting the wrong ones in their hurry. The tall one's hat came down over his ears, the stocky guy's hat perched on top of his head.

'Change hats, boys,' I said. 'And next time you're sent on an errand, act polite.'

They changed hats and beat it. I heard their feet clattering down the stairs. I picked up the desk and put it back in place. I checked the telephone – it still seemed to be working. I looked in the file drawer and found the booze had survived, although one of the glasses was broken. I poured myself a drink in the remaining glass, set fire to a Camel and sat staring into space in a kind of dream.

The sunlight printed the lettering from the office window onto the carpet in reverse. 'Untermeyer Insurance' it said.

I ought to get it changed to 'Thomas Dekker – Investigations', I thought – but was I going to be around long enough to justify the expense? What seemed like a long time later the phone rang and I grabbed it. 'Dekker.'

There was a moment of silence. Then a soft voice said, 'They tell me you make house-calls, shamus?'

'Only for very big clients.'

'Hawthorne Hotel, noon,' said the voice. There was another pause, then the voice added, 'That polite enough for you, *Mister* Dekker?'

'That's just fine, Mr – ?'

The voice said, 'Ask for Al Brown,' and the phone went dead. I hung it back on the stand and poured myself another drink. After all, this was a special occasion. It's not every day you get a call from Al Capone.

Some people said Capone owned Chicago, which was

7

kind of an exaggeration. He owned the little suburb of Cicero for sure though, lock, stock and cops as well.

He'd owned it since the last local elections, when so many bombs went off it was christened the Pineapple Primary.

The bombs and bullets of Capone's hoods had made sure the voting went the right way.

The Mayor and City Council came with the package. To ram the point home, Capone had dragged the Mayor out of his office and kicked him down the steps of the Town Hall for talking back.

The Hawthorne Hotel was a three-storey brown brick joint on Twenty-Second Street, just west of Cicero Avenue. It was a high-class hotel that had gone down in the world – and come up again when Mr Brown picked it for his out-of-town HQ. Now it had all kinds of improvements, like steel shutters at the windows and resident mobsters wall-to-wall.

I parked the Buick by a fire hydrant and went inside.

There was only one way into the Hawthorne, along a passageway that led into the lobby. The front desk, cigar stand and all the lobby chairs faced right down that passageway. The lobby was crowded with hard guys – I could feel myself being watched every step of the way.

I headed for the reception desk. Before I got there a slender, dark man appeared by my side. 'Dekker?'

'That's me.'

'Frank Rio. You're expected. This way.'

He led me across to a row of elevators on the left of the lobby and opened the door with some kind of special key. The lush velvet-lined elevator whisked us up to the top floor. The elevator doors opened onto a thickly carpeted hallway with a mahogany table and a set of double doors on the far side.

There were two armchairs, one each side of the door, a mobster lounging in each one. They had hats tipped over their eyes and looked to be asleep.

I headed for the doors but Rio barred my way. 'The

iron, shamus. No one gets in to see the Big Fellow heeled. Not unless he's on the payroll.'

'What happens if I object? You wake the sleeping beauties?'

I glanced at the two hoods in the armchairs.

'Why bother?' said Rio.

I looked back, and found he was covering me with a Browning automatic.

I glanced back at the two mobsters and found they were suddenly wide awake and pointing black automatics at me.

I shrugged and took the Colt .45 from under my arm, slamming it on the table. 'This one I'd like back.'

I took out the guns that had been weighing down my left and right-hand suit pockets.

'These belong to your messenger boys.'

Rio slid all three guns into the table drawer and slipped the Browning back under his arm. 'Inside.'

I went through the double doors.

The big room beyond was a combined office and parlour. A dictator-sized desk, overstuffed armchairs and sofas, a drinks cabinet against the wall. Steel shutters were folded back on the big windows, and a massive shape stood gazing down at the bustle of Twenty-Second Street.

As the door closed behind me he swung round and came towards me. I was looking at a bulky figure in a pearl-grey suit, cut by the best tailor in Chicago. The tailoring wasn't quite good enough to disguise the belly, but I got the feeling there was more muscle there than fat. The body was topped by a big round head with greased-back hair. The plump, jowled baby-face had a big cigar stuck in the middle.

I was looking at the man who liked to use the alias Al Brown. He was also known as the Big Fellow. He was Scarface Al Capone.

The thought of the nickname made me look for the scars – I'd never been close enough to get a good look at them before.

9

There were three of them: one on the left cheek, one on the jaw, the third on the neck. They'd faded with time and were no more than thin, white lines.

I must have looked a bit too long. The Big Fellow noticed but he didn't seem to mind.

'Spoil my beauty, don't they?'

It was the same soft husky voice I'd heard on the phone.

'Know how I got 'em?'

I decided to act diplomatic.

'I read in the paper how you got them in the Big War, heroically saving your platoon from a Mills bomb.'

Capone chuckled. 'Those newspaper slobs will print anything. I got 'em in New York when I was a kid, working in Franky Yale's bar on Coney Island. A skinny little guy called Galluchio comes in with his kid sister. She's a real hot little piece and I make some crack about her having a nice ass. I mean it like a compliment, but you know how we Italians are about family. Her brother pulls a knife – little bastard really cut me good. I hadda have about thirty stitches.'

'How did Galluchio make out? Is he still around?'

'He's fine. I went looking for him when I got outta hospital, but Joe the Boss made us have a sit-down at the bar. He said I was outta line making cracks about the guy's sister, and Galluchio had a right to be sore but he shouldn't have cut me. We both apologized and that was that.' Capone sighed. 'People had standards in those days, we knew how to behave. These guys today ... You're Dekker, right?'

'Right.'

Suddenly the amiable grin turned to a glare that could curdle bootleg bourbon.

'You take chances, Dekker, bouncing my boys around.'

'I took the chance that if Mr Brown wanted a private eye, he'd want one who wasn't too easy to lean on. Consider the bouncing act my references.'

The grin came back and I breathed again.

Capone went over to the big drinks cabinet and fixed

himself a brandy in a balloon glass you could have taken a bath in.

'Drink, Dekker?'

'Only when I can get it. I'll take bourbon.'

He poured me a slug of Jim Beam – real Jim Beam – and handed it over. He went behind the big desk and sat down in a swivel chair.

'You were a cop, right Dekker? Till you got canned.'

'Till I quit,' I said with dignity.

'How come? Being on the cops is a good racket in this town.'

'That was my problem. I had this dumb idea about a cop being some kind of public servant.'

'So what happened?'

'I busted Pete Gusenberg for putting the muscle on a poor little slob of a saloon keeper. The guy wouldn't change suppliers so Pete broke his jaw. I was having a quiet drink, saw the ruckus and pulled Pete in. He got a little damaged in the process.'

'That Gusenberg, he's an animal,' said Capone disgustedly. 'The times I try to talk sense into him, make a business arrangement, but will he listen? So what happened?'

'Down at the station Pete has a private chat with Reilly, the Precinct Captain. Then Reilly calls me in and tells me he's dropping the charge. He just happens to have an envelope stuffed with greenbacks which he offers to split with me.'

'What did you do?'

'I slugged the Captain.'

Capone chuckled wheezily. 'So they busted you?'

'They wanted to, but I threatened to tell the press boys why I slugged him. So we did a deal. They got my resignation, I got a licence to be a shamus.'

Capone took a last puff on his cigar.

'I got a job for you, Dekker.'

I drew a deep breath. It was now or never.

'I may have left the cops, Mr Capone, but I haven't

11

crossed any lines. So if you want me to drive a beer truck, muscle a saloon keeper or take some guy for a ride . . .'

Capone held up a massive paw. 'Don't insult me, Dekker. For jobs like that I got all the guys I can use. This job's strictly legit. I want you to check someone out for me.'

'Like who?'

'A guy called Doc.'

Why, the very guys that make my trade good are the ones that yell the loudest about me. Some of the leading judges use the stuff.

When I sell liquor it's called bootlegging. When my patrons serve it on silver trays on Lake Shore Drive it's called hospitality.

Al Capone

2

Doc's Place

Capone mashed out the butt of his cigar in a big marble ashtray and took another from a box on the desk. He pushed the box towards me. I shook my head, fished out my cigarettes and set fire to another Camel.

Capone made a big production of lighting another torpedo-sized cigar, biting off the end and using three matches to get fired up. He leaned back in his chair and sent out enough smoke signals to send the Apache nation on the warpath.

'A few weeks ago this guy Doc opens up a night-spot in a house just off Dearborn Street. Small place, high class, good liquor, straight gambling, no hostesses ... To get in you say you feel sick and ask for Doc.'

'Is the joint in your territory?'

Capone shook his head. 'It's kind of in no-man's land. A place where several territories overlap. Me, the Gusenberg mob, the Aiellos, the O'Donnells ...'

'Sounds like this Doc could be in trouble. He have another name?'

'Smith,' said Capone ironically. 'Doctor John Smith. But everyone calls him Doc.'

'So what do you want from me?'

'I need to know about him. Who he is, who his friends are, how much clout does he have. Is he connected, maybe a front man for some New York guys? Do I take him in, take him out, leave him alone? I gotta know. Check him out for me, Dekker.'

I reckoned it was an honest job – about as honest as I was likely to get in Chicago. Beside which, if I said no to

Capone I'd be swimming across Lake Michigan in a cement bathing suit.   ·

'Okay, I'll check this guy out for you. But if you decide he has to go, don't expect me to set him up.'

'Relax,' said Capone. 'All I need from you is information. If I can settle things peacefully with this guy Doc then I will. You know me, I'm a businessman.'

The funny thing was, I believed him. Capone liked to keep things peaceful. Shooting was bad for business. He only killed you if he had to.

'Okay,' I said. 'Now, my daily rate . . .'

Capone pulled out a roll of bills that would choke a Chicago City Alderman and tossed it across to me.

'Retainer. Let me know when it's used up.'

'Right,' I said. 'I'll get right on it, report back as soon as I've got news.'

'Fine,' said Capone. He leaned forwards. 'Those boys I sent to fetch you, Dekker . . .'

'Never send the boys round to do a man's job.'

'Okay, so I underestimated you. But you'd better play square with me on this. I've got better people to send – if I have to.'

'Like Frank Rio?'

'Frank's the best.'

I stood up. 'No, I'm the best. I'll do an honest job for you, Mr Capone. But keep your hoods out of my hair or I'll comb 'em out like dandruff.'

Capone shook his head. 'You really are something, Dekker.'

'That's why you hired me.'

'I could use a guy like you. It's a pity you're straight.'

'Well, nobody's perfect,' I said. 'I'll get back to you, Mr Brown.'

I went out into the vestibule, collected the .45 from the waiting Rio, rode down in the lift, got into the Buick and drove home. I reckoned I was ahead of the game. I had a client, a roll of greenbacks – and I was still alive.

That night I went to take a look at Doc's Place.

It was a modest-looking joint, a compact three-storey mansion in a little side-street just off Dearborn. Lights glowed softly behind curtained windows and there was a faint throb of jazz somewhere. There was nothing else to show it was anything but a private house apart from the number of cars parked outside, and in the vacant lot across the street. I added the Buick to the collection and walked over to the house.

There was a light over the door, a closed shutter at head-height and a big brass bell-pull. I stood under the light and yanked on the bell.

The shutter slid back and a gravelly voice said, 'Yeah?'

'I'm feeling sick. I came to see the Doc.'

The door opened and I stepped into a luxuriously furnished hallway. There was a short passageway dead ahead. To the right an elegant staircase curved upwards. There were ornamental tables and gold-framed pictures on the walls. A classy joint all right.

A gorilla in a tuxedo was closing the door behind me. I looked at the low brow and battleship jaw above the boiled shirt. Happy Harrigan, the biggest, toughest and dumbest thug in all Chicago.

Happy was delighted to see me. 'Hey, Mr Dekker! Who gives you the password?'

'Oh, I just heard it around.'

Happy had a caveman build and a cheerful friendly nature, but he was so dumb he found it hard to earn an honest criminal living, even in Chicago. I'd been his friend ever since the day I left the cops. It just happened to be the day the boys at the precinct had scooped Happy up and put him under the lights down in the cellar. Their plan was to improve the monthly crime figures by bouncing blackjacks off Happy till he confessed to every crime on the unsolved list – believe me there were plenty.

Flattered by the attention, Happy was glad to oblige. The boys didn't even get to use their blackjacks. He'd confessed to enough crimes to draw 99 years in Leavenworth when I heard what was going on and stepped in and spoiled the game.

Happy had just served a short stretch for smashing up a saloon, so he'd actually been in jail when half the crimes he'd confessed to were committed. I alibied him for the rest by saying we'd been singing in the church choir together every night since he got out. The Captain knew he'd be laughed out of court so he let Happy loose.

As we'd walked away from the station house together Happy gave me a worried look. 'What you said in there wasn't true, Mr Dekker. We was never in no choir together.'

I stopped and glared up at him. 'Listen Happy, if the cops ever take you in, like just now you only say one thing. "I don't know nothing about nothing." You're a gangster, aren't you?'

Happy scratched his head. 'Yeah. I guess so.'

'Well, that's what gangsters say.'

I thought it was a stroke of luck, Happy being the doorman at Doc's Place. He owed me one, so he ought to be good for the straight scoop.

'What's the set-up here, Happy?' I asked casually, as he took my coat and hat. 'How much do you know about this guy Doc?'

Happy beamed at me. 'I don't know nuttin' about nuttin', Mr Dekker!' he said proudly. 'Right?'

I sighed and slapped him on the back. 'Right, Happy. Which way's the bar?'

He pointed down the corridor and I went on down.

I pushed open the black velvet-covered double doors and found myself in Doc's Place. It was a high-class version of your basic night-spot. Tables crowded round a postage-stamp dance floor with nobody dancing. On the other side of the floor a jazz combo played quietly as if for their own pleasure. It was early yet and the place was nowhere near full.

A bar ran down the left-hand side of the room with a row of stools, empty except for a dame on the stool at the far end. I went over and perched on the next stool but one. The barman, a silver-haired continental type, stopped polishing an already gleaming glass and glided over.

'What's your pleasure, sir?'

'Straight bourbon – Jim Beam if you have it.'

He reached behind the bar for a bottle, poured a sizeable slug into a glass and put it in front of me.

'We have everything here, sir.'

'You certainly do,' I said.

I was looking at the girl on the bar stool.

She had long, dark hair swept back from her face and she wore a black silk evening gown that was tight in all the right places. She was a good-looking dame, well built and well dressed, but that wasn't why she made such an impression on me. There was something about her. Something about her face maybe, roundish, good cheekbones, fine dark eyes... Not your chorus-line cutie, but a good, strong humorous face.

I've looked at a lot of dames in my time, and they mostly look back. But the way this one was looking at me was different. It was a straightforward, measuring sort of look. She was on the level.

I took out a pack of Camels and held it out. 'Cigarette, lady?'

'I don't.'

There was a big purse on the bar in front of her, but no glass beside it.

'Buy you a drink?' I said.

'I can buy my own.'

'So buy me one, I'm not proud.'

'We're running a business here, soldier, not a charity.'

Which answered one question – somehow I'd guessed she was part of the firm.

'Then let me buy you a drink,' I said. 'Looks like you need the trade.'

The corner of her mouth twitched – it was a nice, wide mouth.

'We're a late-night joint. Still, if you insist.' She nodded to the barman.

'Manhattan, Miss Ace?'

18

'Please, Luigi.'

He got busy fixing the cocktail.

I sipped my bourbon – it made the stuff in my office drawer taste like paint-stripper. I raised my glass to the girl. 'Good booze.'

'Only the best here, soldier.'

'Dekker,' I said. 'Tom Dekker.'

'I'm – '

'I heard. 'You're Ace.'

She grinned. 'I deal blackjack sometimes, upstairs.'

I gave her my smouldering look, 'I bet you play a mean game.'

'Out of your league, Dekker. You couldn't afford the stakes.'

'Try me.'

'Maybe I will.'

Luigi delivered her Manhattan and she sipped at it, looking at me over the rim of the glass.

With an effort I wrenched my attention back to business.

'Doc around?'

She pointed to an alcove just to the right of the bar. It held a table, a chair and a smallish guy in a white tuxedo. He was working through some papers, signing cheques, scribbling the odd note. There was a half-full glass of liquor on the table and a cigarette burning in an ashtray.

'Can I buy *him* a drink?'

The barman was shocked. 'Doc never drinks with the customers.'

I turned my attention back to the girl. 'Now, about that game.'

'You're still talking about cards?'

'What else?'

The doors crashed open and three guys swaggered through. They were brawny, swarthy, flashily dressed. Cheap hoods, Pete Gusenberg's boys.

They were followed by Happy, swaying slightly with blood trickling from his forehead where he'd been pistol-whipped.

19

'These guys,' he said hoarsely. 'I tole them they was the wrong type for a class joint like this but . . .'

'It's all right, Happy,' said the girl called Ace. She put her hand on the big purse.

Happy turned and weaved his way back out of the door. Lucky they'd hit him on the head, I thought. Anywhere else they might have hurt him.

The hard guys bellied up to the bar. The boss seemed to be the biggest and fattest. I'd seen him around, a small-time leg-breaker called Morelli. They called him Swifty, on account of he was fast with a gun.

'Beer,' he grunted. Luigi started filling three tankards from a barrel behind the bar.

I sat hunched over my glass of bourbon. I knew what was coming, I'd seen it a hundred times. They'd drink the beer. They'd spit it out, say it was pigswill, then rough up the barman and the owner if he tried to object. They'd tell them in future they were buying their booze from Pete Gusenberg. Nobody else in the room would make a move and they'd all suffer sudden memory loss if asked about it later.

It was an old, tired act. But today it played a little different. All three thugs swigged their beer – and stood lost in astonishment at how good it was.

Before they could remember they were supposed to complain, Doc left his alcove and strolled over to the bar, hands thrust casually into the pockets of his white jacket.

'Good stuff, eh, gentlemen?'

His voice was quiet. Like the girl's it wasn't quite American. There was a sort of burr in it, Scots or Irish maybe.

'It ain't bad,' said Morelli grudgingly. 'Where'd you get it?'

'I make it in the bath-tub – well, swimming bath actually. I use the bath-tub for whisky.'

'This booze ain't made in no bath-tub.'

'I assure you it's quite a simple process. Once you've synthesized the alcoholic congeners . . .'

20

'Professor!' said the girl. There was a warning in her voice.

Doc smiled. 'Forgive my stupid sense of humour. It's imported, of course, from Germany – the beer that is, not my sense of humour.'

'Well, from now on you buy your booze from Pete Gusenberg.'

'No thank you,' said Doc politely. 'I'm happy with my present supplier. I hear that stuff Gusenberg peddles is pigswill.'

Morelli blinked, then swung a roundhouse right at Doc's head. He was quick moving for a fat guy.

But not quick enough. Hands still in his pockets, Doc stepped aside and the punch missed by the width of a ballpark.

Morelli rushed him.

Doc stepped aside again, sticking out a foot, and Morelli crashed to the ground.

He came up with a gun in his hand – like I said, he was quick. The girl called Ace blew the top of his head off.

The second hood had his rod out by now, but so did I. Before he could shoot, I flattened him with a slug in the shoulder from my .45.

Some people say the old 1911 Model Army Colt Automatic is big and clumsy and noisy, and I guess it is. But hit a man anywhere with the slug from a .45 and he'll go down and stay down.

Luigi stepped from behind his bar and sapped the third thug with a bung starter.

For a moment there was silence, the smell of cordite hanging in the air. I saw Ace slip a black gun back inside her purse.

Doc looked sadly down at the dead hood.

'Did you have to, Ace?'

'He had a gun in his hand, Doc. It was him or me – or you.'

I holstered the .45. 'He was no loss, Doc.'

'Everyone's a loss.'

The doors crashed open again and Happy appeared.

'Doc, the cops!'

Suddenly Happy's bulky figure was grabbed by the collar and hurled aside by an even bigger one. He fell over a table, sweeping it and its two occupants to the ground in a welter of arms and legs and tableware.

It just wasn't Happy's day.

3

Connections

The bigger shape – and bigger than Happy means really big – was that of my old Precinct Captain, Dennis Reilly, resplendent in brass buttons and blue uniform, swinging a nightstick that looked like a toothpick in his massive hand. More uniformed harness-bulls crowded the doorway behind him.

Reilly's huge red face was glowing like a setting sun as he looked at the bodies, one dead, one wounded, one unconscious, on the floor.

'And phwat's all this then, begorrah?' he said in the Mother Machree accent he turned on when it suited him. 'Shootin' and shoutin' marring the peace of our fair city of Chicago! Lucky it is I was passing by at the time.'

'On the job as usual, Captain?' I said.

He swung round towards me, and I wondered how I'd ever gotten up the nerve to slug him. I remembered that my best punch had only rocked him back a little on his heels. I also remembered that it had taken four tough detectives, two on each arm, to stop him tearing my head off.

'So 'tis yourself, Dekker,' he said happily. 'Mixing with bad company are ye? Ah well, 'tis only to be expected of a renegade cop. The boys down at the station house will be glad to see you again – especially as a customer this time.' He raised his voice. 'This joint is closed, illegal gambling and liquor sales.'

Customers started stampeding for the door and at a nod from Reilly the cops let them through. He turned to the rest of us.

'And for you and your friends, Mr Dekker, the paddy-wagon awaits!'

He was as happy as a mugger with a new blackjack.

The girl called Ace was leaning on the end of the bar. 'You're arresting us? What charges?'

He glanced down at the three bodies. 'Oh, we'll think of something. Murder and aggravated assault for a start. And illegal discharge of firearms within city limits.'

Ace's hand slid closer to the purse on the bar and I got ready to jump her. There were five cops on the scene now plus Reilly, and even in Chicago, shooting six cops is a bad move.

Then Doc said quietly, 'You're making a mistake, Captain.'

Reilly looked down at him. 'Am I so? Well, we'll sort it all out down at the precinct house.' He looked hopeful. 'Unless of course you might be thinking of resisting arrest?'

Doc took a silver pencil and a notebook from his pocket and went over to the bar. He scribbled a number, tore out the page and gave it to Reilly, looking up at him with eyes as cold and grey as Lake Michigan on a winter night.

'You might like to call this number first. It's – '

'I know who it is,' said Reilly. ''Tis a number I'm very familiar with.'

Luigi produced a telephone and put it down on the end of the bar. Reilly glared at the uniformed cops. 'And why are ye standing there like statues, ye useless spalpeens?' He kicked the nearest body. Luckily it was the dead one. 'Get this scum out of here and into the wagon.'

'What then, Captain?' asked the nearest bull.

'Then wait till I tell ye!' roared Reilly.

The hood Luigi had sapped was awake and on his feet by now. He looked round dazedly. 'Hey Captain, what gives? Pete said – '

A backhand smash from Reilly shut his mouth and knocked him into the arms of the nearest cops.

'Get him outta here, will ye?'

The cops dragged the two bleeding live bodies and the

24

one dead one out of the room, and Reilly stomped over to the phone.

Luigi put a double slug of Jim Beam on the bar in front of me and fixed another Manhattan for Ace.

Doc leaned on the far end of the bar, a burning cigarette in the ashtray beside him, next to a half-empty glass. I never saw Doc take a drag on the butt or a swig of booze – but the half-full glass and the burning cigarette were always there.

I took a solid swig of the bourbon: bath-tub or not, it was still pretty good. I fished out my pack of Camels, offered them to Ace, pulled it back remembering and lit one for myself.

We all stood there quietly, listening to the low rumble of Reilly's voice on the phone. It was an oddly peaceful moment.

Reilly's voice rose in indignation. 'Sure, and if I'd known he was a such a great friend of yours, your honour –'

He broke off, obviously cut off short by the man on the other end of the line. Then he said soothingly, 'Sure, I'll see to it myself, there'll be no trouble, no trouble at all . . .'

He broke off, obviously realizing he was talking into a dead phone, and slammed down the receiver.

He swung round and lumbered back towards us. 'Well now,' he said softly. 'Maybe I was a mite hasty.' He looked round the bar. 'Let me see if I can be after reconstructing the crime. You good people were having a quiet drink when these three lowlifes forced their way in. They fell to quarrelling amongst themselves, two of them pulled guns, and one ended up wounded and the other dead.'

'Sure, that's right,' I said. 'And the third one sapped himself out of pure meanness. Brilliant, Reilly.'

'That's just how it was,' said Doc. 'Mr Dekker here is joking of course. My barman sapped the third one when he tried to pull a gun on me.'

'Self-defence entirely,' said Reilly heartily. 'And those two yeggs will be after confirming the story when I've had a quiet word with them.'

'Those two yeggs will be on the street in half an hour,' I said. 'Gusenberg will have a mouthpiece with a writ of habeas corpus and the bail money down at the station right now.'

Reilly gave me a look and turned to go.

Doc stepped forward, a bulging brown envelope in his hand.

'I think you dropped this, Captain.'

Reilly took the envelope and tucked it away with the ease that came of long practice.

'Don't forget the Police Benevolent Fund,' I said.

He swung round, nightstick raised, and I saw Ace's hand moving towards her purse. I shook my head slightly, and stood quite still as Reilly patted my face gently with the nightstick.

'I'll be seeing you, Dekker, my bhoy,' he said softly. 'One day we'll be having our little chat down in the station cellar with none of your influential friends to interrupt us – just you and me and the phone book.'

'I'll look forward to it, Captain.'

Reilly marched out, the doors swinging closed behind him.

By now Happy had picked himself up. 'We still open for business, Doc?'

'Why not?'

'Okay, I'll get back on the door.'

Happy went away.

Doc said, 'Can I offer you a drink, Mr Dekker?'

Luigi looked astonished. I nodded at him and he poured me another bourbon. Then he summoned waiters with a snap of his fingers, and started giving orders about getting the place tidied up. A swamper appeared with a mop and swabbed the blood from the floor and the brains from the wall.

The band raised their heads from behind the rostrum – they'd ducked automatically when the shooting started – and started playing. Pretty soon the customers were drifting back in again. When the booze is as good as it was at

Doc's Place, it takes more than a shoot-out and a police raid to discourage the customers.

As soon as things were running smoothly again, Doc went back to his alcove. He waved me over and I sat down at the table.

'Thanks for the help, Mr Dekker,' he said.

'It was nothing.'

Ace carried her Manhattan over and joined us.

'That's exactly right,' she said. 'I didn't need any help, Dekker. Next time don't interfere.'

I shrugged. 'Suit yourself, lady.'

She gave me a hard look. 'Funny how those cops turned up. Quite a coincidence.'

'Coincidence hell,' I told her. 'Reilly's in the bag for Gusenberg, has been for years. The cops were back-up – for Morelli.'

'What was that Reilly said to you about the phone book?'

'You can beat a man up with a phone book,' said Doc. 'Hurts just as much as a blackjack, but doesn't leave any marks.'

'How'd you know an old cop trick like that, Doc?'

'I know a lot of things I wish I didn't, Mr Dekker.'

I took a drag on my Camel and let out the smoke. 'Reilly was all set to haul you down to the station house – if you survived. Lucky you're so tight with Big Bill.'

'Who?' asked Ace.

'Big Bill Thompson, our beloved Mayor. The one who promised to punch King George in the snoot if he ever set foot in Chicago.'

I looked at them for a reaction, but the idea of an assault on the royal snoot didn't seem to bother them any.

'And how about you, Mr Dekker?' said Doc suddenly. 'Do I gather you were once a colleague of Captain Reilly's?'

'I was a cop for a while, but I got fired for honesty. Now I'm freelance.'

'A shamus,' said Doc. 'A gumshoe, a peeper, a private eye.'

27

'There are lots of words,' I said. 'They're only words.'

'And what are you peeping at now?' asked Ace.

'Us, presumably,' said Doc.

They sat back and looked at me, and suddenly I felt cold without knowing why. What's to be scared of, I told myself. A long-haired dark-eyed dame? She had a gun in her purse and she knew how to use it – but I'd handled tough dames before.

Then there was Doc, a skinny little guy who didn't even seem to be heeled. If he packed a gun he hadn't reached for it during the shoot-out. It was like he knew it was safe to leave things to Ace.

Yet somehow I was scared, more than I'd been in the Hawthorne Hotel surrounded by Capone's hoods. Something told me these were two of the most dangerous people I'd ever met, even in Chicago.

Doc must have seen me tense up. He leaned forward and patted my arm. 'Don't worry, Mr Dekker. I'm not sure if you're a friend but I don't really think you're an enemy.'

I was all ready to go into the injured innocence routine. I'm a good convincing liar, it's one of the first things you learn when you're a cop. I'd heard about this new joint with good liquor, so I'd dropped in to take a look. Hadn't I helped out with Gusenberg's thugs?

I looked into those calm grey eyes, and did something completely crazy – I told Doc the truth.

I spilled the lot: the summons from Capone, being given the job of checking up on him.

Doc didn't seem bothered. 'Capone's the major power here in Chicago. It's only natural he should take an interest in us.'

Ace took a different attitude. 'You don't mind working for a crook like Capone?'

'Capone may be crooked but the job isn't. Where do you get off, lady, with this high-and-mighty stuff? I'm still on the right side of the law, which is more than you two can say. Doc's peddling bootleg liquor in an illegal speakeasy. You're carrying a gun for him, same as Franky

Rio does for Big Al – which makes you no better than any other gun-moll.'

Ace got mad. 'That's not true, is it Doc? We're – '

She caught Doc's eye and clammed up.

'Quite right, Mr Dekker,' said Doc. 'I'm just a saloon-keeper trying to earn a dishonest living. Face it, Ace, you're a sleazy Chicago gun-moll!'

He was ribbing her, but I didn't know why or what about, so I let that one drift with the tide.

'Yeah, sure,' I said. 'So what do I tell Capone?'

'The truth,' said Doc. 'I'm a great believer in being openly Machiavellian, Mr Dekker.'

'Come again?'

'Telling people the truth when they don't expect it. It always confuses them. Report back to your employer and tell him everything you've learned about us.'

'Which is nothing!' jeered Ace. 'Some gumshoe!'

'I learned plenty, lady. You've both been around, you can look after yourselves, and you've got connections. The Big Fellow's not going to like that too much, Doc. If he decides you're dangerous, he'll take you out.'

'Then convince him I'm not. I provide my own liquor so I don't buy from anyone else, but I don't supply anyone else either. I've got no plans to expand, this place is all I need.'

'Maybe so, but you've opened up a joint in disputed territory,' I told him. 'Several mobs are fighting over it. No one wants it much, but no one wants to leave it for someone else.'

'Then why not just leave it to me? "Doc's Place" can be neutral ground. A sort of gangland Switzerland.'

I thought for a moment. 'Al might go for it at that. If he does you'll be off the hook.'

'You'd trust Capone?' asked Ace.

'Al's not like the rest of them. Gusenberg's an animal, the Aiellos are mad dogs, the Genna and O'Donnell mobs aren't much better. But Al's a businessman, when he gives his word it's good. He may want to talk to you.'

'I'd be delighted,' said Doc.

I finished my bourbon and stood up. 'Well, I've got places to go and you've got a saloon to run. Be seeing you, Doc.'

I tipped my hat to the girl called Ace, got a cool nod in return, and headed for the door.

As the doors closed behind Dekker, Ace turned indignantly to the Doctor. 'Who does that big ape think he is? And you're no better, Doctor. Sleazy Chicago gun-moll!'

The Doctor chuckled. 'I withdraw the sleazy. But a gun-moll's more or less what you are, Ace – for the moment.'

'Just like you're a saloon-keeper?'

'Exactly.'

Ace brooded for a moment. 'What was all that stuff about getting Reilly to phone the Mayor?'

'Connections, Ace. The Fix. The Mayor recently received a large contribution to his campaign funds. With it came a message that it would be nice if "Doc's Place" could be left alone.'

'Why are we peddling illegal booze in a town full of murderous gangsters? Why did we dump Bernice on that god-awful planet? What was that signal you picked up? And who the hell is Romanadvoratrelundar?'

'Lady Romanadvoratrelundar if you don't mind,' said the Doctor reprovingly. 'Romana for short.'

'So who's Romana?'

'Just a girl I used to know.'

Ace glared at him. 'Doctor!'

'Ace, there's a reason for our being here, just as there's a reason for Bernice being – where she is.'

'Well?'

'I can't tell you.'

'Won't, you mean.'

'Don't want to. Not yet, anyway.'

'Why not?'

'Because if you know what we're after, you won't be able to stop thinking about it.'

'So?'

The Doctor hesitated. 'So then it might come and find you.'

The many-towered city had faded and the screen of the Time Scoop showed only the swirling mists of space and time.

Watched by his fellow conspirators, the hooded figure at the screen checked a spatio-temporal cross-reference on a nearby monitor. With a hiss of satisfaction, he adjusted the Time Scoop controls.

Slowly another picture emerged on the screen.

A single tower, strangely misshapen, standing amidst woods and fields, rising up menacingly against a grey and stormy sky. A primitive village huddled close to the base of the Tower.

The tall figure of the first conspirator leaned over the screen.

'Well?'

'He is here also,' said the figure at the controls. 'Not so strongly present as on Earth. The signal is faint, but clear.'

'And the Doctor?'

'Still on Earth.'

'Has the Doctor found Him?' asked the third figure.

'Not yet, but he will – unless He finds the Doctor first.'

'It matters not,' said the first conspirator. 'So long as our purpose is served.'

They raised their voices in the ritual chant:

'Death to the Doctor!

'Borusa lives!

'Rassilon must die!'

4

The Village and the Tower

Bernice Summerfield looked at the bowl of gruel and shuddered. She poked it experimentally with the wooden spoon.

'Thin green-grey slime with lumps in it,' she muttered. 'Haven't seen the like since military school.'

She looked up at the serving maid, a dull-eyed lump of a girl called Katya. 'This is it?'

Katya wiped a runny nose with the back of her hand, and transferred the results to her grimy apron. 'My Lady?'

'Is this the meal?'

Katya produced a fearsome sniff. 'Oh no, my Lady.' She unloaded the rest of her tray. 'See, there's greenfruit, too. And all the bread and water you want!'

She gave Bernice a gap-toothed smile and clumped away.

Greenfruit was a kind of crab-apple, small and wizened. Bernice bit into one and winced at its bitter tang. The black bread was hard and coarse and sour. Even the water was dank and cloudy with a muddy after-taste.

Bernice reached into the pocket of her jacket and produced a thin silver flask. She poured a healthy slug of Eridanian brandy into her water goblet, drained the mixture and shuddered.

'Brandy and water for lunch. A few more days here and I'll be a drunken degenerate. I might even get to like it.'

Ivo the landlord came over to her table. He was a white-haired giant, still powerful despite his age.

He knuckled his forehead. 'Is all well, my Lady?'

He looked so anxious that Bernice heard herself saying, 'Fine. Terrific. Everything's wonderful.'

'One of the help-maids didn't turn up this morning. Off with her lover no doubt. Gerda's a good girl, but there's no denying she's flighty. And, well, we're not used to guests of quality here.'

Bernice looked round the hall. It was furnished with rows of wooden tables and benches with a kitchen area at the far end.

'Where do your usual customers come from?'

'From the village, and a few farms nearby. In the Old Time this was the Centre, and everyone had to eat here. Now people are free and some choose to take their meals by their own firesides. But others still come for a meal sometimes, and to drink and talk of an evening. More gruel, my Lady?'

'No, this is fine, really . . .'

Bernice stirred her gruel with her spoon, and even made herself eat a little. It tasted just as bad as it looked.

'You said something about the Old Time?'

'Things were very different once,' said Ivo. 'In the time of the Lords . . .' He broke off, shaking his head.

'Go on,' said Bernice encouragingly. 'I'm interested in your history. That's why I'm here.'

Ivo's voice shook with remembered rage. 'The Lords took everything, the food, the wine . . . They left just enough to keep us alive and working.' He paused, rubbing his eyes. 'They took more than the food, they took our children too.'

'To serve them, you mean?'

'Aye,' said Ivo grimly. 'To serve them with their lives. My son Karl . . .' He broke off again. 'Evil days, my Lady.'

'So what happened to change things?'

'A stranger came and helped us. We rose up and destroyed the Lords. After they were vanquished we had better times for a while – until the Troubles began.'

'What troubles?'

'Between those who wanted change and progress, and those who wanted a return to the old ways.'

'Surely no one wants the Lords back?'

'Not the old evil Lords, no. These, we are told, are new kindly Lords who will rule us for our own good.'

'Yes,' said Bernice thoughtfully. 'There have always been plenty of those around. But does anyone follow them?'

'More than you might think, my Lady. Some folk fear change. They like what they are used to, the Lords in the Tower, the peasants in the fields.'

'But your tower is empty, surely?'

'It is,' growled Ivo. 'We have no Lords here, nor do we need any. No offence, my Lady.'

Bernice smiled. 'None taken. Who's in charge then?'

'The Village Council – I myself am headman.'

There was a sound of hoofbeats from outside, the jingle of harness. Ivo ran to the door and Bernice stood up to look out.

A patrol of armed men was riding up to the inn. The riders wore black leather jerkins studded with steel and carried short swords and long spears.

At the head of the patrol rode a thin-faced, fair-haired young man, evidently their leader. He had a better horse than the others, a big black stallion, and he was more richly dressed. He carried no spear and wore a longer sword. He also had a blaster.

'It is the Black Guard,' whispered Ivo. 'My Lady, if I spoke any ill of Lords, I pray you – '

'It's all right,' said Bernice. 'I'm just a passing stranger, you have nothing to fear from me.'

'It is not you I fear, my Lady.'

The patrol drew up outside the inn and dismounted. The leader handed his reins to one of his men and strode into the entrance of the hall. He stared insolently at Ivo. 'And you are?'

'I am Ivo, headman of this village.'

The young man glanced around the hall and noticed Bernice. She ignored him. He looked enquiringly at Ivo who rumbled, 'We have a guest – the Lady Bernice.'

The social system was pretty simple here, thought

Bernice. If you weren't dressed in sackcloth and covered in grime you were an instant aristocrat. She'd been Lady Bernice ever since her arrival.

The Guard leader stalked across to her table and bowed stiffly.

For a moment or two Bernice made a pretence of going on with her lunch. She looked up, giving the young man the insolent stare that he'd given Ivo. Then, in exactly the tone he'd used himself, she drawled, 'And you are?'

Flushing angrily he clicked his heels. 'Captain Varis, my Lady.'

'And why are you here?' Nothing like getting in your questions first, she thought.

'A routine patrol, my Lady,' stammered Varis. 'The Tower here has no Lord and the area is a centre of rebel activities.'

'I understood the villagers governed themselves,' said Bernice coolly. 'Against whom do they rebel?'

'Against their rightful rulers, my Lady. There are too many of these "free villages" as they call themselves. One day there will be a new Lord in the Tower and things will return to normal.'

Ivo gave a sort of choked growl. The Captain glanced coldly at him, then turned back to Bernice.

'May I ask why you are here?'

'I am on a visit of inspection,' said Bernice. 'There have been disturbing reports about this area. You may continue with your patrol, Captain – but I advise you to be careful.'

She went back to her breakfast.

Varis swung round to Ivo. 'I require water for my horses and food and drink for my men.'

'For which you will pay,' said Bernice, without looking up. 'At the usual local rate.'

'Of course, my Lady,' said Varis icily.

'That will be all, Captain,' said Bernice.

He turned on his heel and stamped angrily into the yard.

Nothing like bullying a bully, thought Bernice. I wonder who he thinks I am? She remembered one of the Doctor's

35

favourite sayings: 'In an authoritarian society, people obey the voice of authority. It can be very useful.'

Ivo and Katya brought the patrol food and drink in the yard. They watered their horses, bolted their meal and rode away.

Ivo came back into the inn, jangling a handful of coins.

'They actually paid,' he said, chuckling. 'Usually they take what they want and pay only with blows.'

'Who are they anyway, this Black Guard?'

'They serve the new Lords, and those who would return them to power. They have no rights here – but it is ill arguing with armed men.'

'There are ways,' said Bernice, thinking of a friend of hers. She stood up. 'I must go, I want to take a look at that Tower.' She looked at Ivo's worried face. 'Don't worry, I only want to take a look at it, I'm not going to move in. I'll probably be gone most of the afternoon.'

'Take care, my Lady, it is an evil place. Be sure to return before dark – before the bats start to fly.'

He made a strange ritual gesture, touching ears, eyes and mouth.

'I thought you said the old Lords were gone?'

'Some of their evil may yet remain in the Tower.'

'Don't worry, I'll be back before dark.'

'I shall prepare a special dinner for you, my Lady. Roast marsh-stoat with sourberry sauce.'

'I can't wait. Now, how do I get to the Tower?'

The Tower was easy enough to find. It dominated the village and could be seen from almost every point. The road led along the muddy village street, past houses that were little more than hovels. Occasionally people peered out at her from behind sackcloth curtains.

Bernice saw a grubby child playing with a wreath of white flowers outside one of the huts. She stopped and bent down to talk to it. Before she could say anything, a woman ran out and snatched the astonished child away, carrying it howling indoors.

The child had dropped its wreath of flowers. Bernice

picked it up and sniffed it. The flowers had a harsh, pungent smell. She shrugged and stuffed the wreath into her jacket pocket. She noticed that there were more garlands of white flowers over the doorway and draped across the windows. Beyond the village the road led through ploughed fields. Bernice could see bent figures toiling in the fields. They worked two or three to a field in long straight lines. They were still using the medieval system of farming, each man responsible for his own thin strip of land.

The land looked stony and infertile, the skies were dull and grey and there was a chill in the wind. Bernice turned up the collar of her old safari jacket and hurried on.

This, she thought, has to be the most miserable, backward, poverty-stricken planet I've ever seen in my life.

The path led her into a belt of woodland. Tall trees cut off the light and Bernice hurried uneasily along the shadowy path.

Suddenly she came out of the dark woods and found the Tower looming over her. Bernice had seen a lot of castles in her time but never one like this.

To start with, there was its shape, tall and slender, not a proper castle at all, just one solitary tower. There were two turrets set into the Tower close to the top, miniature versions of the Tower itself. The turrets were set close together, giving an oddly lopsided look, as if a third turret was needed to complete the design.

Shading her eyes with her hand, Bernice looked long and hard at the Tower. Perhaps the third turret had simply decayed and dropped away. She shifted her gaze to the ground at the foot of the Tower. There was nothing, no shattered masonry, no debris of any kind. Had someone taken the turret? But where? And why?

All her archaeologist's instincts aroused, Bernice headed for the Tower.

And here was another oddity, she thought, as she marched steadily towards it. The Tower didn't seem to have any proper defences.

It was surrounded simply by open space, by bare,

parched earth in which nothing grew. No outer wall, no moat, nothing. It was as if its occupants were confident that no one would ever dare to attack them.

But they'd been wrong, thought Bernice. According to Ivo the castle had fallen and its occupants, the mysterious and terrible Lords, had been destroyed.

She came to the arched doorway of the Tower and stood looking up at it. It was made from great blocks of stone covered with moss and lichen. It was ancient, it was impressive and it was added for effect, thought Bernice. Somehow she knew that the arch wasn't part of the original structure.

The door inside the arch was smaller than she'd expected. It was studded with metal, and it stood fractionally ajar. Bernice shoved it hard and it opened with surprising smoothness. She slipped through the gap and the door closed silently behind her, leaving her in total darkness. The Tower had no windows.

Bernice turned and tried to reopen the door. It wouldn't move. She was trapped.

She stood very still for a moment, fighting panic. It served her right, it was ridiculous, poking about on her own like this. She needed a proper expedition. She needed colleagues, assistants, local workers . . .

If you were a proper archaeologist, said a voice deep in her mind. That did it, as always. With a sigh Bernice fished in her many-pocketed jacket and produced a heavy torch. Its beam showed her a circular entrance hall hung with decaying tapestries, a spiral staircase leading up into darkness. A reek of decay hung in the air like invisible fog.

The place was cold and dead and eerily silent. It sent a chill into her soul.

Well, onward and upward, she thought. There must be more than one way in – and therefore more than one way out. She could always leave by the servants' entrance, if she could find it. Meanwhile, since she was here, she might as well take a quick look around.

She began climbing the stairs.

Her footsteps echoed hollowly in the darkness beyond her torch beam, and she had a strange feeling of being watched. Once or twice she thought she heard scurrying sounds behind her, but when she stopped moving the sounds stopped as well. Rats, thought Bernice uneasily. Just rats.

The staircase led her to a corridor, and the corridor to a huge circular chamber on a higher level. Feeling lost in the empty darkness, Bernice swept the beam of her torch around the chamber, revealing more rotting tapestries. On the other side of the room there were twin thrones on a dais. She went over to examine them.

Basically they were high-backed wooden chairs covered with the remnants of once-gorgeous brocade.

Local craftsmanship, thought Bernice. Like the doorway, they didn't quite go with the Tower itself.

A huge painting hung on the wall behind the thrones. It showed two richly robed figures, a man and a woman. Both were tall and thin with white faces and glittering eyes. They reminded her of something and it took her a moment to realize what it was. Then it came to her. They looked like the King and Queen on a pack of cards.

Something caught her eye in the space behind the thrones: a small square opening. She went over to it, shone the light inside and saw a gleaming metal ladder. It led downwards into darkness, and up towards a faint gleam of light.

An inspection hatch and an access ladder – in a tower that wasn't a tower at all.

Taking a deep breath, Bernice slid through the hatchway and got hands and feet onto the ladder. She began climbing upwards, towards the light.

The climb seemed endless and Bernice thought she must be getting very near the top of the Tower. The higher she climbed the lighter it got, and the light was coming from a square of daylight at the very top of the ladder.

At last the ladder came out onto a metal platform, from which rose three smaller ladders. The central and right-hand ladders led to round metal hatchways. The third led into empty space, ending in a circle of light that came from the open sky.

Bernice climbed the central ladder, turned the locking wheel on the hatchway, opened it and slid through the gap.

She found herself in a cramped control room. Bernice shone her torch around the banks of instruments, her suspicions confirmed.

The Tower wasn't a tower at all – it was a spaceship, a mother ship with three smaller scout vessels attached. She was in the control room of one of the scout ships.

She backed out of the hatchway which clanged shut behind her, emerged onto the metal platform and stood looking about her. The right-hand ladder must lead to the second scout ship. The circle of light on the left was where the third and missing scout ship had detached itself.

Bernice started to descend the main ladder. She felt unsafe going down one-handed so she switched off her torch, put it back in her pocket and began climbing down into darkness.

Down and down she went, wondering why the descent which surely ought to be easier seemed to be taking even longer than her climb to the top.

Uneasily she realized the answer. It really was taking longer.

She must have passed the hatchway where she'd joined the ladder. Now she was descending into the depths of the ship. Which wasn't such a bad idea, she thought. That other exit, if there was one, would be somewhere at the bottom.

Suddenly her foot encountered empty space. She had run out of ladder. Scrambling back up a few rungs, Bernice clung to the ladder with one hand, fished out her torch and shone it downwards. With a feeling of anticlimax she saw that the ladder ended a few feet from the ground.

She jumped down, landing with a faint metallic echo, and shone the torch around her. She was in a long metal chamber lined with metal racks. Probably the engine room, she thought. Looks as if the main engines have been stripped out. Curiouser and curiouser.

She became aware of a sound in the darkness, a steady drip, drip, drip . . .

And there was a smell; an odd, coppery smell that brought back memories of battle and disaster. It was coming from the far end of the room.

Shining her torch beam ahead of her, she moved towards the sound.

There was a dim white shape hanging from one of the metal racks. As she got closer, Bernice saw with horror that it was the naked body of a young woman, suspended head downwards, long fair hair just touching the ground. Her throat had been slit. The blood was running into a metal channel, then disappearing though a sink-hole at the end. The fuel tanks must be somewhere below, thought Bernice. Someone, or something, was filling them with human blood.

She heard a faint rustling sound, swung round and saw a tall dark shape towering above her. Its face was white, its eyes glowed red, and it had long pointed fangs.

Claw-like hands reached out towards her.

5

Vampire

Bernice screamed and shoved her torch into the creature's face. It recoiled, hissing, from the light – but not very far. It stood poised, watching her, and Bernice sensed it was nerving itself for a fresh attach.

Shining the torch in its eyes, Bernice studied it while she groped for a weapon with her free hand. Most of its actual shape was concealed by the high-collared black cloak, but she could see that it was tall and skeletally thin. The face was long and white with glittering eyes, a pointed beard and black lips drawn back in a snarl over fang-like teeth. The odd thing about it was that it looked somehow familiar.

Frantically Bernice felt through her pockets and found nothing. Her blaster was still in her pack, back at the inn. Did blasters work on vampires anyway? For it was quite clear that that was what this thing was. She was looking at a myth, a legend – and it was about to attack her.

Her fingers closed on the wreath of flowers dropped by the village child, and the vampire sprang.

Snatching out the flowers, Bernice thrust them into its gaping jaws. The vampire staggered back with a choking scream of rage and fear. Clawing at its face it turned and fled howling into the darkness.

Bernice turned and ran the other way. Shining her torch ahead of her she saw another ladder leading downwards and scrambled down it. She found herself in a small circular chamber with smoke-blackened metal walls. In the centre of its floor was a round hole, rather like a well.

Bernice looked round hopelessly – now what? A scrabbling sound from above made up her mind.

She ran to the hole, slid over the edge feet-first and found herself whizzing downwards in a giant metal tube. She shot out of the end, dropped a few feet and landed on hard rocky ground. Picking herself up she looked round.

She was out of the rocket but not, as she'd hoped, in the open air. She was in a cave, a long narrow cave festooned with stalagmites and stalactites – she could never remember which was which. At the end of the cave there was an archway, and in the centre of the arch was a black altar. Light was coming from the other side of the altar – dull greyish light, but daylight all the same.

Bernice hurried towards it. She stopped to take a quick look at the altar. It was as fascinating a cultural artefact as any archaeologist could wish to find, but Bernice was in no mood to make a lengthy study of it. It was made of black stone and there was a shallow depression on the top, smeared with something dark and thick and sticky. Bernice touched it gingerly, sniffed her finger and recognized the smell that had been in the Tower – the distinctive coppery smell of fresh-spilled human blood.

Somehow she knew that this was where the girl in the Tower's throat had been cut. She had been sacrificed.

Shuddering, Bernice hurried on past the altar and found herself at last in the open air. She was standing on the edge of a huge amphitheatre, a bowl-shaped depression in the ground. All her archaeologist instincts told her that it was a burial ground.

Bernice looked uneasily over her shoulder. There was no sign of the thing that had attacked her in the Tower. Judging by its scream she'd done it considerable harm. The white flower was very like Earth's garlic. Wasn't garlic supposed to be poisonous to vampires? Surely it would stay in the darkness of the Tower where it was safe? Even if it came down into the caves, it wouldn't venture out into open ground, not in daylight.

Bernice felt torn. She felt she ought to head straight back to the village and tell Ivo of her terrible discovery

43

in the Tower. But to an archaeologist – even an unorthodox and unqualified archaeologist – the lure of an untouched burial ground was irresistible. She stared up at the sky. It was hard to tell for sure on a strange planet, but surely there must be several hours before dark. She remembered Ivo's urgings to get back 'before the bats began to fly'.

'Come on, Benny, a chance to make your name,' she whispered. 'Papers, articles in learned journals, a book. Then the holovid series. Just a quick look . . .'

There was something projecting from the earth near the centre of the burial ground, and Bernice walked steadily towards it. It was a metal tail-fin, rusted and corroded with age – the remains of the missing scout ship!

At the edges of the depression the earth was hard-packed and solid, but near the centre it was more and more broken up. There were cracks and fissures, some narrow, some wide and deep. There were sudden hillocks, irregular patches as though the ground had been churned up some time ago. Grass and weeds grew more thinly over these disturbed areas.

Bernice noticed other, more recent irregularities where the earth seemed to be newly turned. With growing outrage she realized that she might not be the first here after all.

As much for the principle of the thing as anything else, she fished pegs and string from her pocket and marked out a square of ground. Another pocket yielded a miniature digger's kit: trowel, hand-fork, probe, stiff wire brush, all rolled neatly into a tool-holder. Bernice began to dig.

Instinct or luck had led her to choose exactly the right spot. Careful digging revealed the shape of a long thin segmented bone. Gently Bernice brushed away the earth. She was looking at the skeleton of a finger – a finger that ended in a long, sharp claw.

With growing excitement Bernice went on working. She uncovered a second finger, a third, fourth and fifth, and finally the skeleton of a giant clawed hand.

She sat back on her heels, considering. Presumably the

rest of the creature was buried here. Using the hand as a basis for estimation it must have been an animal of colossal size.

Some now-extinct beast, the planet's equivalent of a dinosaur or a mammoth? But it had been buried at the base of the Tower, with an altar watching over it. An altar used for human sacrifice. A sacred beast then, something the inhabitants of the planet both feared and worshipped.

Carried away with the excitement of her find, all danger forgotten, Bernice went on digging. She uncovered an immensely long straight bone, the equivalent of the ulna in the human arm. But the radius, the bone that should be connected to it, was missing. Some scavenging animal perhaps? Bernice fished out a magnifying glass and studied the bone. The ligaments connecting ulna to radius were not torn but severed, cut through with a sharp tool.

Bernice was outraged. Not only was she not the first, which was quite bad enough, but the site had been desecrated, vandalized! A potentially priceless specimen had been ruined. And who knew how much more damage had been done?

She raised her eyes to check the site for further damage, and found that someone was standing over her.

She raised her trowel defensively, and then saw with relief that the newcomer was a woman in an expensive-looking grey travelling cloak with a fur hood. She looked neat, elegant and utterly composed. In a crisp, authoritative voice the woman said, 'Who are you, and what are you doing here?'

The voice, the manner and, come to that, everything else about the woman got right up Bernice's nose. Including her appearance – no, especially her appearance. Bernice straightened up, very conscious of her muddy field boots, mud-stained jeans and scruffy safari jacket.

'I might ask you the same questions.'

'You might, but you'd be ill-advised to,' said the woman sharply. 'I know what I'm doing. You presumably don't or you wouldn't be here at all.'

'I'm an accredited archaeologist and I'm making a preliminary study of this site – which happens to have been vandalized.' Bernice went over to the attack. 'Do you know who's responsible?'

'Vandalized? How?'

'Something's buried here, some immensely large creature.'

'I know that. What do you mean, vandalized?'

'At least one important bone is missing from the skeleton. For all I know others may have been taken.'

The newcomer was silent for a moment, staring not so much at as through Bernice. Abruptly she said, 'An archaeologist, you say? Off-planet, presumably? This world doesn't run to such luxuries.'

Luxury indeed! thought Bernice Summerfield. Supercilious bitch! 'I'm on a grant from the Ellerycorp Foundation,' she said, naming one of her old employers at random. 'This is just a preliminary survey. We'll be mounting a full-scale expedition later.'

'Not if you've got any sense you won't. The political situation here is extremely unstable – and there are other problems too.'

'Such as?'

'You wouldn't understand if I told you. Are you staying in the village?'

Bernice nodded without speaking.

'I advise you to get back there straight away. It will be dark soon, and this place isn't safe after dark. Get yourself off this planet and don't come back.' Unexpectedly the woman smiled. 'It's not always a good idea, you know, digging up the past.'

With a nod of dismissal she turned and strode away. Bernice noticed for the first time that a grey horse was waiting quietly, reins dangling, at the edge of the burial ground. The woman swung herself gracefully into the saddle and galloped away.

'I hate horsy women,' muttered Bernice. 'One of the local aristos no doubt, thinks she owns the place and probably does.'

She looked up at the sky, realizing it had got suddenly darker.

'Still, I think I'll take her advice about getting back to the village.'

Giving the blood-stained altar a wide berth, Bernice made her way back to the front of the Tower and set about retracing her route. It was in the woods that things got seriously nasty.

It was really dark between the trees now and Bernice could see shapes gliding and swooping in the shadows. Bats! Suddenly she realized that there was a dark cloud of them above her head – and the cloud was getting thicker.

The bats were making an odd high-pitched chittering sound.

They started diving down at her, swirling about her head, and Bernice felt a sudden irrational fear that one of them would get caught in her hair. She started to run, pounding blindly along the forest path. The chittering rose higher. A bat flew at her cheek and she felt a stab of pain.

Still running, she flapped wildly at it. She rubbed her hand to her cheek and it came away wet and sticky.

'Blood!' she thought. 'Maybe they can smell blood, like sharks.'

She ran faster, gasping for breath now, and suddenly she shot out of the woods and into open ground. She ran on, hoping desperately that the bats wouldn't follow. To her vast relief she heard the chittering sound dying away behind her.

Still running she glanced over her shoulder at the darkening woods, and turned back to find a giant shape looming up in front of her. Before she could check her pace she ran straight into it – and bounced off the solidly reassuring form of Ivo. For a moment she could only look at him and gasp.

'Lady Bernice,' he said in astonishment.

'In person,' gasped Bernice. 'Thanks for coming to look for me.'

'I am glad to have found you, my Lady,' said Ivo solemnly. 'But in truth it was Gerda I was searching for.'

'Gerda?'

'My help-maid, she's been missing since last night.'

'Was she a tall girl with long fair hair?'

'Indeed she was – ' He broke off. 'You said "was", my Lady. I think you bring me ill news.'

Bernice couldn't reply. Ivo took her arm. 'We had best return to the inn, you can tell me there.'

Ivo insisted on settling Bernice in a chair by the fire before he would let her speak. He gave her a cup of rough red wine and Bernice swigged it gratefully.

Then he said, 'If you are ready, my Lady.'

She told him everything that had happened. Her exploration of the Tower, finding Gerda's blood-drained body, the creature that had attacked her, the strange woman at the burial ground.

As Ivo listened despair settled on his face. When she finished he said, 'The one who attacked you, what did he look like?'

'Tall, bearded, glittering eyes...' Suddenly Bernice remembered. 'There was a portrait of him in the throne room in the Tower.'

'Lord Zargo!' said Ivo. 'Perhaps the strange woman was Lady Camilla.' He put his head in his hands and groaned. 'It is true then – they cannot die.'

'Who can't?'

'Lord Zargo, Lady Camilla, Aukon the High Priest. The Old Lords have returned to rule over us.'

'But you said they'd all been destroyed.'

'They cannot be killed,' whispered Ivo. 'They die only to rise again. They are vampires.'

6

The Invitation

It was the end of the night at Doc's Place, the air stale with cigarette and cigar smoke and the smell of spilled booze.

The last customer had weaved his way into the night. Even the musicians had packed up their instruments and gone home. Only Sam the pianist was left, quietly playing the blues for his own pleasure, and Luigi, polishing glasses behind the bar.

It had been a peaceful night on the whole. Only three fights, two with fists, a knife pulled on the third. Ace grabbed the fighters early and bustled them into the vestibule. From there, Happy gave them the bum's rush outside.

The end of the night, thought Ace, with a jaw-cracking yawn – or the beginning of the morning. The Doctor always said sleep was for tortoises: it certainly wasn't for Chicago saloon-keepers. Alert as ever, immaculate in his white dinner-jacket, the Doctor sat in his alcove totting up the night's takings. A half-full glass of whisky stood at his elbow, a cigarette smouldered in the ashtray.

Sam's blues rippled to a conclusion and he closed the lid of the piano. 'Well, that's it, I guess,' he said in his soft smoky voice. 'Night Doc, night Miss Ace.'

'Good night, Sam,' said Ace, and the Doctor raised a hand in farewell.

Luigi placed a steaming cup of coffee in front of Ace and carried another one over to the Doctor. Then he said goodnight and went home. Ace carried her coffee over to the Doctor's alcove.

He looked up as she sat down. 'We're doing well, Ace. Even with what we pay Luigi and Sam and the band and Happy and the relief barman and the waiters – '

'Not to mention our contributions to the Mayor's campaign fund, and Captain Reilly's little envelope and a few extra bucks for the cop on the beat . . .'

'All legitimate business expenses,' agreed the Doctor. 'Even with all that we're still well in profit.'

'Making our own booze in the TARDIS must be a big help.'

'It is. We don't have to run a fleet of booze trucks or pay armed guards to stop hijackings.'

'Meanwhile I can't have a swim because the TARDIS swimming pool's full of bootleg beer.'

'Swim in the beer, the customers won't complain. It'll give it added body.'

Ace winced. 'I'm glad you're making a success of your new career, Doctor. How long is all this going on?'

'Hard to say,' said the Doctor evasively.

'Only breaking up bar-room brawls is a bit of a comedown for someone with my training. There's bound to be a nice little war going on somewhere in the galaxy.'

'There's a nice little war going on right here,' said the Doctor grimly. 'Don't worry, Ace, something's bound to happen soon.'

As if in answer to the Doctor's words the door swung open and a tall figure appeared. Ace's hand was already inside her bag but the newcomer raised his hands shoulder high.

'Don't shoot lady, it's only me!'

'Dekker!' said Ace in mock disgust. 'Who let you in here?'

'Happy's an old friend of mine.'

'Well, if you want a drink, you're too late, we're closed. If you're after breakfast, there's a diner called "Mom's" just down the street.'

'I tried it, the food's terrible. Come on, you can manage a nightcap for an old friend. What do you say, Doc?'

'My pleasure,' said the Doctor. 'But you'll have to help yourself, Luigi's gone home.'

'Helping myself is what I'm best at.' He went behind the bar, poured himself a large bourbon and carried it over to the alcove.

Ace looked critically at him over her coffee cup. A big, tough, ugly man, far too sure of himself. Not her type at all. All the same, there was something curiously engaging about Dekker. Like a friendly gorilla.

Dekker raised his glass in salute and took a swig of his bourbon. The Doctor studied him for a moment. 'Well, Mr Dekker, what's the word?'

Dekker blinked. 'You double as a mind-reader, Doc?'

'I just thought it was time there was some reaction from Mr Capone.'

'There is. Snorky wants you to have lunch with him.'

Ace raised her eyebrows. '*Snorky?*'

'It's what his close friends call him – but not to his face. Means spiffy, neat, smart . . . dapper! On account of Al's always so well dressed.'

'Is that so?' said Ace. 'Well, you can just tell your friend Snorky – '

The Doctor held up his hand: ' – that we'd be delighted. Come on Ace, lunch with Snorky is something not to be missed.'

'Suppose it's a trap?'

'You think I'd set you up?' said Dekker indignantly. 'Capone just wants to meet you, that's all. If he wanted to shoot you he'd shoot you, he wouldn't make an appointment to do it.'

'Oh yeah?' said Ace sceptically. 'Well, I'm coming along too, Dekker. And if there's any funny business, you'll be the first to go!'

Dekker grinned. 'Funny business with you, lady? Nothing could be further from my thoughts.'

In the smoke-filled back room of a North Side speakeasy, a late-night meeting was going on. Those taking part were all men of a similar type, thick-set, blue-jowled, expensively dressed. They wore diamond rings and jewelled tie-pins and smoked fat cigars. They carried guns under their arms and thick rolls of notes in their hip-pockets.

Their names were Pete Gusenberg, Bugs Moran and Hymie Weiss. They were the chiefs of the old O'Bannion mob. O'Bannion himself had been killed by order of Johnny Torrio, then Capone's boss. Now, with Torrio back in Italy, Capone had taken over. If Capone was the king of Chicago, these were the robber barons. No one of them dared stand against Capone alone. But together . . .

They were gathered round a big circular table, cards in front of them, money in the middle of the table, drinks within easy reach. They were talking about a man called Doc.

'I say we take him out,' screamed Bugs Moran. 'Who does he think he is, anyway?' Nicknamed 'Bugs' because of his maniacal temper, Moran always favoured the simple and violent solution.

'That's what we gotta find out,' said Pete Gusenberg. 'If this Doc's just an independent muscling in, we can deal with him. But if he's tied in with Al . . . well, maybe we should watch our step.'

'If he's tied in with Al,' said Weiss deliberately, 'Al's using him as a front to move in on territory that oughtta be ours.'

'So he goes either way,' said Gusenberg. 'I'll see to it myself. The guy knocks off Morelli, smacks my boys around . . . Nobody treats Pete Gusenberg like that!'

The telephone rang.

A tall thin man in a chair by the door got up to answer it. He listened for a moment then said, 'Yeah, he's here. It's for you, Mr Gusenberg.'

Pete Gusenberg got up and went to the phone. He listened for a moment and said, 'Okay, thanks. And keep me posted, I'll make it worth your while.' He hung up the phone and went back to the table, a wolfish grin on his face. 'I gotta contact inside Al's mob. This guy Doc's having lunch with Al. Tomorrow morning in the restaurant at the Hawthorne Hotel.'

The thin man leaned forwards, staring hard at the little group. Just for a moment there seemed to be a red spark in his deep-set eyes. All at once, the atmosphere around the table was charged with bloodthirsty excitement.

'The restaurant at the Hawthorne's on the corner of the block, ground floor,' said Moran. 'Windows face right onto the street.'

Even the normally stolid Weiss was caught up in the blood-lust. 'If we could get them both, Al and Doc together . . .'

Pete Gusenberg jumped up and went to a walk-in closet in the corner. 'Fritz just delivered a consignment of these babies. Cost me two hundred and fifty bucks apiece. Seems like a good opportunity to try them out.'

He emerged from the closet holding a gleaming new Thompson sub-machine-gun.

Doc was already waiting when I turned up around noon the way we'd arranged. He'd swapped the white tux for a snazzy suit, dark blue with pin-stripes, and he was carrying a pearl-grey fedora.

'Ace will be down in a minute, Mr Dekker,' he said. 'She's on her fourth or fifth costume change already, it can't take much longer.'

'You look pretty neat yourself, Doc,' I said.

'A guy's gotta keep up a good front,' said Doc solemnly.

At this point Ace came down the stairs, and however many outfits she'd tried on she'd ended up with the right one. She was wearing a black tailored skirt and jacket, with black stockings and a pillbox hat. There was a big handbag over her shoulder so I guessed she was heeled. The bag was big enough to hold a howitzer.

'Well, we're a classy outfit all right,' I said. 'I can see we're going to impress the hell out of old Snorky.'

As we came out of the house a big black Cadillac saloon, as big as a bus, was pulling up outside. Behind the wheel was Happy Harrigan, grinning like an idiot, a chauffeur's hat jammed onto his bullet head.

Doc opened the door for Ace and she got in. Doc

followed and I went round the other side. We sank into the leather upholstery and leant back, the three of us in a row with Ace in the middle.

'How come I don't get a window seat?' she asked.

I gave her a fatherly pat on the knee.

'Window seats can be dangerous here in Chicago.'

'So can wandering hands. Get your hand off my knee, Dekker, before I shoot it off.'

I folded my arms just in case she meant it, and the car glided away. We crossed Chicago in record time, mostly because Happy drove as though nobody else had any right to be on the road.

Twenty-Second Street was as busy as ever and the kerb outside the Hawthorne was lined with cars. Happy double-parked outside the Hawthorne Smoke Shop – one of Capone's gambling joints – and we all got out and headed for the restaurant.

It was a classy joint for Cicero, marble-topped tables, waiters, the lot, and it was packed with the lunch-time crowd. There was a big table in the window, the best in the place. It held one big, bulky figure and one slender one – Capone and his top bodyguard, Frank Rio.

Rio stood up and stepped back as we headed for the table. Capone didn't move.

'This is Doc, Mr Capone,' I said. 'And this is – '

'I kinda had the idea this was a business meeting,' said Capone. 'Dames and business don't mix.'

Al was trying to grab the initiative, giving Doc the Look, the angry bulging-eyed stare that turned most guys to mush.

It had no effect on Doc whatsoever. He gave Al look for look and said quietly, 'Ace is a full partner in all my enterprises. She's a very skilled negotiator. You could ask Mr Morelli – if he was still available for comment.'

Al turned the Look onto Ace.

'You're the dame that chilled Morelli?'

'If that was his name. He pulled a gun on me, so he wasn't around long enough for us to get acquainted.'

And so help me, she gave Capone back the Look, just like Doc.

Capone laughed. 'You hear that Frankie? This is the dame took out Morelli. You better keep your eye on her.'

'It'll be a pleasure, Mr Capone,' said Rio. He stood there, calm and relaxed, one hand plunged deep in his jacket pocket.

'You can look all you like,' said Ace. 'But keep your hands where I can see them while you're doing it.'

It was Frank's turn to glare now. But he took his hand out of his pocket – empty – and folded his arms.

Al decided to turn on the charm. 'Hey, what kind of hospitality is this? Siddown, all of you.'

We took seats around the big table.

Capone snapped his fingers. 'Where's that goddam champagne?'

A waiter appeared with a bottle in an ice bucket. He popped the cork and started pouring the wine. When all the glasses were full Al said, 'A toast, hey? Peace and prosperity!' He raised his glass. 'Drink up, Doc. This stuff ain't made in no bathtub, it's my own personal stock, imported.'

Doc took a sip of the champagne. 'Krug 21, if I'm not mistaken. An excellent choice, Mr Capone.'

'Hell, what do I know? I started out as a barkeep in the Bowery. But a guy can learn, hey Doc?'

'That's right, Mr Capone. A guy can always learn – if he lives.'

That crack brought the Look back onto Capone's face, and Doc returned it coolly. They sat there staring each other out. Meanwhile Ace and Frankie Rio were eyeing each other as well, wondering who was quicker on the draw. And there I was in the middle. It was about as restful as having a drink in a cage full of tigers.

'Meaning?' said Al at last.

'I think you're in danger, Mr Capone,' said Doc.

The Big Fellow laughed. 'I ain't never been in anything else. Am I in danger from you, Doc?'

I saw Doc smile. 'I'm strictly neutral. All I want is to run a quiet place and have a quiet life.'

'Me too,' said Capone, and he meant it. 'There's enough for all of us in the booze racket. Why spend time knocking each other off when we could all be making dough?'

Doc leaned forward. 'Then why so many deaths? Why all the shootings, stabbings, stranglings, disappearances?'

Al threw out his hands. 'Doc, I wish I knew. I get the bosses together for a sit-down, we agree territories, we make deals – and for a week or two everything runs smooth.'

'And then?'

'Then someone hijacks a booze shipment. Or starts muscling in on some other guy's territory. Or two guys from different mobs fight over some dame and one of them gets rubbed out and the pals of the dead guy take the winner for a ride. And it's getting worse. Just recently guys seem to be rubbing out other guys just the hell of it.'

Doc leaned forward, suddenly interested. 'Killing for the sake of killing?'

Al shrugged. 'Pretty much.'

Something kinda funny struck me. Right from the start this had been a meeting of equals. Which was ridiculous when you came to think about it. Here was Doc, new in town, running one small joint with just Ace and Happy for back-up. No, Ace and Happy and me, I realized. Somehow I'd already chosen sides. And there was Al Capone, the Big Fellow who controlled speakeasies and gambling joints and cat-houses all over Chicago. Capone who owned politicians and cops, who could put an army of killers on the streets.

Doc wasn't big and he didn't act tough. But he was somebody all the same, and Al knew it.

'Doc, what are you after?'

'I'm after whoever or whatever's stopping you from selling your booze in peace, Mr Capone – and turning Chicago into a killing ground.'

'Why? Why should you worry about my problems?'

'Because they're my problems as well. At least, this one is.'

Suddenly something was bothering me and I wasn't sure what it was. A sound . . . I stood up. 'Listen!'

A steady roar of traffic was coming from Twenty-Third Street. Frank Rio said, 'I hear cars. Whaddya expect from a city street, Dekker, hoofbeats?'

Ace was on her feet too. 'No, he's right, I hear it too. Not just passing traffic but a lot of cars, heading this way. Like a convoy.'

A car drove up to the restaurant, its gong clanging. I saw Capone relax.

'It's okay, it's only the cops.' Al had nothing to fear from the police. He owned most of them.

But this was no detective bureau car. I saw a gun muzzle appear at its window. The muzzle belched fire and I heard the stuttering roar of a tommy-gun.

'Duck!' I yelled – and the car sped past, the sound of the tommy-gun fading into the distance.

Suddenly it was very quiet.

'What the goddam hell!' roared Capone. He started for the entrance, Frankie Rio close behind.

'Wait!' said Doc, and there was something in his voice that stopped Capone in his tracks. 'All those shots and not a single hit?'

'They're firing blanks,' snapped Ace. 'That first car was a decoy to get us onto the street.'

Suddenly we heard the roar of the convoy, louder and closer this time.

'Down!' I yelled. 'Everyone down!'

Doc grabbed the tile-topped table we were sitting at and threw it on its side, scattering bottles and glasses. We ducked down behind it.

We heard more cars driving up to the Hawthorne. Then the roar of more choppers, lots of them this time, and they weren't firing blanks.

The front window of the restaurant disappeared in a shower of broken glass.

57

7

The Attack

By now everyone in the restaurant was yelling their head off. Capone, who'd hit the deck at surprising speed for a guy his size, turned his head and bellowed, 'Everybody down, down flat! There's more to come!'

There sure was. Bullets poured into the restaurant in a steady stream, smashing plates and glasses and cups. The tommy-guns stitched neat lines of bullet holes in the walls. Bullets smashed wood-panelling into splinters and brought plaster crashing down from the ceiling.

Me and Ace and Frank all had guns in our hands but there was no point in shooting back – it would have been like spitting into a hurricane. All we could do was keep our heads down and wait for the firestorm to die down.

I raised my head a fraction and eyeballed round the edge of our table. It was a hell of a sight. Ten – I counted 'em – *ten* sedans were drawn up in a long line outside the restaurant, a blazing tommy-gun sticking out of each window. Ten choppers and each drum held a hundred rounds. They musta poured a thousand bullets into that restaurant.

One by one the tommy-guns fell silent. Someone up the front of the line honked three times and the cars started moving away like some goddam procession.

All except the last car, the tenth. The door opened and a man in a brown shirt and khaki overalls got out, clipping a fresh drum onto his tommy-gun. Two more hoods with shotguns jumped out of the back and stood flanking him.

The guy with the tommy-gun took a couple of steps

toward the Hawthorne and started shooting, swinging the blazing chopper from side to side. Taking his time, like he was in a shooting gallery, he pumped another hundred slugs into the restaurant. When the drum was empty he jumped back into the car. The two shotgunners followed, and the sedan started moving away.

Suddenly Ace was on her feet and moving. Gun in hand, she hiked up her skirt, jumped through the shattered window and started shooting at the retreating car. I jumped through the window right behind her and saw two shotgun muzzles appear through the car's back window. I tackled Ace like a Chicago Bears line-backer, carrying her to the ground. Two shotgun blasts boomed over our heads, one of them so close it blew my hat off.

I was lying on top of Ace, catching my breath – and thinking it wasn't such a bad place to be – when an elbow jabbed me in the ribs. She wriggled out from under and got to her feet.

'You big ape, Dekker, when will you stop interfering? I could've shot the driver, caught one of those other hoods and found out who's behind this.'

I got wearily to my feet, picking my hat up out of the gutter.

'You're just overflowing with gratitude, ain't you? All you'd have caught was a faceful of shotgun pellets.'

She was opening her mouth to give me another earful when I shoved my hat under her nose. The shotgun pellets had blasted a big chunk out of the brim.

'That's a ten-dollar fedora there, lady, ruined! And for your information we know who's behind this. That last guy, the one in the overalls, was Pete Gusenberg in person. Pete's a snappy dresser, probably didn't want to spoil his suit.'

I turned and stomped back into the ruined restaurant, where I found Doc, hands in pockets, calmly looking round. It was quite a sight: broken glass, splintered wood and shattered plaster everywhere. Everything in the restaurant had been pretty well shot to pieces and the room was full of hysterical people, laughing, chattering and sobbing.

I fishéd out a Camel and stuck it in my mouth. 'Many dead, Doc?'

'Apart from a few cuts and bruises I don't think anyone's even wounded.' He pointed to a line of bullet holes across the nearest wall. 'They seemed to be aiming about waist-high, and by the time they got going everyone was flat on the floor – thanks to your warning.'

'You worked it out first, Doc. If we'd all run out on the street the way they wanted . . .'

He nodded. 'It was Capone they were after, of course. I got shot at for nothing – just an innocent bystander.'

I looked at him, wondering just how innocent he was.

'You picked a tough town to run a saloon in, Doc. And you keep dangerous company.'

Al Capone stood in the centre of a little group nearby, back in charge as usual, issuing a stream of orders. He put his hand on the shoulder of a little bald guy with a droopy moustache. It was the manager, weeping helplessly at the sight of his ruined restaurant.

'Don't worry, we're gonna have this place fixed up better than new, I'll see to it personally. Frankie, check out things on the street. Anything damaged, anybody hurt, I'll take care of it.'

I heard later that the machine-gunners had put holes in about thirty of the jalopies parked along the kerb and blasted the windows of a number of local stores. Capone paid handsome compensation to the car owners and shopkeepers. Miraculously there had been only one serious casualty out on the street, a woman who'd been sitting in her car with her family when the shooting started. A splinter from the bullet-shattered windscreen got her in the eye. The operation that saved her sight cost Capone five thousand bucks.

Capone turned, saw Doc standing nearby and swept him up in an Italian embrace. He didn't exactly kiss him but it was a pretty near thing.

'You and your friends saved my life, Doc. Anything you want, anything in Chicago, it's yours.'

'Like running my own saloon?'

'You got it, Doc. I'll put the word around. No interference from me or anyone else. Guaranteed. Anything else I can do for you, just name it.'

'Well, you did say something about lunch.'

Capone laughed. 'Service here could be a little slow today. We'll go back to the Hawthorne Hotel, see what the chef can rustle up. Say, Doc, you like Italian food?'

Capone put an arm round Doc's shoulder and led him away. As they left Doc glanced quickly back at Ace, and I got the idea some kinda signal passed between them. Then they moved off, Doc overshadowed by the bulk of Capone.

I turned and saw Ace looking thoughtfully after them.

'Looks like Doc's well in with the Big Fellow,' I said.

'It's a knack he has, Dekker, making influential friends. I've seen him best mates with bigger bosses than Al Capone.'

'You want to go with them? I'm pretty sure we're included. Al's very generous, and he means what he said. If you want a new mink or a new Cadillac, now's the time.'

'I don't approve of fur coats and I'll buy my own Cadillacs. All I need now is lunch, and I think I've had all I want of Al Capone's hospitality. I don't suppose you'd know some place that sells a decent steak and a bottle of wine?'

'Sure,' I said. 'Little Italian joint called Tonio's. Wooden booths, candles on the tables, a violinist. Kinda romantic.'

She gave me a look. 'Just as long as the steaks are good, Dekker.'

'Best in Chicago.'

'Let's go then.'

We walked back to the corner where Happy had parked the limo and found him fast asleep behind the wheel, his chauffeur's cap over his eyes. I rapped on the window and he woke up. He wound the window down and blinked, taking in the crowded street – even the Cicero cops had turned out by now – and the pavements covered with broken glass.

'Has there been some kind of trouble, Mr Dekker?'

'Al didn't like the soup,' I told him. 'Take us downtown, will you Happy? Tonio's on Clarke Street.'

We got into the car and Happy drove us away.

Sinking back into the leather upholstery beside Ace I thought there were two possibilities. Either she'd suddenly fallen for my manly charms, or I'd been right about that signal. Doc wanted to talk to the Big Fellow alone.

Lunch was over, the remains of the meal cleared away, and the Big Fellow and his guest were alone in the luxurious hotel suite.

They sat in adjoining armchairs by the window overlooking Twenty-Second Street, now teeming with cops, pressmen and astonished citizens, all staring in amazement at the bullet-shattered Hawthorne Restaurant. A shootup on this scale was something special, even in Chicago.

A marble-topped table between the two men held a crystal decanter of Napoleon brandy and a box of Havana cigars. As they talked Capone drank and smoked continuously, while Doc sat back in his chair nursing a balloonglass of brandy. Doc didn't seem to be much of a talker but he was a hell of a good listener. Capone was doing most of the talking, holding forth on his favourite subject: himself.

'. . . so I got into a little trouble in New York and I came out here.'

'And you never looked back?'

'Well, I hadda start at the bottom again. Hell, I even worked as a doorman outside the Four Deuces for a while.' Capone lowered his voice to a throaty whisper. '*Looking for a good time, mister? We got some good-looking dames inside . . .*'

'But you got promoted?'

'My timing was right. Me and Prohibition hit Chicago in the same year. You around when it all started, Doc?'

'No, I was out of the country . . . travelling. I've never understood how such a ridiculous law got passed.'

Capone leaned forward, eager to make Doc understand.

'Somewhere back in the '90s this gang of bible-thumping blue-nosers called the Anti-Saloon League decide they want to make booze illegal. Booze! At first everyone thinks they're crazy. But they get bigger and bigger. By the time the Big War breaks out in 1914 they're already picking up a helluva lot of support. By 1920, just two years after the war, they've got enough clout to make Congress pass the Eighteenth Amendment. Suddenly it's illegal to make, sell or transport any drink containing more than half a per cent alcohol. But it ain't illegal to buy it, own it, or drink it – so the customer's in the clear.'

Al Capone sat back and puffed at his cigar, a dedicated businessman discussing his trade.

'*Making* booze is illegal, sure. But there's a helluva demand out there. So whaddya do? You make it anyway, illegally, pay off the cops and the Prohibition boys. There's plenty of breweries turning out real beer, most of them with police guards protecting their shipments.'

'What about the hard stuff?'

'You can make that too, though not the kind you're drinking. Like the Sicilian mob. The Genna boys have put a little still in every kitchen in Little Italy. They pay the family fifteen bucks a day to brew the alky, come round and collect it once a week.' Capone chuckled. 'The stills blow up now and again and the stuff's rot-gut anyway, but it's a good racket. Or you can import. Bring the booze in undercover from Canada or Europe. Costs you more so you gotta charge your customers more but they're getting the genuine article, French brandy, Scotch whisky, good wine. That's *my* speciality – the quality end of the market.'

'So why all the killing?'

'Greed,' said Capone sadly. 'Laziness and greed. You see Doc, whether you make your booze or import it, you got a business on your hands. You gotta run breweries, look after a network of alky cookers, organize shipments and deliveries, and pay off cops, politicians and feds as well.'

'And some people find that too much like work?'

'Exactly. And remember, there's a third way to get hold of booze, the quickest and cheapest way of all. You steal it. So, you get guys hijacking each other's shipments, raiding each other's warehouses. Deany O'Bannion was doing it all the time.' Capone sighed. 'He was a swell guy, Deany, but in the end he had to go.'

'And you took over?'

'I took over Johnny Torrio's operation when he retired on account of getting shot. Weiss, Moran and Gusenberg took over from O'Bannion. They're the ones who pulled that stunt this afternoon.'

'You're sure of that? I mean, you do have other business rivals.'

'Sure I do. Spike O'Donnell's boys, the Gennas, the Aiellos, Saltis and his Polack mob. But by and large we all get along. But Weiss and the rest of those guys can't forget about O'Bannion.'

The Doctor stood up. 'Mr Capone, I want to ask you a favour.'

'Name it.'

'I want you to summon a peace conference. Every mob in Chicago, large or small, including Moran, Gusenberg and Weiss. A meeting to fix territories, stop hijackings, settle grievances once and for all.'

Capone shook his head. 'This ain't the time for it. First I gotta deal with those guys who shot up my place.'

Doc sighed. 'They pull a knife, you pull a gun, they put one of yours in the hospital, you put one of theirs in the morgue, is that it?'

'That's the Chicago way. If they think I'm scared, I lose respect. I hate to refuse you Doc, but I can't do it.'

The Doctor stood over Capone, fixing him with compelling grey eyes. 'Mr Capone, you're the only man who *can* do it, the only one everyone will listen to. And do you seriously think that anyone in Chicago will think *you're* scared?'

Capone brooded for a moment, then rose, his bulky figure towering over his guest. 'Okay, Doc. But I tried this before. What makes you think it'll work this time?'

'I don't,' said Doc surprisingly. 'What I want to know is who's going to try to make it fail.'

8

His Honour the Mayor

Big Bill Thompson slammed his massive fist down on the Mayoral desk, making ashtrays and pen-set jump and jingle.

'Machine-guns blazing on the streets of Chicago!' he boomed. 'Innocent citizens terrified and wounded. It's a disgrace, I tell you.'

A big, handsome man, elegantly dressed and full of vitality, Thompson was a typical politician, strong on sound and fury, weak on effective action. He liked to be known as Big Bill. His campaign slogan had been: 'Vote for Big Bill the Builder – He cannot be Bought, Bossed or Bluffed.'

District Attorney William McSwiggin, plump, bespectacled and serious, gave the expected response. 'Quite right, your honour, a disgrace indeed! Something must be done.' Both men looked sternly at the third man in the room.

Police Captain Dennis Reilly, resplendent in blue uniform and gleaming brass buttons, recognized his cue. 'Investigations are under way at this very moment, your honour. I give you me solemn word the villains responsible shall be brought to justice.'

The formalities were concluded.

Big Bill Thompson, Mayor of Chicago, sworn enemy of crime and upholder of Prohibition, yanked an expensive gold fob-watch from his waistcoat pocket and checked the time.

'It's still a little early but what the hell, it's been a tough day. Let's have a drink. Will you do the honours, Bill?'

District Attorney McSwiggin went to the drinks cupboard in the corner of the oak-panelled office. There was the clink of bottle on glass and he returned with two heavy crystal tumblers brimming with Scotch whisky.

'Irish for you, Dennis?'

'If you please.'

McSwiggin brought Reilly a tumbler of Dewars and returned to his seat.

Big Bill took a cigar from the silver box on the desk, then pushed it towards Reilly and McSwiggin. Both men took cigars and lit up.

For a moment all three sat silent, sipping whisky. Unspoken thoughts hung in the air, as heavy as the coils of blue cigar smoke.

The Mayor knew perfectly well that McSwiggin was Capone's liaison man with Chicago's political establishment. He knew that Reilly looked after the interests of the Moran, Gusenberg and Weiss mob in a similar way.

Both McSwiggin and Reilly knew that Mayor Thompson expected his cut from them and from every other corrupt official in Chicago, in return for running Chicago as an open city for crime.

Thompson had an ever-hungry campaign fund that needed constant topping up. He was serving his third term as Mayor of Chicago and he had his eye on higher things. Big Bill Thompson fully intended to be the next President of the United States. Why not? The man who could run Chicago could surely run America.

'I have to admit that the boys went a bit too far,' said Reilly at last.

'I'll say they did,' said Thompson. 'They tell me it was a war zone over there at the Hawthorne, bullets and broken glass everywhere.'

'Pete Gusenberg's an impulsive fellow, your honour.'

Thompson looked at McSwiggin. 'The question is, what will Capone do about it? If he decides to pay 'em back in kind there'll be a full scale war right here in Chicago. I can imagine what the *Tribune*'s going to make of this.'

The *Chicago Tribune* and its formidable proprietor

Colonel McCormack were a constant problem for Big Bill Thompson. However many inspirational speeches Thompson made, *Tribune* editorials continued to harp on the uncomfortable and unacceptable facts. Over five hundred gangland murders in the past ten years – without one conviction. Hundreds of speakeasies, liquor joints, bars and brothels flourishing all over Chicago and its suburbs. Above all, the constant stream of bootleg money, corrupting the police, the legal system and the politicians alike.

'I don't know,' said McSwiggin at last. 'Al hates all this gun stuff, says it's bad for business. But he's no push-over and he's got a temper, even if he keeps it in check. They give him too much grief, there'll be blood running in the gutters.'

Big Bill Thompson shuddered.

'What about this fella Doc?' asked Reilly.

Thompson shrugged. 'What about him?'

'I hear he was having lunch with Capone when the Hawthorne got shot up. Where does he stand in all this?'

'How the hell should I know?'

'I thought he was a friend of your honour's?'

Thompson shook his head. 'Don't know a thing about him. I got an anonymous campaign contribution. The note with it said it came from a friend of Doc's. Said there'd be more where that came from if Doc was allowed to open up his place and operate in peace.'

'Would you mind if I was after closing him down, and maybe hauling him in for a little chat?'

Thompson thought for a moment, and then shook his head.

'Let's not do anything rash, Dennis. If this Doc's got connections, I don't want them mad at me – I've got enough enemies as it is. Besides, it was a pretty big contribution.'

'Something about that wee feller makes me uncomfortable,' said Reilly. 'He's too damn sure of himself. And he's got this girl Ace that can shoot the eyes out of a fly, so they tell me. And Dekker's tied in with them as well.'

'Forget about Doc,' said Thompson impatiently. 'What's

another speakeasy more or less? It's this feud between Capone and Moran's boys that worries me.'

He put his big hands on the desk and leaned forward.

'Talk to these guys, both of you. Tell them to keep things peaceful. If they don't I'll launch a police crackdown that'll put them all out of business. Remember, I've got the *Tribune* looking over my shoulder. And if it's me or them, it's gonna be them.'

Thompson stood up. The meeting was at an end. Hurriedly draining their glasses, Reilly and McSwiggin got up and said their goodbyes.

'I'm relying on you, boys,' called Thompson as they went out. He slumped wearily behind his desk, thinking about the coming Presidential elections. If the gangster situation in Chicago erupted into a major scandal he wouldn't even win the nomination, let alone the presidency. Capone himself would stand a better chance.

One of his political aides entered, a tall, thin, elegant-looking man. He was carrying a newspaper.

'Yeah, what is it?' growled Thompson.

'The *Tribune*'s bringing out a special edition, sir. I managed to get an advance copy, I thought you ought to see it.'

He spread a sheet of newspaper on Thompson's desk. The thick black ink of the lettering on the giant headline was still wet. The front page of the paper was filled with a big picture of the bullet-shattered facade of the Hawthorne Restaurant. The headline above the picture said: *THIS IS WAR*

Thompson glanced at the article below the headline. It began: *Gang war rages unchecked in Chicago, while a corrupt and inefficient civic administration stands helplessly by. When will Mayor Thompson act?*

Thompson winced and averted his eyes.

'You had the right idea earlier,' murmured the aide.

'I did? And what idea was that.'

'Mobilize the police and crack down on these gangster scum.'

'What's the use of that? They own the judges in this

69

town, they bribe or terrify the juries. We can never convict anyone.'

'Then kill them all,' whispered the compelling voice. 'Shoot them down like dogs.'

'Are you crazy? Do you know how many killers the mobs can call on? Capone alone must have a thousand hoods on the payroll. All of them armed to the teeth. They've got Thompsons, carbines, shotguns, revolvers . . . It'd be a blood-bath!'

'The police have guns as well. When it's all over, you'll be a hero. The man who cleaned up Chicago.'

As the shadows began to gather in his office Mayor Thompson's ears were filled with the harsh staccato chatter of tommy-guns. He saw the bodies of his enemies, twisting and falling in a hail of bullets.

The sound faded and he saw himself taking the Oath of Office on the White House lawn.

The tall thin aide stood over him in the gloom. Just for a second, the eyes of the aide showed a glint of red.

9

The Meeting

Ivo looked round the crowded inn. All the men of the village were there, and as many of those from the outlying farms as they'd been able to reach. Everyone, from grandfathers stooped from a life of toil to boys just big enough to carry a hoe. They stood around the hall in little groups, talking quietly.

Lady Bernice, the stranger, sat beside him at the head of the table. She'd been badly shaken when he'd found her in the forest, but she'd recovered quickly. Now, after food, drink and rest she was herself again.

Ivo found himself thinking of two other strangers, the tall curly-haired man and the small slim woman. Their coming had meant the end of the Old Times. The end of fear. Ivo clenched his great fists on the wooden table, remembering. They had lived with fear in those days, from the time they rose at dawn to toil in the fields till the moment they closed their eyes in exhausted sleep. Fear that their children would be taken at the Time of Selection. Fear of the undying Lords who ruled in the Tower. Now the fear was back.

'But not for long,' vowed Ivo to himself. He had lost his son long ago at the Time of Selection. His wife Marta had died soon after, worn out by grief and a lifetime of toil. He wasn't going to let her suffering go for nothing. This time they would act, before the evil grew too strong.

Ivo raised his voice in a deep-chested bellow that bludgeoned through all the chatter. 'Friends! Your attention, please! If you will gather round . . .'

Slowly the crowd gathered round Ivo's table, some sitting, some perched on tables nearby.

Ivo spoke again. 'This morning my serving-maid Gerda didn't come to work. I thought little of it, it's happened before. She has a lover on one of the farms.'

'Gerda's got a lover on *all* the farms!' shouted a fat farmer.

'I thought Gerda would turn up during the morning,' Ivo went on. 'But she didn't. I waited till near evening and went to her mother's cottage. Her mother said she'd gone out to gather berries in the woods the evening before and hadn't come back. Like me, she thought Gerda had found company for the night and gone straight to the inn next morning. So I went to the woods to look for her, and instead found the Lady Bernice, a guest at my inn.' He turned to Bernice. 'My Lady?'

Bernice looked round the group of villagers. They all looked puzzled and some looked distinctly hostile.

'You don't know me, and I don't know you,' she began. 'I came here from – from far away, to study your history. Tonight I paid a visit to the Tower . . .'

Briefly she told them what had happened after that. When she finished her account there was a stunned and horrified silence.

'The one who attacked you,' said the fat farmer hoarsely. 'You're sure it was Zargo?'

'All I can say is that he looked like the picture in the Tower.'

'And the woman, the one who warned you to go away. Was that Camilla?'

'I can't be sure, but I don't think so. She was dressed differently, she didn't look anything like the portrait and she seemed – well, human.'

A babble of voices filled the hall. The voices were excited and fearful. Some of them were angry.

The fat farmer, who seemed to be some kind of ringleader, shouted, 'Why should we believe all this?'

'Why should I lie to you?'

'We don't even know for sure that Gerda's dead. And

if she is, maybe it was you who killed her! There was no trouble here till you arrived!'

The crowd pressed menacingly closer.

They're frightened, thought Ivo. And they're getting out of hand. Standing up, he raised his voice in a commanding bellow: 'Quiet, all of you!' He glared down at the fat farmer. 'And you, Tubar, that's enough. The Lady Bernice is our friend, and I vouch for her. She's brought us a warning at the risk of her life. Now it's up to us to act on it.'

'Act how?' asked a young farmer called Lothar.

'By going to the Tower and rooting out this evil. If the Old Lords have returned, we shall destroy them once again!'

It took quite a while before everything was decided. Still, that's democracy for you, thought Bernice, sitting silent amidst the chattering crowd. She remembered the Doctor quoting some old mate of his called Winnie – whoever she was. What was it? 'Democracy is the worst form of government, except for all those other forms that have been tried from time to time.'

Meanwhile the debate raged on. There was a strong party, led by the ever-talkative Tubar, in favour of waiting till morning, but Ivo would have none of it.

'We cannot afford a moment's delay,' he boomed. 'Who knows how long this evil has been growing in secret? We must crush it now, before it grows even stronger.'

In the end Ivo had his way. It was agreed that a group of the youngest and strongest men should go at once to the Tower. The very young and the very old would either stay in the village or return to their farms.

'I knew they'd come round,' said Ivo aside to Bernice. 'They're good men, but they're frightened.'

'That Tubar wasn't much help.'

'He's jealous. Wants to replace me as headman one day.'

'And will he?'

'Not if I know anything about it. I've already picked

73

the one to take over, young Lothar. Cautious but steady, he is.'

'What about weapons?' asked Bernice. 'I've got a blaster I can bring along.'

Ivo looked surprised. 'You surely don't mean to come with us, my Lady? The danger –'

'I surely do,' said Bernice firmly. 'And I don't want any of your medieval male chauvinism either. Now, what about these weapons?'

'We've got a few old swords and spears, stuff we took from the Guards in the old days. A couple of crossbows. They're kept in my store-room.'

'Better get them handed out,' said Bernice. 'We'll need torches too, the more light the better. And a sharpened stake.'

'A stake, my Lady?'

'To hammer through the thing's heart, if we catch it. Come to that, there may be more than one of them. Better bring lots of stakes and sledgehammers as well.'

Ivo nodded. 'Anything more, my Lady?'

Bernice struggled to remember the vampire lore she'd gathered from old horror holovids. 'Bring some axes so we can cut off its head. We'd better expose the body to direct sunlight ... And if all that doesn't work we'll just have to put salt on its tail.'

Finally the little expedition set off. Its members were loaded down with axes, swords, spears, sharpened stakes and sledgehammers. In addition, each man carried a blazing torch. The torches were made from bundles of rags tied to the top of wooden poles and dipped in a mixture of oil and tar. They blazed merrily as the line of men, Bernice and Ivo at the head, marched down the village street. The fiery light of the torches flickered on the little huts where frightened women and children and old folk huddled, waiting for the dawn.

It was even darker in the woods, and they were glad of the torchlight. Disturbed by the noise and the light, bats rose in chittering clouds and swirled about their heads.

Men lashed out at them with the blazing torches, driving them away.

Soon, all too soon for Bernice despite her brave words, they had crossed the stretch of open wasteland and arrived at the Tower. Its door stood open.

Bernice turned to Ivo. 'That door closed behind me when I went in. Someone's come out, or gone in, since then.'

Ivo raised his torch. 'Follow me – and stay close. If we are attacked, try to behead the creature or drive a stake through its heart.'

'Or both!' said Bernice.

'Come!' said Ivo. He strode through the open doors and the rest of them followed. By the light of the blazing torches they retraced Bernice's journey. They climbed the staircase to the throne room and saw the rotting tapestries and the decaying, empty thrones. Behind the thrones the wall was bare. 'The portrait,' whispered Bernice. 'It's gone!'

At Ivo's direction they searched the other rooms, the ones Bernice hadn't entered. More state rooms, living quarters, kitchens, store-rooms: all reeked of decay and all were empty and silent, though occasionally small rat-like creatures scurried away at their approach. They searched the upper levels of the Tower and even the scout ship turrets, but there was nothing to be found.

Finally they descended the ladder to the stripped engine room with its metal racks. Bernice was following Ivo and she had to force herself to look as his torch lit up the chamber. But there was nothing there. The girl's body had gone.

Everyone looked at Bernice. Taking a torch from the nearest man, she went over to the place where the body had been hanging.

'Look! There are a few spots of blood, here and here! And there are traces of dried blood in the gutter. Someone tried to clean up, but they were in too much of a hurry to do a good job.'

Ivo, Tubar, Lothar and the others came to join her.

'The blood is old,' said Tubar sceptically.

Bernice wet her finger, rubbed one of the blood spots and held the finger up to the torchlight. The tip was red with blood.

'Yes, *hours* old,' she said. 'Not years and years.'

'Why would anyone move the girl's body?'

'So you'd all do exactly what you are doing,' said Bernice. 'Think I'd made the whole thing up and there wasn't any danger.'

'Gerda *is* missing,' said Lothar slowly.

'That's right. And I can promise you she isn't going to turn up in any farm-boy's bed either.'

'We have found nothing,' said Tubar angrily.

'The Tower is large,' said Ivo. 'Can we be sure to have searched every hidden cranny? The creature that attacked Lady Bernice might still lie concealed. We should go now and return to search by daylight.'

'We should certainly go,' grumbled Tubar. 'And I won't be coming back. I've a day's work to do tomorrow, and small time left for sleep.'

They filed back up the ladder, went through the throne room, down the staircase and out of the Tower. As they trudged back to the village Bernice was thinking furiously. Why had the body been taken – and the portraits as well? She'd stumbled on something that wasn't meant to be seen, not yet. Now someone, or something, was covering its tracks.

They were out of the woods by now – the bats had been strangely silent – and on the outskirts of the village. They'd reached the point where the main street of the village and the road that bordered the fields met at a crossroads.

In the centre of that crossroads lay a huddled body.

Bernice's first thought was that they'd found the missing girl, but as she ran towards it she saw that the shape was black, not white. It was one of the Black Guards, lying face down in the dust of the crossroads.

Ivo came up beside her and helped her to turn the body over. The face of the young soldier stared blindly up at them. His throat had been slit open, almost severing the head, and the skin of the face was a deathly white.

Bernice pushed back the sleeve of the man's tunic. The skin of the arm had the same dead whiteness. The body had been completely drained of blood.

Suddenly they heard the sound of pounding hooves. A patrol of the Black Guard was galloping down the road towards them. As it drew nearer, Bernice saw it was the same patrol that had visited the inn earlier. At least, it had the same Captain, the arrogant young man called Varis.

He reined his horse to a halt a few feet away from them and leaped to the ground shouting, 'Surround them!' The rest of the horsemen formed themselves into a ring, imprisoning the men on the ground.

Varis knelt beside the body, peering into the white face. 'Tolar!' He straightened up, his hand going to his sword. 'You murdering scum!' There was an angry growl from the ring of mounted men.

'This is none of our work,' said Ivo grimly.

With a harsh whispering of steel the sword was in Varis's hand, its point at Ivo's throat.

'No? One of my men goes missing on patrol, and I find him with his throat slit, surrounded by a rabble of armed peasants who've been wandering the woods at night. It seems to me there might just possibly be a connection.'

Ivo didn't budge. 'We found him here moments before you arrived.'

'Look at the body,' said Bernice. 'It's been drained of blood.'

'So?'

'Use your eyes, Captain. There's no blood on the ground around him. It ought to be soaked. He was killed somewhere else and dumped here to make trouble for the village.'

Varis ignored her, pressing the sword into Ivo's throat until a drop of blood welled at its point. 'I'll show more mercy than you deserve. Give me the men who did the actual killing. I'll hang them here and now and let the rest of you live.'

Ivo didn't move or speak.

'Give me the killers,' shrieked Varis. 'Or I swear I'll let my men slaughter the lot of you like the pigs you are.'

Eagerly the mounted men pressed forwards. Suddenly Ivo's right arm swept upwards. His staff struck Varis's sword with terrific force, sending it flying through the air.

'Form square!' bellowed Ivo.

The villagers moved back-to-back to form a rough square: a square which bristled with pikes, axes and swords.

Trapped at the centre of the hollow square, Varis grabbed for the dagger in his belt – and froze when the cold metal of Bernice's blaster touched his ear.

Ivo raised his voice. 'You're dealing with free men here, Captain, not a rabble of frightened farmers. We've beaten the Black Guard before, and we outnumber you. We won't be the ones who get slaughtered.'

'But you will, I promise,' said Bernice, jabbing Varis's ear with the blaster. The most extraordinary feeling was creeping over her. She found herself *hoping* Varis would decide to make a fight of it.

I'll blow Varis's head off for a start, she thought fiercely. Then I'll shoot down as many of the others as I can. We'll drag the rest from their horses and cut them to pieces.

It seemed as if she could already hear the thud of steel against flesh and the screams of the dying, smell the coppery tang of freshly spilled blood. She found herself filled with eager exaltation. Then, as if a relay had been tripped in her mind, she found her head suddenly clearing.

She leaned forward and spoke fiercely to Varis. 'Tell your men to move back, towards the woods. Once the way to the village is clear we'll let you go and join them.'

Varis didn't speak, and Bernice had a sudden fierce desire to press the firing stud. It faded almost at once but Varis must have seen the lust to kill in her eyes.

In a high quavering voice he shouted, 'Strap the body

to my saddle and then pull back to the edge of the woods. I'll join you there. Move!'

Reluctantly the guardsmen obeyed. Wrapping their dead comrade's body in a cloak, they strapped it to Varis's saddle and then cantered slowly back down the road.

When they were a safe distance away, Bernice shoved her blaster back in her pocket and stepped away. Varis swung himself onto his waiting horse and looked down at her.

'You choose to side with rebels then?'

'I choose to try and stop a bloodbath,' said Bernice. 'There's something on this planet that wants to start one. You and these villagers have a common enemy.'

Varis gave her a baffled look. For a moment he seemed about to speak, then he turned and rode away.

Just inside the wood a tall, cloaked figure waited, its mind alert to every nuance of the scene being played out at the crossroads. As the desire to kill rose in Bernice's mind its excitement rose high. The figure's eyes glowed red – and then faded as she recovered control. Disappointment flooded through the watcher's being as the horsemen rode away. The girl had reacted so promisingly and then, suddenly . . . Still, there would be other times. Puzzled and unfulfilled, the tall figure faded back into the shadows.

Bernice shivered. 'I don't know what got into me. For a moment I really wanted to kill him.'

'So did I,' said Ivo grimly. 'But too many others would have died. Come, my Lady.' They made their way back to the village and came to a halt outside the inn. 'Go back to your homes and farms,' ordered Ivo. 'We'll talk again tomorrow.' As the little crowd dispersed, Ivo and Bernice went back inside.

The hall was in darkness except for the glow of the dying fire. In front of it stood an old woman wrapped up in a shawl. 'It's Magda, Gerda's mother,' whispered Ivo.

He went across to her. 'Magda, I'm sorry there's no news yet. We didn't find . . .'

'No, you don't understand,' said the woman excitedly. 'My Gerda's alive – she's come back!'

A white-faced, fair-haired figure came out of the shadows.

10

The Revenant

Bernice stared at the girl in horror. As far as she could see, it really was the girl she'd seen in the Tower. The same physical type at least, tall and slender and fair-haired. Then again, she thought, it's not all that easy recognizing someone walking towards you in firelight, especially when the last time you met they were hanging upside-down with their throat cut.

'More light, Ivo,' whispered Bernice fiercely. 'Quickly!' Ivo took an oil lamp from the mantelshelf and lit it with a brand from the fire. He put it on a nearby table and a pool of yellow light spilled out.

Gerda stopped when the light struck her, blinking uneasily.

'Well, girl, where have you been?' said Ivo harshly. 'Don't you know we've all been looking for you?'

The girl spoke in a dry husky whisper. 'I'm sorry . . . I got lost. I'd been visiting . . . a friend in one of the farms on the edge of the forest. I left just before dawn . . . I wanted to get back here before you got up. I took a wrong turn somewhere and found myself getting deeper and deeper into the forest. It took me all day and most of tonight to find my way back home.'

Her mother came up and put her arms around her. 'There, there, poor child, you're safe now . . .'

Bernice had been looking hard at the girl while she was speaking. The voice sounded curiously lifeless. Now the girl stood stiffly within her mother's arms, making no attempt to return the embrace.

Bernice took Ivo aside. 'There's something wrong.'

81

'It seems you must have been mistaken, my Lady,' said Ivo awkwardly. 'That's Gerda right enough. Perhaps you saw some other girl dead in the Tower. Or perhaps . . .'

'Perhaps I imagined the whole thing? That's what someone wants you to think. Well, I didn't,' whispered Bernice fiercely. 'That's the girl I saw in the Tower all right – and I saw her dead.'

'But how can that be? The dead do not return to us. Unless – ' Ivo broke off, appalled at what he heard himself saying.

'Call the old woman over,' said Bernice.

'Magda, come here!' ordered Ivo.

Leaving her daughter, the old woman came over to them, looking suspiciously at Bernice.

'Tell us exactly what happened – when your daughter came back, I mean,' said Bernice gently.

'I was back at our house, on the edge of the village, waiting for news. I couldn't sleep. Then I heard Gerda calling from outside the house.'

'She didn't come in?'

'No, she was just standing there in the street. She wouldn't come into the house, she was too frightened. So I went out and brought her along here.'

The old woman went back to her daughter, leading her to a bench by the fire.

Bernice was thinking furiously.

'Look at her, Ivo. Just look at her!'

'My Lady?'

'Look at her face, her hands, her clothes. Everything clean and immaculate. If she'd been wandering in the woods all day and all night she'd be scratched and dirty, and her clothes would be in rags. She didn't go into the house, remember.'

'Her mother said she was frightened.'

'But that doesn't make sense either! Why should she be too scared to go into her own house with just her mother there? She must have known you'd be angry with her but she was quite prepared to come and face you, here at the inn . . . Yes, of course!'

'What is it, my Lady?'

'That flower everyone puts over their door and windows . . .'

Ivo nodded. 'The *garil* flower. A superstition from the Old Time. Most of the old people still keep it up.'

'So Gerda's mother would have it over her door?'

'Most certainly.'

'What about you? Is there any over the inn door?'

'To be honest, my Lady, I've never bothered with it.'

'Don't knock it, it really works,' said Bernice grimly. 'I've tried it. Have you got any here?'

'We use it in cooking. There should be some in the kitchen somewhere.'

'Find it then. Quickly please.'

Ivo hurried off to the kitchen and Bernice sat watching mother and daughter huddled on the bench by the fireside. Old Magda had her arm around her daughter, but the girl sat stiff and unresponsive.

'You're so cold, my child,' Bernice heard the old lady say. 'Come closer to the fire.' The girl didn't move.

Ivo returned clutching a rather wizened-looking root from which grew a straggly dried-up flower.

Bernice took it from his hands. 'Bit ancient, but it'll have to do. Stand by, Ivo.'

Bernice went over to the couple on the bench, holding the *garil* plant out before her. Gerda ignored her, gazing sullenly at the ground, but Old Magda looked up eagerly. Before Bernice realized what was happening, she reached out and plucked the plant from her hands.

'Thank you, my Lady, most kind. See, Gerda, the lady has brought *garil* to protect you from evil.'

She tucked the plant into the neck of her daughter's dress.

With a howl of pain Gerda sprang to her feet. Snatching the plant from her dress, she hurled it into the fire.

Her mother jumped up, looking at her daughter in astonishment.

'Gerda, child . . .'

She tried to put an arm round the girl's shoulders. With

one sweep of her arm Gerda smashed the old woman away with so much force that she crashed into the wall beside the big fireplace.

Gerda swung round to confront Bernice – and *changed*. She seemed to grow taller and stronger, reaching out with hands that had become like claws. Her face was a ghastly white, her eyes glittered fiercely and she drew back her lips to reveal long pointed fangs.

Bernice fumbled in her pocket for her blaster, realizing that it was already too late. A bulky shape brushed her aside. The creature that had once been Gerda hurtled through the air towards her – and impaled itself upon the sharpened stake in Ivo's hands.

So fierce was the impact that Ivo was knocked from his feet. He scrambled up and jumped back, dragging Bernice with him.

On the floor before them the vampire howled and writhed, clutching at the stake through its heart. Then with one final convulsive jerk it became still.

For a moment the twisted shape of the vampire seemed to *blur*. Then there was only the dead body of a tall, pretty, fair-haired girl, blood soaking the front of her white dress. Ivo dropped on his knees beside her. 'Gerda,' he said in a choked voice. 'Poor Gerda.'

Bernice went over to Old Magda where she lay crumpled beside the fireplace. She knelt to examine the body.

'She's dead too, I'm afraid. Her head must have been smashed against the wall.'

'Perhaps it's as well,' said Ivo dully. 'She wouldn't have wanted to see what her daughter had become.' He straightened up. 'Poor Gerda – and I killed her.'

Bernice rose and came over to Gerda's body. Steeling herself, she bent down to examine it.

'No you didn't, Ivo. She was dead already. Look!'

Bernice pointed to a thin white line across Gerda's throat.

'She died in the Tower, just as I said. Somehow she was brought back to life and sent here to the village.'

Ivo sank down onto a bench. 'But who would have the power to do such a thing? And why?'

'The why is easy – to discredit me, and my story of what I'd seen in the Tower. To make you all think I'd imagined it all and that there was really nothing to worry about. As for who – that's what we've got to find out.' She thought for a moment. 'Ivo, can you get rid of these bodies? Have them buried secretly, tonight? You'll need help, I know, but try to pick people who can keep their mouths shut.'

Ivo nodded. 'Some of us fought the Lords together, in the Old Time. There are still a few of us left.'

'You'll have to put some sort of story about. Gerda wandered off, got lost in the forest and died of exposure. Her mother went to look for her and died as well. You found the bodies and had them buried in the forest.'

'Wouldn't it be better to tell everyone what's happened, my Lady, warn them of the danger?'

'If we alert the villagers, we alert the enemy as well. I don't think anyone's in danger yet, not if they just carry on as usual. I need a little more time to find out what's behind this.'

'It shall be as you say, my Lady. Leave it all to me.'

Ivo recollected his duty as a host. 'Can I get you food or drink, my Lady? Hot soup? I can rouse Katya.'

Bernice looked at the blood-spattered corpse on the floor and then looked away.

'No, let her sleep. I seem to have lost my appetite. All I need now is rest. Can you find me some more of that *garil* though? No point in taking chances.'

As she prepared for bed, Bernice thought of the compact, incredibly complex signalling device hidden deep in her pack. Was it time to use it? Not quite yet, she decided. It would be nice to get a little further on her own before . . .

She went to sleep that night with *garil* over the door and window, a blaster under her pillow and a sizeable slug of Eridanian brandy inside her.

As Bernice drifted into an uneasy sleep, Ivo stood by

an open wall-locker just beside the door. Inside the locker was the handset of a simple communications device, now worn with age. Ivo was pressing the call button. 'Kalmar! Kalmar, can you hear me? This is Ivo – I need help. Kalmar?'

A reply crackled from the set.

The hooded figure switched off the Time Scoop and sat back, his face twisted with rage.

'Always the Doctor – and if not the Doctor, then one of his interfering friends!'

The second watcher smiled. 'Calm yourself. The woman may have defeated one of His servants, but do you really think she can stand against Him? When it pleases Him, He will snuff her out.'

'Better perhaps if He does not,' said the third watcher. 'When she realizes her danger and her helplessness, she will surely summon the Doctor. Then the Doctor will fall into His grasp – and they will both fall into ours!'

'He can be in many places and many times,' said the second watcher. 'On one planet or the other, our purpose will be fulfilled – for Him, and for the Doctor as well.' The voices of all three watchers joined in their ritual chant:

'Death to the Doctor!

'Borusa lives!

'Rassilon must die!'

When Bernice came down to breakfast late next morning, everything in the inn seemed to be back to normal. The fire burned brightly, the bodies had disappeared and someone had made a very good job of scrubbing the blood from the floor.

Katya served the usual breakfast of gruel, greenfruit and black bread, with the added attraction of some dubious-looking green eggs, fried till they were charred and leathery.

'Marsh-fowl eggs, my Lady,' said Katya proudly. 'I gathered them myself.'

'Thanks a lot,' said Bernice. 'They look almost fresh.' What this planet needs, she thought to herself, is a really good domestic science college. Or maybe you could market the place as an inter-galactic slimming centre. Come to Ivo's Inn – the food's so filthy you're sure to lose weight!

She poured a slug of Eridanian brandy into her water glass, noticing that the flask was half-empty. There was another bottle in her pack but after that . . . Heaven knows what the local liquor's like, she thought. Something made from crushed slugs probably. I'm going to have such a blow-out and booze-up when I get off this planet – if I get off this planet.

She began thinking about the ideal restaurant for the occasion, and was hesitating between Maxim's in nineteenth-century Paris and a fish-bar on Metebelis Three when she noticed that Katya was still hovering, obviously eager to talk.

'Did you hear about poor Gerda, my Lady?'

'The girl who disappeared? What about her?'

'Well, some of the men went searching last night and they found her body. Not just hers but her mother's too. They reckon poor old Magda went off looking for her daughter and she died in the forest as well.' Katya lowered her voice. 'They say the wood-weasels and the blood-bats had been at the bodies. There wasn't enough to bring back, so they buried what was left on the spot.'

'Do you mind, you're putting me off my marsh-fowl eggs.'

Ivo appeared and Katya hurried guiltily away.

Ivo knuckled his forehead. 'Good morning, my Lady. You slept well?'

'Eventually.' Bernice glanced round the inn. 'You can't have had too much sleep yourself. You must have had a busy night.'

Ivo lowered his voice. 'All was done as you said, my

Lady. I persuaded my friends you were right, though it wasn't easy.'

'They weren't keen?'

'It's just that they're suspicious of strangers,' said Ivo awkwardly. 'And in such times as these . . .'

Bernice nodded towards Katya who was sweeping the front doorstep. 'Our story seems to have gone down all right.'

Ivo smiled. 'I told Katya as soon as she came down, and she told the field-workers who came in for breakfast. It'll be all over the neighbourhood by tonight.'

'Good.' Bernice finished as much of her breakfast as she could stomach and stood up. 'I must be off. I want to take another look at that burial ground behind the Tower.'

'My Lady, is that wise?'

'Probably not, but it's my job. That's why I came here in the first place.'

Ivo looked so alarmed that she patted him on the shoulder.

'Don't worry, I'll keep well away from the Tower. If anyone has moved in I'm not anxious to meet them again. And I promise I'll be back here long before it gets dark. I ought to be all right in open country in broad daylight.'

Ivo still looked uneasy. 'It isn't just the Tower and whatever may dwell there, my Lady. There are other dangers.'

'Such as?'

'The Black Guard are still patrolling the area. They'll be in an ugly mood after what happened last night. And there are wild men, outlaws in the woods.'

Bernice tapped the comforting weight of the blaster in her pocket. 'Don't worry, Ivo, as long as it's more or less human I can cope with it. Expect me back about tea-time.'

Ivo looked puzzled and Bernice realized that afternoon tea probably wasn't on the inn's regular menu. Lord knows what they have instead of tea and crumpets, she thought. Boiled bat's urine and toasted cow-pats probably.

Or at least, that's what it'll taste like. Out loud she said, 'I'll be back around the middle of the afternoon.'

Things looked pretty normal, thought Bernice as she made her way through the village. As normal as they ever were in a place like this. At the crossroads outside the village she had to wait while a patrol of the Black Guard rode by. Varis, their captain, glared suspiciously at her as he trotted past on a tall black horse. Bernice simply raised an eyebrow and looked bored, and he finally raised his hand in a reluctant salute before leading his men past. Bernice went on her way, feeling she'd scored a moral victory.

She hurried through the dark and gloomy woods and worked her way round to the edge of the burial ground, steering well clear of the Tower. Rather than excavate a marked-out square, she decided to attempt a general survey, in order to discover the approximate size and shape of whatever was buried there.

Absorbed in her task she worked for several hours, moving about the oval depression beneath the grey and lowering sky. From time to time she looked up at the dark shape of the Tower looming over her. But everything seemed quiet. Nothing emerged from the dark circle of the grotto's mouth and no sinister shape moved about the altar of black stone.

Working inwards from the edge of the burial ground, stopping to make a series of sample excavations, she eventually managed to establish a rough outline of the buried figure. It was large, quite incredibly large, and seemed to be almost triangular in shape. A giant bird perhaps, with outstretched wings? Suddenly Bernice remembered fleeing through the woods, the bats chittering and swooping around her head. That's it, she thought, suddenly certain. Not a bird, a bat – an enormous bat.

But why was the creature so large? Some freak mutation? A giant species that had since become extinct? Why were its remains treated with such reverence? Why was the site a place of worship and of human sacrifice?

And why had the missing scout ship from the Tower

plunged like a great metal arrow into its heart? And who had been pillaging the site, taking away parts of the creature's remains? During her excavations she had come across frequent signs that someone had been there before her. She was convinced that much of the giant creature's skeleton was now missing. But why? Simple vandalism, mindless desecration? Or some more sinister purpose?

A chill wind blew across the burial ground and Bernice decided she had had enough. It was already afternoon and she'd had nothing to eat since breakfast. Searching through her pockets she came up with a crumpled packet of silver foil containing a left-over chunk of dehydrated space rations. It was dry and fibrous, much like eating tree bark, but it was all there was. Washing it down with a swig from her flask, Bernice set off for the inn.

She was all right till she got into the woods. The tree-tops grew into a close canopy, shutting off most of the light, and the trees themselves seemed to crowd round the narrow, twisting path. Bernice kept feeling that she was being watched.

It was all imagination, of course, she told herself. In the gloom her fears made the surrounding trees and bushes seem like human figures. Take that bush on the edge of the path just ahead. It looked exactly like a man in a hood.

The bush stepped onto the path in front of her, and suddenly Bernice realized that it *was* a man in a hood. A tall figure, cloaked and hooded in grey, stood barring her way. A shaft of light glanced down through the trees, gleaming on the blade of the sword in the figure's hands.

11

Resistance

Bernice grabbed for the blaster in the pocket of her jacket, wishing she'd spent more time practising her fast draw. Inevitably the blaster snagged on the lining of her coat and it seemed ages before the heavy weapon was in her hand, levelled at the sinister figure before her.

Not that the sinister figure seemed at all bothered. It stood there, waiting patiently for Bernice to get herself sorted out.

When she'd finished it said wearily, 'Drop the weapon, my Lady. Look around you, you're surrounded.'

Bernice obeyed and saw that the trees and bushes by the path had turned into more grey-cloaked hooded figures, grouped around her in a loose circle. They were armed with a variety of weapons: swords, bows and axes. One or two were carrying long staves.

With her thumb Bernice felt for the controls in the butt of her blaster, struggling to remember Ace's instruction lecture. Although Bernice was always telling her she'd had a perfectly adequate military training at her Academy, Ace never quite seemed to believe it:

'This is your basic military hand-blaster right? Standard issue on hundreds of planets. Dead simple, nothing to go wrong. Power-pack clips into the butt, lasts practically for ever. Two controls, set into the butt, operated by the thumb. The lever has three settings. Setting One produces the effect of a good solid punch, it'll discourage someone without doing any real damage. Setting Two will knock somebody down and probably knock them out as well. Setting Three will kill. The little wheel controls the beam setting. Away from you gives wide-beam, towards you needle-point . . .' And with a final sceptical look, 'It's supposed to be foolproof.'

Setting Two, wide-beam, thought Bernice, frantically adjusting controls. If I can knock enough of them out I can dash through the gap and make a run for it.

'Step aside and let me go on my way,' she called in a voice that quavered a little more than she liked. 'I don't want to use this but I will if I have to.'

For a moment nobody moved. Then the figure before her stepped aside. Relaxing a little, Bernice moved forwards, seeing too late a blur of movement in her eyecorner. One of the figures to her right spun its staff with dazzling speed, knocking the blaster from her hand.

Ace had forgotten to tell her Rule One, thought Bernice bitterly: don't let anyone take your blaster away from you.

Someone snatched up the weapon and two of the hooded shapes moved up behind her, grasping her elbows. Before she could resist a third popped a hood over her head, blinding her completely.

'This way, my Lady,' said someone politely. They bustled her off through the forest.

It was a nightmare of a journey conducted, as far as Bernice was concerned, in total darkness and it seemed to go on forever. The men holding her arms did their best to guide her but they were crossing rough country and she couldn't help slipping and stumbling. Strong hands on her elbows held her up and urged her remorselessly forward.

After a time Bernice got a feeling that they'd come out of the woods and onto open ground. Finally they stopped for a moment or two, and she heard a faint whine of machinery. Then they moved forward again, this time on a smooth surface. She realized that they must be somewhere indoors. Another short walk on a downward sloping surface and they stopped again.

The hood was whipped from Bernice's head and she looked around, blinking in the harsh glare of artificial light.

She was in a large circular chamber that seemed to have been dug out of the ground. Its walls were reinforced with wooden pillars and rusty iron plates, with grass and earth peeping out between the joins.

The room was filled with an assortment of technical equipment. There were control panels, computer terminals and sections of what looked like rocket engines. Bernice thought suddenly of the stripped-out engine room in the base of the Tower – the Tower that was really a spaceship.

The whole place was spotlessly clean and all the different bits of machinery were gleaming and polished. Despite all the neatness and cleanliness, there was something musty and unused about the place. Not so much a control room as a museum.

All around her, her captors were stripping off their grey cloaks and hoods. Underneath they wore rough homespun clothing, much like that of the peasants she'd seen in the village. But there was something different about these men, thought Bernice. It took her a moment to realize that it wasn't a matter of appearance but of bearing. There were only about a dozen of them but every man there looked, strong, confident, capable. The sort of men who'd be natural leaders in their communities.

An incredibly ancient man in a spotless white robe appeared from the back of the room. The leader of Bernice's captors, a tall hawk-faced young man with wiry black hair, came forward to greet him.

'We got her, Kalmar,' said the young man proudly. 'We picked her up in the forest, she'd been snooping around the burial ground.'

'I trust you treated our guest with courtesy, Tarak,' said the old man reprovingly. 'I told you to invite the Lady to visit us, not kidnap her.'

The young man shrugged. 'I was just about to when she pulled a blaster on me. There didn't seem very much point in politeness after that.'

'Well, what do you expect?' said Bernice indignantly. 'You jumped out at me in the woods like a lot of grey ghosts. Of course I was alarmed. I was just trying to protect myself.'

The old man came up to Bernice and bowed stiffly. 'You must forgive Tarak, my Lady, he is young and impulsive.'

'Young and cautious you mean,' said Tarak. 'I don't want to die young like my father. I mean to live to be as old as you are, Kalmar, and I won't manage it by being too trusting with strangers.'

They looked set for a prolonged wrangle, and Bernice decided it was time to ask the obvious questions.

'Look, who are you people? What is this place, and why have you brought me here?'

'We will ask the questions!' snapped Tarak.

Bernice looked at him unbelievingly.

'That's the first time I've actually heard anyone say that.'

'Tarak!' said the old man. 'Please be seated, my Lady.'

He led Bernice to a sectioned-off part of the big room. It had been fitted out as a simple living area with a table, low chairs and a number of metal storage lockers. A simple bed covered with rough blankets occupied one corner.

The old man ushered Bernice to a seat and sat down beside her. The others gathered round, some filling the remaining chairs, others sitting on the ground. Tarak flung himself on the bed, glaring sulkily at Bernice.

The old man went to one of the lockers and returned with a wooden tray holding a number of metallic containers.

'Refreshments for our guest,' he said.

To her astonishment, Bernice saw that the tray held a selection of pre-packed space meals. She peeled the top from a self-heating container and sniffed appreciatively at the hot stew inside. The savoury smell made her realize how hungry she was. Unclipping the built-in spoon from the lid, she started to eat.

'There is drink as well,' said the old man proudly.

Opening a flask-shaped container, he poured liquid into the cup formed by the lid and passed it to Bernice.

She sipped it cautiously and opened her eyes in surprise. 'It's quite a decent brandy, actually,' she said and took an appreciative swig. 'Where did you get all this stuff?'

'I found it all here, long ago,' said Kalmar. 'Everything here was stripped from the Tower in the Dark Time, thrown out and abandoned here in the wastelands. We built this headquarters, furnished and equipped it from the dumps. We have a generator for heat and light and power. We found this food too, which lasts forever and heats itself at need. We keep it for special occasions, there is little of it left by now.'

Bernice went on eating, thinking over what she'd heard.

'I am one of the few left who remembers those days,' said Kalmar. 'I wasn't young even then, but somehow I survive and I tell the others.'

'My father was the leader of the rebels,' said Tarak proudly. 'I bear his name. He died when they attacked the Tower and destroyed the Lords and the monster they served.'

'Not without help, remember,' said Kalmar. 'Had it not been for the strangers – ' He broke off as if he had said too much.

'So this place was the headquarters of the resistance movement,' said Bernice. 'But the old Lords were overthrown years ago. Why do you need a resistance movement now?'

'We didn't, not at first,' said Kalmar. 'When the Tower fell, I stayed on here to look after things. I'd lived here so long I wasn't comfortable anywhere else. The place became a kind of memorial for a time. Then people forgot. They stopped coming and I lived here alone – till young Tarak appeared.'

'I could see signs that the Dark Time was returning,' said Tarak. 'The Lords were trying to restore their rule, the Black Guard were active again, there were even rumours that the Undying Ones had returned.' He touched ears, eyes and mouth in a ritual gesture, and every man in the room did the same.

'So I came back to this place and found Kalmar,' Tarak

went on. 'He shared my fears, so we revived the old movement. We recruited men from the other villages, these men you see here. You do not need to know their names – but I promise you that every man here can call upon many more. This time we are ready. We shall never be slaves to the Lords again.'

'Now you know all our secrets, my Lady,' said Kalmar. 'It is time for you to tell us yours.' He smiled benignly at her. 'I must tell you that unless we are satisfied with your answers, you will not leave this place alive.'

The threat was so unexpected that at first Bernice didn't take it in. But as she looked into Kalmar's faded old eyes, she realized that he meant what he had said. In his own quiet way he was as much of a fanatic as Tarak.

Bernice managed a smile. 'My secrets are soon told. I –'

Kalmar held up his hand. 'One moment, my Lady.' He raised his voice. 'Bring out the Truth Machine.'

A couple of the men jumped up and went over to the other side of the dome. They returned trundling a wheeled trolley on which stood a simple machine. It consisted of a metal cabinet with a vision screen set into the top. Beneath the screen there were two heavy metal hand-holds. There was a row of controls on the front of the machine. One of the men uncoiled a heavy cable and plugged the machine into a power point in the wall of the dome.

Kalmar fiddled with the controls and the screen lit up. Black dots moved across the middle of the screen in an endless line.

'There!' he said happily. 'We are ready, my Lady.'

Bernice regarded the machine suspiciously. 'What is that thing?'

'A Truth Machine, my Lady. In the time when the Tower was a spaceship it was used to interrogate prisoners. I found it and got it working again. This seems a splendid opportunity to test the device. If you will kindly clasp the handholds?'

'I'm not going anywhere near that thing!'

Tarak pushed his way forward. 'There's nothing to be afraid of – my Lady.' He grabbed the handholds. 'Show her, Kalmar.'

Kalmar adjusted controls. 'What is your name?'

'I am Tarak, son of Tarak.'

The dots continued their steady progress across the screen.

Tarak stepped back. 'You see?'

'How does it work?'

'The machine measures pulse, body temperature, muscle tension, perspiration,' said Kalmar. 'As long as you tell the truth – or what you believe to be the truth – there is nothing to fear. My Lady?'

The circle of men around Bernice drew a little closer. She still didn't like it, but there didn't seem to be any way out. Maybe she could bluff the machine – it all depended what they asked her.

Reluctantly she stepped forward and gripped the handholds. Kalmar touched another control and twin clamps slid out of the body of the machine, fixing her hands in place. Alarmed, Bernice tried to pull free but she was held fast.

'Hey, what is this? Let me loose!'

'Shall we begin, my Lady?' said Kalmar. 'What is your name?'

'Bernice Summerfield.'

The dots chugged steadily across the screen.

'Where do you come from?'

'From another planet – from many other planets. I'm a space traveller.' And that's true enough, thought Bernice. So far so good.

'Why are you here?'

'I was brought here.'

Kalmar gave her an impatient look. 'Why did you come to this planet?'

'I'm an archaeologist.'

The machine gave a faint ping and the line of dots juddered a little. Bernice felt a faint tingling sensation.

Tarak leaned forward. 'What does that mean? Is she lying?'

Kalmar frowned, studying the screen. 'Not exactly. But there seems to be some element of doubt involved.'

Bernice bit her lip in anger. Somehow this blasted machine had picked up the trace of self-doubt that never left her.

'*Are* you an archaeologist?' asked Kalmar.

'Yes of course I am,' shouted Bernice. 'I'm a Professor of Archaeology – '

The machine gave a sharp angry ping, the line of dots suddenly peaked – and a jolt of electricity shot through Bernice's body. She gave a yell of pain and rage.

'If you lie the machine delivers a shock,' explained Kalmar.

Bernice felt a wave of humiliation sweep over her. She had lived with that particular lie for so long it had become a kind of truth for her. But her body knew it was a lie. Her body knew that she'd been expelled from school without any proper qualifications, that 'Professor' was a mockingly affectionate title bestowed by the kids she'd helped when she was hiding out in the woods.

Her body knew it and it had betrayed her to the machine.

'*Are you an archaeologist or not?*' asked Tarak. Bernice thought for a moment, choosing her words carefully.

'I am a student of archaeology with a great deal of field experience. I have led expeditions on a number of different planets.'

Tarak looked at Kalmar, who looked at the screen and nodded.

'She's telling the truth.'

'All right,' said Tarak. 'It seems you are an archaeologist of some sort. Now, why did you come to this planet – *Professor*?'

'To study your history with a view to mounting a full expedition – '

Another ping from the machine, another savage jolt of pain.

Bernice gasped and slumped forward over the machine.

'Every time you lie the shock becomes stronger,' said Tarak. 'If you keep on lying the machine will eventually kill you.' He grabbed Bernice by the hair and pulled her upright.

'Now, why did you come to this planet? Who are you working for?'

Bernice clenched her teeth and glared hatred at him without speaking. A third jolt of electricity, the worst yet, convulsed her body.

'The machine punishes silence as well as lies,' said Tarak. 'Well? Why did you come here?'

'All right, damn you, I'll tell you,' shouted Bernice. 'The Doctor sent me here!'

Kalmar stared unbelievingly at the screen. 'She speaks the truth! You fool, Tarak, she comes from the Doctor – and you nearly killed her!'

With a sudden heave Bernice shoved the machine forward, knocking it clean off the trolley. It crashed to the ground amidst a shower of sparks, and the clamps came free from her wrists.

Springing to her feet, Bernice launched herself across the shattered machine, straight at Tarak. She bore him to the ground and sat on his chest, beating his head on the ground. She was banging happily away and resisting attempts to pull her off when a cool voice said, 'May I enquire what's going on?'

Disentangling herself, Bernice got to her feet. Striding towards her from the doorway was a small, neat woman with a high forehead and long fair hair. It was the horsy woman, the one who'd warned her off at the burial ground.

In the same cool tone the newcomer went on, 'Did I hear you mention the Doctor just now?'

'That's right. Do you know him?'

'We used to be very good friends, once upon a time. I'm the Lady Romanadvoratrelundar, by the way. You can call me Romana.'

'I'm Bernice Summerfield,' said Bernice. She looked at

the dazed and battered Tarak, who had just struggled to his feet.

Bernice knocked him down again.

'*Professor* Bernice Summerfield. You can call me Benny.'

They shook hands.

12

Conference

The word was out all over Chicago. They talked about it in high-class hotels and in low-down drinking dives, in speakeasies and in precinct houses.

There was going to be a top level sit-down, a meeting of all the bigshots. The Big Fellow himself had ordered it. There were going to be treaties, agreements, territories laid down and profits fairly divided. No more rub-outs and shoot-ups. Nobody taken for a one-way ride. No more exploding pineapples tossed into saloons and polling stations.

It was all going to be different from now on. Chicago was going to be a city of peace and brotherly love.

That's what they said.

District Attorney McSwiggin said so, on the telephone to His Honour the Mayor.

'I got it from the Big Fellow himself, your honour. He's as tired of all this violence as you are. He's determined to put a stop to it, one way or another.'

'Well, he'd damn well better,' boomed Big Bill Thompson. 'Because if he doesn't, I will.'

McSwiggin put down the phone with a puzzled frown. 'I don't know what's got into the old goat these days,' he told the Assistant D.A. 'If he actually starts trying to run things we'll all be in trouble.'

Captain Reilly discussed it down at the precinct house with his crony Sergeant O'Hanrahan. As they talked, O'Hanrahan was checking the contents of the weekly brown envelope, just delivered by the mob's usual bagman.

'Make the most of it, Patrick, me boy,' said Reilly. 'After today there'll be so much sweetness and light flying around Chicago they won't need any police at all. We'll both be out of a job.'

O'Hanrahan's thick fingers checked through the sheaf of greenbacks with the skill of long practice. 'Do you say so, Dennis?'

Reilly chuckled wheezily, 'To be honest I don't – and I don't much care. As long as the booze keeps flowing and the dollars with it, who cares? After all, they only kill each other.'

'Meself, I'd be happy to have a few less bullets flying about,' said O'Hanrahan. 'A feller could get hurt out there.' He finished his count, peeled off a wad of notes and handed them to Reilly, who tucked them absent-mindedly into his pocket.

As Captain, Reilly had the right to the biggest share. The rest of the money would be divided amongst lieuten-ants, sergeants and detectives, the amount determined strictly by rank, with the odd few bucks left over for the lowly harness-bulls on the street.

'That reminds me,' said Reilly. 'Pete's boys are taking a booze shipment out of one of their warehouses tonight and there's been talk of a possible hijacking. Fix the convoy up with a police escort, will you Patrick? Tell the lads there'll be a few extra bucks in it.'

The forthcoming peace conference was being discussed in Doc's place as well. Ace was in an argumentative mood.

'I mean, what's the point?' she said, unconsciously echo-ing Captain Reilly. 'Who cares if these creeps keep knock-ing each other off?'

It was mid-morning, Doc's place was closed, and they were in the big sitting-room at the top of the house. It was an old-fashioned room with red velvet curtains, lots of solid, overstuffed furniture, a faded Turkish carpet and an excessive supply of china ornaments, elaborate lamps and occasional tables.

The Doctor, elegant in a grey-striped suit, adjusted the angle of his fedora before the big mirror over the fireplace.

'How do I look?'

'Fine. You'll probably win the award for best-dressed mobster.'

'You look very nice too,' said the Doctor politely.

Ace was wearing a tailored black costume with a black silk blouse and a broad-brimmed black hat. She came and stood behind the Doctor, admiring her reflection. She did look pretty good, she thought – and realized she was being distracted.

'Doctor!'

'What is it?'

'Just why are you so keen on Capone holding this peace conference?'

'Peace is always a good thing, Ace, even in Chicago.'

'But it'll never work. These people don't trust each other, they won't keep their word.'

'It's difficult,' agreed the Doctor. 'But it shouldn't be impossible. This peace treaty ought to work, Ace – it's actually in everyone's best interests. But I agree with you – it probably won't.'

'So what are you after, Doc?'

'Someone who wants to make a bad time worse,' said the Doctor enigmatically.

'But this bit of history's not being interfered with, is it? Not like that Nazi-occupied Britain business. I mean, all this really happened. Prohibition, Al Capone, gangsters with tommy-guns . . . I saw it in all those old movies.'

'It's not being totally twisted, but suppose it's being – boosted a little? Just a bit more blood and bullets than is really natural?'

'Why would anyone do that?'

'Fun?'

The hoot of a horn sounded from outside and the Doctor went over to the window.

'There's Happy with the car. Come on Ace, we've got a peace conference to attend.'

The manager of the Sherman Hotel was having the worst day of his distinguished career. His one hope now was that he'd live to see the end of it.

The nightmare had started yesterday with an innocent-sounding phone call. A Mr Brown had booked the hotel's conference room for a meeting of the Chicago Suppliers Institute. No quibbling about cost, money no object.

Earlier this morning, Mr Brown's representative, a dark, soft-spoken gentleman called Mr Rio, had called round to check on the arrangements. Everything was to be the best, food and refreshments to be of the highest standard. Asked discreetly about liquor – the hotel had an excellent bootlegger – Mr Rio seemed amused and said Mr Brown could probably manage to take care of that himself. The hotel could provide glasses, mixers and ice.

The manager had been a little taken aback when Mr Rio had produced an enormous roll of bills and settled all charges in advance in cash, but no doubt these high-powered businessmen had their own way of doing things.

Then Mr Brown had arrived. The manager took one look at the bulky, scar-faced figure and realized that he'd rented his conference room to Al Capone.

Mr Brown had swept up to the suite, accompanied by an entourage of swarthy-faced men carrying cases of liquor – in broad daylight! There was even a cop holding up traffic while more cases were unloaded from waiting cars.

The swarthy men had come down from the suite and arranged themselves around the lobby, while Mr Rio waited by the lifts.

More delegates arrived. The procedure was always the same. A car drew up and a group of tough-looking, expensively dressed men got out and marched towards the lifts. Mr Rio met them, there were a few words of low-voiced discussion. Then one or at most two of the group would get into the lift while the others joined the hard-faced characters hanging around the lobby.

Hovering about by the reception desk, doing his best not to be noticed, the manager shuddered. That the Sherman, of all places, should play host to a gangland convention.

And here were two more of them. A small man in dark suit and fedora and an attractive young woman in a well-tailored costume. The small man was a vicious-looking brute, thought the manager. Every inch a killer. No doubt the girl was his gun-moll.

The manager watched helplessly as Mr Rio came forward to meet the newcomers.

'The lady stays down here, Doc. Principals only, no guns, no muscle, no bodyguards.'

The young woman's hand slid into her shoulder-bag. 'Who are you calling muscle, creep?'

Mr Rio's eyes narrowed and his hand moved towards the bulge in his armpit. The manager prepared to duck.

'Ace, please,' said the man called Doc sharply. To Mr Rio he said, 'Miss Ace is a full partner in my business.'

'Sorry, Doc. For the purposes of this conference she's a gun. That ain't no powder-puff she's about to pull on me.'

He turned to the girl. 'Honest, lady, I'm staying down here in the lobby myself.'

'Do you mind, Ace?' said Doc.

'Mind what?'

'Waiting for me down here. Just keep your eyes open. If you get too bored, have Happy take you home. If I don't see you here I'll see you back there.'

The girl nodded and stalked towards an armchair.

Doc got into the lift and disappeared upwards.

The manager mopped his brow.

The conference room at the Sherman Hotel was a large and splendid room, graced with deep carpets, velvet drapes and a crystal chandelier. Its central feature was a long oval table in polished mahogany, surrounded by high-backed chairs. Before each chair was a leather-bound blotter and a big crystal ashtray.

Capone sat at the head of the table, the Doctor to his

105

right. All around the table were ranged the heads of Chicago gangland. They were tough, hard-looking men, expensively dressed, loaded down with flashy and expensive jewellery. They had cigars, they had drinks, and they were ready to listen.

The Doctor had made it his business to get to know Chicago's gang leaders. He looked around the table, mentally ticking off the list.

There was Hymie Weiss, Pete Gusenberg and Bugs Moran, the uneasy trio that had inherited Dion O'Bannion's Northside mob. There was Ralph Sheldon and Jake 'Greasy Thumb' Guzick, both loyal Capone allies. Jack Zuta and Potatoes Kauffman were closer to the Northsiders.

Klondike O'Donnell and his young brother Miles were both neutral, not daring to challenge Capone. Spike, the senior O'Donnell, didn't care for Capone and had refused to attend the conference. Polish Joe Saltis, a great shambling white-faced lump of a man, was an independent bootlegger and brothel-keeper, too stupid and too violent to have allies. There was Ed Vogel out of Cicero, a loyal Capone man. And there was a sprinkling of minor independents, Marty Guilfoyle, Billy Skidmore, Barney Bertsche . . .

The Doctor heard Capone's voice rumbling in his ear.

'You wanna get things started, Doc? This is all your idea.'

The Doctor would sooner have stayed in the background, but there was no getting out of it now. He raised his voice, cutting through the low-voiced chatter around the table.

'If I could have your attention, gentlemen?'

There was a surprised silence round the table, and the Doctor became the focus of the hard-eyed stares of his audience.

'I'm a newcomer to Chicago,' the Doctor went on. 'You don't know me and there's no reason why you should. I don't operate in your league. I run one saloon called Doc's Place, and that's it. A while back I went for a quiet lunch with Mr Capone here and found myself in a Chicago replay of the Big War.'

A little chuckle went around the table and the Doctor went on, 'Now, that strikes me as a pretty dumb way to run things and I know Mr Capone feels the same. So I ask you to listen to him now.' The Doctor put an edge of menace in his voice. 'In your own best interests.'

Al Capone looked round the table, fixing each gangster in turn with the Look – the bulging-eyed stare that meant business. In a harsh, rasping voice he said, 'You guys know what we're doing? We're turning a great business into a shooting gallery. This is hard and dangerous work, apart from any hate at all. When a guy works hard, he wants to be able to relax and forget about work between times. He don't want to be afraid to sit with his back to a door – or a restaurant window. So I'm telling you now, all this monkey business has got to stop. Because if it don't, I'll stop it.'

'Like you stopped Dion O'Bannion?' said Hymie Weiss bitterly.

The Doctor knew that Weiss and the others had never forgiven Capone for the death of their much-loved leader.

Capone's fist slammed down on the table. 'If I have to, yes! Deany O'Bannion was a great guy, but he was a madman too, a danger to himself and everyone else. So he had to go – but it don't haveta be like that. There's plenty for everyone. Now lissen . . .'

Ace sat back in her armchair, glancing round the hotel lobby. It was crowded with hard-eyed tough-looking men, gangster bodyguards excluded, like her, from the top-level discussion upstairs. They tended to bunch together in little groups, each group keeping a wary eye on the others.

There was a coffee shop just off the lobby and people drifted in and out with mugs in their hands. Ace had a feeling that not all the mugs held coffee.

She became aware that someone was moving from group to group, listening for a while then joining in. A tall man, elegantly dressed, with a long, thin, aristocratic face. A rather unusual type to find in a place like this.

Ace noticed that after a minute or two the tall man seemed to be dominating each conversation, talking urgently while the others listened, frowning. Then he would move away to another group, repeating the pattern there.

Suddenly he was standing beside her.

'Do you mind if I sit down?' His voice was soft and attractive. Ace hadn't noticed the vacant chair, but there seemed to be one beside her now.

'Why not?' she said.

The tall man dropped into the chair.

'Looks like a mobster's convention, doesn't it? The hotel manager is sweating blood, expecting a shoot-out any minute.'

He pointed to a bald-headed and bespectacled man by the desk. He was sweating profusely, mopping at his bald head with a silk handkerchief.

'Are you here on business?' asked the tall man.

'Just waiting for a friend.'

'Of course, you're Doc's girl Ace – the Lady in Black.'

'I'm sorry?'

'That's what they're calling you. Didn't you know? They say you took out Morelli with one shot, that you'd have got Pete Gusenberg at the Hawthorne if someone hadn't stopped you.'

'Seems a lot of fuss about one hit and one miss. You'd think no one ever got shot in Chicago.'

'I guess it's because you're an attractive young woman. All these cheap crooks have got romantic imaginations.' He paused. 'Is your friend Doc going along with this peace talk of Al's?'

'He seems to be.'

He leaned forward confidentially, lowering his voice. 'I'd tell him to be careful if I were you. As soon as he's ready, Al's going to gobble up the independents like Doc, put them all out of business. Al's greedy, wants it all for himself.'

Suddenly Ace became absolutely convinced that he was right, that she ought to warn Doc not to trust Capone. She felt a surge of anger at Capone's treachery.

'Thanks, I'll tell him,' she said. But the tall man was gone. Ace looked round the room. He was nowhere in sight.

She got up and went over to Frank Rio who was talking to a group of Capone's men. He looked warily at her, and she gave him her most dazzling smile.

'Hi, doll,' he said, but he still looked cautious.

'You were talking to a tall man just a little while ago.'

'I was? Yeah, that's right. He was saying Al oughtta be careful about these independents, they were planning to gang up on him.'

'Do you know who he was?'

'Just a guy you see around. Nice feller. I think he's with one of the other outfits.'

'Would anyone else know?'

'I guess so.' He called across to someone in a nearby group. 'Hey Charlie, that tall guy you were shooting the breeze with, know who he was?'

'I thought he was one of your boys.'

'Can you remember what he was saying?' asked Ace.

Charlie frowned. 'Something how about if Hymie Weiss got too friendly with Zuta and Kauffman they could take over our territory . . .'

For some reason Ace felt it was important to find out more about the tall man. She tried asking some of the other groups but she didn't get any further. Everyone seemed to know him but everyone seemed to think he was part of some other outfit. Some people said he was a journalist on the *Tribune*, others that he worked for the Mayor's office. But they all remembered him warning them about someone.

It was odd, thought Ace. Maybe she ought to tell the Doctor about it. Then again, maybe it wasn't worth bothering with.

The memory of the tall man was already fading from

her mind. But she remembered that she had to warn the Doctor about Al Capone. She was quite clear about that.

13
Death Trail

Hands on the table, Capone leaned forward, sweeping the conference table with the Look.

'First of all, territory. Hymie Weiss, Gusenberg, Drucci, Moran, you share everything north of Madison, east of the river. Sheldon operates north-east of the stockyards. Saltis, you keep back of the Yards, like always.' He turned to the two O'Donnells. 'Miles, Klondyke, you take the west side.'

'And what about you, Al?' said Hymie Weiss. 'You ain't leaving yourself out, are you?'

'I look after the whole of the south side,' said Capone flatly.

'What about Cicero and the rest of the suburbs?'

'Them too.'

As everyone round the table knew, the ring of suburbs around Chicago were prime territory for bars and brothels. They offered trouble-free operation too, with police forces and city administrations small enough to be bribed and terrorized.

'It's a big slice of the cake, Al,' said Bugs Moran.

From his place at Capone's side, the Doctor saw the hands on the table turn into massive fists. Capone drew a deep breath.

'Maybe so,' he said mildly. 'But I got people to take care of. Jake Zuta here, Marty, Billy, Barney, they all operate outta my territory. So, is that agreed?'

There were nods of acceptance around the table.

'Okay! From now on everybody sticks to their own

111

territory, no muscling in. That'll cut out most of the trouble right there.

'Next, we start out fresh with a clean sheet. No matter who beat up who, who took who for a ride in the past, we gotta put it all behind us. No settling grudges or paying off old scores. We're a bunch of saps, killing each other off, handing the cops a laugh. One of my guys gets outta line you don't whack him, you tell *me* and *I* take care of him. Same goes for everyone, right?'

Nods and murmurs of agreement from all around the table.

'Right,' said Al Capone. 'That concludes our business, gents. Everyone have another drink, and we'll move on to the Bella Napoli. I'm taking over the whole joint for a celebration. All the Italian food you can eat, enough booze to float a battleship and it's all on me.'

As cigars were lit and bottles passed round, Capone turned to the Doctor.

'How'd I do, Doc?'

'You did fine,' said the Doctor, quite sincerely. 'You'd have made a great diplomat, Mr Capone. Congratulations. Now, if you'll excuse me?'

'You ain't coming to the Napoli?'

Capone sounded quite hurt.

'Better not. I'm still an outsider here really, and this is your big day, not mine. I'll just slip away.'

Quite apart from avoiding the dubious pleasure of a boozy lunch with a bunch of drunken gangsters, thought the Doctor, it wouldn't do to start looking too much like the power behind the throne. It would get in the way of his real mission.

He made his way down to the lobby and found Ace deep in discussion with Frankie Rio, over mugs of coffee with a strong aroma of rye whisky.

'Sure, speed and accuracy's important,' Rio was saying, 'but you gotta have stopping power too. You get some big strong guy coming at you, you can put two or three of those itty-bitty slugs in him and he won't hardly notice it. Okay, so he'll keel over and die later on, but not till he's

112

put you down as well. I don't say you gotta use one of those .45 calibre cannons your friend Dekker lugs around, but anything smaller than a .38 and you're wasting your time.'

Ace shook her head. 'It's not the size of your pistol that counts, Frankie, it's what you do with it.'

'I hate to interrupt a professional discussion,' murmured the Doctor, 'but I think it's time we were on our way.'

Rio jerked his head upwards. 'How'd it go, Doc?'

'Surprisingly well. If everyone keeps the agreement, you two will soon be out of a job.'

Frank Rio smiled. 'Is that so? Well, I won't start worrying yet.'

Ace and the Doctor headed for the door, and Rio watched them move away.

Dingbat O'Berta, one of Saltis's boys, elbowed him in the ribs. 'Some dame, hey Frankie? I think she likes you.'

'Yeah? Well, lemme tell you Dingbat, I've got a little rule. I never make a pass at no dame who can shoot faster than me.'

Dingbat O'Berta was impressed. 'She's that good?'

'So they say. Maybe I'll get the chance to find out someday.'

In the car going back to Doc's Place, the Doctor was telling Ace about the peace conference.

'He handled them brilliantly Ace. Just the right mixture of threat, charm and sweet reason.'

'I don't think we ought to trust Capone,' said Ace suddenly. 'They say he'll swallow up all the independents once he's on top. Maybe we ought to – '

'Ought to what?'

Ace looked wonderingly at him. 'I was going to say maybe we should rub him out before he rubs us out. But we don't do that sort of thing, do we?'

'We most certainly do not. I don't think we ought to stay here too much longer, Ace, you're beginning to go native. Who told you Capone couldn't be trusted?'

'Just someone I was talking to. I can't really remember now. Do you think this peace treaty will hold up?'

'It ought to, it makes good business sense. But we're not dealing with sensible businessmen.'

'So what do you think will happen?'

'I'm not sure ... But if my theory's correct, the peace treaty will hold for a while.'

'And then?'

'Then someone won't be able to stand it – so they'll start giving things a bit of a push.'

'And that's what we're waiting for?'

'Yes,' said the Doctor. 'That's what we're waiting for.'

For the next few weeks peace reigned over Chicago. Nobody was bustled into a car for one last ride, no one died in a hail of machine-gun bullets, not a single bar was blasted by a pineapple.

Naturally, Mayor Thompson took all the credit.

'See?' he told District Attorney McSwiggin. 'I told those mob guys things had to quiet down and they knew I meant business.'

'Absolutely, your Honour,' said McSwiggin. He knew it was Al Capone, not Big Bill Thompson who was keeping the peace, but there was no point in saying so.

McSwiggin decided to go out for a few drinks, make a round of the speakeasies, check things out with some of his underworld connections. Something about the new peace made him uneasy.

In the newsroom of the *Chicago Tribune* Jake Lingle slammed down the phone.

'Nothing!' he said disgustedly. 'I called every damn precinct house in Chicago and they're all sitting there polishing their nightsticks. These days this burg's quieter than a Quaker prayer-meeting.'

Bob Lee, the lanky red-haired city editor, shrugged. 'It won't last, Jake. Does it ever? One of those mugs'll crack wise about some other mug and the lead'll start flying again – just like the good old days.'

114

Lingle stood up. 'Yeah? Well, till it does I'm wasting my time here. It's a nice day and they're running at Washington Park. I think I'll go to the races. See you Bob!'

'Yeah, see you,' said Bob Lee sourly. He watched Lingle's elegant figure stroll away between the rows of desks. Some nerve the guy had, just taking off like that. No other reporter could have got away with it, but Jake Lingle was special. He was the *Trib*'s top crime reporter and the Colonel's blue-eyed boy. Jake Lingle had connections.

He also had dough. That grey suit he was wearing must have set him back a few hundred bucks, and Bob Lee happened to know that Jake Lingle was pulling down just sixty-five bucks a week. The story was that Jake had inherited money from some rich uncle. Lee thought Jake's money came straight from his Uncle Al.

Jake Lingle's connected all right, thought Lee cynically. He's in the rackets, right up to his neck. It'll catch up with him some day.

Picking up a sheaf of papers, Bob Lee went back to his current task: trying to extract some sense from the windy eloquence of Big Bill's latest speech.

In the back room of a Northside speakeasy, Bugs Moran, Pete Gusenberg and Hymie Weiss were dividing a stack of greasy dollar bills.

'You gotta admit it's working,' said Gusenberg, stowing away his share. 'The booze flows out, the dollars flow in.'

'Yeah, just like running a five-and-dime store,' snarled Moran. Money alone wasn't enough for him. He craved the excitement that came with violence. Capone's peace was getting him down.

Hymie Weiss checked methodically through his pile of dollars.

'I still don't buy it,' he said moodily. 'Suppose Al's setting us up? He keeps things quiet till we're off guard – then he moves in and takes over. That's what some guy was saying after the conference.'

'What guy?' asked Moran.

'Just some guy you see around. Tall thin fellow...'
Weiss stood up. 'I gotta meet my lawyer over at the court-house. It's jury selection for Joe's trial today.'

Just before the truce, Polack Joe Saltis had knocked off a rival beer pusher. Typically, he'd committed the murder in public, forcing his victim's car to the kerb and blasting him with a shotgun in broad daylight. With so many witnesses even the Chicago police were forced to take notice, and Joe was arrested. Now he was about to stand trial.

'How come you're involved?' asked Moran.

Weiss shrugged. 'Joe asked me for help. The Polack's dumb but he's tough and he's got some good boys. If I'm right about Al's plans, Joe could be useful.'

'What you gonna do?'

'My mouthpiece has got a contact at the courthouse. If we can get hold of the final jury list, we can maybe influence them a little.'

They were talking about the truce at Doc's place over a late breakfast, down in the bar. Dekker had dropped in, something he'd been doing quite often lately. He would wander in at odd hours, have a few drinks, chat to the Doctor, exchange a few wisecracks with Ace. The quiet times had meant less to do for both of them. One night Ace had taken an evening off and she and Dekker had gone on the town together, returning noisily in the small hours.

Despite all this, their conversation still seemed to consist of swapping insults. The Doctor supposed he was witnessing some sort of courtship ritual. Humans were peculiar, he thought.

Dekker reached out and grabbed the coffee-pot, snaffling the last cup of coffee from under Ace's nose. He added cream and sugar, stirred, and drained his mug noisily.

'Great java, Doc.'

'Sure you're okay?' asked Ace, 'You've only had six cups. Ever think of buying your own?'

'Can't afford it,' said Dekker sadly. 'Peace is breaking

116

out all over. It's not just that these punks have stopped drilling each other. Guys have stopped cheating on their wives, dime-store clerks have stopped dipping in the cash register. A poor private eye could starve to death around here.'

'I hear illegal liquor is still being widely sold,' said the Doctor. 'You could try doing something about that.'

'Then I'd have to come and take you in, Doc. And Ace here would shoot my ears off.'

'I'd shoot something off,' said Ace. She waved the empty pot at Luigi, who took it from her, replacing it immediately with a full one. Ace looked surprised.

'I always put on a fresh pot every time I see Mr Dekker come,' explained Luigi.

'Besides,' Dekker went on, 'my pal Eliot's going to put an end to the illegal booze business.'

Ace poured herself more coffee. 'Eliot?'

'Eliot Ness – also known as Eliot Press, because he's so fond of publicity. Nice young fellow, keen as mustard. Head of a special team of Prohibition Agents. They've got this new secret weapon – they're all supposed to be incorruptibly honest, untouchable by bribery.'

Ace raised an eyebrow and the Doctor explained. 'In Chicago, Ace, Prohibition Agents rate even lower than the regular police.'

'That's right,' said Dekker. 'After all, there are supposed to be *some* honest cops. Now we've got Eliot and his boy scouts as well.' He laughed. 'Hell, Eliot's even got an accountant on his staff, looking into the Big Fellow's income tax returns. How about that? The top bootlegger in Chicago, responsible for a string of murders, some of them in person, and they want to nail him for tax evasion!'

'It's a crazy scheme,' said the Doctor. 'But you never know, it just might work.'

Dekker yawned and stood up. 'Guess I better go out and drum up some work. Maybe I can catch someone stealing five cents from a blind newsie.'

'Keep in touch,' said the Doctor. 'I might have something for you pretty soon.'

'Something gonna break, Doc?'

'Could be.'

'But it's so quiet,' said Ace.

'It's too quiet,' said the Doctor. 'I don't like it.'

Chicago's fragile peace snapped like an over-stretched violin string.

It began with Jake Lingle, happily making his way to the race-track. Tilting his new straw hat to a jaunty angle, he strolled along Michigan Avenue. He bought a racing paper from the news-stand outside the Public Library and then headed down the busy pedestrian tunnel that led to Illinois Central station.

He was about half-way along the tunnel, studying the day's odds in the paper, when he heard footsteps coming up close behind him. He turned and saw a tall thin fellow striding towards him, wearing a straw skimmer much like his own. The guy looked vaguely familiar and Jake half-nodded over his shoulder.

The tall man said, 'Hi Jake!'

He took out a snub-nosed .38 calibre Colt revolver and shot Jake Lingle once in the back of the head. The bullet smashed Lingle to the ground. He fell forward, face-down on the tunnel floor. Knocked from his head by the impact, the new skimmer rolled away.

The tall man turned and ran back down the tunnel, watched by a handful of astonished spectators. Two of them were brave enough to run after him, yelling, 'Stop him! Stop that man!'

Outside the tunnel a passing policeman joined in the hunt. Scattering pedestrians, the tall man ran west along Randolph and then ducked down a narrow alley. Seconds later the policeman, revolver in hand, reached the mouth of the alley.

Raising his gun the policeman yelled, 'Stop! Police –' then broke off in astonishment. The alley was empty. The tall man had vanished.

Anna Rotariu felt she'd been lucky in getting a tenant for

the second-floor front room in her North Street boarding house so quickly. To be honest it wasn't much of a room.

The new tenant seemed happy enough though, and he'd been particularly impressed with the view. The room looked out onto North Street, with a good view of the front of Schofield's flower shop, just next door, and of the Holy Name Cathedral on the other side.

The new tenant's name was Lundin, a tall, thin, aristo-cratic-looking man. He explained that he was a musician, a violinist. He'd be keeping irregular hours, but he promised to enter and leave quietly.

On what was to be the last afternoon of his stay, Mrs Rotariu met her new tenant coming up the stairs. He greeted her with his usual politeness and went on up to his room, clutching his battered black violin case.

Once in the room, the tenant put the violin case down on the bed and went over to the window, pulling aside the grubby lace curtain. He checked the view of North Street, looked at his watch and smiled. He opened the bottom half of the window to its full extent. Then he went over to the bed and opened the violin case, lifting out its contents with loving care.

As Hymie Weiss's car drove along North Street on his way back from court, he was thinking sentimentally about old times.

Schofield's flower shop on North Street, opposite the Holy Name Cathedral, was a sacred spot in gangland history. It had been used by Dion O'Bannion, 'Deany', as a headquarters and a cover for his other activities.

Schofield's became the official gangland florist, selling thousands of dollars worth of blooms when any gangster of note passed away – and they'd been passing away pretty regularly in Chicago for quite a while.

One sad day Deany O'Bannion became his own best customer, shot down by three killers in his own flower shop. Inevitably the killers were never caught, but it was widely believed that two Sicilians called Scalise and

Anselmi were responsible. The third man was thought to have been Al Capone.

Hymie Weiss and the others had never forgotten O'Bannion and Hymie, at least, had never forgiven Capone. They'd kept the flower shop HQ as a kind of memorial to their lost leader.

As he got out of the car, Hymie Weiss was thinking that at least the trip to the courthouse had gone well. His lawyer's source, a bribed court official, had come up with the goods. Hymie Weiss had a list of the names and addresses of the Saltis jury in his pocket right now. Pretty soon those jurors would be subjected to a mixture of bribes and threats, persuading them that a 'not guilty' verdict would be a lot better for their collective health.

Followed by his bodyguard, Pat Murray, and his lawyer, O'Brien, Weiss got out of the car and headed for the shop. Neither of them noticed that a second-floor window was open a little further up the street.

Suddenly the stuttering blast of machine-gun fire came from the open window. Murray, the bodyguard, fell dead in the gutter with seven slugs shattering his head and body.

Hymie Weiss staggered a few steps onto the sidewalk, then collapsed with ten bullets in him.

The lawyer, O'Brien, hit four times in the arm and belly, crawled into a basement stairwell for shelter.

He was lucky. He didn't die.

Coming out of her room to see what was happening in the street, Mrs Rotariu saw her new tenant leaving his room, violin case in hand. She followed him out of the house and saw him jump into a black Cadillac parked just outside and drive away. She heard groans, turned, and saw dead and dying men lying in their blood outside Schofield's flower shop.

District Attorney McSwiggin was having a night on the town. He was riding in a green Lincoln with Miles O'Don-nell, one of the three brothers who ran the O'Donnell mob. The car was driven by a police captain called Duffy. They were all on their way to a joint called the Pony Inn, where the beer was said to be particularly good.

The inn stood on an otherwise vacant lot on Roosevelt. As first Duffy then McSwiggin got out of the car, a black Cadillac drew up. Duffy assumed it was a fellow patron – until he saw the machine-gun projecting from the Cadillac's front window.

He grabbed for his gun. There was a staccato roar as the Cadillac driver opened fire. Red Duffy dropped immediately, his body riddled with bullets. McSwiggin staggered to the Pony Inn and fell dead on its doorstep.

14

Trackdown

I'd been out of town all day on a wandering daughter job.

She was a good-looking kid and kinda wild. The good-looking ones usually are, the plain Janes don't get the opportunity. Apparently she'd been keeping bad company.

Her folks ran a Mom-and-Pop grocery store a few blocks away and they were convinced she'd been grabbed by one of these white-slave operations you read about in the yellow press.

I'd found the girl all right, and her parents were at least half right. The kid was working in a high-class cat-house, one of Joe Saltis's joints. She was there of her own free will, making good money and had no intention of going back behind the counter of the store.

The madam of the joint had said, 'Kidnapped? That's a laugh! Why go to the trouble? In these hard times they're standing in line to get in.'

As I trudged up the stairs to my office, I was wondering what to tell Mr and Mrs Schultz. I decided to tell them I'd had no success in finding their daughter. I also decided to offer to return their twenty-five bucks – with any luck they'd refuse to take it.

As I reached this decision I saw the light was on in my office and the door was ajar. I pulled the .45, kicked open the door and went in. I found myself looking at Ace. She was sitting in the chair on the other side of my desk, wearing the same black outfit she'd worn last time I'd seen her.

She looked up at me from under the brim of her hat as I stowed away the rod. 'You keep late hours, Dekker.'

'I work for a living, lady.'

'Not very successfully, judging by the front you put up.'

'You don't get rich in this business – not if you're honest.'

'And are you?'

'Reasonably.'

I slumped down in my desk chair, got out the office bottle and glass and poured a slug of bourbon. I offered it to Ace, she shook her head, so I swallowed it and poured myself another one.

I fired up a Camel and looked at her through the smoke. 'So you just couldn't resist me, hey kid? I knew you'd crack. This place ain't much but there's a Murphy bed in the wall there.'

She shook her head like she couldn't believe what she was hearing. 'If you really think I've come all the way out to this rat-hole in pursuit of your manly charms, Dekker – '

'And I thought my luck had changed at last. Well, if it's not pleasure . . .'

'Business.' She stood up. 'Doc wants to see you. He sent me to bring you over.'

'Well, you're prettier than the guys Al sent. What's up?'

'There've been some shootings.'

'Yeah, and the sun comes up in the morning. This is Chicago, sweetheart. How many?'

'Three, I think.'

'So much for Al's truce. Mobsters?'

'One of them. Doc said something about a journalist and a D.A.'

'You sure about that?'

'Pretty much. Why?'

'It's against all the rules. Mobsters killing mobsters, that's routine. But like Al says, they only kill each other.'

Ace shrugged. 'Doc will tell you all about it. Will you come, Dekker? Doc said it was urgent.'

'Sure I'll come. Anything for you, doll.'

I finished my drink, stubbed out my Camel and put on my trenchcoat and hat. We went over to the door. I turned out the lights, then closed and locked the door behind me. 'I locked this place up when I left town. How did you get in?'

'It's a cheap lock, Dekker. Took me and a hairpin two minutes.'

I looked hard at her as we went on down the stairs. 'You really have been around, haven't you kid?'

'More than you could possibly imagine.'

Once we were on the street she put two fingers in her mouth and gave a piercing whistle. Doc's big Cadillac rolled round the corner with Happy at the wheel.

He stuck his head out of the window. 'Hi Mr Dekker!'

We got in and the car drove away. It had just started to rain and it was late enough for traffic to be pretty light. The wet streets reflected the streetlights as the big Caddy moved between the skyscrapers, sliding smoothly through the silent city. We passed by the new Carbon and Carbide building on North Michigan. It was pretty spectacular. Black granite and marble trimmed with bronze, a green tower and a gold pinnacle.

'It's a beautiful town,' said Ace softly.

'If you can stand the pace,' I said. 'I like it, but then I was born here.'

She nodded. 'It must be nice to belong somewhere.'

Doc's Place was closed for the night by the time we arrived, but there was Doc in his white tuxedo, wide awake and crackling with energy. The murders seemed to have given him a boost, like something he'd been waiting for had turned up at last.

Luigi was still behind the bar dispensing coffee, and we all settled down in Doc's alcove over cups of java and a bottle of Jim Beam.

'Ace told you what's happened?' he asked.

'Just the facts, Doc. I could use some details.'

Doc rattled them off.

'Jake Lingle, crime reporter on the *Chicago Tribune*, shot down in the Illinois Central subway. Hymie Weiss, machine-gunned from a second-floor window outside

Schofield's flower shop. District Attorney William McSwiggin, found dead inside a bullet-riddled Lincoln in Oak Park. The body of a police captain called Duffy was also in the car.'

My jaw dropped and I just sat there with my mouth open. I guess I must have looked kinda comical. Ace gave me a nudge. 'Dekker? What is it?'

I looked helplessly at Doc, and he smiled. 'Tell her, Dekker.'

I poured a slug of bourbon into my coffee and swigged it down.

'Jake Lingle was a reporter, and there's an unwritten law you don't shoot press guys. Newspapers don't like it, and it makes for bad publicity. Lingle was a Chicago *Tribune* reporter. The *Trib*'s owned by a millionaire, a guy called Colonel Robert McCormack. He's already riled up about Chicago crime, and Lingle was his blue-eyed boy. McCormack has a hell of a lot of clout, and he's going to start using it.

'Hymie Weiss was one of the bosses of the Northside gang, Al Capone's biggest rivals. They've never forgiven Al for knocking off their old boss, O'Bannion – and they're gonna be dead certain he killed Hymie Weiss as well.

'Bill McSwiggin was a special investigator for our beloved Mayor, Big Bill Thompson. With a reporter, a D.A. and a police captain killed, Thompson's just gonna have to do *something* – even though all three of them were up to their necks in the rackets.'

'Tell me something, Mr Dekker,' said Doc in that old-fashioned way of his. 'If you had to pick three men whose murders would be certain to stir up bloody hell here in Chicago, could you have made a better choice?'

'It wouldn't be easy. What's your interest in all this, Doc?'

'I believe all three murders were carried out by the same man, just to cause trouble for his own purposes. I want to hire you to help me find that man. I need your local knowledge.'

I thought for a moment. 'Well, I do happen to be at liberty for the moment. My daily rate is – '

'I'll double it,' said Doc. 'Unlimited expenses as well, naturally. Here's a couple of grand to be going on with.' He took a roll of notes out of his pocket and handed it over.

'It's a deal,' I said. 'When do we start?'

'We've started. We begin by going to see Mr Capone.'

'Right now?'

'Right now.'

I checked my watch. 'It's late, but with all that's been going on, I doubt if Al's having an early night. Okay, let's go.'

I started to stand up, but Ace said, 'Hang on a minute.' She was giving Doc what the guys who write books call a meaningful look.

'What is it, Ace?'

'I don't really know what's going on here, Doctor, though I expect you'll tell me when you're ready. But if it's the kind of thing you usually get mixed up in, is it fair to involve Dekker like this?'

'No, it isn't,' said Doc straight out. 'It's not fair to involve you and it probably isn't fair to involve me either. This thing's too important to worry about fairness.' He swung round to me. 'What Ace means, Mr Dekker, is that this job I'm offering you could turn out to be hideously dangerous – it could land you in the kind of danger you can't possibly understand.'

'Danger is my business, Doc. I'm hired, so I guess I'll stay hired.'

'Thank you, Mr Dekker. Now, if you'll excuse me while I slip into something more suitable . . .'

Doc got up and disappeared upstairs. I turned to Ace and found her glaring at me.

'Danger is my business! Of all the macho posturing . . .'

'I read it in a dime novel somewhere. I always wanted to say it.'

Ace leaned forward. 'Go home, Dekker. Go and look for missing daughters and cheating wives and small-time

126

bank robbers. You don't want to get mixed up with Doc. It's too dangerous. He's got some very nasty enemies.'

'He's got some pretty nice friends, though.'

Ace gave an impatient snort, but I could see she was pleased all the same.

Doc came down in his sharp suit and snap-brimmed fedora. 'We're off for a while, Luigi. Lock up and keep watch. Don't let anyone back in but us.'

Luigi reached under the bar and came up with a double-barrelled shotgun that would've stopped an elephant.

'Don't worry none, Doc. Anyone tries anything, I spread them all over the walls.'

Doc shuddered. 'Not unless you absolutely have to – think of the decorating bills. Come on, you two. Happy's outside with the car.'

We were on our way.

After the Hawthorne got shot up, Al had shifted his HQ to the Lexington Hotel on Michigan Avenue and East Twenty-Second Street. It was a once-posh hotel in a run-down part of town, and as usual Al had pretty well taken it over. He had a suite on the sixth floor and the rest of the place was packed with his boys.

As the car drew up outside, I said, 'Everyone get out real slow and keep your hands in plain sight. Al's boys will be expecting trouble, and that means they'll be nervous. There's nothing more dangerous than a nervous gunman.'

We got out of the car and went into the hotel lobby. Just like the Hawthorne, it was crowded with hard-eyed men in high-priced suits. The desk clerk, a skinny guy with big glasses and slicked-back hair, didn't seem to have heard of Al Capone, Al Brown or anyone else come to that.

I jogged his memory by grabbing his shirt-front and hauling him half-way across his own counter.

'Listen, sonny, just get on the horn to Frankie Rio or whoever else is bodyguarding Al and tell him that the Doc, Miss Ace and Dekker need to see the Big Fellow urgently.'

I let him drop and he scurried to a phone.

We stood waiting by the desk with a dozen hard guys watching our every move. I wanted a smoke but I knew that if I reached for a pocket I'd end up looking like a colander.

After a few minutes of this the doors to the lift opened and Frank Rio appeared. He beckoned us over.

'This better be good, Dekker,' he said as we all got into the lift. 'The Big Fellow's in a bad mood.'

We rode up in the lift, got out in the sixth floor lobby, handed over our guns. I had my .45, Ace had a nine-shot nine millimetre Browning in her purse. Doc wasn't carrying.

We were shown into Al's suite and found him in a huddle round a table with half a dozen other guys. There was Jake 'Greasy-Thumb' Guzick, the money man. The bags under his eyes made him look like a tired old blood-hound. There was Machine-Gun Jack McGurn, Al's favourite, with his round, boyish face. There was Frank Nitti, greased-back hair parted dead-centre, stroking his new moustache, grown as a disguise when he was temporarily on the lam from the tax guys. Al was having a council of war.

In a couple of chairs in the corner of the room, two guys were sitting. One was young and handsome with curly hair swept back in oily waves. The other, stocky and balding, looked like a banker or a businessman.

We'd never met but I'd seen their faces on mug-shots down at Headquarters: John Scalise and Albert Anselmi. They weren't part of the meeting. They were just waiting patiently to be told who to go out and kill. It made no difference to them. These guys were specialists.

Al looked up impatiently as we all trooped in.

'Doc, this isn't a good time.'

'Then let's not make it any worse. I need to ask you something, Mr Capone.'

There was a crackle of authority in Doc's voice that made everyone look up. I could see even Al felt it.

'Okay Doc, ask away.'

'Did you have anything to do with the recent wave of murders?' I saw Scalise and Anselmi's heads turn towards Doc like they were worked by the same wire. I reckon they thought they'd found their next customer. I could feel Ace tense beside me.

Al got up and lumbered towards Doc like a grouchy gorilla. He loomed over Doc, giving him the Look, that bulging-eyed glare that could terrify every mobster in Chicago.

Doc, looking undersized against Al's bulk, returned the look with an expression of polite interest.

In a menacing whisper Al said, 'Suppose I tell you I didn't?'

'Then I'll believe you, of course. I just needed to hear you say it. I never thought you killed them in the first place.'

Al gave a bellow of laughter, then threw his arm around Doc's shoulders, leading him towards the drinks cabinet.

'Then you're just about the only guy in Chicago outside this room who *don't* think I whacked them.' He fixed drinks for himself and Doc, and waved to us to help ourselves. I poured a healthy slug of rye each for me and Ace. I didn't know about her but I needed one.

'Listen, Doc,' said Al seriously. 'I never laid a pinkie on any of them guys. Why would I? McSwiggin and Lingle were on the take. I paid 'em and they delivered. We didn't have any beef. I didn't hardly know Red Duffy existed – strictly small-time.'

'And Hymie Weiss?'

'Okay, so Hymie and I weren't exactly buddies. But if I was moving in on the Northside mob I'd take the lot of them out. If I knocked off just Hymie I know I'd have Gusenberg, Moran and all the rest of those guys out for my blood – which, incidentally, is exactly what is gonna happen now.'

Doc looked round the room.

'I take it you're planning to get your retaliation in first?'

'Sure. Now I gotta get them before they get me.'

'Not necessarily.'

'What else can I do?'

'Nothing.'

Al looked amazed and Doc went on, 'You're an innocent man, Mr Capone, falsely accused! How does it feel?'

Al broke out into a broad grin. 'Hey, that's right. I didn't do it!' The grin faded. 'Suppose the cops try to pin it on me anyway?'

'Since you really are innocent, any evidence against you will have to be fake and can easily be discredited. Just stand fast and tell the world what you've just told me.'

'Hey, maybe that is the way to play it,' said Al thoughtfully. 'What's your angle in this, Doc?'

Doc fed Al the idea he'd fed us earlier, that someone had knocked off these four guys just to stir up trouble.

Al got right to the point. 'Yeah? Why?'

I decided to put in my two cents worth. 'Think about it, Mr Capone. If you and all the other mobs in Chicago are busy blasting each other, and the cops shoot down or lock up whoever's left . . .'

'There's a clear field for someone to move in when the shooting stops,' said Capone. 'Who is this sonuvabitch?'

'That's what I intend to find out,' said Doc. 'With the help of my friends here.'

'Let me do it, Doc. I'll find this guy and tear his head off.'

Doc shook his head. 'If you start asking questions, Mr Capone, people will either start running or start shooting. We may have more luck. I'm here to ask you to let us try.'

'Okay, Doc, you got it. Mind, if I'm attacked I gotta defend myself. Apart from that, I'm just an innocent bystander.'

Outside the suite Ace and I recovered our guns and we all three took the elevator down to the lobby.

'Well, so far so good, Doc,' I said.

Doc nodded. 'I think Al will hold on for a while, but others won't be so patient.'

'How long have we got?' Ace asked him.

'It's a matter of days at most, maybe even hours. We've

got to find our unknown before he triggers off the biggest blood-bath Chicago's ever seen.'

15

The Arrest

'I always wondered how I'd stand up under torture,' said Bernice. 'Now I know. Scream the place down and tell 'em everything.'

'I thought you were doing rather well, actually,' said Romana with her usual calm. 'Not too many interrogations end with the victim beating up the interrogator.'

'That Tarak's a maniac! And that old fool Kalmar's another.'

'They're fanatics, certainly,' agreed Romana. 'But you have to remember that Kalmar survived years of persecution.'

'What about Tarak? What's his excuse?'

'Boyish enthusiasm mostly – and a need to be as big a hero as his dead father.'

They were walking back through the woods towards Ivo's inn. Romana's grey mare trotted docilely along behind them like a well trained dog.

Romana's arrival and Bernice's mention of the Doctor had changed the situation drastically at the rebel headquarters. Kalmar had apologized over and over again, although Bernice suspected he was really far more concerned with the damage to his precious machine. Even Tarak, more humiliated than hurt, had muttered a sulky apology and given Bernice back her blaster.

When the mess and the combatants had been cleaned up, Kalmar had produced a stone jug of some local brew and they'd all drunk a toast to friendship and understanding. Well, several toasts actually. Pretty soon Bernice was feeling no pain.

During the toasts Romana had whispered, 'I came here for a meeting with these people – it's pretty important, actually. We can talk afterwards.'

The toasts over, the meeting had begun. Tarak, Ivo and the other resistance leaders gathered round in a circle to listen to Romana. It was astonishing, thought Bernice, how easily the small fair-haired woman dominated the group of tough, hard-bitten men. There was something about Romana that reminded Bernice very strongly of the Doctor.

'I've come to tell you that everything has been arranged,' said Romana. 'The delegation will arrive at Ivo's inn by tonight. The meetings will begin tomorrow morning. I expect your delegates to be there – unarmed.'

There had been immediate objections.

'Forget it,' growled one small angry-looking man. 'I'm not talking to any Lords without a sword in my hand.'

'It is most unlikely that the Lords will be travelling unarmed,' pointed out Kalmar.

'Exactly!' said Tarak. 'They'll be carrying weapons and they'll have the Black Guard with them as well. Remember, if they can wipe out the people in this room they'll crush resistance for miles around.'

'This is supposed to be a peace conference, Tarak,' said Romana wearily. 'Lord Veran has given his word that there will be no violence.'

'I agree with Zeron. I'd sooner trust my sword than the word of any Lord.'

After what seemed to Bernice like an endless amount of argy-bargy it had been agreed that the resistance delegates could bear arms to the meeting but that they would leave them outside the actual conference room – provided the Lords did the same.

After that there'd been the seemingly endless process of choosing the delegates who would actually attend. Tarak and Kalmar were elected unanimously, and after a complicated series of votes a third delegate was chosen, who turned out to be Lothar, the young farmer from Ivo's village. At last everything was settled and the meeting broke up.

All this had taken so long that it was already beginning to get dark by the time Bernice and Romana were going home through the woods. The bats were already chittering in the trees. Romana looked up and shuddered.

'I've never cared for bats – not since the first time I was here.'

'You came here with the Doctor?'

Romana nodded. 'Quite some time ago. We arrived by accident.'

'Sounds familiar,' said Bernice. 'That's how the Doctor arrives at most places.'

Romana looked curiously at her. 'I take it you've been travelling with the Doctor. You're the latest of his human companions?'

She makes it sound, thought Bernice, as if we were an interesting but faintly eccentric kind of pet. Like cocker spaniels – or newts . . .

'One of them,' said Bernice. 'There's a girl called Ace – you'd just love her. But you're not, are you?' she added challengingly.

'Not what?'

'Human. You're one of the Doctor's own people.'

'How did you know?'

'There's something about you.'

'What sort of something?'

'Oh, arrogance, bossiness, being sure you know what's best for everyone.'

Unexpectedly Romana smiled. 'I know I'm an incorrigible organizer. But there's so much to be done on this planet, and when you can see quite clearly what's needed but you just can't get people to do it . . .' She sighed. 'There's so much to tell you, I don't know where to start.'

'Begin at the beginning,' said Bernice. 'Go on to the end and then stop.'

'You really have been travelling with the Doctor, haven't you?'

Romana went on to tell how she and the Doctor had

arrived on the planet to find it frozen in medievalism, ruled by undying Lords and Ladies who were, in fact, vampires.

'The Doctor really picked out a great place for me to visit, didn't he?' said Bernice grimly. ' "You'll love it," he told me. "Wonderful old castles, a uniquely preserved medieval culture and civilization. An archaeologist's dream!" '

'I'm sure he thought he was telling the truth,' said Romana loyally. 'After all, he destroyed the Great Vampire, and the Three as well. I expect the Doctor thought the planet was vampire-free by now.'

'Well, he was wrong,' said Bernice. She told Romana of her encounter with the vampire in the Tower, and of Gerda's horrifying return to the village.

'And you say this vampire was actually Zargo?'

'It looked like him – like his portrait in the Tower. Then the portrait disappeared.'

'Vampirism is very like a kind of virus,' said Romana. 'Like all viruses it's incredibly hard to kill. You think you've stamped it out and it mutates, reappearing in another, even stronger form.'

'You still haven't told me what you're doing here.'

'The Doctor and I moved on to another planet and got mixed up with a time-sensitive race called the Tharils. They were struggling to free themselves from slavery, and I decided to stay and help them.'

'Why?'

'I don't much care for slavery.'

She was obviously telling the truth – and yet . . .

'Was that all?' asked Bernice.

Romana frowned. It was very clear that she didn't care for being questioned about her motives either. For a moment she didn't answer. At last she said, 'The Doctor can be a little overpowering at times.'

'I've noticed.'

'Perhaps we're too much alike. Two Time Lords in one TARDIS . . . I decided I'd like to do something on my own for a while. I helped the Tharils to sort things out, and found myself with nothing to do. So I thought I'd see how this planet was progressing now they were free of vampires – or so I believed. The Tharils had re-established interplanetary travel and I got them to bring me here.'

'And what did you find?'

'Trouble. The surviving Lords, now free of vampirism, or so they claim, are trying to re-establish control. The free villages like Ivo's are trying to resist them. I made contact with both sides and tried to bring them together. But nothing works. It's as if some unseen force is trying to keep them at each other's throats.'

'The vampires?'

'You'd expect the vampires to ally themselves with the Lords, try to bring back the good old days. This force seemed equally against both sides. Whatever it was I was baffled so I sent a telepathic signal to the Doctor.'

'And he sent me.'

'That's what's puzzling me,' said Romana frankly. 'He did get the signal?'

'Oh, he got it all right. He was brooding over a Time Lord message that had come through to the TARDIS data bank concerning one particular period of Earth's history when he suddenly got very excited. He started jumping up and down shouting, "It's time something was done, and I'm just the Time Lord to do it!" Then all of a sudden he threw this tremendous wobbly.'

'Wobbly?'

'He clutched his head and yelled, "Oh no, Romana, not now! Can't you see I'm busy?" '

'It sounds just like him. Then what?'

'He went all quiet and broody again for a time. Then he took me by the arm and said, "Bernice, I know this terrific planet . . ." You know the rest.'

'He just dumped you down here, without any kind of briefing?'

'He told me to make like an archaeologist and keep my eyes and ears open. So that's what I did. I toured the area, collected quite a few good specimens of local artefacts and finished up at Ivo's inn. You know the rest. Oh, and the Doctor said if things got really hairy I was to use this.'

Bernice fished in her pockets and produced a silver sphere with an inset silver button.

Romana recognized it immediately. 'It's a SPATAB – a Spatio-Temporal Alarm Beacon. Also acts as a homing beacon for the TARDIS. It's also known as a panic button. All you can do with it is yell for help.'

Bernice posed her thumb over the button. 'I know. Let's!'

'No,' said Romana. 'Let's not. If the Doctor's too busy to help them we'll manage without him. Maybe we'll just send for him when it's all over.'

The watcher straightened up from the screen.

'They are refusing to use the device.'

'They will use it,' said the second watcher. 'When their fear is great enough they will send for the Doctor, and he will come to save them.'

'If he lives,' said the third watcher.

'It matters not. On one planet or the other we shall destroy the Doctor. And in the process we shall capture the Other to serve our will. Death to the Doctor!

'Borusa lives!

'Rassilon must die!'

Back at the inn Ivo greeted Romana as an old friend. When the greetings and explanations were over he said, 'So you know each other. And to think that you both know the Doctor! How is he?'

'Changed,' said Bernice. 'Changed in some ways – but in others much the same.'

'Is he too returning to us?'

Bernice and Romana exchanged glances.

'Possibly,' said Romana. 'But not immediately. Is there any sign of the delegation?'

'Not yet, my Lady. But they should not be long. Even Lords do not greatly care to travel after dark.'

Night was falling and they were sitting by the fire, surrounded by the shadows of the darkened inn. Ivo went to the kitchen and returned with bread and cheese and a jug of rough red wine. He brought platters, knives and goblets, and poured wine for them both.

'Something to stay you until dinner,' he said. 'I have prepared my best for the Lords, such as it is.'

Bernice cut a hunk of bread and cheese, took a swig of the rough red wine and shuddered. An interesting little vin du pays with a subtle bouquet of sulphuric acid and swamp-water, she thought. She took another swig and thought it tasted better the more of it you drank. Then again, most things did.

'What do you think of our chances tomorrow?' asked Romana.

Ivo sighed. 'Hard to say, my Lady. Kalmar is for peace and so is Lothar, but Tarak would as soon fight as talk.' He looked almost reproachfully at Bernice. 'Stories of the return of the Undying Ones do not help.' He touched ears, eyes and mouth in the ritual gesture.

'Don't look at me,' said Bernice indignantly. 'I didn't ask to run into your local vampires. According to Romana they're supposed to be extinct.'

'Not all vampires are Lords, Ivo,' Romana pointed out. 'What about your serving girl, Gerda?'

'I know that the Lords claim to be free of the vampire taint,' said Ivo wearily. 'Yet because of the Dark Times, the two stand together in the minds of our people. Some say little has changed. Much will depend on the attitude of the Lords.'

'And here they are,' said Romana.

At first Bernice could hear nothing, and then gradually she made out the sound of hoofbeats coming nearer. Soon she heard the confused noises of a party of riders drawing up outside the inn, shouted orders and the jingle of harness as they dismounted. A figure appeared in the doorway, framed against the darkness of the night.

'Landlord! Some light in this hovel!'

Ivo lit a lamp and came forward holding it up, revealing the newcomer as a thin, sharp-faced man with a neatly pointed beard.

'My Lord?' said Ivo steadily.

'I am Lord Yarven, aide to Lord Veran. He will be here soon. Is all ready?'

'The rooms are prepared, my Lord, and such simple fare as we can command.'

'Do not trouble yourself, fellow, we have brought our own food – and our own cooks.' Yarven caught sight of the wine jug, snatched it up, drank from it, and spat the wine out on the floor. 'And our own wine, thanks be!' He noticed the two silent female figures in the shadows. 'Still, perhaps you can provide us with some simple comforts, eh landlord?' He loomed over Romana. 'What's your name, little wench?'

Romana stood up. 'Good evening, Lord Yarven.'

You could have deep-frozen an ox with her voice, thought Bernice admiringly.

Yarven stepped back. 'Your pardon, Lady Romana. In this cursed gloom I took you for some peasant wench.'

'That does not make your conduct any more excusable.'

Yarven licked his thin dry lips and was silent.

Another figure stamped into the room and saluted Yarven. It was Varis, the arrogant young guard captain Bernice had clashed with some time earlier.

'The men are at their posts, my Lord.' He saw Romana and bowed. 'My Lady.' Then he saw Bernice.

'You, my Lady! I told you we should meet again. The odds are a little different now.' He raised his voice. 'Guards!'

Two black-clad guards marched into the room.

Varis pointed to Bernice. 'Arrest her! Take the man as well.'

More guards appeared and surrounded Ivo. As the men moved forward Romana snapped, 'Upon what charge?'

'The murder of one of my men. Now, take her!'

The guards grabbed Bernice and dragged her to her feet.

16

Summit of Death

'Just one moment,' said Romana, taking charge as usual. 'What were the circumstances of this murder?'

Lord Yarven made a belated attempt to assert his authority.

'Yes, tell us what happened, Captain.'

'What *happened* is this,' said Varis bitterly. 'I found one of my men with his throat slit just outside this village. There was a rabble of peasants around the body, led by the man Ivo and the woman here. They refused to surrender the murderers and the woman held a blaster to my head so they could all escape.' He glared angrily at Bernice. 'I'm not sure if she's responsible for the actual throat-cutting, but she probably knows who is. If she does I'll have the truth out of her.'

Not another interrogation, thought Bernice despairingly. This must be my day for it. I expect this lot prefer good old traditional methods like the rack and thumbscrews and hot irons.

'Is this true?' asked Romana icily.

Not caring much for her tone Bernice said defiantly, 'Yes and no. I made some disturbing discoveries on a visit to the Tower. I persuaded Ivo to take a party of men from the village to investigate.'

Yarven looked at her with sudden interest.

'And did you find anything?'

'Not at the Tower, no. But on the way back to the village we found the body of a soldier at the crossroads. Naturally we stopped to investigate. Then this military idiot turned up and wanted to start hanging people on

141

the spot – in spite of the fact that the man had clearly been killed some time earlier and somewhere else. I was forced to persuade him to go away.'

A soft, amused voice said, 'Indeed, a blaster in the ear is a most effective method of persuasion.'

They turned to the doorway and saw that someone else had come into the room: a big, portly old man with flowing white hair.

'Lord Veran,' said Romana with relief. 'A problem has arisen.'

Veran held up his hand. 'I heard. Captain Varis, does it occur to you that arresting the senior delegate on the other side might not be the most hopeful of beginnings for an important peace conference?'

Not surprisingly, Varis found nothing to say to this. He looked appealingly at Lord Yarven, who remained discreetly silent.

Veran looked at Bernice. 'And as for this lady . . .'

'I can vouch for Lady Bernice,' said Romana quickly. 'She is a visitor to this world, as I am, and became involved with your affairs only by chance.'

'Very well. For the moment we shall accept her story. The murder of this unfortunate soldier must, of course, be fully investigated – *after* the conference. You will make yourself available for questioning in due course, my Lady?'

Bernice managed a fair imitation of Romana's haughty manner.

'There isn't much more I can tell you but I shall be pleased to answer any questions put to me with reasonable civility.'

'Excellent,' said Veran. 'For the moment the matter is shelved.' He waved away the guards and turned to Ivo.

'You must be Ivo, headman of this village. I have heard a great deal about you. I am Veran.'

Ivo fell to one knee and bowed his head. 'My Lord.'

Veran went forward and shook his hand, raising him up.

'No need for that, Ivo. We are equals here, heads of

our respective delegations. Let us hope that between us we can bring some peace to this unhappy land.'

Bernice looked at Romana and grinned, holding out discreetly crossed fingers. After a distinctly rocky start, the peace conference seemed to be back on course.

Dinner that night was the best meal Bernice had eaten for some time. Lord Veran, clearly a man who liked his comforts, had brought along a retinue of servants and cooks, and several pack-loads of food and drink as well. Katya was relegated to an awestricken washer-up while Veran's servants cooked and served an excellent meal of roast venison, fish, assorted pies and pastries, cheese and a variety of sweetmeats.

The meal was accompanied by numerous bottles of a red wine that resembled a most acceptable claret, and a white that was very like a good Riesling.

Ivo, wearing his best jerkin and scrubbed till he positively glowed, was a guest at his own table. Bernice had exchanged her safari jacket for a slightly crumpled basic little black dress from her pack, while Romana was her catlike elegant self. For the visiting team, Veran, Yarven and Varis, all dressed in their best, put up an impressive show.

Veran was an accomplished host who kept the conversation flowing smoothly, making sure that Bernice was included.

'What brought you to our unhappy little planet?' he asked.

Bernice gave him her standard story, that she was an archaeologist on a preliminary field-trip.

Veran shook his head sadly. 'The history of our planet is a dark and bloody one, my Lady.'

'All the more fascinating for that,' said Bernice, who was a little elevated by now. 'You know what they say, Lord Veran. The Draconians had hundreds of years of warfare, terror, murder, bloodshed, and they produced art and architecture to amaze the galaxy. On Dulkis they had

143

brotherly love, democracy and peace, and what did that produce? The egg-timer.'

'It is true that we have many fine castles,' said Veran. 'My own, amongst them. I hope you can visit it one day. But our arts, like our sciences and our very civilization, have been held back by the scarlet thread of vampirism that runs through our history.'

'It's the first thing the Doctor and I noticed when we came here,' said Romana. 'In terms of applied socio-energetics, the society had simply lost its grip on level-two development. It actually seemed to be evolving backwards, clearly as the result of some exceptionally powerful force.'

'And we all know what that was,' said Bernice. The wine had been followed by a really excellent local brandy, and her curiosity was overcoming her tact. 'This vampire business – how did it work exactly? I mean, were all Lords vampires? At one time, I mean,' she added hastily.

Romana shot her a reproving look, but Veran seemed quite ready to answer. 'It's more complex than that, my Lady. Here in this village, which was – forgive me Ivo – the very fount of the evil, matters were simple. Lord Zargo and Lady Camilla were vampires, and as such they ruled, using the people to feed their appetites.'

'My son Karl . . .' said Ivo and his voice broke off. He bowed his head and tears came into his eyes.

After a moment Veran went on: 'Here, at least, the evil was in plain sight. In time the people arose and destroyed their Vampire Lords, led by Ivo here, helped by Lady Romana, whose beauty defies the years, and her friend the Doctor – who I have yet to meet.'

Veran raised his glass to Romana and then continued: 'In other nearby villages, things were much the same. There were other Vampire Lords and Ladies, and as news of the rebellion spread they too were overthrown and destroyed. But elsewhere . . .'

He paused for a moment.

'Elsewhere the evil took a more subtle form. Perhaps just one member of a noble family might be infected by

144

vampirism, or there might be several. No one knew who to trust. The vampires worked behind the scenes, spreading their evil cult. Several noble families took a stand against this evil, vowing to wipe it out. My own was amongst them.'

Veran paused again, then forced himself to go on.

'Just when we thought the battle was won I discovered that my only son, Vetar, had been infected by the evil. I myself drove the stake through his heart.'

The conference started early next morning: far too early for Bernice who was suffering from a certain fuzziness of the brain. Still, she thought, I'd better show willing. She climbed out of bed, groaning a little, and got ready to join the others.

Tarak, Kalmar and Lothar arrived. Tarak, bristling with suspicion, agreed that all three would leave their weapons outside provided Veran, Yarven and Varis did the same. It had been agreed that Bernice should be allowed to attend as an observer. It was a privilege she could have done without.

The conference took place in the main room of the inn. Ivo, Kalmar, Tarak, and Lothar sat on one side of the big table. Lord Veran, Lord Yarven, Captain Varis and Lady Romana sat on the other. At first Bernice was surprised to see Romana sitting with the Lords but a moment's reflection made her see that it was the Time Lady's natural place. But the Doctor would have been on the other side, she thought. Still, the Doctor's different. Bernice was sat at the end in recognition of her neutral status.

The conference began with a speech from Lord Veran, recapping the events of recent history:

'I know how much you all suffered from the old, evil regime, how much you all value your hard-won freedom. Believe me, no one wants to take it from you.'

Kalmar nodded benignly, Tarak looked sceptical and Lothar listened with polite interest.

'I know too that many of your old Lords betrayed your trust, giving themselves over to evil. But that evil has now been driven from our ranks. We ask only to resume our rightful place – to lead and to serve you.'

Veran went on to point out that the destruction of the Vampire Lords had left the planet in a state of chaos. 'If we are to have progress we must have order, and order is best built around the old traditional structures.'

He continued for some time, developing the same theme in a long, eloquent and in many ways convincing speech.

Kalmar was the first to respond when he had finished.

'There is much in what you say, Lord Veran. I myself wish only to pursue my studies, to rediscover the scientific secrets we need if we are to progress. But to do that I need peace and order, and there has been little of that in these parts of late.'

Tarak slammed his fist upon the table.

'There was peace and order enough in the Dark Time – the peace and order of death! Will you sacrifice our freedom for a little security?'

'Without security there is no freedom,' said Lord Yarven. 'If this world is ever to progress we must have order, discipline. Someone must rule, and who better than those of us who were born to the task?'

'Order we must have,' said Ivo slowly. 'But what if the price to be paid is too high?'

'The price of chaos would be higher by far,' said Romana.

'With respect, sirs, and ladies,' said Lothar. He was a shy young man, and he blushed furiously when everyone looked at him.

'The trouble with rule by Lords is this: too much depends upon the Lord. If they were all like you, Lord Veran, we would serve them happily. But that's not so. There are still too many Lords who despise us common folk, and would treat us like dirt.'

He looked defiantly at Yarven and Varis.

'I'm afraid that's just as true of rule by revolutionaries,' said Romana. 'Ivo leads the village council here, and he rules justly because he's a good and wise man. But there are other villages run by revolutionary councils . . .'

'And what's wrong with that?' demanded Tarak.

Romana told him. 'They hunt down and kill every aristocrat they can find – even those innocent of any connection with the vampires. When that's done they split into factions and fight amongst themselves, and the strongest party starts executing political opponents as traitors.'

'I fear that is all too true,' confirmed Lord Veran. 'And do you know how it usually ends up? One man seizes power and rules as dictator – for the good of the people, of course. You end up with a tyrant, as bad as the Lord he's overthrown.'

And that's true as well, thought Bernice. If Lothar takes over from Ivo, things will be fine. But if Tarak grabs power . . .

The arguments raged on, and on and on, with everyone stating and restating their positions. Veran and all the rest of his delegation wanted rule by a Council of Lords, promising that the rights of the common people would be respected. Tarak was passionate for rulers chosen by the common people. He was supported, though with varying degrees of enthusiasm, by Ivo and Lothar. Old Kalmar just wanted peace and quiet.

Bernice sat back and let the arguments roll over her. More from boredom than anything else she started trying to work out some kind of solution. Dragging her attention back to the meeting, she heard Veran's weary voice.

'We seem to have reached deadlock. I suggest we break off for a time and resume later. If no one has anything to add?'

'Aah, herrum!' said Bernice.

'Lady Bernice,' said Veran politely. 'You have something to suggest?'

'As a matter of fact I have. Is there any chance of a drink?'

Romana gave Bernice a disapproving look. 'Is that it?'

'No entirely, no. I do have some ideas that might help.'

Yarven snapped his fingers and servants appeared with

147

wine and sweetened oakcakes. The refreshment was welcome and for a few minutes the delegates concentrated on eating and drinking.

Veran brushed crumbs from his white beard. 'And now, my Lady?'

'Der trumble uz,' said Bernice indistinctly. 'Sorry!' She washed down the last of her oatcake with a swig of wine. 'The trouble is that both sides are in the wrong. This is complicated by the fact that both sides are also in the right.'

She beamed at their astonished faces and took another swig of wine, then pointed to Lord Veran.

'You lot want to turn the clock back. Can't be done. There's a lot in what you say about the benefits of tradition, but the peasants have tasted power and they're not going to give it up.'

Tarak thumped the table. 'Well said, my Lady! Power to the people!'

Bernice's accusing finger swung round to point at him.

'No need to look so smug, Tarak, your lot are no better. The Lords want to live in the past, but you want to abolish it. That can't be done either. The Lords are still here and they're not going to go away. Any new system you set up won't work unless it takes them into account.'

'Exactly so,' said Lord Veran. 'We accept that our role has to change, but a role we must and will have!'

'So far all you've given us is a definition of the problem,' said Romana. 'What about the solution?'

'It's a bit of a mad scheme,' said Bernice. 'But I think it just might work. You set up not one but *two* groups of rulers.'

Kalmar stroked his beard in puzzlement. 'Why two, my Lady? Will they not fight?'

'One group will be made up of the heads of all the great families. The other will be formed from delegates chosen by the common people. You could call them, oh, I don't know, the Lords and the Commons. The Commons decide what needs to be done, then they pass the idea to the Lords. Things only go ahead when both Houses agree.'

'Houses, my Lady?' asked Veran.

'They'd need special buildings to meet in, close together but entirely separate. Nobody from one side goes to the other side's House unless they're invited.'

'Suppose the two Houses don't agree,' said Tarak. 'Who wins?'

'The Commons. The Lords can turn down any idea twice, but the third time the Commons get their way.'

'So!' said Lord Yarven. 'We would not have supreme power.'

'No, but you'd have enormous influence – enough to get your way quite a lot of the time.'

'A House of Commons and a House of Lords,' mused Veran. 'A strange idea indeed. What do you think, Ivo?'

Ivo rubbed his chin. 'I was thinking that when the load is extra heavy you yoke two horses to the cart.'

'That's so,' said Lothar. 'At first they fight and kick, but in time they grow used to the work and pull together.'

These gems of rustic wisdom were followed by a thoughtful silence. Bernice seized her opportunity and stood up.

'Well, there you are, I've given you the broad outline. You can work out the details for yourselves. I need to go and write up my notes.'

Unobtrusively picking up a nearly full wine bottle and a goblet, Bernice went out of the room. Soon the delegates were deep in discussion once more.

They went on talking, discussing Bernice's ideas with ever-growing enthusiasm. It was close to dinner time when the formal meeting broke up, in a far more hopeful state than ever before. Lord Veran invited everyone to be his guests at dinner.

Kalmar however wanted to get back to his beloved machines, and Lothar, who had little liking for luxury, was anxious to return to his farm. Both promised to return early next morning. Tarak, who seemed to have a taste for high life, agreed to stay and Ivo promised him a room at the inn.

As the others were saying their goodbyes, Lord Veran put a fatherly hand on Tarak's shoulder. He recognized Tarak as the real force in the opposition party and was anxious to reach an understanding.

'Suppose we continue this discussion between ourselves? There are one or two points that might be easier to settle with just the two of us.'

Flattered by the invitation, Tarak agreed and the two left the room together, deep in conversation.

Lord Yarven watched them go, an expression of sour disapproval on his face. It was beginning to look as if this conference might succeed. For certain very private reasons of his own, Yarven intended that it should fail. His mind numbed by hours of talk, Yarven stamped out of the main door of the inn, hoping that fresh air might clear his head.

Ignoring the salutes of the sentries, Yarven wandered round to the little smallholding at the back of the inn, staring gloomily at the scattering of barns and sheds.

Somewhere along the way a fellow Lord had joined him, a tall thin, elegant man in a black cloak. Yarven couldn't quite place him, but he was clearly attached to the delegation.

'Things are going badly for us,' said the stranger.

'It's a disaster,' said Yarven. 'Give these peasants a toehold in government and they'll swamp us. We should crush them now before they grow too strong.'

'Why don't you?'

'How can I with that old fool Veran mad to make peace with them? He's the head of our delegation.'

The tall stranger stared down at Yarven with eyes that held a fiery spark of red in their depths.

'Then why not remove the head?'

'That's easier said than done.'

'Not if you use the right tools,' said the stranger.

He flung open the door of a rickety shed to reveal a rack of gleaming agricultural implements. Ivo was a conscientious worker and he always kept his tools clean and sharp.

Like a man entranced, Yarven stretched out his hand.

150

Seconds later he was striding back towards the inn, something hidden beneath his cloak.

The tall man watched him go, red fires burning deep in his eyes. Then he turned and hurried away. He had work to do.

As he came to the head of the old wooden staircase, Yarven saw Tarak come out of Veran's room, walk along the corridor and disappear into his own room. Moving stealthily after him, Yarven slipped into Veran's room. The old man turned in alarm, and then relaxed when he saw who it was.

'I've just been having a private word with young Tarak. That boy's got the makings of a politician. I think we can work together . . .'

Lord Yarven stood with his back to the door. He was facing the window, his white face caught by the feeble rays of the setting sun. He stared at Veran with bright glittering eyes.

'Did I ever tell you that your late son was my very good friend?'

'I'd no idea you'd ever met.'

Yarven smiled, revealing curiously long white teeth.

'We shared certain interests.' He brought something shining out from under his cloak.

Veran backed away. 'Yarven, no!'

He opened his mouth to shout for help but the shining blade swept across the room and cut him off.

17

Flight

Bernice lay stretched out on her bed, snoring lightly, her notebook in her lap, the half-empty wine bottle on the wooden table beside her bed.

She awoke suddenly with the feeling that something had disturbed her. There was a vague memory of a cry, a thud, something rolling across the floor. Was it real, or had she dreamed it? She realized the room was in semi-darkness. She must have dozed for quite some time.

There was a tap on the door.

'Come in,' she called.

The door opened and Romana appeared, carrying a smokily burning oil-lamp. She looked around the room, put the lamp on the table and sat on the room's single wooden chair.

'Hard at it?' she said amiably.

Bernice struggled to a sitting position. 'Sorry, must have dropped off. How's the conference going?'

'Very well, thanks to your contribution. Where did you pick up that extraordinary idea about two linked legislative chambers?'

'From a long lecture by the Doctor about the political history of his favourite planet. I didn't think I was listening but some of it must have sunk in.'

'I think it tipped the balance,' said Romana. 'You must try to remember some more for tomorrow's session. Are you coming down? I think there's supposed to be some social chit-chat before dinner.'

'Yes, sure, just give me a minute.'

There was a jug of cold water in a basin on the table.

Bernice tipped water in, splashed her face and hands, dried them on the rough towel and dragged a comb through her hair. She wondered how Romana always managed to look so aggravatingly immaculate.

Probably licks her paws and washes her face like a cat, she thought. 'Okay, I'm ready,' she said out loud.

They went out of the room, Romana leading the way with the lamp, and saw Tarak coming along the corridor from his room.

'Ah, good, there you are,' said Romana with her usual bossiness. 'Come along, we'll be – ' She broke off, kneeling down and holding the lamp just a little above the floor. They were immediately outside the room between Bernice's and Tarak's room.

A trickle of blood was running from underneath the door.

'That's Lord Veran's room,' said Tarak. 'We were talking in there not long ago.' He opened the door and they went inside.

Romana held the lamp up high, illuminating the room.

Veran's head was in the basin on the table beside the bed. Wide eyes stared sightlessly at them and his mouth was open in a silent scream.

His body lay sprawled across the floor, the stump of the neck towards the door. Blood poured in a stream from the severed arteries in the neck, forming a pool beside the bed and sending tendrils of blood out under the door.

'Get on the other side of the room,' ordered Tarak. 'Don't step in the blood.' He ripped the blanket from the bed, soaked one end of it in the water from the jug and swabbed up the trickle of blood in the corridor. Closing the door again, he rolled the blanket and stuffed it along the bottom of the door like a draught-excluder.

Avoiding the blood, Bernice reached out and took Veran's wrinkled old hand. 'The body's still warm and the blood's absolutely fresh. This was done just minutes ago.'

She shuddered, remembering. 'I was dozing, and something woke me up. A cry, a thud, the sound of something heavy rolling across the floor . . .'

'He was killed with this,' said Romana. She held out the lamp and pointed to a curved billhook, tossed carelessly in the corner, its curved blade dulled with Veran's blood.

She looked at Tarak. 'You say you were just talking to him. You didn't . . .'

'Disagree on a point of procedure and lop off his head with a billhook I just happened to have about my person? Of course I didn't, you stupid bitch.'

'Someone did,' said Bernice.

'Someone who wants the conference to fail. That's not the point, not at the moment. I don't know who killed him, but I know who's going to get the blame for it.' Tarak tapped his own chest. 'We left the conference together, he was killed with a peasant's weapon. If I'm here when they find the body, Varis will hang me out of hand.'

'What are you going to do?' asked Bernice.

'I'm going straight out of that window, heading back to our HQ and sending out a call for my men.'

'But if you run it will make everyone sure you killed him,' said Bernice. 'Don't you want to prove your innocence?'

'I'll worry about that when I'm safe, my Lady. It's hard to put up a good defence when you're dangling from a tree.'

Romana looked hard at him, but she didn't say anything.

'I really didn't do it, you know,' said Tarak more gently. 'I liked the old man and the talks were going well. Do you think I'd still be here if I'd killed him?'

Romana nodded. 'What about the rest of your delegation?'

'They both left right after the conference, remember. And Ivo's been downstairs in plain sight all the time. I'll see they're warned.'

A heavy fist rapped on the door.

It rapped again and a voice called, 'Lord Veran!' It was Captain Varis.

Romana handed the lamp to Bernice. Stepping carefully around the pool of blood she opened the door just a crack, slipped through and closed it behind her.

They heard her voice in the corridor, cool and assured as usual. 'Less noise please, Captain! Lord Veran is a little unwell, and has asked that dinner be delayed. He will come down as soon as he feels better.'

'But there are important matters . . .'

'They must wait, Captain. Lord Veran particularly asked not to be disturbed. Will you give me your escort downstairs?'

As the two moved away, Bernice heard Romana saying, 'I don't think there's any real cause for alarm. Lord Veran is no longer young, and it has been a rather tiring day . . .'

Bernice turned to Tarak and found that he'd already disappeared, presumably out of the open window.

'Great!' she thought. 'They all clear off and leave me with the headless corpse. Now what?' She considered following Tarak, but it didn't seem right just to abandon Romana.

Trying not to look at the severed head in the basin, she stepped carefully around the pool of blood and slipped out the door, trying to disturb the folded blanket as little as possible, and went back to her room.

The first thing to do was to change, she thought. There was no way she was going on the run in a little black cocktail dress. Stripping it off, she climbed back into the familiar comfort of trousers, work-shirt, safari jacket and boots, and immediately felt much more herself.

She looked longingly at her pack but decided she daren't take it. Instead she rifled it for everything that might be useful, stuffing everything into the many pockets of her jacket.

Picking up the lamp, she started on her way downstairs. There was still a damp patch outside Veran's door, but there didn't seem to be any more blood, not yet.

The inn's big main room was lit by several lamps, and she found Romana chatting to Varis and Yarven by the fire. They all greeted her, and Yarven gave her an enquiring look.

'Not leaving us, my Lady?'

'How could I bear to do that?' said Bernice, despising herself for the mock-flirtatiousness in her tone. 'No, it's just that I heard dinner will be delayed, so I thought I'd go for a walk. Can I persuade you to join me, Lady Romana?'

Romana hesitated, just long enough to give the impression of someone being landed with a rather tiresome social chore. 'Of course, I'd be delighted.'

'Why don't we all go?' suggested Yarven.

'Please don't trouble yourselves,' said Romana firmly. 'I'm sure you don't really want to leave the wine and the fire.'

'We'd best wait here for Lord Veran,' said Varis. 'I'm sure he'll be coming down soon.' With his head tucked underneath his arm, thought Bernice, and realized she was getting hysterical.

'I don't advise you to wander too far afield, not after dark,' said Varis. 'I'll detail some of my men to escort you.'

'No need for that,' said Bernice hastily. 'We're just going to take a quick stroll around the inn. We'll be back with you in no time.'

Yarven made a great business of helping Romana into her hooded cloak, settling it attentively around her shoulders. Romana and Bernice went out into the darkness.

'I thought we'd never get out of there,' said Bernice. 'Come on, let's get going!'

'Going where?'

'No idea, I thought you'd know that. Away from here, that's all.'

Romana stopped moving. 'I'm not so sure I want to go anywhere,' she said with exasperating calm.

'Even though you're a murder suspect?'

'Nonsense! They'll all think Tarak's guilty.'

'You really are just like the Doctor, aren't you?'

'Am I?'

'You both think you can talk your way out of anything. Well, you can't. They'll think we're all guilty. You most of all, you were seen by Varis coming out of Veran's room.'

'The murder could have happened after that.'

Bernice felt like shaking her. 'Oh, don't be so daft! With a brutal murder like this everyone's going to be too angry to pay any attention to logic. You're involved, and you'll be suspected. So will I, just by being there. Pretty soon someone's going to find Veran's body. If it's not found by accident, the murderer will find it on purpose. After that it'll simply be a case of "Round up the usual suspects".'

Romana still didn't look convinced. Bernice added the clincher. 'Do you really want to be interrogated by Yarven? I'm sure he'd enjoy it, but I doubt if you would.'

'Perhaps you're right.'

The decision taken, Romana became her old bossy self. 'I must find Ivo and warn him. Then we'd better join Tarak at his HQ. We'll be as safe there as anywhere until things cool down a bit. My horse is in the stables and most of my things are still in the saddlebags. Can you ride?'

'After a fashion – if I had a horse.'

'We'll have to borrow one for you. Wait here!' Romana disappeared through the back door of the inn.

Bernice waited nervously, shivering in the night air. After what seemed like far too long a time, Romana reappeared.

'I've warned Ivo, he's going to join us when he can. Come on, let's not hang about chattering.'

Romana strode off towards the stables. Bernice followed, muttering curses under her breath. There was no one about at the stables, and Romana led out her grey mare. It nuzzled her affectionately.

'Pick a nice quiet one for yourself,' she ordered.

Defiantly Bernice picked Varis's black stallion.

Romana finished saddling her mare, strapped on the

saddlebag and came to help Bernice finish saddling the stallion. It whickered and stamped its feet.

Romana swung lightly into the saddle. 'Are you sure you can manage that beast?'

In a dignified silence, Bernice scrambled onto the stallion. It reared and threw her off into a pile of straw.

Romana sighed and slid down from the saddle. She caught the stallion, soothed it, patted its nose and breathed into its nostrils. The stallion calmed down, and stood meekly waiting. Bernice picked herself up and Romana handed back the reins.

'He'll be all right now. Come on!'

A guard came around the corner of the stables and stopped short in amazement.

'It's all right,' said Romana brightly. 'We're just going for a little ride.'

'After dark? And that's the captain's horse.'

'So it is,' said Bernice and handed him the reins.

As he stood holding them, she slipped round behind him, took her blaster from her pocket and slugged him hard behind the ear. Grabbing back the reins as he fell, Bernice climbed back on the black stallion.

Romana was already in the saddle. They galloped away towards the darkened woods.

Back at the inn time dragged past slowly. Yarven and Varis had long ago run out of polite conversation. The two women didn't come back from their walk, and Lord Veran didn't come down from his room. Lord Veran's cook said if the dinner was delayed much longer it would be a disaster. At last Varis said, 'Perhaps I'd better go up. Lord Veran may be more ill than we think.'

'He may indeed,' said Yarven.

Varis picked up a lamp and made his way upstairs.

Yarven stood staring into the fire, sipping his wine and waiting. He heard a terrible choked cry, raced upstairs and found Varis, white-faced and horror-struck, holding up the lamp in the doorway of Veran's room.

158

Yarven turned and ran to Tarak's room, glanced inside and returned to Varis.

'Tarak has gone. He did this! Come on, man!'

He led the way downstairs. As they reached the bottom of the stairs a bruised guard staggered into the room. 'The women have gone, Captain. One of them took your horse.'

'They've all gone,' said Yarven savagely. 'Tarak, the women, the two others – a clean sweep.' He grabbed Varis by the shoulder. 'Don't you see, Captain, this whole conference was a trap, a trick to destroy us. We're lucky we're still alive. We must find them before they kill more of us.'

'These peasant scum have a headquarters in the wastelands,' said Varis hoarsely. 'It was secret once, but everyone knows where it is now. That's where they'll be. We must find them and burn them out.'

'How many men have you, Captain?'

'A full company.'

'It will have to do. If we strike quickly . . .' Yarven looked round. 'Where's that damned landlord? He must be in this too.' But Ivo was nowhere to be found.

To her surprise, Bernice found herself enjoying the mad gallop through the night. There was something exhilarating about it in a loony kind of way.

They rode through the dark woods, crouched low in the saddle to avoid lashing branches, and across the rough broken ground of the wasteland. It was a difficult and dangerous ride, and Bernice had to fight to stay in the saddle. Ahead of her, Romana's grey mare flitted surefootedly through the darkness.

At last they cantered up to the mound that concealed what had once been the headquarters of the peasant resistance movement. The usually hidden doors stood open and light flooded out from the tunnel entrance.

Romana reined in the mare and jumped down. A little more slowly, Bernice did the same. Letting the reins dangle, they left the horses and moved slowly down the brightly lit tunnel.

'I can't understand it being left open,' said Romana. 'It's not particularly secret these days, more of a museum, but Kalmar is always so careful with his precious machinery.'

At the end of the tunnel Bernice found the circular chamber to which she'd first been brought as a captive. It looked very different now.

The place was ruined, wrecked, ravaged, as if a hurricane had been raging inside the underground chamber. The whole room was littered with scattered clothes and papers, shattered furniture, smashed and twisted fragments of machinery. It seemed as if nothing had been left whole or in its proper place.

They picked their way across the room, looking round them. 'Kalmar!' called Romana. There was no reply. 'His room's over here,' she said, and led the way to the sectioned-off part of the dome. Kalmar was there, staring up at the ceiling. His old body had been hacked and stabbed and sliced with maniacal frenzy, until his once-white robe was soaked with red. In a final savage gesture a sword had been thrust through his heart, pinning him to the floor. It was a long sword with an ornately jewelled handle. The kind of a sword worn only by Lords.

They heard movement behind them and saw Tarak running across the ruined room. He came up to the alcove and stared down at Kalmar's body.

'No,' he whispered. 'No . . .'

For a few minutes Tarak knelt beside the old man's body, struggling to control his feelings. Then he pulled aside Kalmar's bed to reveal a concealed hatchway.

'At least they didn't find this . . . You'll be avenged, old friend.' He lifted the hatch to reveal a power switch. He threw the switch, a light flashed, and a low, regular electronic tone pulsed through the room like a drumbeat.

'What is that thing?' asked Bernice.

Tarak looked at her with unnaturally bright eyes. 'It's an alarm-signal – a war drum. There's one like it in every resistance HQ for miles around. Everyone who hears it will arm himself and come here. When they arrive we'll march on the village and kill every Lord and every soldier we can find!'

It was quite clear that it was no use talking to Tarak.

Bernice took Romana's arm and drew her aside. 'Does it strike you there's something familiar about all this?'

'Is there?' said Romana impassively.

'It's a replay of the earlier murder, only in reverse. First a much loved Lord is slaughtered with a weapon that shouts peasant. Now an equally loved peasant leader, butchered with a sword used only by Lords.'

'Go on.'

'We're pretty sure the peasants didn't kill Veran. I don't think the Lords killed Kalmar either.'

'Then who did?'

'I think the same person is behind both deaths. Someone who wants to set the two sides at each other's throats.'

'I think you're right – in fact I know you're right. The Doctor knows it too. That's why we're both here.'

Deep in the forest a tall cloaked figure stood with arms outstretched, savouring and increasing the waves of hate and anger and blood-lust that swirled around it.

At the inn angry soldiers prepared to set off. Yarven had paraded them before Veran's body and they were filled with the lust to kill.

At the rebel HQ silent angry men were gathering, hiding weapons beneath their cloaks. One by one Tarak took them to see Kalmar's broken, blood-soaked body, and the fire for revenge burned in every man's heart.

Not far away, dark creatures were stirring. Wars and policies meant nothing to them. They were simply eager to slake the blood-lust that was their own.

The cloaked being stood for a long time, savouring the feast that was to come. But it was not quite ready. And in another time and another place, there were other matters to be attended to. Slowly the tall figure faded away, becoming one with the darkness.

18

Private Investigations

'Three crimes, three private eyes,' said the Doctor. 'If Mr Dekker will grant us honorary status, that is?'

'Be my guest, Doc,' said Dekker, through a mouthful of English muffin. They were having a breakfast conference at Doc's Place, and the Doctor was laying out plans for the day.

Ace was sipping her third cup of coffee and watching the Doctor suspiciously, in case he tried to keep her out of the action. 'Okay Doctor, so who goes where?'

'I want Mr Dekker to concentrate on the McSwiggin murder. Most of the witnesses seem to be mobsters, and he knows how to talk to those kind of people.'

Dekker tapped the bulge of the .45 automatic under his armpit. 'I'll have 'em singing like birds, Doc.'

'Try not to kill anyone,' said the Doctor dryly. 'I'm trying to cut down the death rate, not boost it. That applies to you as well, Ace – in fact, especially to you.'

Dekker grinned. 'You know what Al Capone always says, Doc? "You get further with a kind word and a gun than just a kind word alone." '

'What about me?' asked Ace. 'What do I do, apart from not kill people?'

'I want you to go over to Schofield's flower shop on 738 North State Street. Hymie Weiss got killed outside – '

'Yeah, and Deany O'Bannion got killed *inside* a while back,' interrupted Dekker. 'That place is owned by the Northside mob, Doc. She starts nosing around there, you'll end up buying flowers for *her*.'

'I can look after myself, Dekker. If anyone needs flowers it'll be you, not me.'

'It's an interesting point, that,' said the Doctor, ignoring the squabbling. 'The site of the murder, I mean. Most people think Capone had O'Bannion killed. Isn't that right, Mr Dekker?'

'Sure. It was probably Anselmi and Scalise, those two guys in the corner at the meeting last night. There was a third guy too. Some people say it was Al in person. Anselmi and Scalise were actually arrested and tried for it. They got off – not enough evidence.'

'A Capone murder, at any rate. Now Mr Weiss, one of Mr O'Bannion's leading successors, gets killed almost in the same spot. Why there, of all places?'

'Because if Al's telling the truth and he didn't have Hymie Weiss knocked off . . .' said Dekker slowly.

'Someone wants very much to make it look as if he did,' concluded Ace.

The Doctor regarded his two assistants with benign approval. 'Exactly. I want you to keep an eye out for that kind of misdirection. I think it could be a feature of all three cases. Oh, Ace, try the boarding-house next door to the flower shop as well, the place the shots were fired from.' He paused for a moment. 'One final thing. I don't want you trying to bring anyone in, officially or unofficially. This is just a reconnaissance. I want you to help me to find the common denominator behind these three murders. It could be the killer, or perhaps just the organizer. If you come across any suitable candidates, all I want is a description and, if possible, a place where they can be found.'

The Doctor got up, smoothed the lapels of his black and white striped suit and took a trenchcoat and a snap-brim fedora from a nearby hatstand.

'What are you going to do?' asked Ace.

The Doctor shrugged into his trenchcoat. 'Whereas your two affairs are low, sordid mob murders, the Jake Lingle murder is a highly political case involving some of the highest in Chicago. Naturally I shall attend to it myself.

163

I'm afraid I'll require Happy and the limousine, Ace. Got to keep up my image.'

'I'd give you a ride but I'm heading the other way,' said Dekker.

'Great. So how do I get to this flower shop?'

'It's a nice morning,' said the Doctor. 'You could always walk.'

'Me, walk?' said Ace. 'Not bloody likely. I shall go in a taxi!'

A little later that same morning, Al Capone was giving a press conference at the Lexington Hotel.

Before Al's time most gang-leaders scuttled past the press with collars turned up and hat-brims pulled low. Intrusive photographers got their cameras – and often their heads – smashed. But Al Capone loved publicity. He was the first of the mobsters to realize that he was a public figure, and that it was just as easy to make the press his friends.

The suite was crowded with journalists, knocking back the free booze, filling their pockets with the free cigars and taking down Al's every word.

'I ain't no squawker,' he said. 'But I'll tell you all I know about these murders – which is nothing. Billy McSwiggin was a friend of mine. He was having a drink with me and some friends right here, just a few days ago. We could've killed him then – if we'd wanted to – and no one would ever have known.'

One of the bolder reporters said, 'There's a story you were sore at him for prosecuting your friends Anselmi and Scalise for the O'Bannion murder.'

'Why should I be sore? He was just doing his job. Besides, they were acquitted, weren't they? You guys won't print this because your bosses won't let you – but I paid McSwiggin and I got what I paid for.'

As everyone in the room knew, McSwiggin's less than enthusiastic prosecution had had a lot to do with getting the two killers released.

'What about Hymie Weiss?'

'Me and Hymie had some problems, sure, but that was all in the past. We made an agreement, I kept it and so did he. I didn't have any beef with Hymie.' Capone held up his hand. 'And before you ask, I didn't have anything to do with the Jake Lingle killing either. Come on, fellers, me kill a reporter? You guys are sacred to me – like priests!'

There was some laughter and Capone went on, 'The police want to shove these murders onto me because they can't find the men who did the jobs and I look like an easy goat. If they've got anything on me except hot air, let them use it. I'll answer anything they ask me about these murders. Okay, that's it. Enjoy your drinks.'

Flanked by his bodyguards, Capone left the room. As the ever-thirsty reporters refilled their glasses, one of them said wonderingly, 'I've got a weird feeling the sonovabitch was actually telling the truth!'

An enterprising reporter telephoned Mayor Thompson for a comment on Al Capone's press conference. The Mayor fired off an inspiring speech hinting that dramatic developments were about to break very soon. 'I've created a special police squad to deal with these murders,' he announced. 'Captain Dennis Reilly will be in charge. No efforts will be spared . . .'

The interview over, Thompson slammed down the phone.

'Dammit, Reilly, I want Capone arrested. He's a suspect in three murders and *he's* holding press conferences, saying all we've got is hot air. He's making fools of us – of me!'

The good Lord himself did that long ago, thought Captain Dennis Reilly, but he had too much sense to say so. Instead he said soothingly, 'If your honour wants Capone arrested, then arrested he'll be. I'll take a squad down to the Lexington and bring him in meself. But you know what'll happen. A gang of expensive lawyers will turn up waving writs, and he'll be out in a matter of hours, giving more press conferences about his wrongful arrest.'

'Surely you must have something to hold him on?'

'Between ourselves, the feller's right. We've got nothing at all but hot air. The Hymie Weiss business looked promising, what with all the bad feeling between Hymie and Al. Unfortunately, all the witnesses have come down with a bad case of Chicago amnesia.'

'With what?'

"Tis a common ailment in mob murder cases,' said Reilly solemnly. 'No one saw anything, no one recognized nobody – or if they did they've had a sudden lapse of memory.'

'But there must be something. What about the McSwiggin case?'

'The more I probe into the McSwiggin case, Mr Mayor, the more people start asking me what was your District Attorney doing out on the razzle with a group of known gangsters?'

'He was doing criminological research,' said Thompson uneasily. 'Tell them that.'

'Well, I can *tell* them your honour. But there are things people won't believe, even in Chicago.'

There was a moment of silence. Both men knew that if the full extent of McSwiggin's involvement with the underworld came out, the resulting scandal could be bigger than that of his murder. 'What about the Jake Lingle killing?'

'There's nothing to connect Capone with the Lingle case at all – and as far as I can see, no motive either. What's more, Jake Lingle was no angel. There's a lot of political mud to be stirred up there too.'

The Mayor's secretary appeared in the doorway that led from his outer office. She was a classic dumb blonde – the Mayor picked his secretaries for looks rather than character – and she was rather flustered. 'There's a gentleman who insists on seeing you, Mr Mayor, even though I've told him – '

'There, there, my dear, don't trouble your pretty little head,' said the Doctor, slipping neatly past. He took off his hat and coat and handed them to her with a beaming

166

smile. 'Look after these will you, my dear? And a cup of coffee would be most welcome.'

Thankful that Ace wasn't around to witness his outrageously sexist behaviour, the Doctor turned to the two men in the room. 'This is an honour, your honour. And it's a great pleasure to meet you again, Captain Reilly.' He glanced at Reilly's expensive suit. 'Plain clothes, I see.'

Proudly Reilly stroked his lapels. 'And haven't I been promoted? Head of the Special Detective Task Force no less!'

'Well deserved, I'm sure. Though it's a pity in one way. Nothing sets off a fine figure of a man like a uniform.'

'Sure, it's a silver tongue you have Doctor,' said Reilly. 'Where would you be from now, originally?'

'Well, I've travelled a great deal but I'm originally from a place called Gallifrey.'

'Sure I know it well!'

'You do?'

'A little town in Ireland, not too far from Dublin. I've a cousin there meself.'

Deciding it was better not to go into that one, the Doctor turned back to the Mayor. 'I must apologize for this intrusion your honour but I'm here on important business.' The Mayor stared at him in amazement and the Doctor added, 'Party business.' When the Mayor still boggled the Doctor said, '*Republican* party business.'

The dime dropped at last and the Mayor said, 'I see. Captain Reilly, if you will excuse us?'

Reilly looked suspiciously at the Doctor. The Doctor smiled blandly back at him. Reluctantly, Reilly heaved himself out of his deep leather armchair. 'Very well, your honour. But I'll take the liberty of reminding you that the City of Chicago has no need for gold bricks – and the Brooklyn Bridge is definitely not for sale!'

He stomped out of the office.

By now the Mayor was thoroughly confused. 'What the devil's got into Reilly?'

'Strain,' said the Doctor soothingly. 'Great responsibilities, difficult times.'

167

Big Bill Thompson rubbed a weary hand across his face. 'You can say that again, Doctor.'

Resisting the temptation to do just that, the Doctor went on, 'And of course, no one suffers the burden of that strain more than you do, your honour.'

'Damn right,' said the Mayor. The pretty blonde secretary came in with a silver tray holding a silver coffee pot and cups and saucers of fine bone china. She put it on a nearby table, poured out two cups, smiled at the Doctor and went out.

Thompson watched her go, sighed and said, 'How about a little something to liven up the coffee, Doctor?'

'Just a touch,' said the Doctor resignedly.

Big Bill went to the drinks cabinet, splashed expensive Napoleon brandy into crystal and handed one to the Doctor. He raised his glass. 'Chin chin!'

'Chin chin!' said the Doctor solemnly, taking a sip. If he stayed in Chicago much longer, he thought, he'd be the first alcoholic Time Lord in Gallifreyan history.

'Now then,' he said sternly, 'to business. Last time we, er, made contact, I was unable to be too specific about my reasons for being in Chicago. Since then events have moved on. As you know, Calvin Coolidge, our beloved President, has announced that he feels unable to stand for a further term. With elections on the horizon the party has been forced to cast round for a suitable candidate. Its eyes have fallen upon Chicago.'

Eyes shining, Big Bill Thompson leaped to his feet. 'I shall be proud,' he boomed, 'nay honoured – '

The Doctor held up his hand. 'We must not be premature – I am not yet empowered to make any specific offer. My task here is to observe, and to recommend.'

Disappointed but still hopeful, Big Bill subsided. 'I understand, Doctor. If there is anything, anything I can do . . .'

Glitz would have been proud of him, thought the Doctor. Then again, conning someone as vain and stupid as Big Bill Thompson was almost too easy. Remembering

Glitz's motto, 'Never give a galactic sucker an even break,' the Doctor went on, 'If I may be frank, your honour?'

'Please do.'

'The situation in Chicago gives some cause for concern. It's a question of the public image, you see. Chicago the booming city of industry and commerce, under the leadership of Big Bill the Builder is one thing. The Chicago of tommy-guns and gangsters is quite another.'

Big Bill was on his feet again. 'I am planning a clean-up that will scour the filth of crime from the face of our fair city . . .'

'Please,' said the Doctor wearily, 'Save the speeches for the voters. As long as this Prohibition nonsense lasts, there will always be bootleggers. The appetite of the people for drink and gambling and – other diversions has to be satisfied.' The Doctor leaned forward. 'But it must be satisfied discreetly in quiet, well run establishments. It is open, blatant crime which must be put a stop to – and when it comes to the murders of three prominent citizens in swift succession . . . I have been asked to enquire what you are proposing to do about it.'

'I have set up a Special Task Force, under Captain Reilly.' The Mayor scrabbled on his desk. 'His reports are here, if you'd care to see them.' He picked up three files and waved them at the Doctor.

'May I?' The Doctor whisked the files from Thompson's hands and returned to his chair. He flicked through them with apparent carelessness, taking in every word and committing the files to memory.

The McSwiggin and Weiss files contained little of interest. The witnesses in each case had apparently seen little and remembered less. Dekker and Ace would just have to dig deeper, thought the Doctor. But in the Lingle murder the assassin had been seen by a traffic policeman, a certain Anthony L. Ruthy, and his report was in the file. He was home on sick-leave at the moment, and the report gave his address.

Officer Ruthy was reluctant to talk to the Doctor at first:

169

he was all talked out, he said. But the Doctor's hint that his newspaper, the London *Times*, provided a handsome expense account, did the trick. He was invited into the seldom-used front parlour of the Ruthys' little house, and they talked as the Elevated rumbled by.

'Though it's little enough I can tell you,' said Ruthy. He was a bulky man with a round face and strangely child-like blue eyes. 'I heard a shot, heard people shouting "Stop him, stop him!", and saw this feller running away.'

'What did he look like?'

'Nothing special. Tall and thin.'

'Then what?'

'I chased him and he turned down a blind alley. I had him trapped. He swung round on me . . .' His voice faltered. 'Then he disappeared.'

'How, exactly?' asked the Doctor gently.

'That's what I can't tell you. One minute he was there staring at me . . . Then he was gone.'

The Doctor nodded. 'Why are you home on sick-leave, Mr Ruthy?'

'It's the visions,' said Ruthy simply. 'I can't get his eyes out of my mind. Since then I've been seeing things, every-one from the good Lord himself down to Abe Lincoln.' He shook his head. 'Now, I know I never met Lincoln in my life! Then there are the dreams, slaughter and blood-shed and all kinds of horrors . . . What's happening to me?'

'You've suffered a kind of psychic shock,' said the Doctor authoritatively. 'Just take it easy and the dreams and visions will fade. You'll be back on duty in no time.'

He thought for a moment, then took a silk handkerchief from his pocket. In it was wrapped a miniature, a portrait of a man in eighteenth-century clothing – not surprisingly, since the portrait had been painted in the eighteenth century.

'Would you be good enough to take a look at this for me?'

The policeman took the miniature and peered hard at

it. Then he looked up, the blue eyes wide with horror. 'It's him,' he whispered. 'It's the very man!'

19

The Trail

When Ace got out of her taxi outside Schofield's flower shop, she saw a tall bald-headed old negro scrubbing at the sidewalk with the help of a stiff broom and a bucket of soapy water. She paid off her taxi and went over to him.

'Won't it come out?'

He rested on his broom. 'Blood don't shift easy, missy. It kinda soaks into things.'

'You sound as if you've had lots of practice.'

'I surely have. I mopped up inside here when they shot down Mr O'Bannion a few years back. Want to see? I'm about done out here.' He picked up the bucket and led her inside the shop.

It was a sizeable place about twenty-five feet wide and a good fifty feet deep. There were plants and ferns all around, and a huge display rack in the centre of the room. It was filled with red roses – the colour of blood, thought Ace.

'Them's American Beauty Roses,' said the old man. 'Same kind we had in the shop that day.' He pointed to a faint stain on the floor just in front of the rack. 'That's where I found Mr O'Bannion's body. I been scrubbing that floor quite a few years now and I still can't get all the blood out.'

'What happened?' asked Ace.

'Mr O'Bannion was in here fussing with some chrysanthemums. We had a big funeral order coming in. You know that man really loved flowers? Lots of people thought he bought this place just for a front, but that ain't so, he had a real gift for the work. He liked to do all the big displays himself.'

There was something distinctly odd about the idea of a gangster with a talent for flower-arranging, thought Ace, but she didn't say anything. The old man went on with his story. Ace realized that he enjoyed telling it, that he'd probably told it hundreds of times.

'There was a whole mess of petals all over the floor. Mr O'Bannion he says to me, "Bill, you mind cleaning up those petals?" He was always very polite, Mr O'Bannion. So I sweeps up the petals into a big dustpan and carries it out the back. Just as I go through the workroom door I hear some people coming into the shop, and Mr O'Bannion says, "Hi boys, you here for the flowers?" I go on out to the trashcan in the back alley, and suddenly I hear all these shots. I run back into the shop and there's Mr O'Bannion lying there dead, and three guys disappearing out of the door. I hear a car engine, and by the time I get to the door they're gone.'

'So you didn't really get a good look at them? Didn't recognize anyone?'

'I'm still here, ain't I?'

Ace nodded understandingly, and suddenly realized she was investigating the wrong murder. 'What about when Mr Weiss was shot?'

The old man chuckled. 'That time I *really* didn't see anything. I was working out the back when I heard one of them tommy-guns blazing away. By the time I got out front Mr Weiss was dead on the sidewalk. I didn't really know Mr Weiss too well, he wasn't friendly like Mr O'Bannion.'

'I hear the shots came from the boarding-house next door?'

'That's what they say.'

Ace took a five-dollar bill from out of her purse and slipped it into his hand.

He looked at it in surprise. 'A fin – that's way too much.'

Ace smiled. 'My pleasure.'

As the old man tucked the bill away in his overalls

pocket, a young man came out of the back of the shop. He wore a grey suit, a loudly striped shirt and a flashy tie held down by a jewelled tie-pin. One of those round straw hats called skimmers was stuck on the back of his head and there was a cigar between his teeth. Ace could see the bulge of a gun under his left lapel.

'Still playing tour-guide, Bill?' he said in a loud raucous voice. 'How about earning your pay for once? Get out back and clean up some of that mess in the workroom.' The old man looked at him without replying, then picked up his broom and went out through the back of the shop.

The flashy young man gave an uneasy laugh. 'I don't know why we keep that dumb old nigger on here. Can I help you, lady?'

His contemptuous dismissal of the gentle old man made Ace feel like killing him on the spot. She remembered the Doctor's warning and forced herself to smile. 'Sorry, that was my fault. I was asking the questions.'

'How come?'

'Just another curious tourist.'

The young man nodded. He was used to dames from out of town looking for a few cheap thrills from Chicago's sinful reputation. He usually did pretty well with them, and this one looked classier than most.

'If you want the low-down on life in Chicago, lady, you've found the right guy.'

'I have?'

'Sure thing. I could tell you stories would curl your hair.'

'Stories about the Hymie Weiss murder?'

'Sure, I was there, I saw the whole thing.'

Ace was pretty sure he was lying to impress her, but she decided to play him along just a little longer. She gave him a seductive smile. 'Really?'

He came closer. 'Sure! Why don't we talk about it over a drink? There's a speakeasy just down the street.' He grabbed her by the shoulders and pulled her close. 'They got rooms as well.'

Information or no information, thought Ace, enough

was enough. There were limits to what she was prepared to do to help the Doctor in his mission – whatever it was. She brought her knee up hard.

The young man bent forward with an agonized whoop – and encountered a three-fingered strike to the solar plexus that left him paralysed. Ace was tempted to follow up with a heel-strike to the septum that would drive splinters of bone into his brain, but she remembered the Doctor's words. Restraining herself, she delivered a chop to the upper lip that started a spectacular nosebleed, and a rabbit-punch that slammed him to the floor.

Ace picked up the iron bucket, still half full of soapy water, tipped it over him and went out of the shop.

The young man's name was Tony Ricotti and he was a very minor member of the Gusenberg mob. As he came painfully back to consciousness, he became aware that someone was helping him to his feet. It was a stranger, a tall thin fellow. He must have just come into the shop. He was somehow familiar – Ricotti had a vague idea he was one of Polack Joe Saltis's boys.

'Lousy dame sucker-punched me,' said Ricotti thickly.

'I saw it,' said the stranger.

'When I get my hands on her . . .'

'She went into the boarding-house next door,' said the stranger calmly. 'She's still there now, nosing around, asking questions.' He handed Ricotti a towel.

The mobster rubbed a mixture of blood and soapy water from his face and dried his dripping hair. 'Yeah?' He clawed for the gun under his arm. 'I'm gonna go round there and fill that bitch full of holes.'

'Take it easy,' said the stranger. 'Don't you know who that was? She's the one they call the Lady in Black, works for a guy named Doc.'

'That's the dame took out Swifty Morelli?'

'That's right. And you know how fast he was. Go after her and you're liable to wind up dead, not just damaged.'

'But we gotta do something. Swifty was a pal of mine.'

'I can tell you how to get her, and get her good.'

'Yeah? How?'

'She's a good-looking dame.'

'So?'

'Joe's cat-houses can always use a little new talent. Listen . . .' The stranger began to speak in a low, persuasive voice.

Ricotti listened with eager attention, saying, 'Yeah, right!' as the scheme unfolded. He went to the back of the shop, unhooked the wall phone and made a number of urgent calls. When he'd finished he said, 'It's all set.'

Ricotti broke off, looking around the shop in astonishment. The stranger had disappeared.

Ace was getting nowhere fast at the boarding-house. The owner, Mrs Rotariu, had gone off somewhere and in true Chicago style the other tenants knew nothing about anything.

They didn't know where the landlady had gone or when she was coming back. They didn't know anything about the tenant of the now-empty first floor front. No one had spoken to him, no one seemed to have even seen him.

The first floor tenant, a burly white-haired old railwayman, invited her into his kitchen for coffee and explained why.

'Had a young nephew once, worked on the railway like me. Nice kid, kinda straight-arrow, keen church-goer. One night he's coming home off the late shift, sees two guys toss a dead man out of a car. Kid's got good eyesight – too good. He gets a look at the two guys, takes down the car number. Police find the guys and pull 'em in, kid picks 'em out of a line-up. They get arrested, sent for trial.'

Eyes staring bleakly into the distance, the old man took a swig of coffee.

'Then the phone calls start. They begin by telling the kid he can make a pile of dough just by having a lapse of memory. He turns 'em down. Then come the threats, saying what's gonna happen to him if he testifies. Kid's tough, he doesn't crack. Tells 'em to go to hell. Few nights later he's coming home off the late shift, big black Caddy comes round the corner, smashes him off the sidewalk. Kid dies on the way to hospital, driver of the Caddy's never found. No witnesses, no case, the killers walk. Lady, if someone guns you down right here in this goddam kitchen I won't see or hear anything and neither will anyone else.'

'And the killers go on killing,' said Ace.

The old man shrugged. 'That's Chicago. At least if you leave 'em alone they only kill each other.'

'Thanks for the coffee,' said Ace, and went on her way.

Back in the corridor she decided to take a look at the now-empty flat used by the machine-gunner. It was locked, but a few minutes work with a hairpin fixed that.

It wasn't much of a room. The brass bedstead was creaky and tarnished and the dressing-table mirror was fly-blown. There were a couple of rickety wooden chairs, a gas hot-plate, a tin food safe and that was it.

Still, thought Ace, the room's former tenant had probably been more interested in the view than in the amenities. She went to the window and looked out, checking the field of fire with a professional eye.

Down and to the right there was a pretty good view of the front of Schofield's flower shop. Unfortunately the front of the shop jutted out, shielding the actual door. Nevertheless, there was a clear view of the sidewalk and of the road in front of the shop. You could be pretty sure of getting someone arriving by car – the way the unknown machine-gunner had got Weiss.

Even so the angle was awkward. You'd have to lean quite a way out, exposing yourself to counter-fire. Personally Ace would have been happier mounting the ambush from a vantage-point somewhere opposite. However the only building opposite was the cathedral – and there might be problems in setting up a machine-gun nest in a cathedral, even in Chicago.

As Ace turned away from the window the door opened and a woman came into the room. She was small and plump with brassy yellow hair and red fingernails, and she wore a tatty-looking fur coat. She didn't look in the least like the conventional idea of a landlady.

The woman glared suspiciously at Ace. 'What the hell are you doing here?'

'I heard there was a room vacant,' said Ace innocently. 'I thought I'd take a look at it.'

'Pull the other one, sister. A dame like you don't wanna live in a crummy joint like this. What are you after?'

'All right. I'm trying to get a line on the guy who had this room. Do you know where he is?'

'Who wants to know?'

'What do you care who wants to know?' asked Ace. 'So long as you get yours?' She took a roll of greenbacks from out of her bag and riffled through it.

The woman's eyes fastened greedily on the money. 'How much?'

'Depends what you've got to sell.'

'The guy told me he was a musician. Okay, I knew he had a chopper in the violin-case that last day, but not all the time. I useta hear him playing sometimes. I reckon he really was a musician, maybe it was his cover.'

'What did he look like?'

'Just average,' said the woman hurriedly. 'You wouldn't notice him in a crowd. I know the name of the place where he works. They called when he was out one time, left a message to call them back.'

'Where is it?'

'It'll cost you.'

'How much?'

'Couple of centuries.'

Ace peeled twenty ten-dollar bills from the roll, and held out the money. 'Go on, spill it.'

'Palace Hotel on West Fifty-First Street,' said the woman, snatching the money.

Ace went to the door, struggling to remember the dialogue from late-night B-movies. 'Okay, sister, but this better be the straight dope. If it's not, I'll be back.' She went out of the room.

The blonde woman struck the money into her coat

pocket. 'I don't think you will, honey,' she said softly. She began to laugh.

Ace came out of the boarding-house and saw that the old man was back in front of the shop, sweeping the sidewalk. He looked up and waved. 'All right, missy?'

'Fine, thanks. And you?'

'Oh, I'm fine. Young Mr Ricotti ain't too good though. He's gone off looking all bruised and battered. He ain't walking so good neither.'

'Dangerous places, flower shops. He must have trodden on a rake.'

The old man chuckled. 'That rake sure beat the hell out of him.'

'Can you tell me where I can get a taxi round here?'

'Well they usually goes right past the end of the street – say, there's one!'

A taxi appeared on the corner and Ace put two fingers in her mouth and gave a piercing whistle. The taxi drew up and the old man opened the door for her. Ace reached for her purse, but he shook his head. 'You take care now.'

'You too.' Ace leaned forward to speak to the driver. 'Palace Hotel, West Fifty-First Street please.'

'You don't want to go there, Missy,' said the old man. 'That's a *bad* place . . .'

But it was too late. The taxi was already drawing away.

The Palace Hotel had a kind of faded grandeur, like a society lady who'd fallen on hard times. As Ace paid off her taxi, the driver said, 'Hey lady, you sure you wanna go in there?'

'Why shouldn't I?'

'Well, it ain't the kind of place where ladies usually go.'

'You mean it's a men-only hotel?'

'No, no,' said the taxi-driver hurriedly. 'There's ladies there all right, plenty of 'em.'

'So what's the problem?'

The driver, a burly bald Chicagoan, actually managed to look embarrassed. 'It's just that the ladies are there

179

already, if you see what I mean, and the guys come to visit them – for a while . . .'

'Are you trying to tell me this is a whorehouse?'

'You said it, lady.'

'Oh well,' said Ace, 'there's a first time for everything.' She went into the hotel.

There was nobody about in the lobby, which held a few shabby armchairs and dusty potted palms and a wide staircase curving upwards. Still a bit early for the lunch-time trade, thought Ace, and was annoyed to find herself blushing.

A door off to the right led to what had once been the hotel bar, and probably still was, despite the hand-scrawled notice 'Coffee Room' tacked over the door. Ace went inside and found herself in a long room filled with a scattering of tables and chairs, all empty. There was a bar to her left. Behind it a seedy-looking little man in a grubby white apron was studying the racing page of the *Tribune*.

Ace went up to the bar and perched on a stool. 'Coffee, please.'

The man spoke without looking up. 'Rye coffee or bourbon coffee?'

'Just coffee coffee please.'

The man gave her a look of faint surprise, got up and went over to the coffee urn behind the bar. He turned away from her and Ace heard a hiss of steam and the chink of crockery. He turned back and put a steaming mug of coffee in front of her. The coffee smelled surprisingly good, and Ace took an appreciative swig. She realized she was hungry, and helped herself to a hard-boiled egg from a bowl on the bar.

'I'm looking for someone,' she said. 'One of your musicians.'

'Musicians don't come in till tonight,' said the little man in his flat toneless voice. 'Guy comes in for a lunch-time quickie, he don't need to hear no band playing.'

'I suppose not,' said Ace. She was surprised to find her head nodding, and took another swig of coffee to wake herself up. The little man had put down his paper and was studying her curiously. Ace looked back at him, and saw his ratty features beginning to blur. Realizing too late what was happening to her, she reached for the Browning in her shoulder-bag. It was on the bar, close to her hand, but as she reached for it, the bag seemed to move further and further away. Ace slumped forward onto the bar, her head between her arms.

A door behind the bar opened and Tony Ricotti came through. He had changed his clothes for another, equally garish outfit and dried his hair, but his upper lip was bruised and puffy.

'Old Mickey Finn gets 'em every time,' said the barman with professional pride. 'This the dame gave you the fat lip?'

Ricotti didn't answer. He came around the end of the bar, scooped the unconscious Ace off the stool and carried her out of the bar and up the stairs.

20

Rescue

I had to visit a lot of dives and spend a fair amount of Doc's money before I found the witness I wanted. I had to down a lot of drinks as well. Okay, so it's a tough racket, but someone's gotta do it.

I started off with a visit to my old Precinct House, a much safer business since Captain Reilly had been moved up to the Mayor's new Detective Task Force. A couple of swigs from my hip flask and a few bucks from Doc's bankroll persuaded Sergeant Mulrooney to let me take a look at the McSwiggin file.

I made myself comfortable in Reilly's empty office and had a good look through the file. It didn't take long. McSwiggin and a cop called Red Duffy had been found dead in a green Lincoln sedan in Oak Park. Car and corpses had been riddled with machine-gun bullets, but the detectives on the case reckoned both men had probably been killed elsewhere, brought to Oak Park in the Lincoln and dumped.

That's when I hit the speakeasies. Gangsters love to gossip, and everyone was ready to hash over the McSwiggin murder. I'd only met McSwiggin a couple of times and I didn't know Red Duffy at all. Now I'd officially left the cops the mob guys were a lot more willing to talk to me. I soon learned that Red Duffy had been crooked even for a Chicago cop, running booze for the O'Donnell mob as well as operating a barber shop on the side. It didn't leave him much time for police work.

The O'Donnell boys ran a whole string of joints, but

the biggest and best was the Pony Inn on Roosevelt. I decided to move on to there.

The Pony Inn was a two-storeyed joint built from cream-coloured brick, on the south side of Roosevelt. As I parked the Buick I noticed the little tree in front of the building looked kind of bedraggled. I got out of the car and went over to look at it. The wood of the trunk and the lower branches was all chipped and splintered. That tree had been all shot to pieces.

I checked the front of the building behind the tree and found a neat line of bullet-holes stitched across the front. Someone had been loosing off with a tommy-gun at the front of the Pony Inn. Either we had a mystery tree-hater on the loose, or the unknown tommy-gunner's target had been something human – like Captain Duffy and District Attorney McSwiggin.

I shoved at the door of the inn and found it was closed. I stepped back and looked up at the building. The shutters were up at the windows and there was no sign of life. That told me something screwy was going on. Why else would the O'Donnells close down their most profitable joint? If they'd had any sense they'd have kept the place running normally, but then most mobsters are pretty dumb.

I leaned on the bell-push till my thumb was sore, then started thumping and kicking the door just for a change. After a while I heard shuffling footsteps and a blue-chinned cigar-smoking thug opened the door a crack, releasing a cloud of smoke and a smell of bourbon. 'G'way, we're closed,' he croaked.

I gave the door a shove that knocked him back off his feet, stepped inside the entrance hall and slammed the door shut behind me. 'So now you're open.'

He scrambled to his feet, reaching for the gun in his belt, but by that time I had the .45 in my hand. 'Just hold it.'

A voice from above me said, 'You hold it, bright boy.'

I turned and saw a tall bony character in a light grey suit coming down the stairs. He was wearing a straw skimmer, smoking a cigar and carrying a pump-action shotgun which was pointing in my direction.

I raised my hands. 'Don't shoot, Colonel. I'm out of season.'

The shotgun man said, 'Take his rod, Jake.'

Jake reached up and took my .45. Once it was in his hand he drew it back to pistol-whip me, but I kicked him hard in the shins and he hopped away howling.

'Just the gun, Jake,' said the man with the shotgun. 'Fun and games later. This way, bright boy.' He gestured ahead with the shotgun and I went through the door into the main saloon. I'd been to the Pony Inn before, and at this time of night the place should have been jumping, but the big room was empty, the roulette and blackjack layouts deserted.

'Must be costing you a bundle, having this place shut down.'

'We're closed for redecoration.'

'Is that what the guy with the chopper was doing – decorating the outside?'

The bony hand waved me into a chair. He perched on a bar-stool, the shotgun cradled in his lap, its muzzle towards me. He held it with casual ease, like it was something he was seldom without.

'Okay, bright boy, what's the pitch? Are you a cop?'

'Private. The name's Dekker.'

He nodded. 'I heard of you.'

'I heard of you too,' I said. 'You're Spike O'Donnell.'

Spike was the oldest and the toughest of the three brothers who ran the O'Donnell outfit. He was one of the few men in Chicago not afraid of Al Capone, and had once invited Big Al to 'Step out in the open and fight like a man.' Al turned down the invitation, but soon after that one of Al's boys opened up on Spike with a tommy-gun, while he was buying a paper. He missed. There were two other brothers, Bill, known for some reason as 'Klondike', and Myles, the baby of the family.

Spike gave me a hard stare. 'So what are you after? Is this some kind of shakedown?'

184

'I'm not after money, Spike. Just information.'

'What about?'

'The McSwiggin killing.'

'Why come to me?'

I took a gamble. 'Because he was killed outside your joint.'

'You saying I killed him?'

'On your own doorstep? Not hardly. But I think someone may be trying to make it look like you did.'

'Who? Why?'

I told him about Doc's theory that someone was trying to stir up trouble, so as to take over when the shooting died down.

'All Doc wants to know is who really killed McSwiggin and the others. We don't think it was you – but believe it or not, it wasn't Capone either.'

Spike O'Donnell sat thinking for a moment. He slipped off the stool and said, 'This way, shamus.'

He led me out of the bar, up the stairs, along a carpeted corridor and into a comfortably furnished bedroom. A slim, fair-haired young man in striped pyjamas was lying in, or rather on top of the bed. The sheets were all twisted and tangled like he'd been thrashing about.

'How's the boy, Myles?' asked Spike gently.

'Oh, not so bad,' mumbled the young man. 'If I could just get some sleep . . .'

'Kid was in the car when McSwiggin got it,' said Spike. 'Right outside here, like you said. He ain't been right since. Says he has nightmares about battle and bloodshed and stuff.'

'Tell me what happened,' I said.

Myles propped himself up on one elbow, eyes glittering feverishly. 'Me and Red Duffy are bringing McSwiggin over here to meet Spike. We pull up outside and Red and McSwiggin get out. I'm just gonna follow when this Caddy pulls up and starts spraying lead, so I duck down in the car. The shooting goes on and on . . . I raise up and look and there's Duffy and McSwiggin laying out in front of the door, wriggling and twitching in their own blood. And there's this guy in the Caddy, standing up in the front seat and hosing them with lead from a tommy-gun. And he's laughing. He sees me watching him and swings round the gun, but the drum's empty. He kinda glares at me, then tosses the tommy-gun in the back seat and drives away.'

'You were lucky, kid,' said Spike.

Myles didn't seem so sure. 'I keep seeing his eyes, red and glaring like fire. And I get these dreams, people screaming and dying and all this blood . . .' He fell back on the bed.

'By the time I got outside it was all over,' said Spike. 'I brought the kid in here, had some of the boys put the two stiffs back in the Lincoln and dump it over in Oak Park. I don't want no dead D.A.s on my doorstep.'

I leaned over the bed. 'This guy in the car, Myles. What did he look like?'

'Long and thin,' muttered Myles. 'Long thin hands, long thin face. McSwiggin and Duffy were jerking and twitching and flopping around in their blood and he was *laughing . . .*'

'And that's about it, Doc,' I concluded. 'I managed to convince Spike O'Donnell I was no danger to him, and got out of there in one piece.'

I was back in Doc's place reporting to my client. It was still early and the place was empty.

Doc seemed to think I'd done a pretty good job. 'Excellent work, Mr Dekker. What's more, it ties in nicely with my own discoveries.' He told me about the cop's description of the guy who'd gunned down Jake Lingle.

'Even if we find this guy, it's going to be pretty hard to get a conviction,' I warned him. 'I doubt if Myles will testify even when he's recovered, it's against the gangster's code. And this cop sounds kinda screwy as well. Say, isn't it strange that both our witnesses seem to be cracking up?'

'No,' said Doc, 'it isn't strange at all. And I'm not concerned about a conviction. When we find our – quarry, I shall deal with him myself.'

In spite of Ace's warning, I just didn't figure Doc for a killer. 'You're gonna knock him off?'

'I shall – neutralize him.'

Doc looked at me with his calm grey eyes and my blood started forming icicles. Maybe this little guy was a killer after all.

'What about Ace?' I asked. 'Has she turned up some tall skinny guy too?'

'It wouldn't surprise me. But whatever she's found out, she hasn't been able to tell me yet.'

'You haven't heard from her?'

'Not since this morning. And there have been no messages – Luigi has been here all the time. I'm getting rather worried about her.'

'You should be. I told you that flower shop joint was dangerous.' I finished my beer. 'I'll get over there and check.'

'Wait, I'll come with you.' Doc turned to Luigi. 'Can you manage here for a while? I'll leave you Happy on the door, in case there's any trouble.'

Luigi reached under the bar and pulled out a sap and a sawn-off shotgun, and an old Colt Peacemaker. 'I can manage, Doc. There won't be any trouble.'

We grabbed our hats and coats and began to leave. 'Just a moment, Doc,' I said. 'Are you heeled? I may need some back-up.'

'I disapprove of guns, Mr Dekker, but I suppose under the circumstances . . . Luigi, may I?'

'Take the sawn-off, Doc,' I advised.

Doc picked up the shotgun, Luigi handed him some spare shells and we were on our way.

Traffic was light and we made good time across Chicago. When I pulled up outside Schofield's an old black guy was just putting up the shutters. 'Hey, you,' I yelled.

The old guy ignored me.

I was about to jump out and shake some sense out of him when Doc touched my arm. 'Allow me.'

He got out of the car and raised his hat to the old

negro. 'Excuse me for bothering you, sir, I can see you're busy. We're looking for a friend of ours, a young lady, and we understood she was coming here.' He gave the old guy a quick description of Ace. 'Have you seen her, by any chance?'

The old guy chuckled. 'Oh, I seen her all right. Mr Ricotti in there, he seen her too!'

'Something happened?'

'Mr Ricotti he got a little fresh and the young lady she mashed him up pretty good.'

'That's our girl,' I said. 'What happened after that?'

He pointed next door. 'She went into Mrs Rotariu's boarding-house, stayed quite a while.'

I jumped out of the car. 'Okay, let's go.'

Doc stayed right where he was. 'You said she stayed quite a while. Did you see her come out then?'

'I sure did. Came over and said goodbye to me. Then she called a taxi. Boy, that lady sure can whistle!'

'I don't suppose you happened to overhear ...'

'Palace Hotel on West Fifty-First Street,' said the old guy.

Doc looked at me. 'Do you know it?'

'I know it,' I said. 'We'd better get moving.'

Doc still didn't move. He was looking hard at the old man. 'If there's anything else you can tell us ...'

'I don't like to mess in other folks' business, but that young lady treated me real nice. You sure you're friends of hers?'

'I give you my word.'

'After she mashed Mr Ricotti and went off next door, some other man appeared in the shop and helped him up. They was whispering together quite a while, then Mr Ricotti made some phone calls. I was out in the workroom so I couldn't hear so good. But it sounded like they was planning something – something to do with the lady. Mr Ricotti went and got changed, then he drove off in his car.'

'What about the other man?' asked Doc.

'He just kind of disappeared. Didn't see him come, didn't see him go.'

'What did he look like?'

Somehow I knew the answer, even before the old man spoke. 'He was a tall, skinny guy . . .'

'Thank you,' said the Doctor and jumped back in the car. I reached for my pocket but the old man shook his head. 'You just go and take good care of that young lady.'

As we drove away I said, 'She'll be okay, Doc. I'll be surprised if the place is still standing.' I tried to sound cheerful but I was worried sick.

Doc wasn't fooled. 'I know just how capable Ace is, Mr Dekker, but she's inclined to be headstrong. And from what we've heard, she was walking into a trap.'

Ace awoke with a thick head and a furry tongue and found she was looking at herself.

The self she was looking at lay flat on its back on a purple quilt, and it was wearing black silk teddies: a combined vest-and-pants garment Ace had bought when she first came to Chicago. That was all the figure was wearing, and Ace wondered fuzzily how she came to be lying on a strange bed in only her underwear.

She remembered the doped coffee and came wide awake. She was looking at her own reflection in a mirror on the ceiling – and someone was looking down at her. It was the blonde woman from the boarding house. She'd changed her ratty fur for a shabby red silk evening gown.

Ace struggled to a sitting position, hugging her knees under her chin. 'Who took my clothes?'

'I did, honey,' said the woman. 'With some help from Tony Ricotti – the guy you beat up in the flower shop. I think he enjoyed it.' She saw the look on Ace's face and laughed. 'Don't worry, nothing else happened, not yet. Tony wanted you to be awake so's you'd enjoy it, and Little Charley downstairs made the Mickey too strong.'

'Give me back my clothes.'

'They're in the pawnshop, honey, three blocks away. You won't need many clothes in your new career.'

189

Ace swung her legs off the side of the bed and stood up.

The woman backed away. 'Where do you think you're going?'

'Out of here.'

'Like that?'

'I'm not shy,' said Ace.

The woman pressed a bell in the wall and Tony Ricotti appeared. There was another man with him, a shambling pasty-faced giant with a round head and blobby features.

'There you are, Joe,' said Ricotti. 'Ain't she worth every last dollar you paid me?'

The man called Joe nodded. 'Sure is!' he said in a husky voice.

'Only me first, right?' said Ricotti.

'Maybe you better let me give you some help, on account of she's so tough . . .'

The two men moved towards her.

Ace backed away. There was so little room, and there were two of them, three with the woman.

They heard shots from downstairs.

I parked the Buick by a fire-hydrant right outside the Palace Hotel and we both jumped out.

'When we get inside just let me handle things,' I said.

Doc wasn't listening. We marched through the lobby and into the bar where a handful of hard-looking types were sitting down at the tables, knocking back their booze and chatting to a bunch of dames who looked even tougher than they did.

I'd planned to order drinks and make a few discreet enquiries, but Doc was in no mood for discretion. He pulled the sawn-off from under his coat and fired one barrel into the ceiling. 'If I could have your attention please?'

He had that all right. It was as quiet as a morgue in the off season.

'We're looking for a young lady who's being held here

190

by force,' said Doc. 'Hand her over and we'll be on our way. No one has to get hurt.'

The bartender grabbed for something under the bar. Doc blasted liquor bottles from the shelves, firing close enough to the guy's head to part his hair with buckshot. He broke the sawn-off and reloaded in one swift movement.

I reached over the bar and took the gun from the stunned bartender's hand. 'Hey Doc, this is Ace's Browning!' I grabbed the bartender's tie and hauled him over the counter. 'Where is she, creep?'

He was choking too much to answer, but he pointed frantically upwards.

We heard a shot and a scream from upstairs.

'Cover me, Doc!' I yelled, and saw him backing towards the door. I pulled out my .45 and ran for the stairs, a gun in each hand. I took the stairs two at a time and paused at the top. Another scream came from down the corridor, and I saw light spilling out from an open door.

I sprinted along the corridor and looked into the room. There was a blonde dame by the door, a gun on the floor and a heaving pile of bodies on the bed.

I kicked the gun into the corner, threw the dame out into the corridor and she squawked and ran off. I turned my attention to the bed. The pile seemed to made up of two guys, with a lot of bare female arms and legs underneath. The guy nearest to me had a big round head I thought I recognized. I slammed the barrel of the .45 against it hard. Joe Saltis grunted, went limp and rolled off the bed.

I grabbed for the other man, but Ace was already taking care of him. She had two long bare legs wrapped around his neck in a scissor-lock. As I watched she gave a final squeeze and the guy went limp. Ace disentangled herself and scrambled to her feet.

'What kept you, Dekker?'

I looked admiringly at what was left of her outfit. 'You certainly take this Lady in Black thing seriously.'

She gave me a belt on the ear, threw herself into my

arms and kissed me, then burst into tears. I stood hugging her for a moment and I'm damned if I wasn't nearly crying too.

Ace looked up at me and smiled through her tears. 'What the hell's going on here, Dekker? We're supposed to be tough.'

'We are tough,' I said. I yanked open the wardrobe, grabbed a purple silk robe and tossed it to Ace, passing her the Browning at the same time.

She slipped into the robe and we ran along the corridor and down the stairs. Doc was still making like Wyatt Earp at the door to the bar. He heard us coming down and backed towards us, still covering the bar with the shotgun.

We crossed the lobby and just as we reached the main door a voice croaked, 'Hold it, you bitch!'

I looked up and saw the guy Ace had throttled at the top of the stairs. He looked in pretty bad shape, but he'd got his breath and his gun back. He shook his head and staggered a little, the gun barrel waving to and fro.

We all three froze – but we all had guns in our hands. I could feel Ace tense as she prepared to fire.

Doc said, 'Ace.'

In a low voice Ace said, 'He took off my clothes when I was unconscious. He was coming back to rape me.'

'Is that a reason to kill him?'

Ace sighed. 'I suppose not.'

'The hell it isn't,' I said.

The guy fired – and missed. I put two slugs through his pump and he fell backwards out of sight. We went out of the door and headed for the Buick. No one followed us.

21
The Battle

A group of armed and angry men had gathered in the rebel HQ. A fierce debate was raging. Some wanted to dig in and defend the dome. Others, led by Tarak, were all for going on the attack.

Romana suggested a third option. 'Why don't you send a messenger under a flag of truce and ask for a meeting?'

'I won't ask anyone to volunteer to be killed,' said Tarak. 'The Black Guard would hang any messenger from us on sight.'

'I'll go myself if you're all afraid.'

Tarak shook his head. 'There's nothing to say, not now.' He glanced towards Kalmar's cubicle, where the old man's cleaned-up body lay in state, candles burning at head and feet.

'Of course there is,' said Romana. She looked round the circle of angry faces. 'Tarak, did you kill Lord Veran? Did anyone here kill him?' There was no reply. 'Exactly – and yet the Lords and the Black Guard are all convinced you did, just as you're all convinced the Lords killed Kalmar.'

'So they did,' said Tarak. 'Them or their damned Black Guard.'

'Suppose you're both wrong? Suppose some third force killed them both, to get you and the Lords slaughtering each other?'

Tarak had different ideas. 'I think Lord Veran genuinely wanted peace. Some other Lords didn't agree. One of them killed him, knowing I'd get the blame, and killed Kalmar as well to make sure we'd fight. Well, if war's what they want they can have it. Once we've defeated them, we can talk peace from a position of strength.'

'If there's anyone left to talk,' said Bernice, but no one took any notice.

There was the sound of voices at the entrance and Ivo came into the dome.

Romana hurried over to him. 'Ivo, where have you been? I was beginning to worry.'

'When you told me what had happened, I slipped away and hid out near the inn. I was able to get close enough to overhear their plans.' He turned to Tarak. 'They're going to attack you here, tonight. The whole Company, led by Varis and Lord Yarven.'

'How long?'

'They were just starting to form up when I left.'

'Then we can't stay here,' said Tarak. 'They'll just bottle us up and wait till we come out to be slaughtered or starve to death. We'll split up into small groups and take them in the forest, it's our only chance.' He clapped Ivo on the shoulder. 'Like old times with my father, eh Ivo?'

'I'd hoped those times were over,' said Ivo. 'Still, if we must fight, we must . . . and we'd better win.'

As the guerillas made their plans, Bernice said disgustedly, 'No use talking to them now. Once men start playing soldiers . . . What do we do now?'

'I'm going to slip away as soon as I can. You'd better come with me.'

'Where to?'

'There's another Tower, a real one not a spaceship, on the far side of the forest. It belongs to one of the wealthiest and most powerful of the Lords. His name's Sargon.'

'Whose side is he on?'

'He's been neutral so far. He's a scholar, a student of the Dark Times. He says that before the planet's past can be dealt with it must first be faced. He's even got a vampire museum in his castle. If we can only get him on our side . . .'

Bernice became aware of the weight of the signalling device in her pocket. 'Shouldn't we send for the Doctor?'

'And land him in the middle of a pitched battle? What could he do except get killed? No, the situation's still too confused and we know too little. When things calm down and we've got more information . . .'

'You'd like to settle all this without the Doctor if you can, wouldn't you? Send for him when it's all over and say *voilà*!'

'Yes, as a matter of fact I would,' said Romana frankly. 'But I'm not going to be stupid about it. As soon as I'm convinced the Doctor can help I'll send for him.'

Bernice wasn't entirely convinced, but she decided to bide her time. Already Tarak's men were slipping away into the darkness in little groups. As the last party left Tarak said, 'I'd advise you two to stay here. I can't leave anyone to guard you, I need every man.'

'We don't need looking after,' said Bernice. 'We can take care of ourselves.'

Tarak hurried away, but Ivo lingered for a moment.

'Goodbye Lady Bernice, Lady Romana. I'm sorry it's come to this in spite of all your efforts. I must go with them now, or young Tarak will get them all killed.'

'We tried, Ivo,' said Romana. 'When the time comes, we'll try again. Take care.'

As Ivo hurried away down the tunnel, Romana turned to Bernice. 'We'll give them a few minutes to get clear, then be on our way.'

The Company of Black Guards rode through a dark and windy night, with a pale moon only occasionally visible through the storm-tossed clouds. On the edge of the forest, Captain Varis halted his men. 'Take extra care from this point, all of you. In open country the advantage is with us, and we'll be in the open again when we get through the forest. Until then, keep a good look out.'

'No need to worry lads,' said Lord Yarven. 'The peasants will still be skulking in their den. Let's go and burn them out!' Varis gave him an angry look, but there was nothing he could do. Yarven's rank allowed him to say and do what he wished with no fear of reproof.

The Company rode into the deeper darkness of the woods. On and on they rode, the trees seeming to close in around them. But there was no sign of the enemy.

Varis and Lord Yarven rode at the head of the column. Varis was tense and alert, gazing continually about him, looking back over his shoulder to check that the column was keeping together. Lord Yarven however trotted along easily, as if he was out on a hunting trip or some pleasure jaunt.

He caught Varis's anxious gaze and smiled, teeth gleaming white in his bearded face. 'I tell you there's nothing to worry about, my boy. This peasant rabble won't dare to attack a full patrol.'

Varis wasn't so sure. Arrogant and overbearing as he was, he was an experienced soldier and a good commander. All his instincts told him that this was the time of maximum danger for his men.

'I'll be happier once we're out of the woods,' he said, and suddenly realized the origin of that all too common phrase.

A forest is an uneasy place for mounted men. Confined to paths and tracks by the trees, they lose their freedom of action. With no room to turn they can't even retreat. They must ride on to face whatever awaits them. What awaited most of the men of this Guard Company was death.

It came first in the brief glimpse of a cloaked figure between the trees and the hiss of an arrow. A guard clutched his throat and fell from his horse. The horse reared, panicking those in front and behind it, and cursing riders fought to keep control of their horses.

More arrows sped through the trees and more men fell. A rope snaked out and dragged a rider choking from his horse. The waiting knife of a grey-cloaked guerilla finished him off before he could rise.

Ivo stepped from cover and swung his great staff like a club, smashing a rider clean out of the saddle.

In a fight in the open a cavalryman's main weapon is his horse, which he uses to ride his opponent down. Here in the forest the plunging, rearing horses were useless, as Varis soon realized. 'Dismount, lads!' he roared. 'Let the horses go and fight on foot. Form squares, back to back and defend each other!'

The soldiers slid from their panic-stricken horses and let them gallop clear. Back to back, in little groups of two and three, they met the attacking guerillas on foot.

Very soon the battle in the darkness started to even out. The soldiers were better armed, better disciplined, better protected in their jerkins of steel and leather. They might not be able to defeat their half-seen attackers, but at least they could stand them off. Swords and pikes flashed in the forest gloom as the desperate soldiers fought savagely for their lives, cutting and thrusting at the grey-cloaked figures.

Varis ran his sword through the body of an over-confident guerilla, kicked the dying man away with a booted foot and wrenched his sword free. Beside him Lord Yarven fought with ferocious efficiency, running his opponent neatly through the throat.

The guerillas began to fall back and some of the soldiers started to follow them. Varis saw the danger at once. In the depths of the forest the little groups of soldiers risked being cut off and cut down. 'Fall back!' he called. 'Fall back and regroup at the edge of the forest!'

As the retreat began, Varis thought grimly that at least he'd managed to avoid *total* disaster. True, he'd lost all his horses and some of his men – just how many he couldn't yet tell. But a fair number seemed to be still on their feet somewhere around him, falling back through the forest.

Then the vampires came.

They appeared silently from out of the darkness of the forest behind the retreating soldiers, sinking long sharp fangs into unprotected necks between jerkin and helmet. The spurting blood looked black in the fitful moonlight that filtered down between the trees.

Swinging round to face this new enemy, Varis saw shadowy figures all around him, cutting off any retreat. The figures had white faces, glittering eyes and long white

197

fangs – though by now many of the fangs were red with blood. Some of the vampires wore flowing black cloaks, others were dressed in the rotting finery of their rank, richly ornamented robes and tunics now mouldering and decayed.

'Grave clothes!' thought Varis. 'These are the clothes they were buried in, and now they've come back.'

He saw one of his soldiers thrust a knife into the ribs of an attacking vampire, a tall, gaunt female whose skeletal limbs showed horribly through a tattered ball-gown of rotting silk. He saw the vampire pluck the knife from her side, smiling horribly, and launch herself at the terrified soldier, sinking her fangs deep into his neck.

Distracted by the horrible sights all around, Varis failed to see the guerilla who appeared behind him, sword raised.

A black-cloaked vampire sprang up before him, launching itself at his throat. Varis leaped aside, and the vampire collided with the attacking guerilla, bearing him to the ground. Just as satisfied with its new prey, it sank eager fangs into the guerilla's throat.

'At least they're impartial,' thought Varis. 'They're going to kill us all.'

He turned and saw Lord Yarven at his side. Yarven had sheathed his sword and stood quietly watching the slaughter around him.

Varis grabbed Yarven by the arm. 'Don't just stand there, run! We must get clear of the woods or we'll all be killed!'

Yarven didn't move. 'I assure you I am in no danger. Why should I fear my brethren?'

He smiled and Varis saw red lips and long white fangs in the bearded mouth.

It was the last thing he saw.

Smashing aside all who opposed him with his great staff, Ivo broke through into a little clearing and found himself facing three robed figures.

There was a man and a woman, both tall and thin with

white faces and glittering eyes, both gorgeously robed. Between them stood a smaller man, bearded and more plainly dressed. Their glittering eyes seemed to glow brighter as they fixed upon Ivo.

Ivo froze on the spot, giving a great sob of fear. 'Lord Zargo,' he whispered fearfully. 'Lady Camilla and Lord Aukon. The Three Who Rule.'

Ivo was a brave man but it is hard to face your enemies when you have seen them die once already. Breaking the spell of fear with a mighty effort he crashed on through the forest.

The three vampires were about to follow but at that moment three soldiers, united in flight, blundered into the clearing. They stopped in astonishment at the sight of the three robed figures.

For a moment the vampires hesitated – but Ivo was moving away, their hunger was great and here was hot fresh blood for the taking. The vampires hurled themselves upon their prey.

Blundering on through the woods, Ivo felt mingled feelings of relief and shame. He had escaped but men were dying all around him. He came to a path and saw a vampire crouched over a prone figure. Almost without thinking Ivo snapped his great staff in two and thrust the jagged end of one broken half deep into the vampire's left side, piercing the heart. With a terrible shriek the dying vampire rolled from its victim, and Ivo saw he had saved the life of one of the Black Guard. It didn't seem important which side the man was on: there was only one side now.

He helped the man to his feet. Staring at his rescuer, the dazed guard drew his dagger but Ivo plucked it from his hand. 'Time for that later. We've a common enemy now.'

Ivo snatched a branch from a tree, trimmed it with the dagger, sharpened the end and thrust it into the guard's hand.

'Come on, there's work to do! Remember, it must be

in the heart! A spear might do. Or find an axe and behead them. Tell the other soldiers.' They headed back towards the battle.

Not far away, Yarven rose from Varis's body, wiping bloody lips, and found himself facing Tarak. The guerilla leader had a bow in his hands, arrow nocked in the string. As Yarven advanced towards him Tarak drew back the bowstring and fired.

The arrow thudded into Yarven's heart. Yarven staggered back for a moment – and then sprang for Tarak's throat.

Bernice and Romana were galloping along the road that skirted the forest. Just ahead of them rose the summit of a low round hill. For quite some time they'd been hearing the confused sounds of battle and the screams of dying men. The terrible sounds faded at last as they left the battle behind them.

They'd found their horses where they'd left them, and no one had tried to stop them from getting away, but Bernice still felt uneasy. She rode up alongside Romana. 'Shouldn't we go back and try to do something?'

'What sort of something?'

'Intervene – break it up. I've got a blaster.'

'And what do you propose to do with it? Shoot down people from both sides till they all agree to behave? They'd kill you first. No, if they're hell-bent on slaughtering each other – and they are – there's really nothing we can do.'

Romana could be as ruthlessly practical as the Doctor himself.

Bernice still felt guilty. 'All the same, those screams . . .'

'Those screams are the best possible reason to keep going.'

'What do you mean?'

'That's not the kind of noise men make when they're fighting. Those were screams of fear. I think there's something worse than a battle going on in those woods tonight.

It sounds more like a massacre. I want to get as far away from the Tower as I can. I'll feel better once we're over that hill. I shan't really feel safe until it's daylight.'

'You don't really think they'd follow us this far?'

'You don't know how fast those things can travel.'

'Rubbish,' said Bernice, more to reassure herself than anything else. 'We've been riding for ages and . . .'

Suddenly her horse reared up, almost throwing her, and Romana's grey mare reared up as well.

Three ghastly figures had appeared on the track ahead of them. There was a man and a woman, both tall and thin with white faces and glittering eyes, both gorgeously robed. Between them stood a smaller man, bearded and more plainly dressed.

With an effort, they regained control of the nervous horses.

'It's them,' whispered Romana. 'Zargo, Camilla and Aukon. The Three Who Rule.' She glared indignantly at the three vampires.

'Go away, you're dead! You're just piles of dust. I saw you die!'

'We do not die,' said Zargo in a flat, dead voice.

'We always come back,' sighed Camilla. 'Always!'

Aukon said softly, 'And now we have come for you.'

22

Sargon's Castle

Bernice struggled to control her fear. 'Won't you introduce me to your friends? Though, come to think of it, one of them does look familiar.'

'They're Vampire Lords,' said Romana steadily. 'Zargo and Camilla and Aukon, their High Priest. They lived in the Tower when the Doctor and I first came here. I rather thought we'd dealt with them.'

'Not very effectively, it seems.'

In the road ahead, the three vampires waited, smiling. Camilla toyed with a little silver dagger at her waist.

'Have you got any of that *garil* flower?' asked Romana.

'Used it all up on my last vampire. I'm fresh out of sharpened stakes as well.'

'Then we've got just one chance – and I don't pretend it's a very good one.'

'Which is?'

'Ride straight at them – ride through them if you can, and on over the hill. If we can escape them till dawn . . .'

Romana leaned over, whispered in the grey mare's ear, and touched it lightly with her knees. The grey mare sprang forward. Bernice, not so well acquainted with her mount, had to use less subtle methods. She jabbed her heels into the black stallion's flanks, slapped it hard on the rump and yelled 'Hiiii-yah!' into its ear. The already nervous stallion shot forward after the mare.

The three vampires waited unmoving as the two horses thundered towards them. At the last possible moment they floated aside and up into the air. Then Zargo and Camilla swooped down upon the two riders.

Bernice became aware that there was someone on the saddle behind her, thin white arms gripping her fast. She looked over her shoulder and saw Camilla's white face, saw red lips draw back to reveal pointed teeth.

With a yell of fear Bernice hurled herself backwards from the saddle. She crashed to the ground, thankful that the vampire was underneath to break her fall. Camilla's body felt incredibly strong and wiry, as if made from springs and hard rubber. The impact of the fall knocked them apart and Bernice rolled over and got to her feet. Camilla stood waiting in front of her.

She saw Zargo drag Romana from the saddle and hurl her to the ground. She helped Romana up and they backed away from the advancing vampires, only to find Aukon cutting off their retreat.

Bernice and Romana stood back to back as the vampires advanced, claw-like hands outstretched. Bernice drew her blaster. She knew it was hopeless, but it was better to go down fighting.

Suddenly a deep voice rang out: 'Begone, accursed creatures of the night!'

A white-bearded, white-robed figure stood on top of the hill. Behind him appeared soldiers with blazing torches.

'Begone!' boomed the white-robed figure again. Its arm swept down and a ball of flame sizzled down from the hill, exploding at the feet of the vampires in a blaze of golden light that lit up the surrounding countryside like day. The vampires fled.

The bearded man ran down the hill towards them, followed by torch-bearing soldiers. Two of them recaptured the grey mare and the black stallion, a third led up a great white horse for the old man.

'Quickly,' he said. 'These evil creatures fear the light of fire, since it reminds them of dawn, but they can bear it if they must. We must leave here before they realize that mine was but a false dawn.'

Even in the middle of a life-and-death crisis, Romana didn't forget her manners. 'We owe you our lives, sir,' she said. 'May we know the name of our rescuer?'

'I am Lord Sargon,' said the old man simply. 'And you, I think, are the Lady Romana.'

'We were just coming to find you!' cried Bernice.

'Fortunately, my dear, I was also just coming to find you,' said the old man courteously. 'Now, I suggest we leave this evil place before the vampires come back and find all of us.'

He swung himself easily into his saddle, and Bernice and Romana did the same. They rode to the top of the hill where more soldiers waited, holding horses. When everyone had remounted, the old man led the way down the hill and across the flat plain beyond, Romana and Bernice riding close behind him. The soldiers followed, their torches blazing a fiery trail across the darkness.

Bernice was never sure how long they rode. The events of the night and the last-minute escape from the vampires had left her curiously light-headed and she felt no fatigue. The first pale streaks of dawn were in the sky by the time they rode up to a many-turreted castle on the brow of a low hill. They clattered through a stone arch into a cobbled courtyard, and castle guards armed with blasters came forward to take the horses. More servants ushered them into a big kitchen with a blazing fire, where they were given hot soup and soothing cordials.

'No formality tonight,' said Lord Sargon firmly. 'Tomorrow, when you have both rested, I shall receive you in a more fitting manner.'

Bernice was shown to a tapestry-hung chamber with a fire in the hearth, fur rugs on the stone floor and a curtained four-poster bed. A maid helped her into a sleeping robe and before she knew it she was sound asleep.

When she awoke next morning the sun was already high in the sky. A maid appeared with a steaming mug of herbal tea. When she'd finished it, she was shown to an adjoining chamber, the floor of which dipped to form a giant bowl filled with bubbling water.

Bernice braced herself for a cold plunge, and was amazed to find the water pleasantly warm. Wrapped in a vast towel she looked around for her clothes. Her safari jacket was hanging on a carved chair, but everything else seemed to have vanished.

'Your garments are being washed, my Lady,' said the maid. 'There are others for you to wear meanwhile. When you are ready, Lord Sargon and Lady Romana await you on the terrace.'

The other clothes consisted of an assortment of under-dresses and robes that left Bernice feeling like a fairy princess in a holovid historical. As soon as she was dressed, the maid led her along the stone-flagged corridors of the castle. It was a pleasant, airy place built from an attractive pale grey stone, with frequent windows and archways to let in the light. It was quite different from the Tower, thought Bernice. No doubt that was because it was a proper castle, not a converted spaceship. They climbed endless flights of winding stone stairs and came out onto a sunny terrace. There she found Lord Sargon and Romana sitting around a stone table enjoying bread and cheese and fruit, and drinking wine from silver fla-gons. She sat down to join them.

The terrace looked out over rolling green countryside that looked very much more pleasant than anywhere else she'd seen so far. She said as much to Lord Sargon.

'You must not judge us by Ivo's village and the Tower,' he said. 'That part of the country is tainted by the evil that it harboured for so long.'

'And is harbouring again,' said Romana. 'Those crea-tures you rescued us from were the original Three Who Rule, though how they have managed to survive and return . . .'

'If there is one thing I have learned about vampires,' said Lord Sargon, 'and I like to think that I've learned a great deal, it's that they cling with incredible strength to life – or rather, to their own version of life, which is living death. They seem to have re-established themselves in the Tower. There must be a sizeable colony of them.'

'More than just the three we saw last night?' asked Bernice.

'I fear so,' said Sargon gravely. 'As soon as the sun rose I sent a scouting party back to the area. They have just reported back.' He paused for a moment. 'There are bodies all over the woodland area: a patrol of guards and a considerable number of armed peasants. All dead, and all drained of blood. For the vampires to overcome so many . . .'

'They were helped by the fact that guards and peasants were busy killing each other,' said Romana bitterly. She gave Sargon an account of the background to last night's events.

'I'm sure you're right,' said Sargon when she'd finished. 'When the fighting was at its height, the vampires must have attacked both sides at once. Even so, such slaughter could only be the work of a considerable number.'

'It's odd though,' said Bernice. 'I only ever saw one vampire actually in the Tower. The tall one from the three we saw last night.'

Romana nodded, remembering. 'Lord Zargo.'

'And right after that I got a party of villagers to search the whole place. We didn't find a single vampire, let alone a nest of them.'

'No doubt their hiding-place eluded you,' said Lord Sargon. 'They are very cunning.' He paused for a moment, stroking his beard with a long white hand. 'The terrible events of last night do offer a ray of hope. The fact that the peasants and the guards, the soldiers of the Lords, all suffered alike may unite them against a common enemy.'

'I'm afraid it's not that simple,' said Bernice bluntly. 'As far as I can gather, Lords and vampires are all mixed up in people's minds. They're going to need a lot of convincing that you're not just trying to bring back the bad old days.'

Romana gave her a reproving look. Lord Sargon smiled sadly. 'I am afraid that what you say is all too true. Many of the Great Houses bore the taint of vampirism. When the vampires were overthrown many Lords over-reacted. They tried to pretend that vampires did not exist, had never existed. Naturally enough, they were not believed.'

'But you thought differently?'

'I felt that no problem can be dealt with unless its existence is admitted. So against much opposition, I started my vampire museum. Would you care to see it?'

Bernice felt she'd had enough vampires to last her for a while but Romana, polite as ever, said, 'We'd love to.'

The old man led them down several flights of stone stairs to a large chamber underneath the castle. It had a vaulted stone roof supported by stone pillars and to Bernice's astonishment it was lit by softly glowing glass globes in holders on the walls.

The room was filled with display cases holding maps, charts and all kinds of exhibits. Proudly the old man showed them round. 'If we begin here, the cases tell the story in the correct historical order ...'

The early cases concerned the history of the planet. Before the arrival of the Great Vampire it had been a still-traditional society, but one in the middle of a sudden flowering of scientific and technological breakthrough – like Earth, thought Bernice, in the late eighteenth and early nineteenth century.

'We had discovered steam power,' said the old man proudly, pointing to a case of early designs and models. 'I have managed to recreate some of these discoveries. We have a generator beneath the castle which gives us light and heat.'

He took them to another case filled with cumbersome-looking muskets and blunderbusses and enormous bell-mouthed pistols. 'We had discovered projectile weapons too, and simple explosives.'

'That thing you chucked at the vampires!' said Bernice.

'An invention of my own,' said Lord Sargon. 'It is a great success at village festivals, and as you saw, it has other uses.'

He led them to an alcove which was covered with a curtain.

'Then the Great Abomination descended upon our world and the Age of Darkness began. A giant vampire appeared above our planet, wounded, apparently dying.

207

Here is the moment as the greatest of our ancient artists imagined it.'

He drew back the curtain to reveal a horrifying picture. A great beast, part man part bat, hovered in space, blood dripping from a gaping wound in its leathery-skinned side. It had huge wings and a massive rat-like head, with great savage fangs.

23

Vampire History

Bernice swallowed hard and forced herself to examine the painting. 'How big was it, exactly?'

Sargon led them to another case. It held an enormous claw-like hand, blackened and twisted as if in some catastrophe.

'You can judge from this. I recovered this from the burial ground close to the Tower.'

'So it was you,' said Bernice sharply. 'Did you make off with a lot of other bits as well?'

'It's true I took specimens of various bones,' said Sargon apologetically.

Bernice looked round. 'Where are they then? I don't see them here?'

'They crumbled when I tried to prepare them for display. The claw was all I could manage to preserve.'

'Well, you've ruined an extremely valuable specimen,' said Bernice crossly.

Romana was clearly embarrassed. She turned to Lord Sargon, as if to make amends for Bernice's rudeness. 'It's a wonderful picture, Lord Sargon, and a wonderful museum. As it happens I can tell you where the creature came from. We don't usually talk of these things, but if anyone has a right to know then you do.'

'I should be eternally grateful, my Lady.'

'It all goes back to the early history of the Time Lords – the Doctor's people and mine. There was once an entire race of these creatures. According to the Doctor, each one had the strength to drain the energy from an entire planet. We fought a war with them and destroyed them, all except one, their leader the Great Vampire. It fled, wounded, from the last battle and disappeared.'

'And now we know where,' said Bernice. 'What happened next?'

Lord Sargon said, 'The creature buried itself beneath the soil of our planet. But its body was not dying but dormant, and its mind was still alive and possessed of incredible powers. It used those powers to bring to our world a ship that travelled through space. That ship landed close to the buried monster's body. With the power of its mind it corrupted the ship's crew. They became vampires. Over long years their ship became the Tower and they became the Lords of the village and all the country around – the Three Who Rule.'

'Zargo, Camilla and Aukon,' said Romana. 'They were still there, all those years later, when the Doctor and I came to this planet.'

'Their vampirism gave them great strength, long life and a savage determination,' Sargon continued. 'For generations they drained the blood of the peasants who served them, feeding their buried master, who they called the Great One, with their blood. From this evil centre the taint of vampirism spread out to corrupt our world. Just as the vampires had become Lords, so many of our Lords became vampires. By now the peasants were beginning to demand their freedom. To their eternal shame the Vampire Lords used their powers to crush them, plunging our planet into an age of darkness. Many Great Houses were as corrupted as the Three themselves. Others were only partially tainted, with a single vampire working behind the scenes.'

'Like Lord Veran's son,' said Bernice.

Sargon nodded. 'Some families resisted the taint entirely. Mine, I am proud to say, was one of them.'

'Even though your castle is so close to the Tower?' said Bernice. 'That can't have been easy.'

Romana took up the story. 'All this time the Three Who Rule were following their master's plan. They stored the blood of the peasants in the ship's fuel tanks, and pumped it into the burial ground to feed their master. On the Day of Arising, the Great Vampire, his strength restored by the blood of generations, would return in all his glory. Then he would summon his vampire servants and lead them in an assault on the entire planet. When it was drained, he would use his powers to take his vampire horde back into normal space, where they would have a whole universe to feed on, swarming over planet after planet.'

'But you and the Doctor turned up,' said Bernice. 'And the Day of Arising never arrived.'

Romana nodded. 'The Doctor discovered the old Record of Rassilon in the TARDIS. It revealed that Rassilon had destroyed the Great Vampire with bow-ships, specially constructed to fire "a mighty bolt of steel".'

'I suppose the Doctor just happened to have one handy?'

'No, but he improvised – as usual. He activated one of the little scoutships attached to the Tower and programmed it to go straight up and straight down again. It plunged right through the Great Vampire's heart and destroyed it.'

'Well, it's certainly dead enough now,' said Bernice, giving Lord Sargon a reproachful look. 'What with bits of its body scattered all over the countryside . . .'

'It's odd though,' said Romana. 'When the Doctor's scoutship pierced the Great Vampire's heart, the Three crumbled to dust.'

'If they crumbled they've been reconstituted,' said Bernice. 'Instant vampire – just add fresh blood and stir.'

That night they joined Lord Sargon for dinner in a small comfortably furnished dining room in one of the castle turrets. The afternoon had been spent in an item-by-item tour of the museum, with Romana politely attentive and Bernice openly bored.

Over dinner, a simple meal of omelette, salad and venison, Romana and Lord Sargon indulged in an extensive discussion of the local nobility, all of whom Romana seemed to know intimately.

Feeling left out and bored, Bernice ate in sullen silence, downing frequent goblets of the excellent local wine.

By the end of the meal Sargon and Romana had run out of noble families, and the conversation was flagging a little.

Suddenly Bernice leaned forward. 'Lor' Shargon – sorry, *Lord Sargon*,' she said, speaking with exaggerated distinctness. 'Does the *garil* plant grow around here? I don't seem to have seen any in your castle.'

Romana gasped. 'Bernice, really!'

Lord Sargon smiled. 'It grows in great profusion, I assure you.' He summoned one of the servant girls and whispered in her ear. She hurried away.

'It's not usually found in the living quarters, of course,' Lord Sargon went on. 'But we use it a good deal in cooking. The omelette we all enjoyed earlier was flavoured with it – and so was the venison.'

The servant girl reappeared with a bunch of fresh *garil* flowers, and Sargon took them from her. 'Ah yes, here we are!' He buried his nose in the flowers and took a deep breath.

'A humble everyday flower,' he said. 'A little sharp, a little pungent. Not to everyone's taste, but not entirely unattractive all the same. I'm very fond of it myself.'

He rose and presented the bouquet to Bernice with a flourish of his long white hand. 'Now if you will forgive me, ladies?'

He bowed and strode elegantly from the room. With a toss of her head, Romana rose and followed him.

Left alone at the table Bernice emptied her goblet and decided reluctantly against another one. She stared rather blearily at the bunch of *garil* flowers. 'Worth a try,' she said defensively. 'I mean, you never know.'

When she eventually managed to find her room again, Bernice found her own clothes, washed, pressed and neatly folded on a chair. Her boots were underneath, all gleaming and polished.

'Ha!' said Bernice. She went into the adjoining room, filled a stone hand-basin with cold water and plunged her head into it. She came back into the bedroom, dried herself on the coverlet and started climbing into her own clothes.

She was struggling with her boots when Romana came into the room and said, 'Really, Bernice!'

'Oh shut your face,' said Bernice. 'I had an instructor at Military Academy who used to say "Really!" in that tone. That's why I ran away.'

Romana struggled to keep her temper. 'I've told you how important it is to us to gain Lord Sargon's support, and you practically accuse him of being a vampire at his own dinner table and – what are you doing?'

'Getting dressed.'

'Why?'

'I want to take another look at that museum.'

'You didn't seem to enjoy it much the first time.'

'I don't think we saw the most interesting bits. Coming?'

'I'm certainly not letting you roam round on your own.'

Romana nipped next door into her own room and reappeared surprisingly quickly, dressed in her own clothes.

They moved quietly along the darkened corridors of the castle, lit now by the occasional glowing light-globe. It wasn't hard to find the museum. They just kept heading downwards until they reached the big underground chamber and went inside.

The place was strangely forlorn-looking as if waiting for crowds who would never come.

'Well?' said Romana.

Bernice dropped down and pressed her ear to the floor. 'Come and listen!'

Romana sighed and lay down beside her. She put her ear to the flagstone and heard a faint steady hum of power. There was something else behind the hum, a steady pulsing sound. Romana found it strangely familiar.

They both got up.

'He said there was a generator,' said Romana.

'That's no steam generator, it's something much more hi-tech. The thing is, how do we get to it? I'm pretty sure there's an entrance in here.'

Bernice roamed around the museum until she found herself standing before the portrait of the Great Vampire. She drew back the curtain and rubbed her finger across the bottom of the painting. It came away smudged with paint. 'Ancient artist,' she muttered. 'It's so new the paint's still wet. So why bother, unless . . .' She gripped the edge of the painting and pulled. It swung open like a door, revealing a real door behind it: a perfectly ordinary door, made of shining steel. She opened it and revealed a metal staircase leading downwards. She looked at Romana and started to descend the steps. Romana followed.

The metal steps led them down into an enormous, brightly lit underground chamber. Romana and Bernice stopped at the bottom of the steps and stood looking around them.

The centre of the chamber was occupied by a colossal glass tank. The tank was filled with a dark swirling fluid, at the heart of which floated a huge, dimly seen form. A low steady pulsing sound came from the tank, like the beat of a great heart. One end of the room was filled with a complex-looking bank of instrument consoles, humming with power.

Around the other three sides of the chamber were upright glass coffins. The coffins were occupied by vampires, white-faced and bloody-fanged, eyes closed and hands folded on their breasts.

They heard the slam of the door and turned to see Lord Sargon looking down at them, no longer old and white-haired but young and handsome. He smiled, stroking his chin with his long white hand. 'You were right, after all,' he said. 'Instant vampire – just add fresh blood and stir.'

He seemed to float down the steps toward them, and Bernice instinctively snatched the blaster from her pocket.

'Keep back!'

Sargon smiled and kept coming. Thumbing the blaster to the 'kill' setting, Bernice fired.

Sargon's body absorbed the energy bolt with no apparent effect. He reached out and plucked the useless blaster from Bernice's fingers, tossing it aside.

Faced with a smiling and apparently invulnerable enemy, Bernice reached into her other pocket, found the Doctor's signalling device and did the only thing possible.

She pressed the panic button.

24

The Quarry

It was closing time at Doc's place, and the last customer had just left. Ace was bathed, dressed, fed and her old stroppy self again. She'd had a couple of celebratory drinks with Dekker and sent him home, and she was ready to confront the Doctor.

He was sitting in his usual alcove, immaculate in his white dinner-jacket, whisky glass by his side, cigarette burning in the ashtray. Ace sat beside him in a new black evening gown, the black velvet bag with the Browning automatic inside close at hand.

They were tourist attractions by now, the mysterious Doc and his Lady in Black. Rumours about the events at Schofield's flower shop and the Palace Hotel were already circulating, and that night Doc's place had been busier than ever. Ace was beginning to worry that their images were taking over.

'All right Doctor, I've been drugged, kidnapped, shot at, beaten up and almost ravished, and that's just this afternoon. Don't you think it's time you told me what this is all about?'

'Yes,' said the Doctor. 'I suppose it is.' He took a small crystal sphere from his pocket and handed it to Ace.

She took it cautiously. 'What is it?'

'It has several uses. For you it's a kind of snapshot album.'

Ace stared into the sphere which was full of swirling mists, and suddenly she was somewhere else. Several somewhere elses in fact, in rapid succession.

She was on a balcony overlooking a bakingly hot city

square scattered with blazing bonfires. Eager crowds watched human figures writhing in the heart of the flames. Beside her on the balcony stood an elegant figure in a black robe and hood, a tall man with a long thin face and long white hands. He was savouring the smoke and the screams like perfume, and he was smiling.

She was on another balcony overlooking another square in another place and another time. Wooden carts rumbled along the street beneath, filled with white-faced men and women in tattered finery. At the centre of the square was a scaffold built around a tall framework holding a triangular blade. As the carts reached the scaffold the prisoners were bustled out, formed into a line, thrust up the steps and strapped under the framework, all with a ghastly well-practised efficiency.

The blade came down, the head dropped into the basket, the executioner held it up by the hair for the delectation of the crowd. There was a roar of approval and another victim was hustled up the steps. Beside her on the balcony, a tall elegant figure, neat in black velvet, stroked its chin and smiled.

She was on a hillside, overlooking a plain where a battle raged. She saw an aide, tall, thin, immaculately uniformed, hand a dispatch to a baffled officer. She saw him point a long white hand. 'There lies your enemy!'

She saw the officer lead a charge of cavalry straight into the mouths of a battery of cannon, heard the screams of dying men as the surviving horses trotted by with blood-spattered empty saddles. The aide flicked a speck of dust from his cuff with a silk handkerchief and smiled.

She was on another hill, overlooking a mud-filled trench filled with grimy, weary soldiers. The rumble of artillery filled the air. A car arrived from the rear and a tall thin staff officer got out, wearing the red tabs of a brigadier. He summoned a tired young officer and gave orders.

The officer led his battle-weary men out of the trench, across a strip of barren ground strewn with barbed wire, and into the fire of a concealed machine-gun nest. As the men twisted and writhed and died in the choking mud, the staff officer smiled.

She felt the Doctor take the sphere from her hand, the stream of horrifying images faded and she was back in the alcove.

Ace found she was shaking with anger. 'It was the smile,' she said. 'That damned superior smile.'

'Yes,' agreed the Doctor. 'It's the smile that gets you.'

'Who was – who is he?'

'It's "is", I'm afraid. And not so much who as what. He, or it, is sometimes called Agonal, it's as good a name as any. It's a Greek word, means "the agony of death".'

'Doctor – '

'Bear with me Ace, this is difficult.' The Doctor paused, concentrating his thoughts. 'There are beings in the universe, call them elementals, spiritual in essence, but with the power to interact with the physical world. Some are very powerful, some so weak you hardly notice them. Some are what you'd call good, some bad, some completely neutral. With me so far?'

'Not really, but go on.'

The Doctor sighed. 'I told you it was difficult. Perhaps if I used more familiar names. The good ones might be called gods, or angels or earth spirits; the bad ones devils, or demons or ghouls. The feeble ones like poltergeists can only manage to smash cups and slam doors in the night.'

'And this Agonal is one of the powerful and bad ones?'

'Yes, but in a very odd way. He doesn't cause anything. He just magnifies evil.'

'How do you mean?'

'What did you see in the sphere?'

Ace told him and the Doctor nodded. 'The Spanish Inquisition burning heretics, the Terror in the French Revolution, the Charge of the Light Brigade in the Crimea, the First World War ... Agonal didn't cause any of those events, he just takes advantage of them.'

'He caused that charge, and he got those soldiers killed.'

'That's right. But the wars were happening already. No doubt he stirred up the Spanish Inquisition to resume

218

religious persecution, and helped whip up revolutionary terror. Don't you see, Ace? He chooses his period in history and intervenes to make bad things worse.'

'And he's intervening here, now, in Chicago?'

'It's perfect for him. A turbulent period which ought to be settling down by now. Everyone's getting fed up with the violence, even Capone wants to sell booze not kill people, but one incident after another keeps the pot boiling.'

'So he's behind these three murders, the ones we've been investigating?'

'He killed Lingle, the reporter, and Dekker found a witness who saw him kill McSwiggin. I'm pretty sure he machine-gunned Hymie Weiss, and he was certainly behind your kidnapping – which means he knows I'm after him.'

'Why are you after him, Doctor? What got you involved?'

'An anonymous message from Gallifrey,' said the Doctor. 'It suggested Agonal might be likely to be operating in Chicago in this time-period. I decided to establish myself here and trap him.'

'Why dump poor Benny on that peculiar planet first?'

The Doctor sighed. 'This is where it gets a bit complicated. Just as I got the report from Gallifrey I got another message as well – a telepathic one from a Time Lady who travelled with me for a while.'

'Romanathingy?'

'The Lady Romanadvoratrelundar. She felt things were going wrong on a planet we'd visited earlier, she was a bit vague about why. I didn't want to put off dealing with Agonal so I dropped Benny off to look round and give Romana a hand. As soon as we're finished here we'll go and find her and sort things out. I don't suppose there's very much wrong. It's probably just Romana panicking.'

'This first message,' said Ace. 'The one from Gallifrey. Did you say it was anonymous?'

'It was probably from some unknown well-wisher in the Earth Section of the Bureau of Historical Observation.'

'Why tell you?'

'I've been urging the Time Lords to do something about Agonal ever since I first started studying human history. But until now they didn't seem to think he was important enough. He doesn't change history, you see, just makes the bad worse.'

'Why?'

'Because it amuses him,' said the Doctor simply. 'Some elementals nourish themselves on the emotions of living beings. Agonal feeds on agony and death.'

'So he kills people, or gets them killed, just for kicks?'

'Yes – and you know, Ace, I find that quite intolerable.' The Doctor's voice was shaking with anger. 'The universe is all too full of pain and suffering – and that someone, some abominable *thing* should increase that pain for its own selfish pleasure . . .'

'All right Doctor, I'm with you, we'll find him and scupper him. What are we up against? What are this thing's powers?'

'Pretty formidable, I'm afraid. He isn't human but he can assume a human body. Luckily for us he always seems to choose very much the same appearance, tall, thin, aristocratic-looking, just out of vanity, I think.'

'Wait a minute,' said Ace. 'I've seen him – I even spoke to him!'

The Doctor leaned forward. 'Where?'

'At that peace conference, when I had to stay downstairs. He was going round chatting to people. He warned me not to trust Capone. Everyone seemed to know him . . . I even felt I knew him from somewhere myself.'

'That's one of his gifts. He clouds people's minds. He can turn up anywhere, make people accept him, even think they already know him, and influence their behaviour. Then he fades away and they forget he was ever there.'

'Any other tricks I should know about?'

'Well, he's trans-dimensional: he can move through time and space pretty much as he likes. Vanish from one planet, reappear on another. Makes him hard to catch.'

'So how do we? Catch him, I mean?'

'We use his one weakness – his vanity. He knows I'm here and he knows I'm hunting him. He can't resist a challenge. He's already tried to strike at me through you. No doubt he'll try to kill us both in some frightfully amusing way, and he'll want to be there to enjoy it. That's when we'll get him.'

'So we're using ourselves as bait? If we do catch him, can we kill him?'

'He can't be killed but he can be confined, in this.' The Doctor held out the sphere. 'This is a sensosphere with a built-in force-field. As you saw, it holds a record of the suffering Agonal's caused. He'll find it irresistibly attractive. Once he touches it, it will absorb and imprison him.'

'Like a genie in a bottle?'

'Exactly,' said the Doctor. 'Like a genie in a bottle!'

But as yet, the genie was still unconfined.

'I don't want any more arguments from you, Captain Reilly,' shouted Big Bill Thompson. 'I want a total crackdown, starting first thing tomorrow. You can call on the other precincts for all the men you need. Every speakeasy, brewery and illegal beer joint you can find. It's time these hooligans learned who's boss around here! Oh, and Reilly – you don't have to be too gentle about it. If one or two of these guys get hurt or even killed resisting arrest, well, it all helps to relieve the pressure on the courts.'

At the other end of the phone, Reilly said, 'If that's what you want, Mr Mayor, that's what you'll get. I'm to hit everyone, you say? No exceptions?'

'No exceptions!'

'What about Doc?'

Thompson looked up at the tall, thin aide standing at his shoulder. The aide whispered briefly in his ear.

'Hit Doc's Place as well,' bellowed the Mayor. 'I've been talking to a guy who knows, and these Washington connections Doc talks about are all fake. He's just a cheap hoodlum like the rest of them!'

Thompson hung up the phone.

'That's telling them, Mr Mayor,' said the tall aide standing at his shoulder. 'I can just see the headlines: "Mayor Thompson Cracks Down on Chicago Crime!" When they see those headlines in Washington it won't be Mr Mayor, it'll be Mr President.'

Lost in dreams of Presidential glory, Big Bill Thompson sat sipping scotch in his darkening office. He didn't even notice when the tall aide faded away into the shadows, leaving him alone.

25

Crack-down

Early next morning, Captain Reilly was addressing an astonished gathering of his fellow Chicago police captains, all big, beefy prosperous-looking men much like himself.

'The orders come straight from the Mayor,' he said. 'If you don't believe me you can call him up and check.'

He looked round the circle of angry and resentful faces. 'Now, I know what you're all thinking. This is going to mean an interruption in the weekly pay-packet, and I don't mean the pittance you get from the City of Chicago. There'll be no more brown envelopes coming our way for a while. But I've been thinking things over, and for once his honour is right. He's under a lot of pressure, and he has to do something to make himself look good. Besides, these fellers have been getting above themselves entirely. There's poor Red Duffy killed, one of our own, and McSwiggin and Lingle as well. A police captain, a D.A. and a journalist! It could be one of us next!'

He paused, watching his words sink in. 'And remember this – it can't last long. The good citizens of Chicago have to have their booze or his honour will lose their votes. Before very long it'll be business as usual. When it is, the cost of operating will have to go up. Believe me, they'll be so glad to be open again, they'll pay up and like it!' He stood up. 'So be off with you now – oh, and just one more thing. You can hit where you like, and be as rough as you like, but no one's to touch Doc's place. That's a pleasure I'm reserving for myself – a little treat at the end of the day.'

223

Inspired with a new sense of civic duty, Chicago's finest went out to bust a few heads.

Ace slept in next morning. When she came down, the Doctor and Dekker were drinking coffee in the alcove, Happy was mopping the floor and Luigi was polishing glasses behind the bar. Luigi poured her a cup of coffee, and she went over to join the others.

'Mr Dekker says the police are on the rampage,' said the Doctor.

'I got the word straight from my pal Eliot,' explained Dekker. 'He's like a kid in a candy-store. Total crack-down, no exceptions, no mercy. I thought I'd better come and warn you.'

He reached down beside his chair and came up with an elaborate card embossed with a heart-shaped box of chocolates and a bedraggled bunch of flowers. Proudly he presented them to Ace.

She looked at them with distaste. 'What the hell is all this garbage, Dekker?'

Dekker looked hurt. 'Presents for my best girl. Don't you know it's St Valentine's day?' He leaned over and gave Ace a quick kiss. Automatically she raised her fist to thump him, decided against it and kissed him back. She was getting much too used to Dekker.

'About this crack-down,' she said. 'I thought all the cops were on the take?'

'Most of 'em are,' said Dekker. 'But cops have a natural hatred for hoods. Being paid off only makes it worse. A lot of old scores could get settled in the next few days.'

The Doctor said, 'It sounds as if we'd better stay closed for a while.' He waved Luigi over to the table. 'Luigi, we're closed down till further notice. Tell the staff they'll all be paid as usual till we open again. Lock up tight and don't let anyone in, especially the police.'

'Sure Doc, me and Happy will take care of things. Hey Happy?'

'Sure thing, boss. We'll clean the joint up real nice and have a grand reopening.'

'What are we going to do if we don't have to work?' said Ace.

'Easy,' said Dekker. 'If it's okay with Doc, I'll take you out and show you the town.'

You could hear the scream of police sirens, the sound of shattered wood and breaking glass, the shouts and gunshots and the dull thud of police nightsticks thumping criminal skulls all over Chicago.

Squads of police burst into countless bars, speakeasies, saloons and soda parlours, seizing stocks of booze, rousting the customers, arresting the owners. Seven breweries were raided and padlocked, and notices nailed to the doors: CLOSED FOR ONE YEAR FOR VIOLATION OF NATIONAL PROHIBITION ACT.

Eliot Ness and his squad of Untouchables got hold of a heavy truck, reinforced the front bumper and drove straight through the locked door of a booze warehouse.

Police cells were filling up all over Chicago.

In Schofield's flower shop, Pete Gusenberg and Bugs Moran held a crisis conference.

'I tell you it's the straight dope,' Moran was saying. 'I got it from this guy works in the Mayor's office.'

Gusenberg frowned. 'Oh yeah? Which guy?'

'Tall, skinny guy, I don't remember his name. Anyway, he says this clean-up is all a fix, see, between Thompson and Capone.'

'The way I hear it Capone's joints are getting hit as well.'

'Sure, the cops'll knock over one or two of Al's places to make it look good, but we're the real targets. When all this is over, we'll be outta business and Capone will be sitting pretty.'

'Maybe it's time we did something about Al,' said Gusenberg. 'We oughtta take care of him before he takes care of us all like he did poor Hymie, right out there on that sidewalk. I'll talk to some of the boys.'

Moran shook his head. 'No, this is too important. We'll do something about Al all right – and we'll do it ourselves.'

Later that day, as Al Capone's Cadillac was pulling up outside the Lexington Hotel, a black Packard drove by, a tommy-gun sprouting bullets from the open window. Capone's car was sprayed with .45 calibre bullets from end to end. Had it been any ordinary vehicle those inside would certainly have been killed. But Capone's new Cadillac weighed seven tons. It had armour-plated bodywork and its windscreen, side and rear windows were made of bullet-proof glass three inches thick.

When the shooting stopped and the Packard had disappeared, Capone got out of the car unhurt and stomped into the foyer of the hotel. He stopped for a moment and spoke to Frank Rio, who was at his side as always. 'You get a look at them?'

'Moran and Gusenberg. Gusenberg driving, Moran handling the chopper.'

Capone said, 'Okay, that does it. Enough is enough. Send for Anselmi and Scalise. And put some of the boys onto tracking those guys down.'

Al Capone was alone when he got into the lift, yet somehow he wasn't surprised to see the tall thin man lounging in the corner. This was one of his best men, a trusted adviser. Who else could it be?

'You took the right decision, boss,' said the tall man as the lift swept upwards. 'Those guys have been asking for it.'

'Anselmi and Scalise will take care of 'em,' grunted Capone. 'The problem's going to be finding them.'

'I know how we can find them,' said the tall man. 'And I know how you can get them exactly where you want them.'

North Clark was a shabby, ordinary sort of street lined with shops, rooming houses and small businesses. Number 1222 was a grubby one-storey brick building with black-painted windows. A placard on the door read SMC Haulage Company.

The front part of the building was partitioned off to form a small shabby office. The rest of it formed a garage, entered by double doors from the back alley. The garage was owned by the Northside mob, used for the storing and distribution of bootleg booze. So far it had escaped the attention of Reilly's crack-down squad.

That morning the garage held a couple of empty trucks. One of the trucks was jacked up, a mechanic working underneath. His name was John May, and he'd brought his alsatian, Highball, tying it to the wheel of the truck.

Watching him work there stood a small group of men in overcoats and hats. Pete Gusenberg and his brother Frank, a small-time gunman called Jim Clark, Frank Snyder the garage owner and a failed optician called Schwimmer, a minor hanger-on.

A stocky man in a brown hat and grey overcoat came into the garage. His name was Al Weinshank, a speakeasy owner who handled liquor distribution for the gang. In build and appearance he was very like Bugs Moran, and the two were very often mistaken for each other.

(The mistake was being made now. In a diner across the street a watcher picked up a telephone, dialled and said, 'Moran's just gone in.')

Weinshank looked around the garage. 'They ain't here yet?'

'They'll be here,' said Pete Gusenberg.

They were waiting for a hijacked consignment of Old Log Cabin whisky. The unknown hijacker had offered the Northside mob a good deal, saying there was plenty more where this came from. In these hard times it was a deal not to be missed. The fact that the booze had been hijacked from Al Capone made the deal all the sweeter.

The hijacker had insisted on dealing with Pete Gusenberg and Bugs Moran in person. Although he lived in the Parkway Hotel just round the corner, Bugs Moran, luckily for him, was late.

A black car drew up outside the front of the garage. It

was a black seven-seater Cadillac like the ones used by the detective squads. It had a siren and a gong and a gun-rack behind the driver's seat. Five men got out, leaving the driver at the wheel. Witnesses later described the fifth man as being especially tall and thin. Two of the men who got out were in police uniform. They were carrying shotguns.

Bugs Moran and his bodyguard Ted Newberry appeared around the corner just as the men in police uniform got out of the car.

'Ah hell, a raid,' said Moran disgustedly. He hesitated for a moment.

'No point getting pinched for nothing, boss,' said Newberry.

'Yeah, you're right. We'll go back to the Parkway and call a mouthpiece.'

They turned and went back the way they came.

The two uniformed men in the lead, the group of raiders forced open the flimsy door, went through the empty office and down the narrow passage that led to the garage.

At the sight of the blue uniforms, Peter Gusenberg echoed Moran's words, 'Ah hell, a raid. Okay boys, no trouble.' For bootleggers a police raid was just a professional hazard. All it meant was a bit of pushing around from the cops, a few hours in a cell, a speedy release when the mob mouthpiece turned up with *habeas corpus* writs and bail money.

'What are you trying to pin on us?' said Frank Gusenberg. 'There ain't even any booze here yet!'

One of the men in uniform said, 'Up against the wall in a line, hands up. He pointed to the mechanic. 'You too.'

Covered by the two shotguns, the gangsters obeyed.

Schwimmer the little optician tried to protest. 'Officer, I'm not really –'

'Shaddup. In line with the rest.'

When the line was formed one of the uniformed men went down it, taking guns from the Gusenbergs, Clark,

Snyder and Weinshank and tossing them to one side. Schwimmer and May, the mechanic, were unarmed.

'Okay. Now turn to face the wall.'

Hands still high above their heads the seven men faced the brick wall of the garage. It was to be the last thing they saw.

Two of the men in plain clothes took tommy-guns from under their long overcoats. They formed a second line, two tommy-gunners in the centre, a shotgunner at either end.

The fifth man, the tall one, stood a little apart, watching. Then he smiled and raised his hand.

The garage exploded in a roar of sound, the harsh chattering of the tommy-guns punctuated by the boom of shotgun blasts.

The first sweep of sub-machine-gun bullets took the line of men at shoulder level, later sweeps riddled them lower across the body. Repeated blasts of buckshot made doubly sure. Four of the men fell straight forward, lying at right angles to the bullet-pocked wall. Clark half-turned and fell sideways, Pete Gusenberg slumped face-down across a wooden chair. One of the machine-gunners fired a final burst, spraying the prone bodies at head level.

The noise died away and the five men walked out of the garage, leaving the way they had come. The alsatian dog Highball, still tied to the wheel of the truck, howled miserably, struggling to reach his dead master where he lay in a spreading pool of blood.

Several people heard the noise of shooting, but gunfire wasn't so unusual in Chicago. A lady in the apartment house opposite was cleaning her front room window. She saw three men come out of the garage, covered by two policemen with shotguns, and assumed she was seeing an arrest.

'They all got in the car and drove away,' she said later. 'The funny thing was, one of the fellers being arrested, the tall thin one, was *smiling*.'

In his hotel suite, Al Capone was listening to the report

of his adviser. 'So, you missed Bugs – still, you got both Gusenberg boys. Two out of three ain't bad.'

'The danger isn't over,' said the tall man. 'There are still people out to get you and some of them are the ones you trust the most.'

He began to talk in a low hypnotic voice. Capone listened appalled as the extent of the treacherous plotting against him was revealed at last.

The anger turned to a fierce delight as his friend, his one trusted friend, explained how he could take vengeance on his secret enemy. 'Who'da thought it'd be him all along,' whispered Al Capone. 'Well, I'll take care of him. I'll take care of them all.'

The Doctor sat alone in the empty bar, grey eyes staring into nothingness. He was letting his mind range through time and space and events.

The anonymous message from Gallifrey, the summons from Romana. He ought to do something about that soon and about Bernice as well, but he was close, so close . . .

It was like playing three-dimensional chess in the dark with an opponent who could become one of the pieces at will. Or even several of the pieces.

But was there another game behind the game? A voice inside his head whispered, 'To lose is to win, and he who wins shall lose.'

There was a distant ringing sound and the Doctor became aware that someone was calling him. It was Luigi from behind the bar.

'Telephone for you, Doc.' He lowered his voice. 'It's the Big Fellow.'

The Doctor got up and went over to the telephone that stood on the bar. 'Hello?'

A rich throaty voice said, 'That you, Doc? This is Al.'

'How are you, Mr Capone?'

'Fine, Doc, fine . . . if it wasn't for them lousy cops. They hit your joint yet?'

'Not yet. I've closed down for a while just to be on the safe side.'

'Smart move. Me, I'm taking a little vacation till things blow over. Going down to my little place in Miami. Listen Doc, you know that line you fed me about some guy stirring things up so he could take over? Well, I think you're right and I think I know who it might be.'

'I'd be very interested to hear.'

The voice became confidential. 'I don't wanna talk over the phone, Doc. Listen. I'm giving a little dinner party tonight, over at the Lexington. Why don't you come? We'll have a quiet word and I'll spill all I know. Bring Miss Ace as well.'

The Doctor thought for a moment. 'I'd be glad to,' he said. 'I can't speak for Ace, she isn't here, but I'll certainly pass on your invitation.'

'Swell. I'll leave word at the door. Oh, and it's formal – tuxedo, the works. Be seeing you, Doc.'

The Doctor put down the phone. For a moment he stood lost in thought. 'Tell Happy I'll be needing him to drive tonight, will you, Luigi? I'm going to supper with Mr Capone.'

Ace had to admit it, she was having quite a day. Dekker had driven her all over Chicago, showing her everything from dazzling new skyscrapers to tenement houses where immigrants cooked alky for Capone in illicit kitchen stills.

They'd talked to cops and crooks and all kinds of people in between. Dekker seemed to know everyone. They'd seen police cars tear down the streets with howling sirens, and seen axe-wielding cops smashing up a speakeasy.

She'd met Dekker's friend Eliot Ness, an astonishingly young-looking man with an honest, square-jawed face like a clean-cut boy scout leader. They'd even gone on one of his raids, riding in the cab of the truck as it smashed through booze-warehouse doors, leaping out to help arrest the astonished gangsters inside.

They'd had lunch at a hot dog stand and dinner at their favourite Italian restaurant, where prohibition didn't seem to interfere with the flow of Chianti.

It was evening by the time they got back to Doc's place, and she invited Dekker in for a drink.

'Quite an offer,' he said. 'You and a bar, all to myself. Any chance Doc'll have an early night?'

'You're out of luck, Dekker. I don't think he sleeps at all.'

They went into the half-darkened bar and Luigi appeared from behind the scenes with a note from Doc. Ace read it, shrugged, and turned to Dekker. 'Sorry, I have to go to a party.'

'Have to?'

'I think I'd better. Doc's already there.' Dekker looked so crestfallen that she added, 'Why don't you come too?'

'I was planning on a smaller party, just the two of us.'

'Some other time – maybe. Have your drink while I change.'

Dekker sipped his bourbon and picked up a copy of the evening paper lying on the bar. He was still studying it when Ace came back down in one of her snazzy black evening numbers, so absorbed he didn't even notice the dress.

'Take a look at this – things are really busting loose. Seven guys gunned down in a garage on North Clark. Seven! They're calling it the St Valentine's Day Massacre.'

Ace studied the story. 'They're hinting Capone's behind it.'

'Al will have an alibi from here to breakfast. But the guys that got it just happen to be some of his worst enemies.' Dekker frowned. 'It's not like Al to pull something like this. He must have gone crazy.'

'That's nice,' said Ace. 'We're going to his party, and Doc's already there.'

26
Farewell Party

Looking like a slightly undersized James Bond in his immaculate evening dress, the Doctor stood sipping vintage champagne and observing Al Capone's party. It was a strange affair, he thought, with some very odd undercurrents. It was taking place in a private dining room on the same floor as Capone's suite. There was an elaborate buffet, smoked salmon, cold chicken and caviare, and waiters circulated with glasses of champagne. Most of the guests were men, solidly built, hard-eyed mobsters, though there was a scattering of what were usually referred to as party girls with short skirts, frizzed hair and cupid-bow mouths.

The focus of the affair seemed to be two men sitting at a corner table, one dark and sinisterly handsome, one like a balding middle-aged banker. Scalise and Anselmi, Capone's Sicilian killers. Quite clearly they were the heroes of the hour.

The Doctor became aware of Al Capone's vast bulk looming towards him. There was something strange about Capone tonight. He gave off a feeling of secret excitement, of powerful repressed energy, like a volcano on the point of eruption.

'Having a good time, Doc?' wheezed Capone.

'Yes indeed,' said the Doctor politely. 'I'd be grateful if we could find a moment to talk though – that little matter you mentioned over the telephone?'

'Later, Doc, later,' said Capone vaguely. 'We got a little ceremony to take care of first. You'll enjoy it.'

He raised his hand in a signal, and hard-eyed young

men began bustling the small fry out of the room. All the waiters went, all the party girls, and some of the men as well. When only a small select group was left, the doors were closed and locked and two guards stood with their backs to them.

Suddenly the room had gone very quiet. Capone went over to Scalise and Anselmi's table, and stood behind the two seated men.

'I just wanna say a few words about our two guests of honour,' he said. 'John Scalise and Albert Anselmi. They've done a lot of good work for me in the past. Deany O'Bannion coulda testified to that a while back, or the Gusenberg boys today – only unfortunately they ain't around any more.'

There was a ripple of knowing laughter and Capone went on, 'I think it's time these two boys got what they deserved, and I'm gonna give it to 'em – with this!'

Capone stretched out his hand and a waiting henchman put a baseball bat in it. Raising the bat high, he smashed it down on Scalise's skull. There was a dreadful cracking sound like someone smashing a coconut on concrete. Anselmi, spattered with his partner's blood, swung round in astonishment – and the bat rose and fell again.

'No!' shouted the Doctor and took a step forward. Something hard and metallic jabbed him in the ribs and Frank Rio's voice growled, 'Forget it, Doc!'

The Doctor's fingers flashed to Rio's wrist in a nerve-crushing grip. The gun thudded softly to the deep-pile carpet.

But it was already too late. The baseball bat was still rising and falling, and Scalise and Anselmi were beyond all help now. They lay slumped forward on the table, their ruined heads turning the white tablecloth scarlet.

The astonished bodyguard snatched up his automatic. Ignoring him, the Doctor stayed where he was.

Capone tossed the blood-stained bat aside. 'If you wanna know why they deserved what they got, they took on one assignment too many. That assignment was me. Someone offered them fifty thousand bucks to kill me –

well, you saw what it bought them.' He glared around the shocked and stunned assembly. 'Now I want you to meet tonight's real guest of honour. The man who offered these mugs that fifty grand. The man who came here talking about peace while all the time he was playing us off one against the other, so he could take over.' Capone's finger pointed. 'My old pal Doc!'

The crowd moved menacingly towards the Doctor.

The Doctor said, 'Wait! Listen to me!'

Somehow the authority in his voice stopped the gangsters where they stood. The Doctor stared unflinchingly back at Capone.

'Some of what you said tonight is true. Someone *has* been manipulating you all, stirring up trouble deliberately. But that someone's been lying to you, about your friends, about your enemies and above all about me! And he's skulking here tonight, revelling in the bloodshed he's caused. I dare him to show himself.'

The long drapes billowed in the corner of the room and suddenly a tall, thin man in evening dress was standing there.

'I am here, Doctor,' he said. 'I have come to savour your death.'

'Have you?' The Doctor took a crystal sphere from his pocket, tossing it up and down. 'And I have come to see the end of you!'

Up and down, up and down went the crystal sphere, higher and higher, caught in the Doctor's sure fingers and tossed again.

The tall man began walking towards it, hand outstretched, drawn by a yearning he could not control.

Ace and Dekker got into the Lexington easily enough. Ace's name was on the guest list, and when Dekker grabbed the minor thug on the lift by the necktie and growled, 'I'm with the lady,' the thug decided not to argue. Let them sort it out upstairs.

It was when they got up to Capone's floor that things got tricky. The doors to the dining room were locked and guarded by two Capone thugs. Ace caught Dekker's eye and they marched up to the guards.

'Sorry, sister, private party,' said one of them.

Ace gave him a sweet smile, a knee in the groin and a chop to the neck. The other turned his head to look and Dekker's fist caught him neatly under the jaw.

They dragged the bodies aside and listened at the door. Nothing came through it but a sinister silence.

They drew their guns, stepped back, and hurled themselves forward.

One more step, thought the Doctor. One more step and he'll touch the sphere, and I've got him.

The doors crashed open and Dekker and Ace appeared, guns in their hands. The spell broken, the tall man disappeared. The Doctor said something extremely coarse in Old Low Gallifreyan.

The crowd came to life and bodyguards' hands started moving towards their armpits.

Ace sprang across the room and stuck the muzzle of her Browning under Capone's jowly chin. 'Okay, we're leaving now. Mr Capone will see us down to our car.'

An ambitious bodyguard tried for a fast draw. Dekker spotted the move from the doorway and shot him in the right shoulder, blasting him to the ground.

As the crash of .45 died away Capone yelled, 'Okay, nobody move!' He started walking towards the door, Ace at his side.

The Doctor followed, they picked up Dekker at the door and made for the lift. It was pretty crowded with four of them inside, especially when one of the four was Al Capone, but they made it, and the lift sank down to the ground floor.

By the time they reached it, Dekker's gun was back in its holster and Ace's was in her bag, but the bag was jammed against Capone's side. They walked across the crowded hotel foyer, Capone's presence causing the usual stir.

Outside on the sidewalk Capone clapped the Doctor

on the shoulder, completely ignoring the threat of Ace's gun. 'Well, goodbye, Doc, thanks for coming. Swell party, eh? Drop by any time.' He nodded affably to Ace and Dekker, turned and went back into the hotel.

Dekker and Ace looked at each other in astonishment.

'It's all right,' said the Doctor. 'He's back to normal – or as normal as he ever is. Well, come on, can't you?'

They made their way back to Dekker's Buick. Dekker got behind the wheel, Ace got in the front passenger seat and the Doctor climbed in the back. He sat grumpily silent as they drove back towards Doc's Place.

Finally Dekker said, 'So don't go all mushy on us, Doc. I mean, I know it was pretty heroic of us to bust into Al Capone's HQ, rescue you and shoot our way out again, but you don't have to overwhelm us with gratitude this way.'

'Gratitude!' said the Doctor. 'You ruined everything! I almost had him. Then you two came bursting in and broke the link and he got away.'

Ace wasn't in the mood for any nonsense. 'That's tough, Doctor. You may have had *him* but Capone had you! All we knew was that Capone had gone on some kind of killing spree, and you were locked up in his hotel. Maybe we should have gone out for a few drinks and talked things over, but it seemed better to take some action.'

'Didn't I see two guys with their heads bashed in at a corner table?' said Dekker. 'Looked like what was left of Anselmi and Scalise. If Al's turning on his old friends like that, he could have gone back to bat, with your head as the ball.'

There was a moment of silence.

'You're absolutely right, both of you,' said the Doctor. 'My apologies, Mr Dekker. Let me make amends by offering you a nightcap.'

Dekker grinned at Ace. 'Hey, maybe the evening's back on course.'

They pulled up outside Doc's Place and went inside. Even Happy and Luigi had gone home by now, and Doc went behind the bar and served the drinks himself, two bourbons and a scotch.

'I think I'm getting a taste for this stuff,' he said gloomily. He picked up the paper which was still on the bar and read the account of the St Valentine's Day Massacre.

' "One of the killers was described as being particularly tall and thin." Well, we know who that was, don't we? He's winning every move, Ace. If I don't find him soon . . .'

'I thought you said he'd come and find us?'

As if in answer to her words, there came a thunderous knocking at the door. 'Open up – in the name of the law!'

'Oh no,' said the Doctor wearily. He rose to go to the door.

Dekker grabbed his arm. 'Take it easy, Doc.' He tapped the newspaper. 'There's been one lot of fake cops operating today at that garage massacre – if they were fakes, that is. Some people think they were real cops, paid by Capone.'

The hammering came again. 'Open up, or we'll bust it down!'

'There's something familiar about that voice,' said Dekker.

'Let's take a look from upstairs,' said the Doctor. They went up to the gaming room on the first floor and looked out. It was quite a sight. Doc's Place was ringed with armed police. The front of the place was lit up by a police searchlight. In front of the ring of police stood Captain Reilly, resplendent in his police overcoat and cap. Beside him was a tall thin man in civilian clothes. His overcoat was open to reveal evening dress.

Reilly was yelling through a police megaphone: 'We've got the place surrounded, front and back. Come out with your hands up, or we come in shooting. We know who you really are now, and we'll be taking no chances.'

The Doctor opened the window a crack and yelled, 'Who am I?'

'You're Doc McCoy, wanted for bank robbery in three states. We know you're armed and dangerous. Come out with your hands up, or we come in shooting.'

Dekker couldn't believe what he was hearing. 'Reilly's lost his marbles!'

'He's being influenced,' said the Doctor. 'Our thin friend tells a very convincing yarn.'

'He's nuts,' said Dekker. He stuck his head out of the window. 'Hey, Reilly, it's me, Dekker!'

There was the harsh chatter of a machine-gun and the window shattered into fragments.

'Hit the deck!' yelled Dekker, and they threw themselves down.

'He must have thought you said Dillinger,' said Ace. She had her gun out and was taking careful aim at the machine-gunner.

Dekker pushed down her arm. 'We're in a bad spot, Doc. There's too many to shoot our way out – and even if we did we'd be branded cop-killers. If we surrender . . .'

'We'd probably be shot trying to escape,' said the Doctor. 'They don't mean to take us alive, not if our thin friend has anything to do with it.'

'Well, in that case,' said Ace.

'Yes, I know. Mr Dekker, we're going to escape and you'll have to come with us. I apologize in advance for the shocks in store.'

The Doctor wriggled away from the window, got up and unlocked a door in the corner, revealing an empty store-room. In the middle of the room stood a square blue box.

Dekker looked at it in amazement. 'What's that?'

'Our way out,' said the Doctor. 'Questions later, Mr Dekker. Ace, could you fire out of the window without hitting anyone?'

'If you insist.' Ace fired a few shots out of the window, one of which knocked Reilly's cap off. There came a fusillade of shots in reply.

The Doctor flung open the window and yelled, 'Come and get me copper!' He left the window, went back and added, 'You dirty rat!' Then he returned to the others. 'I've always wanted to do that,' he said happily. 'Come along!' He bustled them into the TARDIS.

After repeated shouts and threats produced no reply,

Reilly's men broke open the door and piled nervously inside brandishing their weapons. They searched the place from attic to cellars, but there was no one there.

'It's impossible,' said Reilly. He looked round for the tall man who'd revealed the Doc's true identity but he'd faded away.

'There's just one thing,' said a nervous young recruit.

'Well?'

'I was in the front as we came in and I thought I heard a strange kind of sound from upstairs.'

'What sort of a sound?'

'It's hard to describe, Captain. It was kind of, I dunno, a sort of wheezing, groaning sound.'

'Get away with you,' said Reilly in frustration. 'Wheezing and groaning ... What kind of an eejit would make up a description like that?'

27

Escape to Danger

Romana and Bernice were in a dungeon.

It wasn't too bad, as dungeons go. It was light, clean and dry rather than dark, slimy and rat-ridden. There was a table and two wooden chairs. There was a wooden bed to sit on, a window to the outside world (small, high and barred), and an adjoining cell with basic sanitary facilities.

Nor were they being starved. Delicious meals from Lord Sargon's kitchen were brought to them with embarrassing regularity.

'Compared to some of the dungeons I've been in,' said Romana, pushing aside her plate, 'this is positively luxurious. The food is really rather good.'

Bernice, who had lost her appetite for once, was stretched out on the bed, hands behind her head. 'Suspiciously good if you ask me. I think we're being fattened up, and you know what for.'

After their capture by Sargon they had been marched off by the castle servants, locked up and more or less ignored.

Bernice took out the Doctor's signalling device. 'I wonder if this thing is still working? Maybe the batteries have run down.'

'It'll have an eternal power pack,' said Romana, who could be literal-minded at times. Bernice gave the signalling device an irritable shake. 'They took my blaster when they searched us. I wonder why Sargon didn't take this away from me?'

'Perhaps he didn't know what it was?'

'With the technology he's got in that laboratory? No, if

I've still got it, it must be because he wants me to have it. Maybe we should shut it off?'

'We can't. Once it's activated it stays on till it's deactivated from the TARDIS. And those things are practically indestructible.'

'Didn't you say you'd contacted the Doctor by telepathy? Can you do it again?'

'I tried. There was some kind of barrier.'

'Then if this thing's still transmitting,' said Bernice, 'and we can't stop it, we're leading the Doctor into a trap.'

When they got inside the TARDIS, the Doctor reacted swiftly and dramatically to a flashing light on the many-sided control console. 'Good grief, poor Bernice. Poor Romana too, come to that. I should have checked earlier. Well, that settles our destination.'

Ignoring the others, the Doctor became busy at the console.

Ace tried to explain things to Dekker, who had spotted the hatstand and hung up his trenchcoat and hat. Now he was looking around him with the mild interest of an American tourist in yet another European cathedral.

'It's bigger on the inside than on the outside, you see.'

Dekker nodded. 'Sure is.'

'That's because it's dimensionally transcendental,' Ace persevered. 'You see, it's really a sort of disguised ship. We're travelling through time and space.'

'That right?'

'We're going to help some friends of ours who are in trouble. They're on another planet in another time.'

'Okay by me, I need a vacation. Chicago's been bad for my health recently. Too much lead in the air.'

'What does it take to impress you, Dekker?' said Ace. 'The TARDIS is one of the wonders of the universe. Not too many people from Earth get to travel in it. The ones that do usually fall about in respectful amazement.'

'Yeah? Maybe they weren't from Chicago. Is there a drink on this ship of yours?'

'A drink?' Ace grinned. 'Dekker, we've got a whole swimming pool full of beer!'

'The Doctor has escaped – again!'

'Not for long. He goes where Agonal awaits. The Doctor had too many allies on Earth. On this planet he will be almost alone, and Agonal will be the stronger.'

'This time Agonal will surely destroy the Doctor.'

'And we shall take Agonal and use him for our great purpose. Is the device functional?'

'Fully functional.'

'Excellent! Death to the Doctor!

'Borusa lives!

'Rassilon must die!'

Dekker came back into the TARDIS control room. 'Ace is just changing, she'll be along in a moment –' He broke off. 'I see you've changed as well, Doc.'

The Doctor had changed out of his tuxedo and was now wearing a crumpled cream linen suit. A battered fedora with a paisley hatband was stuck on the back of his head and a colourful scarf was tucked into the neck of his cream silk shirt. A snazzy pair of two-tone brogues completed the outfit. He was carrying an umbrella with a question-mark handle, and there was a rather tired-looking bunch of white flowers tucked into his lapel.

'Swell outfit, Doc,' said Dekker politely.

'Oh just a few things I threw together. It's more me, really.'

Ace came into the control room wearing a black leather combat suit with a high collar. She wore gauntlets and knee-high boots. Her belt held a collection of pouches and gadgets Dekker didn't recognize and something he did: a holster and some weird kind of hand-gun. She gave Dekker a challenging look.

'I guess it's Hallowe'en where we're going,' said Dekker.

'It's practical, Dekker. Maybe you'd prefer a pink gingham dress with a white lace collar?'

'Depends on the occasion. How about a pair of black silk teddies?'

'Maybe I'm wearing them underneath.'

Dekker looked at the tight-fitting black-leather outfit and shook his head sadly. 'I don't know how a guy would ever find out. Not without a can-opener and a blowtorch.'

'How about you, Mr Dekker?' said the Doctor hurriedly. 'The TARDIS holds a wide variety of clothes and weapons. I'm sure we could find something to suit you.'

'Thanks, but I'll stick with what I'm used to, Doc.' Dekker went over to the hatstand, put on his battered soft hat and his shabby trenchcoat. He took out his big Colt .45 automatic, checked it over and put it back under his arm.

'A hat, a coat and a gun,' said Ace wryly. 'That's all you need to face the dangers of an alien planet?'

Dekker shrugged. 'Can't be much worse than downtown Chicago on a Saturday night. Ready when you are, Doc!'

The Doctor looked at the gizmo in the centre of the console. Its rise and fall was slowing down.

'Good,' he said. 'We're about to land.' He fished a faded bouquet of white flowers out of his pocket, divided it in two and handed one half to Ace, the other to Dekker. 'Wear these, will you?'

Dekker sniffed the flowers. 'Don't care for the smell, Doc.'

'Neither do some of our enemies.' The centre column stopped moving. 'We've landed,' said the Doctor. He opened the TARDIS doors.

The TARDIS had materialized on the edge of a wooded clearing. It was dusk, with the sun just sinking below the trees. Birds twittered, settling down for the night, and there was a distant chittering that might have been bats.

Dekker looked round. 'Like I said, a vacation in the country.'

244

'I do believe we've landed in the very same spot,' said the Doctor delightedly. 'Even though she hasn't actually ever been here before.' He patted the side of the TARDIS approvingly.

Shading his eyes, the Doctor peered across a stretch of open country beyond the woods. 'Look!' He pointed with his umbrella. Ace and Dekker looked. In the distance they saw an oddly shaped tower with a cluster of low buildings nearby. 'The Tower and the village,' said the Doctor. 'Come on!'

He led them along the edge of the woods and took a path that led past some agricultural land.

'I don't understand, Doctor,' said Ace. 'Where's Bernice? If you homed in on the signal . . .'

'Ah, but I didn't, not quite. I thought it might be wiser to find out more about the situation rather than charge right into the middle of it. Bernice is very near, I promise you.' He took out a device like an old-fashioned pocket watch and flipped it open. 'I took the precaution of bringing a tracer with me. We can find Bernice as soon as we like.'

They left the cultivated land and came to a crossroads. 'This way, I think,' said the Doctor. The road he chose led them to a village, silent buildings lining the one central road. There was no one about.

'Nice peaceful spot,' said Dekker.

An arrow whizzed into the ground before their feet. From somewhere ahead a voice called, 'Halt! Who are you?'

Ace and Dekker had already drawn their guns but the Doctor held up his hand. 'Please, don't kill anyone, it's not the best way to make friends.' He raised his voice. 'It's the Doctor and two friends. We are all wearing *garil*. Is Ivo in the village?'

Grey-cloaked figures appeared from between the huts and surrounded them. They carried bows with arrows already on the strings. One of them who wore the tattered remnants of a guard's uniform had a blaster.

'Best take 'em to the inn,' he said.

The Doctor and his friends were marched to a bigger building further down the street. It looked more like a field-hospital than an inn. A fire burned in the big fireplace and wounded men lay on improvised beds. Others, with arms, legs and heads bandaged, sat at long wooden tables while peasant girls served them with soup and bread.

'Strangers, Ivo!' called the man with the blaster.

A white-haired giant of a man came forward, carrying a massive tureen of soup. He put it down and advanced on them, looking suspiciously at the odd trio. 'Who are you? What do you want?'

The Doctor seized his hand. 'Ivo! How are you? I'm the Doctor. This is my friend Ace, and this is Mr Dekker.'

Ivo just stared at him. 'The Doctor? You?'

'Don't you remember the night we took the Tower? And the way you were rude to K-9 and I made you apologize?'

It took a lot more reminiscence before the Doctor's identity was established, but eventually Ivo accepted him.

'Where's Romana?' asked the Doctor.

'The Lady Romana was here until just a short time ago. She has hardly changed at all.' Ivo looked at the Doctor in sorrowful amazement. 'But you, Doctor . . . What have the years done to you? Your curly hair, and flashing teeth, all gone! And your fine clothes. And you've even shrunk!'

'Looks aren't everything, you know,' said the Doctor impatiently. 'There's a lot to be said for being inconspicuous. Now, I think you'd better tell me what's been going on around here. And how about some of that delicious soup?'

Dekker and Ace drank their soup and listened while Ivo told the Doctor of recent events, and of Bernice and Romana's part in them. His story ended with the failed peace conference and the bloody battle in the woods. 'We have been searching for the dead and wounded and bringing them in,' said Ivo. 'It has taken us most of the day.'

The Doctor looked at the mixed group of guards and guerillas. 'At least you're all working together.'

'At the end of the battle we joined forces and fought together against our common enemy. It was what saved us – that and the rising of the sun.'

'This guy Ivo's story reminds me of Chicago,' said Dekker. 'There's these guys trying to make peace but every time they get near it something happens, and always the worst possible something. Don't it strike you as kinda familiar, Doc?'

'Yes it does, Mr Dekker – which means my friends are in worse danger than I thought. Oh dear.' The Doctor took out his tracking device, studied the quivering needle and then pointed. 'What lies over that way, Ivo?'

'The castle of Lord Sargon.'

'Have you ever seen him?'

'He passed through the village once. A tall man, very thin.'

'That's our man. Can we raise a rescue force from this lot?'

'We can try, Doctor.' Ivo's voice became a bellow. 'Listen to me, all of you. This is the Doctor. Some of you will have heard of him. He helped us before. Now he needs help from us.'

The Doctor stood up. 'I believe Lady Romana and Lady Bernice are being held prisoner at the castle of Lord Sargon. If we can defeat him you'll have a real chance for peace, especially now you're working together. I'm looking for a few good men – a commando force, not an army. If anyone has the strength for one last fight, will they please come forward?'

For a moment no one moved. Then one by one, weary and wounded as they were, a handful of guards and guerillas came forward.

Ace surveyed them with a professional eye. 'Bit of a scratch lot, Doctor,' she whispered.

'They're all brave men, Ace, and they're all we've got.'

At sunset, Romana and Bernice were taken from the dungeon and brought back into the laboratory to stand before Lord Sargon.

247

Flanked by castle guards, he waited for them beside the great tank, looking proudly up at the winged horror that floated within.

'I rather think it's gloat time,' whispered Romana. 'Try to keep him talking. Lay the flattery on with a trowel.' Raising her voice she said, 'Congratulations, Lord Sargon. I thought only Time Lords had mastered regeneration technology to this extent.'

'A simple matter,' said Sargon. He pointed to the glass coffins holding Zargo, Camilla and Aukon. 'These three old friends of yours, Lady Romana, I regenerated from three piles of dust I found in the caves beneath the ship.'

Romana shuddered, remembering how the three vampires had crumbled to dust when the detached scout ship, the Doctor's 'mighty bolt of steel', had plunged down to pierce the Great Vampire's heart. Now here they were again, as large as death, and the Great Vampire was about to be restored as well.

'The experiment was not a great success,' Sargon went on. 'It appears that much of the brain tissue did not survive the regeneration process. These three are no longer the Zargo, Camilla and Aukon that you knew. They live only to kill, to feed... A few basic thought and speech patterns seem to remain. Camilla cut the throat of a soldier near the village with that little dagger of hers. Zargo killed some unfortunate village girl and drained her of blood in the Tower. Harking back to the good old days, you see.'

'And I suppose you brought the poor girl back to life as a vampire?' said Bernice.

'Of course.' Sargon waved at the other cases. 'It amused me to recreate still more vampires, from such remains as I could find. I tried them out last night, not without some success. One or two were lost.' He indicated a row of empty coffins. 'However, it will be easy enough to make more.'

'And what about the Great Vampire himself?' said Bernice. 'He can't have been easy. That really is an achievement.'

'You're very kind. Of course, I did have better material to work with.'

'The bits of the original body you took from the burial ground?'

'Exactly. I have hopes that my recreation of the Great Vampire will be a complete success. He will arise in all his former glory to rule this planet. I will make more and more Great Vampires. They will swarm out of E-Space and overrun galaxy upon galaxy.'

'Why?' asked Bernice. 'Why do all these horrible things?'

Sargon seemed to grow taller and stronger, glowing with evil energy. 'Because it amuses me, just as it amused me to encourage the miserable criminals of Earth to slaughter each other. Because I choose to feed upon the pain and death of inferior beings. Because I am Agonal!'

The Doctor's commando force met with surprisingly little resistance – which, as Ace pointed out, was just as well considering the shape it was in.

Limping and lurching along, they staggered through the night, reaching the outskirts of Sargon's castle just before dawn. A near-silent bolt from Ace's blaster disposed of the guard outside the main gate. She produced a rocket-gun with line and grapnel from a belt pouch, shot the grapnel over the wall, climbed the line and opened the gate from the inside. The little party crossed the court-yard to the inner door, which was locked. Another of Ace's pouches produced a silent plastic explosive which blew open the main door with a low thump.

The commandos staggered inside the main hall. An astonished guard opened his mouth to give an alarm and dropped with an arrow through his chest. Two more appeared and fell, one to Ivo's club and the other to the barrel of Dekker's Colt automatic.

The Doctor studied his tracer. 'This way!'

The device led them to the museum and straight up to the portrait of the Great Vampire. It took the Doctor only a moment to find the secret door. He turned to Ivo. 'You and the others stay here and guard our backs. Ace, Mr Dekker, come with me.'

As the Doctor went through the door he heard a hateful voice saying, 'And now we come to your part in our ceremony, ladies. It is time for the Great Vampire to arise. But first he must feed, not upon artificial nutrients, but upon his natural food – blood. I have a large quantity in store, but I propose to add an extra delicacy: your blood, ladies. The blood of a Time Lady will be particularly nourishing.'

From the top of the stairs, the Doctor saw Romana, Bernice and the tall figure of Agonal. All stood with their backs to him, staring at the floating horror in the tank. They were surrounded by a semicircle of armed guards – four of them.

The Doctor heard Romana's high clear voice. 'Exactly what are you planning to do?'

'I shall revive the Great Vampire and drop you into the tank with him. He will react to your movements, clasp you in his claws and feed. It should be an interesting spectacle.'

'Ace, take out the guards,' whispered the Doctor. 'Blaster on stun, please – as quick as you can. Mr Dekker, come with me.'

The Doctor and Dekker clattered down the staircase. 'Romana, Bernice, this way!' yelled the Doctor. Even as the little group started to turn, Ace began a deadly accurate fire over the Doctor's head. One of the guards dropped before he could reach his blaster. Of the remaining three, two fell with blasters half-drawn. Only the last guard got off a shot, and that went into the ceiling.

Romana and Bernice were running towards the bottom of the steps. For a moment Agonal watched them, frozen in disbelief. Then he swung round, pointing a long white finger, and hissed a command. The lids of the upright glass coffins holding Zargo, Camilla and Aukon swung open. The three vampires stalked forth, eyes glowing, fangs bared, claw-like hands reaching out.

28

Gallifrey

The three vampires glided after Romana and Bernice with incredible speed. By the time the two women reached the bottom of the stairs their ghastly pursuers were close behind them.

The Doctor heard Ace coming down the steps. 'Don't shoot,' he called. 'Energy weapons don't work. It's up to you, Mr Dekker. In the heart, remember – it must be in the heart!'

'Okay, Doc.' Dekker raised his .45, the heavy automatic steady in his big hand. 'Get down, ladies!'

As Romana and Bernice flung themselves down at the foot of the steps, Zargo sprang. Dekker fired twice, *Blam-blam* and Zargo was slammed back, a red stain spreading on the breast of his robe.

Aukon attacked next. The gun roared twice in quick succession and Aukon fell, his white robe flooded with red.

Camilla sprang – and just for a moment, Dekker hesitated.

In that moment Camilla was upon him, white arms clasping him with incredible strength, long fangs lunging for his throat.

'Shoot, Dekker!' shouted Ace. 'She's not human!'

With a mighty effort, Dekker flung the vampire away from him, and as she sprang back to the attack he fired twice, *blam-blam*! The impact flung the vampire across the laboratory, and she crumpled and fell in a bloody heap.

Some people say the old 1911 Model Army Colt Auto-

251

matic is big and clumsy and noisy. Maybe it is. But hit them in the heart with two slugs from a .45 and they go down and stay down. Even if they're vampires.

All this happened so quickly that Agonal had no time to react. The Doctor stepped forward quickly, tossing the glowing crystal sphere in the air. 'Agonal – look!'

Agonal's eyes fastened on the sphere, and he froze. The Doctor tossed the sphere, up and down, up and down. Agonal began taking slow steps towards him, drawn by a force he could not resist.

Then something extraordinary happened. A pyramid of blackness appeared in the laboratory. Spinning over and over, it engulfed Agonal and whisked him away.

For a moment the Doctor stood there, amazed and enraged.

'Timescooped!' he yelled. 'Of all the interfering...' With an effort, he dragged his mind back to present problems. He whirled round. 'Ace! Get everyone out of here – those guards as well. Tell Ivo to get everyone else out he can find, friend or foe. You've got about five minutes!'

'What are you going to do?'

'Turn up the pressure cooker. Move!'

No situation, however urgent, could override Romana's aristocratic politeness. She paused at the bottom of the steps looking at the odd-looking little man who had turned up to save her. 'I really must thank –' Her eyes widened. 'Doctor?'

Briefly the Doctor smiled. 'Later, Romana. Now go!'

Romana turned to Dekker, who was holding onto the rail of the metal steps. 'I must thank you too.'

'My pleasure, lady,' said Dekker, and slid gently to the ground. Only then did they see the handle of Camilla's little silver dagger projecting from his left side.

The Doctor took in the situation in one quick glance and gave a stream of orders. 'Don't touch the dagger. Find a stretcher, get him back to the TARDIS. Everyone out. Now!'

Ace took charge. 'Hello Benny!' She kicked the stunned

252

guards into consciousness. 'You lot, move – help me to get him up the steps.'

Romana and Bernice hurried away while Ace chivvied the dazed guards into carrying Dekker's body up the metal staircase.

The Doctor hurried over to the bank of controls. Their function was quite familiar to him, he'd done some work in this field himself a long time ago. This was Time Lord technology.

It didn't take the Doctor long to achieve the results he wanted. It was basically a matter of turning everything up to maximum. As the control room started to shudder and throb he turned to look at the thing in the tank. It was stirring, flexing its great leathery wings. The green eyes opened and glared at him with unutterable malevolence.

'Nice to meet you too,' said the Doctor. He turned and ran swiftly up the metal steps.

It was almost dawn when the Doctor came out of the castle. At the foot of the hill he found Ace, Bernice, Romana and Ivo, and a mixed band of guerillas and guards. The four castle-guard prisoners were holding a rough stretcher on which lay Dekker's body. Ace had pulled open his shirt and was clamping a flat metal disc onto his chest, close to the wound. Dekker's body arched for a moment and then slumped back, motionless. A thin rime of frost began spreading over his face.

'Field cryogenics,' said Ace, in answer to Bernice's enquiring look. 'He's in stasis now. He'll stay like this, no better no worse till we can get him proper medical attention.'

'We'll get him the best, Ace,' said the Doctor.

'He won't die,' said Ace fiercely. 'I won't let him.'

'Look!' shouted Ivo. 'The castle!'

The castle was shaking itself apart. A spider-web network of splits appeared across the main facade. Turrets crumbled and fell, their masonry crashing into the courtyard.

As the main building fell in upon itself a great fountain of blood arose, shooting many hundreds of feet into the

253

air. Borne aloft on that fountain was the hideous form of the Great Vampire.

As the fountain fell, the immense blood-stained form of the Great Vampire stayed aloft, unfurling its great leathery wings and flapping them in triumph. The green eyes glared down at them and it gave a loud, hissing cry. In a moment it would swoop down and choose its prey.

Bernice grabbed the Doctor's arm. 'You've revived it, not destroyed it!'

'Wait!' said the Doctor. But he looked a little worried all the same.

The sun rose over the hill and its first rays touched the Great Vampire's bloody wings. It shrieked, flapped its wings and rose higher – and began to disintegrate like the castle from which it had arisen.

Its body melted into shapeless globs of rotting meat, and its bloody remains showered down upon the ruins of the castle.

Romana swallowed hard. 'What was it, Doctor, the sunlight?'

'Not entirely, though it helped. I forced the regeneration – and besides it was inherently unstable. Agonal was using borrowed technology. He didn't really know what he was doing.'

The ground began to shake beneath their feet and the Doctor yelled, 'Quick everyone, move!'

As they hurried away from the castle a great pillar of fire erupted from the ruins and rose high into the sky.

'That's the main power source,' said the Doctor with satisfaction. 'Fire's a great cleanser.'

The little procession hurried away.

Lord Yarven staggered wearily towards the inn. He had plucked Tarak's arrow from his heart, and the wound was healing well. He had feasted on the blood of the dying with his fellow vampires and he knew he would soon regain his strength. But at the moment he desperately needed rest. Rest and darkness.

Thankful that the place seemed deserted, he lurched into the dark shadows of the barn behind the inn.

'There are probably still a few of the old true vampires left,' said the Doctor. 'Apart from those *ersatz* creations of Sargon's, I mean. But without Sargon stirring up trouble all the time, you should be able to hunt them down. The important thing is for peasants and Lords and Black Guards all to work together.'

He was standing with Romana and Ivo outside the inn, waiting for Bernice to get her things together so they could leave. At Ace's insistence they had carried Dekker straight to the TARDIS. She was waiting there for them now.

'We'll try, Doctor,' said Ivo wearily. 'It means going back to the beginning.'

'Not quite,' said the Doctor. He raised his voice so that those around them could hear. 'You've worked together already, guards and peasants in alliance, to defeat Sargon. That's something to build on.' He looked round impatiently. 'What's keeping Bernice?'

'I'll find her for you, Doctor,' said Ivo and hurried away.

Romana looked round at the weary little group of men, drinking Ivo's rough wine and talking over their victory. 'That's why you asked for their help, isn't it Doctor?' she said quietly.

The Doctor smiled. 'My half-crippled commandos? Maybe I didn't really need them. I had Dekker, and Ace is a one-woman army in herself. But now they've got a victory to share.'

Bernice came round from behind the inn. She had her pack on her back and she was followed by Ivo and the four castle-guards who were carrying an enormous wooden packing case between them.

'What's that?' demanded the Doctor.

'My archeological specimens,' said Bernice defiantly. 'I did manage to collect a few interesting local artefacts before I got involved with vampires. That's why you sent me here, remember? What's the matter, not enough room in the TARDIS?'

'All right, all right,' said the Doctor. He held out his hand. 'Goodbye, Ivo. Good luck.'

The Doctor and Ivo shook hands.

Romana held out her hand graciously and Ivo went down on one knee and kissed it. While he was down there, Bernice flung her arms round his neck and kissed him, making him blush furiously.

They set off for the TARDIS.

The TARDIS was in flight and there was little to do but wait. Ace came back into the control room and found Bernice sitting on her packing case, which she couldn't be bothered to move. The Doctor and Romana were standing on the other side of the console.

'How is he?' asked Bernice.

Ace sat down the packing case beside her. 'Much the same, but that's the idea. The Doctor says the Time Lords have the finest doctors in the galaxy on Gallifrey.'

'Well, they would, wouldn't they?' said Bernice. 'Talking of Time Lords . . .'

Ace looked across the control room. The Doctor and Romana were standing face to face, arms outstretched, fingertips resting lightly on each other's temples.

'Sickening isn't it?' said Ace. 'She's not staying, is she?'

Bernice shrugged. 'She might. She's the only one of the Doctor's companions who's not – ordinary.'

'I'm not ordinary,' said Ace. 'Neither are you.' She stood up. 'I've got a bottle of bootleg booze in my room. Come and have a drink and I'll tell you about Chicago.'

As they left the room the Doctor and Romana lowered their arms and stepped back. They stood silent for a moment, each absorbing the flow of information.

'Well,' said the Doctor at last. 'You have had a time.'

'So have you, Doctor. Several times in fact.'

The Doctor smiled. 'So the Tharils are all free?'

'Most of them. Now the ones that are free are busy freeing the rest of them.'

'And you discovered they didn't need you?'

'I discovered they needed to do it on their own.'

'That's the hardest lesson – learning to walk away. And K-9?'

'He's Biroc's Lord High Administrator. He runs things on very logical lines.' Romana studied the controls. 'We seem to have left E-Space. Isn't that a problem?'

'Not any more. K-9 worked out the mathematics just before you both left. Then we got blasted back into normal space, and I didn't need to use them. It's easy enough once you know how.'

'Most things are.'

'Did you ever build another TARDIS to K-9's specifications?'

'I was very busy,' said Romana a little defensively. 'I never quite got round to it. Still it doesn't matter now does it, Doctor? Now we're going home.'

'Gallifrey?' said the Doctor. 'Home?'

'Agonal is ours at last!' The speaker's voice was exultant.

'But can we hold him?' asked the second figure.

'Long enough – at least until the Doctor arrives.'

'Ah yes, the Doctor,' said the third speaker. *'He will be here soon. We must arrange for his reception.'*

'Death to the Doctor!'

'Borusa lives!'

'Let's dispense with the ritual chant for once, shall we?' said the first speaker irritably. *'It's beginning to get on my nerves.'*

The approach of the TARDIS had been registered on one of the most advanced security scanning systems in the universe. Since it was undoubtedly a Time Lord craft, and it was transmitting an emergency distress signal the transduction barriers were lowered and it was allowed to land. Now two puzzled technicians in Security Control were wondering what to do next.

'It's a Type Forty,' said one of them. 'A Type Forty – and still operational!'

The other was hastily skimming the flow of data across a screen. 'According to this, there's only one Type Forty still in use – by someone known as the Doctor.'

'And who's he, when he's at home?'

'He isn't very often, seems to spend most of his time roaming the universe. As to who he is, the records are rather confusing. At one time or another he's been a wandering fugitive, a suspected traitor and assassin, and Lord President of Gallifrey. Present status and whereabouts uncertain.'

'I don't know about status,' said the first technician. 'But I can tell you his current whereabouts – right in the centre of the Capitol. He's just landed.'

'Better call out the guard then.'

'I already have.'

'Hang on, there's a fresh note on the file. "Any information regarding the Time Lord known as the Doctor is to be reported immediately to the Committee of Three".'

The Type Forty capsule, in the form of a large blue box, was located at a corridor junction close to the centre of the Capitol. It was immediately surrounded by a squad of Chancellery Guards under Commander Leran, young, keen and desperately determined to do the right thing.

The door of the blue box opened and four strangely dressed people emerged, carrying a stretcher between them. On the stretcher lay a large man covered with the white rime of cryogenic stasis.

As Leran opened his mouth to bark commands and questions, the man at the front of the stretcher said, 'Well done, you've wasted no time. Have four of your men take this stretcher and conduct us immediately to the Chief Hospitaller. If I got the landing details right, we should be very close.'

Commander Leran shut his mouth, opened it again and said, 'I must insist – '

There was a blur of movement at his side. The tall girl

in black leather, who was holding her corner of the stretcher with her left hand, drew a laser-gun with her right and stuck it in Leran's ear.

In a voice colder than the cryogenic rime she said, '*Do as the Doctor says.*'

'It's all right, Ace,' said the Doctor. To Leran he said, 'I am the Doctor, one-time President of Gallifrey and Special Envoy of the High Council.' With his free hand he fished a gleaming gold badge from his pocket and showed it briefly to the bemused young man. 'Just take us to the Hospitaller. I take full responsibility.'

The magic words did the trick. At a barked order from Leran four of his men took over the stretcher and he led them away down the corridor. The four strangers followed, and the rest of the guards fell in behind.

Ace holstered her blaster. 'What did you show him, Doctor?'

'My old Reichsinspektor General badge. In an authoritarian society – '

' – people obey the voice of authority. Yes, I know, Doctor. This had better work.'

They marched along an immense echoing marble corridor, passed through an archway and entered into an area of high-ceilinged white-walled rooms filled with quietly humming machinery. A white-robed meditech appeared and Leran barked, 'The Chief Hospitaller, please. Immediate and urgent.'

After a wait which had Ace reaching for her blaster again, a tall beaky-nosed old man in a high-collared white robe appeared, followed by a large and respectful entourage of meditechs.

The Doctor stepped forward. 'Chief Hospitaller, I have a patient for you.'

'Good grief,' said the old man mildly. 'An actual patient – a live one?'

'That's right,' said Ace. 'And he'd better stay that way.'

Ignoring her, the old man snapped, 'Details?'

'Adult male human, thirties, knife wound close to heart,

dealt by vampiric entity, field cryogenic pack applied soon after wounding,' said the Doctor rapidly.

The old man sniffed. 'Sounds straightforward enough.'

'Recovery estimate?'

'Oh, eighty per cent, maybe eighty-five. Slightly lower if the blade was poisoned.' The old man peered at him, making brief mental contact. 'It's the Doctor, isn't it? Another regeneration I see, and in trouble as usual.'

'I'd like to ask a favour, Chief Hospitaller. This man has done me and Gallifrey great service on a dangerous mission – which is not yet concluded. If anything happens to me, I'd be grateful if you'd see that he's cured and sent home to his own time.'

'Very well, Doctor, I'll attend to it.'

'Word of a Prydonian?'

'Word of a Prydonian.'

As the old man and his entourage bore Dekker away, the Doctor said, 'He'll be all right now, Ace, whatever happens. That's an unbreakable oath.'

'Isn't it time we made contact with the authorities, Doctor?' asked Romana.

Bernice pointed down the corridor. 'I think the authorities are about to make contact with us.'

A squad of six black-clad soldiers was marching down the immense corridor towards them. They looked a very different kind of soldier from the first lot. The elaborate red, white and gold uniforms worn by the aristocratic young men of the Chancellery Guard had a reassuringly comic opera look about them. These hard-faced troopers reminded Ace of the SS.

Their leader handed Commander Leran a scroll. 'I am Lieutenant Zorell of Special Security, Commander. You will hand your prisoners over to me – by order of the Committee of Three.' As Leran and his guards marched away, Zorell beckoned the young meditech who had first received them. 'I understand there is a fifth prisoner. Fetch him out.'

Ace tensed, but the Doctor patted her arm reassuringly. 'There are no prisoners here, only patients,' said the meditech. 'Your committee holds no authority over them. You will please leave this area immediately.'

After a very long pause Zorell said, 'Very well. Your attitude will be reported to the committee.' He turned to Ace. 'Your weapon please. The belt as well. It is illegal for aliens to carry arms in the Capitol.'

Ace took off the belt with its holstered blaster and passed it over.

'Before you ask, the rest of us aren't armed,' said the Doctor. 'Now, Lieutenant, I need an audience with the President immediately. If she's not available, take me to a senior member of the High Council.'

'All in good time, Doctor.'

The Doctor glanced at Ace, raising his voice. 'I tell you I *must* see the President!'

Zorell ignored him and Romana stepped forward. 'Lieutenant, I am the Lady Romanadvoratrelundar and I should like to know the meaning – '

'We know who you are,' said Zorell. 'You defied an order to return to Gallifrey, did you not? You are a renegade and a fugitive like the Doctor.'

'What about me?' asked Bernice.

Zorell looked disparagingly at her. 'Omega knows. You look like one of those Shobogan bitches to me.'

'Thanks very much. Is that a crime?'

'Unfortunately not. But consorting with known felons is – not to mention unauthorized entry to the Capitol precincts. Sergeant, take two men and put these women in the custody suite.' Zorell turned back to the Doctor. 'As for you, Doctor, you are summoned to appear before the Committee of Three – immediately.'

Separated from his companions, and flanked by two black-uniformed soldiers, the Doctor was marched away.

29

The Three

The custody suite turned out to be a large, luxurious room, elaborately over-decorated in typical Time Lord style. There were ornately designed chairs, tables, couches, lamps and mirrors. There was a wallscreen and audio unit. There was even a dial-anything-you-like food and drink dispenser much like the one on the TARDIS.

Ace's quick check of the rooms off the main area revealed bedrooms, bathrooms, a gymnasium and a small swimming pool. Everything except a way out.

'What is this place?' she asked disgustedly. 'The Gallifrey Hilton?'

Romana went over to the wallscreen and switched it on. It was showing a Public Record Video programme, the ceremonial inauguration of President Flavia. The President, a small, neat woman, looked lost in the middle of the swirling crowd of tall colourfully robed Time Lords. Romana switched off the wallscreen and threw herself gracefully onto an overstuffed couch.

'Beats the last place we were locked up in,' said Bernice. She went over to the dispenser and dialled herself a large brandy. 'What do you think, Romana?'

'I think it's an oubliette.'

Bernice frowned. 'Like those tiny cells in castles? Chuck in awkward prisoners and forget all about them?'

'Yes, only we Time Lords are so much more civilized. We provide food, drink, sanitation, entertainment, exercise ... Don't you see, this isn't just some temporary holding area, they can leave us here forever.'

Bernice sipped her brandy. 'Like "*Huis-Clos*".'

Ace was studying the double doors by which they'd entered. 'Come again?'

'An Old Earth play I read once. Somebody dies and goes to hell and finds it's this room with two other people in it – forever!' Bernice swigged down the rest of her brandy and shuddered. 'They wouldn't do that to us, would they?'

Romana shrugged. 'I'm not sure what they might do. Things seem to have changed for the worse since I was last on Gallifrey.'

The doors were made of some gold-coloured metal, decorated with elaborate scroll-work. They were designed to slide apart, only there was no control on the inside. They were in a very superior prison.

'Well, I don't know about you two,' said Ace, 'but I'm not stopping. You heard the Doctor. He said he had to see the President, and he was looking at me when he said it.'

She reached up to her high collar and began peeling off the edging.

The Doctor had been taken to a small windowless conference chamber somewhere deep beneath the Capitol. The room held a long table on a raised dais at one end, with three high-backed chairs behind it, and one uncomfortable-looking metal one in front of it. The metal chair was fastened to the floor.

The Doctor was thrust into the metal chair. Wrist-clamps slid out from the arms, holding him fast. Zorell and the black-clad guards took up positions by the door.

The Doctor waited. After a while he started singing an old Earth ballad in a loud tuneless voice. The words of the ballad consisted of the phrase 'Why are we waiting?' sung over and over again.

'Silence!' bellowed Zorell. The Doctor ignored him.

In a cell not far way, Agonal was imprisoned in a cone of light. Three cloaked and hooded figures watched him from the darkness beyond. A wallscreen showed the Doctor imprisoned in the metal chair.

The taller of the three figures said, 'As you see, the Doctor is our prisoner. The Doctor who scorns you, who has hunted you, who has ruined your schemes, who has twice almost captured you. Aid us and he is yours.'

Agonal did not speak.

The second figure said, 'We helped you to regenerate the vampires, even the Great Vampire, with our technology. The Doctor destroyed your work, frustrated your plans.'

The third speaker said, 'Help us and you shall have your revenge.'

There was a long silence. Then Agonal spoke, his voice a little muffled by the immensely powerful energy-field that held him captive. 'What would you have me do?'

Ace had pulled all the edging from her jacket, leaving her with a long strip of soft black material rather like old-fashioned liquorice. She slipped a knife from her boot and began packing the long black strip along the fine line that marked the meeting point of the two doors.

Romana and Bernice looked on admiringly.

'You're certainly not without resources are you?' said Romana.

'Amateurs,' said Ace scornfully. 'Hand over your gun-belt and that's it? Amateurs!'

She finished packing in the black stuff, put her jacket back on and pulled off two of the buttons.

'Time to take cover. This next bit is best viewed from behind the sofa.'

Feeling rather silly, Bernice and Romana ducked down behind an oversized couch. Ace stuck the buttons at the top and bottom of the strip of black stuff and then pressed down hard on the centre of each one in turn. The buttons started pulsing with light, and Ace ran to join Romana and Bernice.

Peering over the back of the sofa, they watched as a fierce white light ran out from the buttons and along the strip. When the two lines of light met there was a flash and a dull *crump* – and the doors gaped open.

Ace jumped up and slipped through the gap. Hurriedly Bernice and Romana followed.

A hidden door slid open behind the table, and three figures emerged and took their places in the three chairs. They wore the elaborate high-collared robes of members of the High Council. The Doctor regarded them with polite interest.

The councillor in the central chair was tall, broad-shouldered and handsome, with a great beak of a nose and golden hair. He wore the orange and scarlet of the Prydonian Chapter.

The other two councillors were considerably less impressive. The one on the Doctor's left wore the green of the Arcalians. He was small and wizened with a pinched, mean face. The one to his right, robed in the heliotrope of the Patraxes, was plump and sleek with thick lips in a round, sensual face.

The central figure spoke. 'I am Councillor Rath,' he said. He waved a hand towards the plump figure on his left. 'This is Councillor Elar.' He nodded to his right. 'This is Councillor Morin. We are the Committee of Three – a special committee of the High Council responsible for matters of security.'

'With a squad of bully boys to back you up?'

'The functions of the Chancellery Guard, Doctor, as you must know, are largely ceremonial –'

'That's how I like my soldiers: aristocratic, decorative and useless. Much safer for everyone.'

Elar said, 'We wish to know why you have returned to Gallifrey, Doctor.'

'We *insist* on knowing,' said Morin.

The Doctor ignored them. He was staring hard at Rath. 'You're very like your elder brother, aren't you? I knew Chancellor Goth very well.'

'You ended his career, Doctor – and his life.'

265

'I understood that Chancellor Goth died in a heroic attempt to capture the Master?'

'That was the cover story. My committee uncovered the truth.'

The Doctor was silent for a moment. 'Then you know that the Master used your brother as his champion against me in the Matrix – and sacrificed him. Your brother died because his mind was burnt out by the strain.'

'After you had defeated him! I have a second, even better reason to hate you, Doctor, you and all your previous selves. Not that I will allow the fact to prejudice me against you.'

The Doctor's gaze swept scornfully across the little group. 'So, what have we here? An ambitious Prydonian, with his career blocked through guilt by association. Oh, I know there was a cover story but the people who mattered knew the truth, they always do. So he allies himself with an Arcalian and a Patraxean – a couple of insignificant high-benchers.'

Elar and Morin reacted angrily to the insult. Time Lords of any importance sit on the lower levels of the benches that run round the great circular Council Chamber. Only the insignificant perch up near the roof.

'And what do this precious trio do?' asked the Doctor rhetorically. 'They form themselves into a nice little committee and take over security – an area no right-minded Time Lord could be bothered with. Gradually they get their hands on more and more power. What's the final plan, gentlemen? Shoot down the Chancellery Guard and oust President Flavia in a coup?'

Elar sprang to his feet. 'We have far more ambitious plans than that, Doctor – '

At an angry look from Rath he subsided into his seat.

'Our plans do not concern you, Doctor,' said Rath. 'It is your plans that concern us. Why did you return to Gallifrey?'

'I can disclose that only to the President.'

'We can compel you to speak, Doctor.'

At a sign from Rath, Zorell's two guards wheeled forward a sinister-looking contraption consisting of a set of controls with a metal helmet suspended above them.

'Oh no,' said the Doctor wearily. 'Not the mind-probe!'

Romana, Ace and Bernice were hurrying along endless echoing marble corridors.

'Are you sure you know where the Presidential office is?' demanded Bernice.

Romana looked worried. 'I used to, but I've been away for quite some time.'

A tall, blond and handsome captain in the Chancellery Guard came round the corner and marched straight towards them. Ace went instinctively for the knife in her boot, but Romana pushed her hand away.

'Oh Captain!' she called in her highest, most aristocratic voice.

The captain hurried up to her. 'My Lady?'

'I am the Lady Romanadvoratrelundar.'

He gave her an elaborate salute. 'I don't think I've had the honour of meeting you before.'

'I've been away from Gallifrey, on a mission to the outer planets.' She lowered her voice. 'I've brought a delegation from the Barbarian Women's Committee back to meet the President and I just can't seem to find her office.'

'Allow me to escort you, my Lady.'

He led them along the corridors, looking curiously at Ace and Bernice. 'I admire your courage, my Lady. To dare to leave the civilization of Gallifrey for the barbarism of the outer planets – and to mingle with such creatures as these! Can they talk?'

'Oh, just a few simple phrases. Actually, they're quite sweet when you get to know them.'

Ace chucked the astonished captain under the chin. 'Me Jane! You Tarzan?'

He blushed. 'I'm sorry?'

'It's a mating call,' said Bernice. 'I think she likes you.' She smiled seductively at him. 'I like you too!'

The captain increased his pace.

* * *

Summoning up all his resources, all his mental barriers, the Doctor stared straight ahead as the mind-probe helmet was lowered over his head. He could, he knew, resist the mind-probe for a time. But not for ever. Nobody could.

'Why did you come back to Gallifrey?' asked Rath.

'I will speak only to the President.'

An agonizing jolt seared through the Doctor's brain.

'Why did you come back to Gallifrey?' Another searing jolt, a little stronger this time.

'Why did you come back to Gallifrey?'

It went on for some time like this, getting steadily worse. As he felt consciousness slipping away, the Doctor sensed that his interrogators were simply going through the motions. They didn't really want to find out why he'd come back to Gallifrey. Either they already knew or they didn't care.

They were torturing him just for the fun of it.

Lady Flavia was hard at work in her office, her enormous desk piled high with papers, scrolls and micro-records, the extraordinary mixture of old and new that was Gallifreyan bureaucracy. Since she had given strict orders that she was not to be disturbed on any account, she was surprised to see Secretary Pogarel enter her office, followed closely by several complete strangers.

'What is the meaning of this, Secretary Pogarel?' she said without looking up. 'Why have you brought people to see me against all my orders?'

Pogarel, a lean, precise Gallifreyan bureaucrat, spoke with his usual dignity. 'For two good reasons, Madame President. Firstly, one of them, the Lady Romanadvoratre-lundar, convinced me that the matter was indeed one of great importance.'

'And the second?'

'The tall young lady in black is holding an extremely sharp knife between my ribs.'

President Flavia looked up. She waved her secretary

aside and studied the strangely assorted trio. A thought struck her.

'You wouldn't be friends of the Doctor by any chance?'

The voices seemed to come from very far away.

'I'm afraid he's fainted, Councillor Rath. No use going on till we can revive him. It'll take a little time.'

'I'm afraid we don't have time, Lieutenant. We have a vital mission to complete – the culmination of all our plans. I'll have to leave him to you. See if you can soften him up for me before we get back.'

'My pleasure, Councillor.'

'Don't get carried away, though. I need him alive.'

Opening his eyes with an immense effort, the Doctor saw the three councillors disappearing through the door by which they had entered.

He slipped back into unconsciousness.

In the secret chamber the wallscreen showed the unconscious Doctor slumped back in the metal chair, black-clad figures grouped around him. One of them slapped his face, again and again.

Rath, Elar and Morin confronted the imprisoned Agonal.

'You see the Doctor, a helpless prisoner in our hands,' said Elar.

'You see his suffering,' said Morin. 'He can suffer more, much more before he dies.'

Agonal said nothing, but for a moment a spark of red glowed in his eyes.

Rath said, 'You will do as we ask? We are agreed?'

'We are agreed,' said Agonal. 'And when it is done, you will give me the Doctor. He shall suffer agonies of torment for all the rest of his Time Lord lives.'

Rath touched a control and the cone of light faded, leaving Agonal free. The three stepped back, wary of the force they had unleashed. Agonal did not move.

Rath touched another control and a transmat-booth lit

up in the corner of the chamber. 'If you will come with us?'

'I have no need of such devices,' said Agonal. 'We meet at the Tomb.' He stood regarding them scornfully for a moment and then faded into nothingness.

The Doctor felt Zorell's hand under his chin, shoving his head back.

'Good, he's coming round. Look, this is getting boring. Let's put up the power two levels each time. That'll make him talkative.'

'Or an idiot,' said the first guard.

'Or a talkative idiot!' said the second.

Zorell laughed. 'They only said he had to be alive. They didn't say he had to be sane.'

The main door of the chamber was flung open and a burly, broad-shouldered figure strode in. The newcomer wore plain robes and a close-fitting helmet. He had a barrel-chest, big hands and a stern, weathered face with a heavy jaw. He was Castellan Spandrell, Commander of the Chancellery Guard, and he was Gallifrey's version of a tough cop. He and the Doctor were old friends.

'Good old Spandrell!' thought the Doctor muzzily. He wondered if he was dreaming.

Castellan Spandrell strode over to Zorell and swatted him, a bear-like backhanded blow that knocked him off his feet. Zorell staggered back up, clawing for his blaster, and Spandrell clouted him again, so hard that he went down and stayed down.

By now the two guards had drawn their blasters. Ignoring the weapons, Spandrell grabbed each one by the collar and knocked their heads together with a resounding clunk, dropping the unconscious bodies to the floor.

If it was a dream, it was quite a good one, thought the Doctor. Chancellery Guards were flooding into the little room. 'Clear out this rubbish and lock them up,' ordered Spandrell. 'Come along, Doctor.' He released the clamps and lifted the Doctor's limp body from the metal chair.

* * *

When the Doctor came round he was in a high-backed chair in President Flavia's office, with the President herself holding a silver flask to his lips.

The Doctor took a refreshing sip and felt an almost miraculous sense of strength and well-being flooding through his body.

He tried to push the flask away. 'The Elixir of Life,' he whispered. 'Madame President, it is too precious . . .'

'Drink, Doctor,' said Flavia firmly. 'A little is kept for emergencies, and no one deserves it more.'

The Doctor took a measured sip and handed back the flask. He looked up and saw Romana, Ace and Bernice looking anxiously at him. He held out his hands and they crowded round him.

Romana said, 'I hope you are somewhat recovered, Doctor?'

Ace touched him briefly on the shoulder. 'All right, Doc?'

Bernice hugged him and burst into tears.

'Your friends' methods are vigorous but effective, Doctor,' said Flavia. 'They broke free of confinement and told me of your danger. You owe them your freedom.'

'I owe them my sanity,' said the Doctor. 'And very probably my life as well.' He patted Bernice awkwardly on the back. 'Well, this is all very nice but we can't just sit here. There's work to be done.'

'You need not exert yourself further, Doctor,' said Flavia. 'Castellan Spandrell has matters well in hand. Before long the entire Special Security squad will be under arrest. Their leaders have fled, but the transduction barriers are up and they cannot leave Gallifrey. Their capture is only a matter of time. All is well now.'

'Don't you believe it, Madame President,' said the Doctor. 'Our troubles are only just beginning.'

30

Rassilon

In an anteroom of the Tomb of Rassilon, Morin and Elar were adjusting a complex but compact machine which looked rather like an electronic cannon. Rath stood watching them impatiently.

Agonal appeared beside him. 'What is this machine?'

'It's a Time Gun – a temporal force-field generator. If Morin's calculations are correct, it will disrupt the temporal stasis around the Tomb itself.'

'Why do we delay?'

'They need to build up the energy levels and fine-tune the field. It's a complex business.' Rath gave Agonal a look of agonized concern. 'When we start to use the Time Gun, Rassilon will awake. None of us can stand against him.'

'None but I,' said Agonal. 'I shall make his strength my own.'

President Flavia sat patiently behind her Presidential desk while the Doctor strode up and down the Presidential office, watched by Romana and Castellan Spandrell. Ace and Bernice had gone to see how Dekker was getting on.

'The trouble is, I still don't know what they're really up to,' he said. 'There's a hidden agenda, I'm sure of it!'

'A simple take-over, surely,' suggested Spandrell. 'I've had my eye on them for quite a while. These movements crop up from time to time, Doctor – boils on the body politic. Calls for stronger government, for a policy of more active Time Lord intervention in the affairs of the cosmos.'

'You accuse us of wanting only to observe the universe,

Doctor,' said Lady Flavia. 'We charge you with wishing to meddle with it – with the best of intentions of course. People like this want to rule it, and order it to their liking.'

'Rath, Morin and Elar,' muttered the Doctor. 'You'd think even they must know they're not up to it.'

He sat down by the Presidential desk, and Romana drew up a chair close beside him.

'Let's take it from the beginning,' said the Doctor. 'The Three leaked me that report from the Temporal Observation Bureau, saying Agonal was probably going to be active in 1930s Chicago. They knew Agonal was an old obsession of mine so they could be pretty sure I'd go after him. By a useful piece of sychronicity, Romana came across evidence of something disruptive happening on the Vampire Planet. I was determined to follow the Chicago trail, so I sent Bernice Summerfield to look into it and hold the fort with Romana until I could get there.' He looked round. 'Clear so far? Right! Agonal realized I was after him in Chicago, and made several attempts to get me killed. I tried to capture him, missed, chased him to the Vampire Planet and missed again – *because the Three Timescooped him to Gallifrey!*'

Flavia looked shocked. 'They have reactivated the Time Scoop?'

Spandrell was punching up records on a terminal. 'Morin and Elar are first-rate temporal engineers. They've both worked in Temporal Control.'

'They used me as a stalking horse,' said the Doctor. 'They wanted *me* to find Agonal so *they* could take him. They knew I'd follow so they wanted me here as well – but why?'

'To kill you, surely,' said Romana. 'Rath hated you because of what happened to his brother.'

'He said he had two reasons to hate me,' muttered the Doctor. 'To hate all my selves ... Can you check Rath's political record, Spandrell old chap?'

Spandrell stabbed at the keyboard with blunt fingers, then looked up from the screen. 'When the Goth business put a crimp in his career, he attached himself to Borusa's party. When Borusa became Lord President, Rath was one of his loyalest supporters.'

'Then you turned up and defeated Borusa too,' said Romana. 'In his eyes you'd destroyed his big brother and his beloved leader.'

The Doctor nodded. 'No wonder he hated me.'

Castellan Spandrell chuckled. 'Oh, he hated you all right, Doctor, they all did. According to one of my informants, they even included you in the chant that ended their meetings.'

The Doctor looked mildly interested. 'Really? How did it go?'

'I hardly like to, Doctor . . . ladies present.'

'You have my permission, Castellan,' said President Flavia.

Spandrell cleared his throat. 'It goes:

"Death to the Doctor!
Borusa lives,
Rassilon must die ' '

There was a shocked silence at the blasphemy of the last line.

Spandrell said, 'Well, I must go and supervise the rest of the round-up. With your permission, Madame President?'

Flavia inclined her head, and Spandrell hurried away.

The Doctor rose, staring into space. 'Borusa lives!' he whispered. 'Rassilon must die!' He looked wildly from Flavia to Romana. 'I know what they're going to do!'

The Time Gun was giving off a low hum of power, a light sequence flashing on its control panel.

Elar stood up. 'Best we can do, eh Morin?'

Morin nodded his agreement.

'Then let us begin,' whispered Rath. 'For the last time. Death to the Doctor!'

Morin and Elar took up the chant:

'Borusa lives!

'Rassilon must die!'

Carrying the Time Gun between them, Morin and Elar set off for the heart of the Tomb. Rath followed.

Behind them came Agonal.

The Doctor, President Flavia and Lady Romana stood looking up at the ancient painting that hung in the Inner Council Room, close to the President's office. It showed a mysterious cowled figure, reputedly Rassilon himself, playing a harp against the background of a wild and romantic landscape.

There was a music-stand in the picture, bearing a parchment sheet on which music was inscribed. Despite the painting's great age, the detail of the picture was so clear that you could distinguish the actual notes.

Close to the picture stood a pillar upon which stood an ancient Gallifreyan harp, exactly like the one in the painting. There was an inscription at the top of the pillar: 'Here is the Harp of Rassilon.'

The Doctor took down the instrument and handed it to Romana.

'As a well brought-up young Time Lady, you must have been taught to play the harp?'

Romana ran her fingers across the strings. 'What would you like me to play?'

The Doctor pointed to the music in the painting. 'Play that!'

Romana peered up at the painting and began to play, tentatively at first. After a few bars she smiled. 'Oh, I know this. It's an old ballad called "Rassilon's Lament".'

Playing with increased confidence now, Romana finished the tune. There was a grinding of concealed machinery and the hidden door beneath the picture slid open, revealing a flight of steep and narrow stone steps.

Taking the harp from Romana's hands, the Doctor placed it gently back on its pillar. Then he went through the door and down the steps. Flavia and Romana followed him.

They found themselves in a gloomy underground control room. Even now, thought the Doctor, the air still felt thick with ancient evil and long-ago cruelties.

The great Game Table stood in the centre of the room.

Its surface formed a replica of the Death Zone, dominated by the central model of the Dark Tower. On the other side of the chamber stood a huge and clumsy-looking piece of ancient machinery.

The Doctor moved over to it. He touched an ancient keyboard and a central screen lit up. 'The Time Scoop,' said the Doctor. 'Apparently back in full working order – thanks to Elar and Morin no doubt.'

He flicked controls at random and a picture appeared on a screen, a muddy swamp with drifting mists. Suddenly a great roaring head burst out from beneath the surface. It looked like a giant worm with a dog-like head and far too many teeth.

'A Drashig!' said the Doctor almost affectionately. His fingers moved over the controls and a black obelisk appeared, containing the monster's image. The Doctor looked at Flavia.

'One touch of a button, Madame President, and that delightful creature will be rampaging around the Capitol corridors.'

'No thank you, Doctor,' said Flavia firmly.

'Perhaps you're right. Drashigs make awkward pets. They're no trouble to feed, mind you. They eat anything – and anybody, of course. They ate a space-freighter once.' As he spoke the Doctor's fingers stabbed at the keyboard and the machine went dead.

'I ordered that device to be deactivated,' said Flavia.

'You should have ordered it to be destroyed.'

The Doctor led them over to a booth in the corner. 'A basic transmat link – one destination only, I fancy. I'd better go. I may be too late, but I'll do what I can.'

'I'll come with you, Doctor,' said Lady Flavia. 'If I order the Three to abandon their evil scheme . . .'

'They've gone too far for that. Besides you're too valuable to risk.'

'I'm not,' said Romana. 'I'll come, Doctor. I'd like to see the end of this.'

'It may be the end of all of us,' said the Doctor with uncharacteristic gloom.

'Wait, Doctor,' pleaded Flavia. 'Let me find Castellan Spandrell, send guards with you.'

'Later if you must,' said the Doctor. 'But guards won't help us now. This will be a struggle of the spirit.'

He stepped into the transmat booth and Romana joined him. The Doctor touched the control, the booth lit up and they faded away . . .

. . . to reappear in a booth set deep in a darkened alcove. They stepped out of the booth, went through a high stone arch and found themselves at the heart of the Tomb of Rassilon.

It was a vast cathedral-like chamber, lit only by a shaft of light that slanted down from above, picking out a massive stone bier. On top of the bier lay a motionless form dressed in ancient ceremonial robes. Figures were set into the side of the bier – a long row of Time Lords, arranged in a kind of fresco. At first Romana thought they were carved into the stone. Then she saw that their eyes were alive.

'Who are they Doctor?' she whispered.

'Time Lords who wanted immortality – and got what they wanted. The one in the centre is Borusa. I helped to put him there.'

The Tomb had been desecrated. A device like a squat silver cannon had been set up, aimed directly at the imprisoned Borusa.

'The idiots have made a Time Gun,' whispered the Doctor.

Two black-robed figures crouched beside the device. Two taller ones stood beside them. One of the tall figures was Rath, in the black ceremonial robes and head-dress of the Old Time. Beside him, tall and elegant in a black robe, stood Agonal.

The air before the Time Gun seemed to be pulsing, flickering as the beam of temporal energy assaulted the bier.

The Doctor stepped forward. 'No!' he called. 'Stop it you fools! Do you wish to face the wrath of Rassilon?'

Agonal turned. 'I do not fear your Rassilon, Doctor. When I have destroyed him, I shall destroy you – slowly!'

Ignoring him, the Doctor spoke to Rath. 'Don't you know the one strength this wretched meddling entity has, the one thing that makes it really dangerous? *In any direct confrontation he draws power from the strength of his opponent.* Don't you see? If he absorbs the strength and energy of Rassilon, and overcomes him, you'll have created a monster of quite incredible power. He'll turn the universe into a blood-bath for his amusement!'

A deep voice said, 'So you are here at last, Doctor. Now the game of Rassilon can begin!'

The voice didn't come from anywhere, it just *was* inside their minds and all around them. It was as if the whole great chamber had spoken.

'No, Lord Rassilon,' cried the Doctor. 'You don't realize the danger. Even you – '

'*LET THE GAME BEGIN!*' The booming voice seemed to shake the stone walls of the Tomb.

Agonal stepped forward, standing alone before the bier. 'I challenge you, Rassilon!'

A great wave of psychic energy drove out from the bier.

Agonal withstood it, absorbed it – and sent it back.

The Doctor and Romana and the three renegade Time Lords stood forgotten spectators as the battle raged. It seemed that nothing Rassilon could do would serve to overcome Agonal. He seemed to grow taller, stronger, glowing with malevolent power as the waves of psychic energy raged about him.

The Doctor watched in helpless agony. Was this the end of Rassilon? The end, perhaps, of the Time Lords?

There was a sudden shattering explosion. Overloaded by the colossal energies that played around it, the Time Gun had exploded. As the echoes of the explosion died away, Rath gave a triumphant shout. 'Lord Borusa! You are free!'

The Doctor turned and saw Borusa, his old teacher, standing beside the bier. The space that had imprisoned him was empty.

Rath ran to kneel before his lost leader. 'Lord Borusa, we have set you free! It was all for this. Now you can return to lead us, and we shall rule the cosmos . . .'

His voice tailed away as he saw the anger on Borusa's face.

'Return to lead *you*?' said the old man scornfully. 'Return to the madness that put me here? I may have been wicked but I am not entirely a fool. I have had time, very considerable time, to reflect on the past. I do not wish to repeat it.' Rath's face seemed to crumble as his idol rejected him, and he turned away sobbing.

Suddenly the Doctor felt the power of Rassilon flowing through him. Somehow he knew it was flowing through Romana too, and above all through Borusa – the old Borusa, with all his strength and wisdom. Together they confronted Agonal and the power of Rassilon swept through them, mingled with their own spiritual strength and blasted Agonal into nothingness, like a candle in a hurricane.

With a howl of pain and rage, Agonal disappeared.

A deep silence fell.

The Doctor ran forward and grasped Borusa's shoulder. It felt sinewy and strong, utterly real. 'Is it really you?'

'It seems to be, my boy.'

The Doctor fell to one knee and kissed the old teacher's hand. Borusa patted his shoulder. 'There there, my boy. It's good to see you again.' He raised the Doctor to his feet and stepped back, looking upwards.

'I am ready to resume my place, Lord Rassilon.'

'No!' shouted the Doctor, ready to defy Rassilon himself.

But Rassilon's voice said, 'That place is already filled, Lord Borusa.'

The Doctor and Borusa turned together and saw that Agonal had taken Borusa's place on the side of the bier. The long thin form, the long elegant face were part of the fabric of the pedestal. Only the eyes were furiously alive.

Rassilon spoke again. 'Come with me, Borusa old friend. We shall find you a better place.'

Borusa turned back to the Doctor, raised his hand in farewell and faded into nothingness.

Rassilon's voice boomed out. 'You, who call yourselves the Three. You are not worthy to stand here. Return to the Capitol and submit to the judgement of your fellow Time Lords.'

Rath, Morin and Elar turned and trailed disconsolately away. Romana at his side, the Doctor stood waiting before the bier.

'Still here, Doctor? Can't an old man have any peace?'

'You knew, didn't you?' said the Doctor indignantly. 'You knew what was going to happen all along.'

'This is the Game of Rassilon. To lose is to win, and he who wins shall lose . . .' An enormous yawn rolled around the Tomb. 'Come and see me again some day, Doctor. The cosmos would be a duller place without you.'

As the Doctor and Romana turned away, a deep silence fell upon the Tomb. Rassilon had returned to his long sleep.

The Doctor and Romana stood waiting by the TARDIS in the Capitol corridor where they had first landed.

'What happened to Borusa, Doctor?'

'I think he went sane.'

'Is he dead?'

'Is Rassilon dead? What is death anyway? Write on one side of the paper only.'

'And what about the Game of Rassilon?'

'It's all a game to Rassilon,' said the Doctor. 'And he's always at least six moves ahead of anybody else. What do you plan to do, now you're back on Gallifrey?'

'I think I'll stay for a while, Doctor, and resume my studies. I'm a Gallifrey girl at heart, you know.'

A procession was approaching along the corridor. It consisted of Dekker, sleeping peacefully on a stretcher carried by four meditechs, with the Chief Hospitaller himself in attendance, and Ace and Bernice fussing over the patient.

'A full recovery, Doctor,' said the Chief Hospitaller.

'Your friend is as good as new – rather better in fact. We took the liberty of making a few minor improvements. He will never be ill, and he will recover quickly from any wounds. If he survives his hazardous times, he will live to a great age – for a human.'

The Hospitaller and his staff installed Dekker in the TARDIS, emerged and said goodbye, making light of the Doctor's thanks.

'His memories may be a little vague when he awakes in his own place and time,' said the Chief Hospitaller as he moved away. 'But perhaps that will be just as well.'

Another little procession appeared, this one consisting of Lady Flavia, Secretary Pogarel and Castellan Spandrell.

'I've spoken to Temporal Control,' said Lady Flavia. 'Your TARDIS will be on a Temporal Guidance Beam. You'll arrive back on Earth at precisely the right place and time.'

'I can manage that sort of thing perfectly well for myself, thank you,' said the Doctor rather ungraciously. He was getting tetchy. He hated goodbyes. He held out his hand. 'Goodbye, Romana. I got you back to Gallifrey eventually – even if it was by a roundabout route.'

'Roundabout another universe,' said Romana. 'Goodbye Doctor, take care.' In an astonishing display of affection – for Romana – she kissed his cheek.

Castellan Spandrell held out a big hand. The Doctor was about to shake it when Spandrell said, 'My Gallifreyan Army Knife, Doctor. It went missing the last time you were here.'

Rather shamefacedly, the Doctor fished in his pockets, produced the knife and handed it over.

'I sometimes wonder if you're entirely honest, Doctor,' said Spandrell, but he smiled as he said it.

'Goodbye, old friend,' said the Doctor.

Spandrell gave the Doctor a salute and a bone-crushing handshake and went on his way.

Ace and Bernice popped out of the TARDIS.

'Are we going or what?' said Ace.

Bernice gave Romana a hug. 'Goodbye, Time Lady.'

281

Romana and Ace shook hands. Ace and Bernice went back inside the TARDIS, leaving the Doctor and Lady Flavia alone.

'I suppose it's no use asking – ' began Flavia.

'You're a much better President than I could ever be,' said the Doctor.

'You'll have to come home one day,' said Flavia.

'I will,' said the Doctor. 'When I find out where it is.'

They shook hands, and the Doctor went back inside the TARDIS, like a rabbit popping back down its burrow. The seldom-heard sound of a Type-Forty dematerialization echoed around the corridors, and the Doctor was gone.

As Romana was walking back to her new quarters, she bumped into a fellow Time Lady who was hurrying round a corner.

They exchanged apologies and Romana studied her new acquaintance with interest. She was tall and straight-backed, wearing a neat black trouser-suit and a silver belt. Fashions had changed since Romana was last on Gallifrey. She had sharp inquisitive features, scraped-back black hair and she wore a necklace of golden spheres.

'Ruathadvorophrenaltid,' she said formally, adding as one did if one was prepared to be friendly, 'Ruatha.'

'Romanadvoratrelundar,' said Romana. 'Romana.'

'I was hurrying to see the Doctor,' said Ruatha. 'I heard he'd had an encounter with some vampires, and vampirism is a particular study of mine.'

'I'm afraid you've missed the Doctor,' said Romana. 'But perhaps I can help? I spent quite a lot of time on the vampire planet myself.'

31

Sweet Home Chicago

After the shoot-out with Reilly's cops, I woke up in a bed at Doc's Place with Ace looking after me. Apparently I'd stopped a slug and been out of it for a while. It couldn't have been anything much. The wound had pretty well healed and I never felt better in my life.

Then Ace told me she and Doc were leaving Chicago, and for a while I never felt worse.

We had a farewell party their last night. I sat on a stool at the bar watching Ace while Luigi filled me in on all the news.

Al Capone was taking the sun at his place in Miami, and Bugs Moran had disappeared after his near miss on St Valentine's Day. Nobody had seen Anselmi and Scalise around, and nobody was missing them. Nobody seemed to have shot anyone for a while, and it looked like recent violent events had worn everybody out. Mayor Thompson's clean-up campaign had run out of steam, and most of the joints were back in business again. I guess nobody was ever gonna close down Chicago.

Half-way through the evening, my old friend Captain Reilly came in. He was alone and in plain clothes and he wasn't looking for any trouble. He even bought me a drink.

'I was hoping for a word with Doc,' he said, and I took him over to Doc's alcove.

Reilly sat down and raised his glass to us both. 'God save all here,' he said, emptying it. Doc beckoned to a waiter, who brought him over another one.

'And what can I do for you, Captain Reilly?'

'Well, to begin with I want to apologize for that little bit of a misunderstanding we had a while back.'

'Think nothing of it,' said Doc.

Reilly leaned forward. 'The truth of it is I was given a bum steer by that tall skinny feller, him that went round causing so much trouble. No one seems to have seen him for a while.'

'They tell me he's out of circulation.'

'Took care of him, did you?'

'In a way.'

'Well now, since everything's back to normal again,' said Reilly. He gave Doc a hopeful look.

'Ah, the police benevolent fund! Of course.'

Doc produced a well-stuffed envelope and Reilly made it disappear. He had a couple more drinks and disappeared himself.

I looked at Doc. 'Only in Chicago.'

'Just a matter of business,' said Doc. 'Oh, and speaking of business.' He handed me a sheaf of important-looking papers.

'What's this?'

'Half a saloon. You're co-owner with Luigi – a silent partner. Prohibition won't last very much longer, and when it ends you can go legit.'

I tried to argue, but you just can't argue with Doc. We called Happy Harrigan off the door and gave him a drink.

'Meet your new bosses, Happy,' said Doc. 'Luigi and Mr Dekker.'

Happy was pleased, but a little worried too. 'Maybe Mr Dekker don't want no ex-con working here, him being a private cop and all.'

I pounded him between the shoulder-blades. It was like hitting a brick wall. 'Happy, as long as we've got a saloon, you've got a job. Right, Luigi?'

Luigi smiled. 'Wouldn't be Doc's Place without you, Happy.'

It was going to be Doc's Place without Doc soon, I thought – and without Ace.

It was quite a night. By the end of the evening even

the band got tired, and Doc took over from Sam. Doc played a mean piano, and some friend of his, a helluva nice dame called Benny, sang the blues like she knew what they meant.

Me and Benny were having a drink at the bar later, and getting on real well when Ace came by and gave Benny one of those looks dames give other dames. Benny gave me one of those 'some other time' looks and drifted away.

Ace took over her stool. 'Buy me a drink, soldier?'

She was wearing the slinky black number I'd first seen her in, and carrying the same black purse.

I raised a finger to Luigi and a couple of Jim Beams appeared. I tried to pay but Luigi shook his head. 'Owner's privilege.'

I looked at Ace. 'Doc gave me half the joint.'

She nodded. 'I know.'

We sat sipping our drinks.

'I could stay, you know,' said Ace.

'Sure you could. I could get a house in the country with a white picket fence and you could buy a pink gingham dress with a lace collar.'

Ace sighed. 'It's not us, is it?' She looked around the crowded, noisy, smoky joint. 'We've still got Chicago.'

'We'll always have Chicago.'

Ace put her hand over mine. 'And we've still got tonight.'

Doc was over at the piano with Benny. I looked over and caught his eye, and he raised his hand in salute.

Benny saw us too, and smiled and waved.

'Well, no one seems to need us here,' I said.

We finished our drinks. As we left the bar, Doc was playing, and Benny was singing the blues.

Epilogue

But that wasn't the end – not quite.

Much later that same night Bernice Summerfield, who was in a somewhat elevated state by now, remembered she was an archaeologist and that she had a crate of largely unsorted specimens in the TARDIS control room.

She had a bourbon-fuelled fancy to have a preliminary look at them and borrowed the TARDIS key from the unsurprised Doctor. He never seemed to sleep himself, and didn't expect anyone else to.

Bernice opened the TARDIS door and stared owlishly at the crate. She could unpack it in the control room, but the Doctor probably wouldn't like it. She could take it right into the TARDIS, but that seemed like too much trouble. The simplest thing seemed to be to drag it out of the TARDIS and into the empty store-room. So that's what she did. As she said later, it seemed a good idea at the time.

She'd had no time to nail up the crate, so it was easy enough to lift the lid. She did so and saw Yarven staring up at her, eyes glowing and bloody fangs gleaming. She screamed and jumped back and he sat bolt upright like a jack-in-the-box.

As he sprang out of the crate, Bernice gave another scream, a real glass-shatterer. Yarven, who seemed as frightened and confused as she was, made no move to attack her. He flung himself out of the store-room, right across the empty gaming room and out of the still-closed front window.

She ran to the window and saw him scramble to his

feet and stagger away, disappearing into the shadows of the vacant lot.

Her screams and the sound of shattering glass produced first the Doctor, then Dekker wearing a sheet and a Colt .45, followed by Ace wearing a Browning and an extraordinary garment in black silk, followed by Happy Harrigan in night-gown and shotgun.

The Doctor shooed them all away, calmed Bernice down and managed to get a coherent story out of her. He took her back down to the now empty bar and gave her a drink to steady her nerves.

When she realized what had happened, Bernice was appalled. 'He must have hidden in the crate sometime after the battle – when it was still stored in Ivo's barn.'

'Very probably,' agreed the Doctor, not seeming at all perturbed. A thought struck him – or rather, a memory.

'Of course . . . So that's how . . .'

'But don't you see, Doctor, he must have been one of them – a real vampire! We brought him back to Earth and now he's free. You've got to do something!'

The Doctor smiled. 'It's already done.'

Bernice stared at him. 'Already – but how . . .?'

'Don't worry, Bernice,' said the Doctor. 'I took care of it ages ago.'

CAT'S CRADLE: WARHEAD
Andrew Cartmel

The place is Earth. The time is the near future – all too near. As environmental destruction reaches the point of no return, multinational corporations scheme to buy immortality in a poisoned world. If Earth is to survive, somebody has to stop them.

ISBN 0 426 20367 4

CAT'S CRADLE: WITCH MARK
Andrew Hunt

A small village in Wales is visited by creatures of myth. Nearby, a coach crashes on the M40, killing all its passengers. Police can find no record of their existence. The Doctor and Ace arrive, searching for a cure for the TARDIS, and uncover a gateway to another world.

ISBN 0 426 20368 2

NIGHTSHADE
Mark Gatiss

When the Doctor brings Ace to the village of Crook Marsham in 1968, he seems unwilling to recognize that something sinister is going on. But the villagers are being killed, one by one, and everyone's past is coming back to haunt them – including the Doctor's.

ISBN 0 426 20376 3

LOVE AND WAR
Paul Cornell

Heaven: a planet rich in history where the Doctor comes to meet a new friend, and betray an old one; a place where people come to die, but where the dead don't always rest in peace. On Heaven, the Doctor finally loses Ace, but finds archaeologist Bernice Summerfield, a new companion whose destiny is inextricably linked with his.

ISBN 0 426 20385 2

TRANSIT
Ben Aaronovitch

It's the ultimate mass transit system, binding the planets of the solar system together. But something is living in the network, chewing its way to the very heart of the system and leaving a trail of death and mutation behind. Once again, the Doctor is all that stands between humanity and its own mistakes.

ISBN 0 426 20384 4

THE HIGHEST SCIENCE
Gareth Roberts

The Highest Science – a technology so dangerous it destroyed its creators. Many people have searched for it, but now Sheldukher, the most wanted criminal in the galaxy, believes he has found it. The Doctor and Bernice must battle to stop him on a planet where chance and coincidence have become far too powerful.

ISBN 0 426 20377 1

THE PIT
Neil Penswick

One of the Seven Planets is a nameless giant, quarantined against all intruders. But when the TARDIS materializes, it becomes clear that the planet is far from empty – and the Doctor begins to realize that the planet hides a terrible secret from the Time Lords' past.

ISBN 0 426 20378 X

DECEIT
Peter Darvill-Evans

Ace – three years older, wiser and tougher – is back. She is part of a group of Irregular Auxiliaries on an expedition to the planet Arcadia. They think they are hunting Daleks, but the Doctor knows better. He knows that the paradise planet hides a being far more powerful than the Daleks – and much more dangerous.

ISBN 0 426 20362 3

LUCIFER RISING
Jim Mortimore & Andy Lane

Reunited, the Doctor, Ace and Bernice travel to Lucifer, the site of a scientific expedition that they know will shortly cease to exist. Discovering why involves them in sabotage, murder and the resurrection of eons-old alien powers. Are there Angels on Lucifer? And what does it all have to do with Ace?

ISBN 0 426 20338 7

WHITE DARKNESS
David McIntee

The TARDIS crew, hoping for a rest, come to Haiti in 1915. But they find that the island is far from peaceful: revolution is brewing in the city; the dead are walking from the cemeteries; and, far underground, the ancient rulers of the galaxy are stirring in their sleep.

ISBN 0 426 20395 X

SHADOWMIND
Christopher Bulis

On the colony world of Arden, something dangerous is growing stronger. Something that steals minds and memories. Something that can reach out to another planet, Tairgire, where the newest exhibit in the sculpture park is a blue box surmounted by a flashing light.

ISBN 0 426 20394 1

BIRTHRIGHT
Nigel Robinson

Stranded in Edwardian London with a dying TARDIS, Bernice investigates a series of grisly murders. In the far future, Ace leads a group of guerrillas against their insect-like, alien oppressors. Why has the Doctor left them, just when they need him most?

ISBN 0 426 20393 3

ICEBERG
David Banks

In 2006, an ecological disaster threatens the Earth; only the FLIPback team, working in an Antarctic base, can avert the catastrophe. But hidden beneath the ice, sinister forces have gathered to sabotage humanity's last hope. The Cybermen have returned and the Doctor must face them alone.

ISBN 0 426 20392 5

BLOOD HEAT
Jim Mortimore

The TARDIS is attacked by an alien force; Bernice is flung into the Vortex; and the Doctor and Ace crash-land on Earth. There they find dinosaurs roaming the derelict London streets, and Brigadier Lethbridge-Stewart leading the remnants of UNIT in a desperate fight against the Silurians who have taken over and changed his world.

ISBN 0 426 20399 2

THE DIMENSION RIDERS
Daniel Blythe

A holiday in Oxford is cut short when the Doctor is summoned to Space Station Q4, where ghostly soldiers from the future watch from the shadows among the dead. Soon, the Doctor is trapped in the past, Ace is accused of treason and Bernice is uncovering deceit among the college cloisters.

ISBN 0 426 20397 6

THE LEFT-HANDED HUMMINGBIRD
Kate Orman
Someone has been playing with time. The Doctor Ace and Bernice must travel to the Aztec Empire in 1487, to London in the Swinging Sixties and to the sinking of the *Titanic* as they attempt to rectify the temporal faults – and survive the attacks of the living god Huitzilin.

ISBN 0 426 20404 2

CONUNDRUM
Steve Lyons
A killer is stalking the streets of the village of Arandale. The victims are found each day, drained of blood. Someone has interfered with the Doctor's past again, and he's landed in a place he knows he once destroyed, from which it seems there can be no escape.

ISBN 0 426 20408 5

NO FUTURE
Paul Cornell
At last the Doctor comes face-to-face with the enemy who has been threatening him, leading him on a chase that has brought the TARDIS to London in 1976. There he finds that reality has been subtly changed and the country he once knew is rapidly descending into anarchy as an alien invasion force prepares to land . . .

ISBN 0 426 20409 3

TRAGEDY DAY
Gareth Roberts
When the TARDIS crew arrive on Olleril, they soon realise that all is not well. Assassins arrive to carry out a killing that may endanger the entire universe. A being known as the Supreme One tests horrific weapons. And a secret order of monks observes the growing chaos.

ISBN 0 426 20410 7

LEGACY
Gary Russell
The Doctor returns to Peladon, on the trail of a master criminal. Ace pursues intergalactic mercenaries who have stolen the galaxy's most evil artifact while Bernice strikes up a dangerous friendship with a Martian Ice Lord. The players are making the final moves in a devious and lethal plan – but for once it isn't the Doctor's.

ISBN 0 426 20412 3

THEATRE OF WAR
Justin Richards
Menaxus is a barren world on the front line of an interstellar war, home to a ruined theatre which hides sinister secrets. When the TARDIS crew land on the planet, they find themselves trapped in a deadly reenactment of an ancient theatrical tragedy.

ISBN 0 426 20414 X

ALL-CONSUMING FIRE
Andy Lane
The secret library of St John the Beheaded has been robbed. The thief has taken forbidden books which tell of gateways to other worlds. Only one team can be trusted to solve the crime: Sherlock Holmes, Doctor Watson – and a mysterious stranger who claims he travels in time and space.

ISBN 0 426 20415 8

Also available in July 1994 is *Goth Opera* by Paul Cornell, the first in a new series of Missing Adventures.